A DEAL WITH THE DEVIL

"Would you be Maggie Cayton, the woman in need of my services?"

His voice sent chills down her spine, but in a way she wouldn't have expected. His was not the voice of a killer. Her name which had always sounded painfully plain and unattractive had sounded amazingly soft and melodious as it rolled from his throat in that husky, whiskey whisper. She had the alarming sensation that she had just been stroked by his voice, as if it were as tangible as the hand resting on the gun.

Quickly, very quickly, Maggie reminded herself that she'd just heard the voice of a man practiced in the art of illusion and trickery. Beneath Sackett's attractive outer shell he was nothing but a bloodthirsty, heartless killer.

His services? Indeed. Yet why had his question sounded as if he was offering something much more pleasant and fulfilling than a gun?

"The scenes between Seth and Maggie ignite in a gentle way . . . a really good book."
— THE PAPERBACK TRADER

TODAY'S HOTTEST READS
ARE TOMORROW'S SUPERSTARS

VICTORY'S WOMAN   (4484, $4.50)
by Gretchen Genet
Andrew—the carefree soldier who sought glory on the battlefield, and returned a shattered man . . . Niall—the legandary frontiersman and a former Shawnee captive, tormented by his past . . . Roger—the troubled youth, who would rise up to claim a shocking legacy . . . and Clarice—the passionate beauty bound by one man, and hopelessly in love with another. Set against the backdrop of the American revolution, three men fight for their heritage—and one woman is destined to change all their lives forever!

FORBIDDEN   (4488, $4.99)
by Jo Beverley
While fleeing from her brothers, who are attempting to sell her into a loveless marriage, Serena Riverton accepts a carriage ride from a stranger—who is the handsomest man she has ever seen. Lord Middlethorpe, himself, is actually contemplating marriage to a dull daughter of the aristocracy, when he encounters the breathtaking Serena. She arouses him as no woman ever has. And after a night of thrilling intimacy—a forbidden liaison—Serena must choose between a lady's place and a woman's passion!

WINDS OF DESTINY   (4489, $4.99)
by Victoria Thompson
Becky Tate is a half-breed outcast—branded by her Comanche heritage. Then she meets a rugged stranger who awakens her heart to the magic and mystery of passion. Hiding a desperate past, Texas Ranger Clint Masterson has ridden into cattle country to bring peace to a divided land. But a greater battle rages inside him when he dares to desire the beautiful Becky!

WILDEST HEART   (4456, $4.99)
by Virginia Brown
Maggie Malone had come to cattle country to forge her future as a healer. Now she was faced by Devon Conrad, an outlaw wounded body and soul by his shadowy past . . . whose eyes blazed with fury even as his burning caress sent her spiraling with desire. They came together in a Texas town about to explode in sin and scandal. Danger was their destiny—and there was nothing they wouldn't dare for love!

Available wherever paperbacks are sold, or order direct from the Publisher. Send cover price plus 50¢ per copy for mailing and handling to Penguin USA, P.O. Box 999, c/o Dept. 17109, Bergenfield, NJ 07621. Residents of New York and Tennessee must include sales tax. DO NOT SEND CASH.

LINDA SANDIFER

CAME A STRANGER

ZEBRA BOOKS
KENSINGTON PUBLISHING CORP.

Prologue

The White Raven Ranch, Wyoming

The booming blast of a rifle report brought Maggie Cayton upright in bed, disoriented and frightened. From outside, the frantic yell of men's voices confused her even more. Inside, a strange red shadow swayed on the bedroom wall like the rearing head of a Chinese dragon. Strands of hair had fallen from her thick, auburn braid and she pushed them back from her face while trying to make sense of what she was hearing and seeing. But it took another gunshot blast to clear the remaining fog from her brain. Tossing back the covers with haste now, she hurried to the window.

Her heart leaped to her throat, forcing up a stifled gasp of fear and dismay. She automatically cringed away from the swelling red flames that, even though a considerable distance away, seemed to inhale the night sky as if it alone was the fuel for its momentum. Below in the yard, the cowboys were scrambling from the bunkhouse, pulling on pants and boots over their underwear while others started a bucket brigade from the watering trough to the burning barn. The terrified screams of trapped horses came from inside the barn before more men raced through the huge double doors to release them.

Maggie whirled from the window. Fumbling in the red glow of the fire that offered the room's only light, she hastily lit a lamp with shaking hands. She pulled on her slippers and dressing gown and exited the room. With the white cotton cloth of the gown billowing behind her, and the lamp cutting a narrow corridor of light in front of her, she hurried down the hall, flinging open the doors of her childrens' rooms.

"Natalie! Lance! Alison! The barn's on fire! Everybody up!"

By the time she reached her mother's room on the first floor, her children were right behind her, firing more questions than she could answer.

For all the haste she had exhibited just moments before, Maggie entered her mother's room quietly. Gently, she tried to wake the sixty-year-old woman without causing undue alarm or stress. But when Maggie received no response but groggy mutterings, she knew her mother had once again taken the sleeping draught the doctor had prescribed over four months ago. It kept Catherine Marshall in her own safe world away from the responsibilities she had uncharacteristically come to fear since she had been made a widow three years before.

Maggie shook her harder, but to no avail. The woman mumbled again and turned to her side, sinking back into the drug-induced sleep.

Maggie turned to fourteen-year-old Natalie, the second of her three children. "It's very unlikely that the fire will spread across the yard to the house," she said, trying to ease the fear in her children's eyes. "You stay here with Alison and your grandmother. Lance, wake the servants and then stay here with your sisters. I'm going outside to see if I can help the men get the horses out of the barn."

"I can help the men," Lance objected, jutting his chin out belligerently. "Besides, you could get hurt out there."

Lance had just turned sixteen and at every opportunity he rebelled at being treated like a child. And, with Trent's death nearly a year ago, Maggie had indeed taken many of the responsibilities that her husband had borne and had placed them on her son's shoulders. He was tall and strong and eager, and she needed his help now more than ever.

"Wake the servants, Lance," she repeated firmly. "Then join me in the yard."

She hurried from the house. A wide dirt thoroughfare separated it from the yard and outbuildings. A stream ran to one side of it, supplying water for the stock. She ran across the wooden bridge that spanned the waterway and visually searched the faces of the frantic men until she spotted the ranch foreman, Sonny Haig. He was easy to see, not for his height, but rather his lack of it. Without his boots and ten-gallon hat, he wasn't much taller than Maggie. He was with the men who were trying to lead the remaining horses out of the blazing barn.

Lifting her dressing gown up past her ankles, she hurried to join him. "How many horses are left inside?" she shouted above the deafening roar of the fire.

"Just a couple. And Trent's horse in the end stall!"

Even as they spoke, the two horses in question were brought out, snorting and dancing sideways with fear. Maggie was jolted by the piercing scream of the last horse remaining in the barn, the big charcoal-gray stallion named Shadow that Trent had raised from a colt, trained himself, and had claimed as his personal mount.

Abandoning Sonny's side, Maggie ran to the huge barn door but the intense heat made her shrink back, shielding her face with an upraised arm. Sonny, Lance, and the other men joined her, but their repeated efforts to enter were thwarted by the scorching flames rapidly consuming the loft. A burning timber fell, igniting more straw on the ground floor and bursting into scores of smaller fires whose red-orange tentacles quickly and uncontrollably scurried in all directions to block the alley that led to Shadow's stall at the rear of the barn.

"We've got to get him out!" Maggie cried desperately. Not waiting for the men to take action, she started into the barn herself. Almost immediately Sonny's iron grip closed around her arm and she was hauled back.

"Don't be a fool, Maggie! Look at the roof. It could go any second! You can't chance going in there!"

"I've got to try!" She struggled to free herself, but he pulled her back, folding her arms across the front of her in the fashion of a straightjacket. She fought

him harder, laying blows to his knees and shins, but
the assault from her slippered toes hurt her worse
than it did him.

"Let me go, Sonny. I've got to get him out!"

"You'll die if you go in there now."

"It'll hold. Let me go!"

"Even if it held, there's no way through the fire!"

"He's right, Mom," came Lance's voice from behind her. "It's too dangerous! The fire's everywhere."

"Damn it, let me go." Her voice now held a
threatening edge. "You both know how much that
stallion meant to Trent."

Lance stepped in front of her, blocking her view
of the alley, the flames leaping across it, and the
screaming horse in the red darkness beyond. He
placed his hands on her shoulders and shook her the
way she'd gently shook her own mother earlier.

"Yes, I know, but Dad wouldn't expect you to
risk your life to save Shadow's. He'd expect you to
think of yourself, of me and the girls, of Grandma,
and of the White Raven. Think about it! If you go
into that barn, you'll be giving Big Ben Tate exactly
what he wants!"

Maggie looked up into her son's young, implor-
ing eyes filled with fear but with wisdom too. His
words were sobering but true. God, so true. With
Trent gone, everyone on the White Raven depended
on her now. Lance was right, but still she glared at
him. Why did he have to be so damned level-
headed? How could he and the other men stand
there when Shadow was screaming for help?

"Then go in from the other side," she shouted.

"Get some axes! We'll get him out through the back!"

Obviously no one had thought of that, but the men tore into action, heading for the tool shed and any implement they could use to hack their way in through the back. Before they got far, though, more wood snapped and popped overhead; another beam fell, grabbing more tinder on the ground and rapidly gobbling it up. The men ran faster, and in the chaos everyone yelled orders to everyone else. Shadow's screams increased, piercing the night and sending chills down Maggie's spine. The big animal hurled his body against the sturdy poles of the stall, struck it with his hooves, and still the wood wouldn't give beneath the onslaught.

Before the men could do anything with their picks and axes, there was a terrible groaning from the massive wood structure, accompanied by a ripping sound that drew everyone's attention upward. Clawing flames swirled around the big beams, sucking out the fiber and strength of them with what seemed a vicious obsession. For a moment, Maggie, Sonny, and Lance stared mesmerized with both horror and fascination.

Then Sonny yelled, "Run!"

Rocks bit into Maggie's slippered feet as she found herself being dragged along by Sonny and Lance almost faster than her legs could carry her. Behind them above the roar of the fire they could hear a terrible groaning and rumbling, followed by the cracking and popping of the big beams that had once held the immense barn upright. At last, as if a mighty earthquake had struck, the ground shook beneath the weight of the collapsing structure. Sonny flung Maggie down, throwing his body over hers protectively, shielding her from the pieces of burning wood and sparks sailing down to the ground. One caught the hem of her nightgown but he quickly beat it out with his hat.

The horse's screams were a nightmare Maggie knew she would hear forever. She covered her ears, unaware she was weeping convulsively. No one could have possibly known that Shadow had been her very important link to Trent. It may have sounded stupid to the cowboys, but to Maggie, as long as the horse remained alive then something of Trent had remained alive, too. She had lost her husband, and now she was losing everything that he was, everything he'd built, everything he'd owned, everything they'd dreamed together. Little by little it was being stolen from her. Would her memories, too, be stolen one day?

After a time, when the screams had stopped, and all that could be heard was the roar of the fire, Maggie staggered to her feet. Sonny and Lance came with her, ready to grab her again if she should try something foolish.

But she only stared at the heap of burning timbers, glowing blood red in the night. "He'll pay for this," she said quietly, but with certainty. "Ben Tate will pay. If he thinks he can scare me off the White Raven by poisoning my cattle, intimidating my men, and burning my barn, he's sadly mistaken. I've been here for twenty years and I've fought things a sight tougher than him. If he wants me off Cayton land he'll have to kill me . . . the same way he killed Trent."

Sonny Haig shifted uneasily. "What do you plan to do, Maggie?"

She turned away from the fire. Any gentleness she had possessed was gone in that moment, taken from her by Trent's murderer and by the acts of violence that were coming closer and closer to her children. Like any mother whose offspring is threatened, Maggie Cayton would fight. She'd done it before. And, by God, she'd do it again.

When she finally replied, it was with a cold and dangerous edge to her voice. "I want you to find me a hired gun, Sonny. Big Ben Tate has crossed his last line."

Chapter One

Two seconds after the thunder rolled, a purple wave of sheet lightning undulated across the advancing black shoulders of the storm. After the sun had dropped below the Big Horn Mountains, darkness had come swiftly, dripping downward like paint from a watercolor picture that has been hung too soon.

Maggie stood at the window of her second-story bedroom and watched with fascination the rippling play of light and dark across the Wyoming sky. For twenty years she had witnessed similar storms rushing over the mountains, thundering toward the White Raven. But for all their awesome ferocity, and despite their grandiose threats of terror and destruction, the storms came on the hooves of a familiar horse that no longer frightened her.

This storm, like the others, would do what it set out to do. And, as was the way of Mother Nature in this harsh and wild land, it would leave man—or woman—to accept whatever it rendered and to cope the best way possible.

"Do what you can," Trent used to say. "And if you can't do anything else, just pick up the pieces and start over."

Yes, and they'd done that plenty of times over the two decades of their marriage. They had built the White Raven, literally, with blood, sweat, tears, bullets, and a lot of blisters. She had stood by Trent's side fighting Indians, rustlers, blizzards, droughts, diseases, even insects. And he had stood by her side through the birth of their three children, and through the burials of two other babies.

She and Trent had struggled through the years of financial hardships, and when things had finally started to look good for them, they had lost fifty percent of their cattle in the blizzards of '86 and '87. But Trent had held on and rebuilt his herd while others had given up and sold out. He'd taught her how to be strong, how to not give up in the face of all odds. Even though they had lost on some occasions, their perseverance had ultimately made them emerge victorious.

They had been young and full of dreams when they'd come to this savage land whose only gentleness seemed to be in the grassy slopes of the foothills and the gentle curves of the valleys strutting alongside the creeks and rivers. Sometimes the shining light of their dreams had dimmed through the blur of tears and discouragement, but Trent had never let the light go completely out. Now, could she go on without him? She was strong—this land allowed little else from a person, save death. But Ben Tate was strong, too, and he was surely just as stubborn and determined.

Worry knotted her stomach. The weight of the burden she carried alone now was beginning to rest much too heavily on her shoulders. Although the Indians had been subdued, the battle with the land, and over the land, was not truly won, nor would it ever be.

"It'll work out, Trent," she whispered. "I won't let him take the White Raven." *But I wish you were here. God, how I miss you, darling.*

A streak of lightning knifed down toward the ranch, startling her from her musings. It was time to do something, and the ranch's record books had been waiting a long time for a good rain storm that would keep her inside.

She turned from the window, but movement below caught her eye and her curiosity. She reached for the curtain again to lift it out of the way. When she did, a chill rippled through her, as if the storm had found its way through the window's glass panes and to the very marrow of her bones.

From beneath the heavy mantle of the evening sky, almost as if he had stepped from the belly of the storm itself, came a stranger. His blood bay horse moved steadily toward the ranch, silently urged on by the reins wielding the power. She saw no facial features at this distance except a black Stetson pulled low and a long black coat covering him from head to toe, its collar pulled up against the wind that pummelled his back. She sensed he sat in the saddle with tense awareness of everything that moved and didn't move on the ranch, even though she saw him look neither left nor right. An aura of danger crackled around him with the same power and foreboding as the invisible forces of electricity that sizzled through the black clouds.

Her hand automatically curled around the butt of Trent's old Starr double-action revolver that now hung in the holster on her hip. Her heart gathered speed. She knew who the stranger was. Now that he was here there was no turning back. The final round of the game had begun.

She left her room. As she hurried down the stairs to the foyer her legs felt as weak as jelly, revealing her nervousness. She wanted to meet the stranger herself. She hadn't told her mother and the girls about hiring a gun, and she didn't know yet how she would break the news to them. Perhaps she would be able to convince them that he was just another hired hand.

Through the oval glass in the front door she watched him dismount in front of the house, looping a rein only once around the hitching rail. The wind was picking up, spattering the first drops of moisture onto his dusty, long black coat, and he tilted his head to keep the wind from snatching his hat. When he did, she caught a glimpse of a man who gave no quarter, and asked none.

Yes, she despised him for what he did and what he stood for; she even despised herself for stooping so low in her desperation that she had felt compelled to hire him. But Seth Sackett was a necessary evil, and without him, everything she and Trent had worked for would be lost to the clutches of Big Ben Tate. She could only hope that the end would justify the means.

As if sensing her piercing, contemptuous gaze, he

turned his head to the oval window. From the distance she could read nothing in his narrowed eyes—eyes that she presumed were accustomed to vigilance and scanning distant horizons for the hidden gun that would one day bring him down.

She watched while he pulled his long coat away from the gun on his hip, snagging it behind the holster and exposing the weapon for easy accessibility. His gaze shifted warily around the ranch yard before he finally advanced to the house. She waited while the unhurried booted feet finally took the wooden steps and crossed the creaky boards of the old porch. He walked silently, like a jaguar stalking its prey, and she recognized in those tense moments the absence of the jangling spurs most cowboys always wore. But Sackett was not of the same breed as Sonny and the men in the bunkhouse, and she was sure she would be reminded of that time and again before she paid him his final salary and sent him on his way.

She didn't wait for him to knock. There was no point; he knew she was there. She swung the door wide and the cold wind, like a house-trained cat, scampered into the house. On its rush past her it lifted the hem of her black riding skirt, rippling it up to her knee and exposing the polished black length of her riding boots. But the chill was quickly displaced by the intimidating heat of the gunslinger's tall, dark form filling the doorway, and by the intense gray fires in his eyes that now—on closer inspection—seemed to be half-shuttered in a perpetual squint against the sun, or possibly against the probing eyes of others who sought to intrude on the secrets in his mind.

Those eyes, gray and sharp like the edge of a well-honed knife, didn't miss the wind's invasion of her riding skirt. They went from there to the Starr revolver on her hip and finally lifted indolently to her face. Her back stiffened automatically in retaliatory defiance at the trace of derision she saw in his eyes. So he found the gun on her hip amusing? Well, let him think what he would. She was no gunslinger, but she could fire the damn thing, and more often than not she managed to hit what she was aiming at.

While she nurtured a new wave of contempt for him, he filled the gap of silence. "I'm over from Deadwood, ma'am," he said, his gaze hypnotically pinned to hers. "Would you be Maggie Cayton, the woman in need of my services?"

His voice sent chills down her spine, but in a way she wouldn't have expected. His was not the voice of a killer. Her name which had always sounded painfully plain and unattractive had sounded amazingly soft and melodious as it rolled from his throat in that husky, whiskey whisper. She had the alarming sensation that she had just been stroked by his voice, as if it were as tangible as the hand resting on his gun.

Quickly, very quickly, she reminded herself that she'd just heard the voice of a man practiced in the art of illusion and trickery. He had to be to have survived and to have acquired a reputation so notorious that it preceded him. Beneath his attractive outer shell he was nothing but a bloodthirsty, heart-

less killer. A man just like him—perhaps even one
of his friends—had killed Trent in cold blood.

She forced her eyes to the gun on his hip, just to
keep her perspective clear. His practiced hand
rested on its butt, and she knew inherently just how
fast he could draw it, how guiltlessly he could pull
the trigger. It didn't matter that she hadn't hired
him to kill anyone. He would do it without a qualm;
all she had to do was ask.

His services? Indeed. Yet why had his question
sounded as if he was offering something much more
pleasant and fulfilling than a gun?

She nodded to his question, stiffly. "You're Sackett?"

"Yeah. Seth Sackett," he said in a pronounced,
slow drawl. "And you never did say if you were
Mrs. Cayton."

"I am."

His gaze slid over her again from head to toe.
Even though it wasn't leering, it was bold, and she
shifted uneasily beneath his silent perusal, wondering if in her attempt to allay trouble by hiring him,
she had only bought herself more.

His eyes lifted to hers again and she sensed that
he could read every thought there, every fear, every
nuance of emotion. For all her bravado, she
doubted she could conceal her true thoughts from
him, and, because of that, her dislike for him deepened.

"We've been expecting you. You're three days
late," she said with flint in her eyes, as well as in her
voice. "I hope you'll be more dependable in the
future."

There was only a flicker of reaction to her words, but it was enough to make her realize that he wasn't a man who would tolerate too much highhandedness, even from an employer. If she wanted to keep him on, she would have to do a better job of hiding her contempt for him. But she wouldn't be meek. She hadn't been from the day she was born and she wouldn't let some gun-slinging sonofabitch make her start now. He might be used to controlling people with nothing more than their fear of him, but he wouldn't control her. For a moment she met those stormy eyes of his, cold stare for cold stare, just to let him know.

She turned on her heel and left him to follow. "Come to my office and we'll discuss your employment."

She heard the door latch softly. The booted feet barely made a sound as he crossed the gleaming hardwood floor and the small braided rugs scattered along the way. She felt the chill of his presence behind her like a cold wind pushing her to take cover. She had to be crazy to have hired him in the first place, let alone invited him into her home. Yet, what choice did she have unless she wanted to lose this home?

In the office, she settled herself behind the desk where Trent had conducted his business and managed the diverse affairs of the White Raven. Sackett paused in the doorway of the small room, blocking the opening almost completely. There was a window behind her, and for the first time in her life Maggie found herself thinking of it as a means of escape.

"Take your hat and coat off and hang it there on the coat tree," she waved a hand toward the corner where it stood. "I'll give you your retainer now and the rest when you complete the job."

She avoided meeting his eyes and busied herself unlocking the top desk drawer. From her peripheral vision she saw him remove his raincoat, but not his hat. He wore all black. Only a white shirt beneath a black vest broke the continuity of color from head to toe. He settled in the leather chair across from her and quietly waited. Outside, the rain suddenly began to pour. Driven by the wind, it lashed viciously at the window behind her. The sound of the rain and the occasional crack of thunder was the only relief from the uneasy silence hanging stagnant in the air.

She knew it would have been better manners to invite him into the parlor for tea or coffee, or to even offer him a shot of whiskey to warm himself, but she simply didn't want to be friendly or sociable with his sort. He would most likely read more into it than she intended. Besides, she was anxious to have him out of the house.

From the top drawer of the desk she removed the bills totalling five hundred dollars and handed them to him. Immediately she realized she should have slid them across the desk for when his hand reached out to accept them, his fingers brushed hers. The startling heat of those long, tanned fingers streaked to every part of her body as swiftly as a sizzling lightning flash. Her gaze shot upward, meeting his, and she realized too late that the spontaneity of her reaction had betrayed her awareness of him. She felt a flush rise to her cheeks and saw an enigmatic glow darken his eyes.

"Count it if you'd like," she said, hoping to shift the direction of his interest from her face to the money.

It didn't work. He barely seemed to notice the money. He took it and tucked it into his inner vest pocket, saying, "I trust you." Yet his eyes belied his words. There was an essence in them that made another chill run down her spine. He trusted her, indeed. If the complete five hundred wasn't in there when he did get around to counting it, he would probably come back and put a bullet through her without giving it a second thought.

He came to his feet, slowly, towering over her to such a height that she, too, stood up. He sauntered back to his coat and shrugged it on. She found herself nearly hypnotized by the shift of muscles in his back and arms as he drew the garment back on. He was a big man, broad in the shoulder, narrow in the hip, and he stood at least six foot three.

"Where are my quarters, Mrs. Cayton?"

She pulled her eyes from his chest, thinking there was probably a lot she should be discussing with him, but her mind seemed to have become a gray void. She did remember that Sonny had returned from Deadwood with the word that Sackett wanted his retainer in cash, no bank drafts, and that he wouldn't take the job unless he could have his own quarters. Apparently he was unsociable and didn't want to bunk with the hired hands. Either that or he was afraid one of them would put a bullet in his head in the middle of the night.

"There's a place in the tack building where we put our extra hired hands during roundup," she said. "It's not the best, but as you can see the barn burned so it was about our only alternative."

"No extra rooms in this big house, Mrs. Cayton?"

She stiffened. His eyes held a glint of amusement. Was he joking, or was he serious? Did he actually believe that what he did was an honest profession and should be treated as such? He might act polite, even like a gentleman, but as far as she was concerned, there was only one true side to a man who killed for a living, and everything else he presented, or tried to present, was pure bullshit.

She felt the hair bristle on her scalp. "Maybe we should get one thing straight right now, Sackett," she suddenly heard herself saying. "I hired you to do a job, but you're not here to become friends with me or my family. As a matter of fact, I would prefer it if you would use another name. I'm afraid your own could bring us more problems than we already have."

He smiled, but there was no humor behind it. "Surely your ranch hands already know all about me. I doubt your foreman could keep a secret any better than the next person."

"I told him not to say anything."

"And you trust him to obey?" When she didn't respond he continued. "As I said, your hired hands probably already know who I am, and your family will know soon enough. You call me by my name or I'll just give you back your money, and you can find somebody else to do your dirty work."

His eyes were as intimidating as the gleaming end of a poisonous arrow. If Maggie had had feathers, they would surely have been ruffled. She had the sudden urge to march around the desk and slap him good and hard across his arrogant face, but she had the good judgment of keeping the big oak desk between them.

"My dirty work? Well, maybe that's what it is, Sackett, but then that's what you're used to doing. Isn't it?"

He seemed to know she didn't want an answer and he didn't give her one, but she didn't overlook the mounting fury in his eyes.

"Don't play games with me," she continued, "and I won't play any with you. I know what you are, and I don't care if another gunman's bullet finds you one day—it would be justice. But I don't want it happening before you finish what I've hired you for."

He took the two steps back to the desk and with knuckles pressing against the polished wood, he leaned toward her until only inches separated their faces, but Maggie refused to back down to him in any way.

"I like people who are honest, Mrs. Cayton," he said, "so I'll be honest with you. Your little war doesn't mean shit to me. I don't care if you win or if Ben Tate wins. All I care about is the thousand dollars you promised to pay me. So naturally I'll try to keep you alive so I can collect. But in order for me to remain loyal to you, you'll have to keep me happy here at the White Raven or I could just go to Tate. I'm sure he'd be happy to up the price."

If Maggie hadn't needed the insolent bastard so much she would have fired him on the spot, but something kept her reined in. She would be stupid to make an enemy of a man like Sackett—if she hadn't already.

"I don't know what Sonny Haig told you, Mr. Sackett, but my husband was killed by one of Tate's hired guns." She couldn't keep the bitterness from her voice. "I won't apologize for my feelings about men in your line of work."

The room was too dim now, and she wished she'd lit a lamp. His perusal suddenly seemed too encompassing. She felt as vulnerable as if she had been stripped naked beneath the onslaught of his silent assessments, whatever they were. His expressions seemed never completely discernible, and she wondered if they were always just a hint of this, a bit of that. When he finally spoke, it was in a tone barely above a whisper and she had to strain to hear what he said over the rumble of the thunder and the rain lashing the windowpanes.

"The way you feel is understandable, Mrs. Cayton. But now I can see it's not a hired gun you want. It's a champion, a knight on a white horse who'll charge into the thick of battle and lay down his life for you and your cause. Frankly, I don't care anymore about your petty little range war than you care about my life." He yanked the bills from his vest pocket and slapped them back down on the desk. "Good day, Mrs. Cayton."

Before Maggie realized what had happened, Sackett was no longer standing in the doorway of her office. By the time she had collected herself and recovered from the verbal slap to the face, he had shown himself to the front door. Her voice caught him just before he exited.

"Sackett."

He turned, glaring at her. His eyes were not totally successful this time at concealing his anger. At least there was one emotion he was no good at hiding. He waited for her to speak. Outside, thunder and lightning struck at the same time, making her jump. He didn't even wince.

"The last thing I want is someone to lay down their life for me, Sackett," she said. "It's a burden I don't need added to the ones I'm already shouldering. All I want is your presence and your muscle to keep Tate in line. And if things should escalate to a war, I'll need your expertise. I'm hoping to prevent that from happening. I don't want to see any more people die. I only want to keep my land and my home."

Sackett obviously didn't make any hasty decisions, nor any hasty pardons. It was several moments before he responded to her apology and her offer of employment. "The only reason I'm here now, Mrs. Cayton, is because I felt you were standing on the right side of the law and that Tate wasn't. I won't help you fight this battle if you step over that line."

She couldn't help but find that amusing. "You hardly strike me as a saint, Sackett. Why should you care which side of the law I stand on?"

"Because I have to live with my conscience, Mrs. Cayton, even if you have the luxury of transferring yours."

His eyes penetrated hers again and she felt a challenge in their stark, gray depths. She didn't comprehend the nature of it, but knew it made her highly uneasy, as everything about him did. Before she could stop him, he was gone again, this time closing the door in her face.

With bitter fascination, she watched him saunter across the muddy yard, leading the bay gelding to the loafing shed where the other saddle horses had taken cover from the rain. She had no idea if he was going to stay or go, or if he was just going to wait out the storm on her property. She would know in the morning what his plans were, but she wouldn't ask him a second time to accept employment.

He removed the gear from his horse and turned the animal in with the others. Lugging the saddle on his shoulder, and bowing his head against the rain, he turned toward the tack building, seeming to know inherently which one it was. But when he opened the door, he paused, glancing over his shoulder at her. In a gesture that seemed purely mocking even from the distance, he touched the brim of his hat and nodded to her. Hastily she stepped back inside, firmly closing the door behind her.

For all her good intentions, though, Maggie could do nothing but walk the floor of her bedroom well into the night. As the clock downstairs rang out twelve rings, she glanced to the tack building and saw that Sackett's light was still burning. The storm was gone now and the moon rode high in the sky, casting a ghostly silver sheen over the hills.

Knowing it was totally foolish, she nonetheless

changed back into her clothes. She had to be certain he wouldn't leave at first light. Her problem still loomed like the circling black shadow of a buzzard. For as much as she hated to admit it, she still needed him.

So, gathering up the money from her office desk, she slipped quietly into the night.

Chapter Two

When the wicked cometh, then cometh also contempt and, with ignominy, reproach. Proverbs 18:3

The rapping on the tack room door brought Seth Sackett to immediate attention. The Bible closed in one hand while, as if by magic, his Colt .45 Peacemaker appeared in the other. He slid the Bible under the pillow and came to his feet.

He didn't like being disturbed when he was alone in his quarters, and he was always wary when his privacy was invaded, especially at odd hours. He had learned long ago that friends were harder to find than enemies, and the two would separate themselves like cream from milk soon enough. But while he had not yet found either friend or foe here at the White Raven, he knew from experience it was seldom the former who came in the middle of the night.

"Who is it?" he demanded in an irritated growl. "Can't a man get any sleep around this place?"

"It's me . . . Maggie Cayton," came the softly

spoken reply. "I need to speak to you, Mr. Sackett. I saw your light was still on."

He relaxed. So the lady boss had come to beg? He'd expected as much, but oddly found no satisfaction in it. People who begged were essentially weak or foolish, certainly without pride, and he had no respect for those particular flaws of human nature.

Your pride will be your ruination, boy. It'll send you right straight to Hell.

Maybe so, Pa, but at least it won't be self-righteousness that puts me there.

The stinging memory of his father's hand cracking across his face jarred Seth from his neutrality. He took the steps to the door and pulled it open, but with caution, and with his gun still in hand. Mrs. Cayton was a beautiful woman, but sometimes women could be more deadly than men. He'd learned that lesson the hard way and still had the knife scar on his back to remind him of a beautiful French whore who'd led him on a merry chase of love and deception. The rigid set of Mrs. Cayton's shoulders, however, reminded him he was not dealing with an over-powdered paramour.

His gaze slid over his pretty visitor, absorbing once again the perfect curves beneath the fitted shirtwaist and black riding skirt. He took another amused glance at the revolver still slung on her shapely hips. The auburn hair she'd had coiled on top of her head earlier had been released from its pins and fell in a thick, luxurious shawl over her shoulders. The dim light of the kerosene lamp gave it depth and richness that reminded him of firelight playing on brandy.

Perhaps she hadn't come to beg at all, but rather to seduce. If she had, it wouldn't be the first time a woman had acquired, or tried to acquire, his services through insidious means.

His eyes lifted to the emerald shine of hers, but he saw nothing of seduction in their depths. He saw only an edge of steel, stubborn determination, defiance, and pride. Ah, yes—pride and rebellion. His father, Ezra Sackett, a self-appointed savior, would have had a heyday trying to exterminate those two particular evils from Mrs. Maggie Cayton and mold her into his concept of goodness and godliness, the changes he would have deemed necessary before she could meet her savior with sufficient meekness. For the meek shall inherit the earth, so said He. Seth always thought it odd how the rule had never applied to Ezra himself.

Seth stepped back, opening the door wider and dropping his revolver back in its holster. "Come in, Mrs. Cayton. Did things get lonely up at the big house?"

Maggie Cayton was quick to recognize the mocking, sexual suggestiveness in his tone, but she pretended not to notice. She stepped inside the tack building, suddenly wondering if she'd used extremely poor judgment by coming here. But it was too late to retreat now.

She moved away from Sackett to the center of the building which measured about thirty feet square. She'd never paid much attention to the low roof and the exposed, big-beam rafters, but her attention was drawn to them now because they barely cleared Sackett's head.

There were three cots in the room pushed up against one long wall. They were used during those times of year, such as fall roundups, when more men were needed than what the bunkhouse would accommodate. Sometimes even more cots had to be brought in. A small table, next to the cot Sackett had chosen to occupy, held a lamp, ashtray, basin, and water pitcher. Every wall was taken up with bridles, harnesses, halters, and ropes, all neatly coiled and draped on large nails. Beneath them were shelves that held neat's foot oil, tools, and medicines for the horses. Lined up along the perimeters of the plank floor, rows of sawhorses supported the ranch's saddles as well as the cowboys' personal gear.

It had stopped raining, and Sackett had opened a window, so along with the usual smells of leather and oil, salves and tonics, came the fresh mountain air spiced with damp earth and the lingering scent of rain. She also detected the aromatic tinge of tobacco smoke and saw the remnants of a ready-made cigarette in the ashtray.

She gave Sackett's cot a brief surveillance, noting his saddlebags tossed there, unbuckled, but she couldn't see the contents. On nails on the wall he'd hung his duster and hat. He'd used one of the empty sawhorses for his saddle and bridle. There was nothing, however, in his meager possessions that told her any more about him than she already knew, or surmised.

She turned finally to find him watching her, waiting for her to make the first move. Without his hat she could see his face and hair clearly now. The latter was wavy and dark, nearly black, and the former was as handsome as the devil would have made his own if he had set out to woo a woman to his bed. The shadow of black stubble was deep but not deep enough to conceal the strong facial lines and hard jaw. His height and breadth was almost ominous in the dim lamplight, and she wished, with uneasiness, that she hadn't allowed him to position himself between her and the door.

"Are the quarters acceptable, Mr. Sackett?"

"I've seen worse," he replied nonchalantly. "But I hardly think you came here to inquire after my comfort, Mrs. Cayton. So to what do I owe the pleasure of this midnight visit?"

She didn't care for the smoldering glow in his eyes as he spoke. A man with that look, even as indiscernible as it might be, was a man who deserved a woman's utmost attention and wariness, for in the dark smokey depths of a smoldering fire lay hidden coals of danger, ready to burst into destructive flames.

"You left the first half of your payment in my office," she replied, handing him the packet of money.

His razor-sharp eyes took a bold measure of her before lifting indifferently from the money to her face. He looped his thumbs in his gun belt, ignoring the money. "I thought I made it clear I wasn't accepting the job."

"I need you, Sackett," she said bluntly. "Reconsider."

His weight shifted to one long, lean leg. "It might cost you more than that now, Mrs. Cayton," he said in a soft, low tone. "Or . . . should I call you *Maggie?*"

She felt the brush of his whisper again over her senses, touching her with his voice as if he'd touched her with his hands. Unnerved by the peculiar sensation of it, Maggie lowered her arm back to her side. "How much more, Sackett? One hundred? Two?"

"Oh, I think much more than that."

He moved toward her, slowly, until the toes of his boots were touching the toes of hers. At such close proximity his presence was even more daunting. Though only inches separated his brawny chest from the rapid rise and fall of her bosom, Maggie refused to back down to him. She might feel like a doe cornered by a mountain lion, but she knew that one step in retreat would be a lethal mistake. Predators always leaped when their prey took flight.

Those probing gray eyes, touched by faint crow's feet, seemed focused entirely too intently on hers, and if he had been a magician she was sure she would have fallen under his spell. What frightened her the most was that she knew she was no match for him in any way that was physical. The only way she could ever possibly win a battle with him would be by the sheer manipulation of his mind.

His hand curled around her wrist, startling her. The touch of his fingers branded her. Her first impulse was to pull away, but she forced herself to remain motionless. It was apparent he was accustomed to intimidating people, but she wouldn't be one of them. He lifted her hand upward until it was between them, her fingers gripping the money much tighter than necessary.

But he didn't look at the money; his eyes remained trained on hers. Almost imperceptibly his gaze slid to her lips, and her heart began to pound viciously. She wanted to run. God, how she wanted to run! But something told her—perhaps it was that mocking, sultry glow in his eyes—that running was exactly what he was daring her to do. She didn't know if he wanted to hurt her or merely humiliate her in some sadistic way, but she was positive he was trying his best to frighten her.

The slightest pressure on her wrist pulled her unerringly closer to him until she felt the heat of his body emanating into hers, scorching her. The hard length of his legs brushed the folds of the riding skirt, and his loins edged closer, coming within a fraction of an inch of her own. His nearness alone induced a steady, hard throb in that area, causing her cheeks to blaze with shame at her body's reaction to him.

She didn't want to look at his lips, graced by the thick, black moustache, but like a magnet her eyes were drawn there nonetheless. His mouth was set in a firm, distinctly masculine line, and she could read nothing of his thoughts by the set of it. He merely waited like a hawk, watching the subtle movement that would signal the moment to attack. And suddenly he saw it. His lips swooped down, covering hers, while arms of corded muscle closed around her, dragging her against his chest and forcing all the air from her lungs. His lips scalded hers. His tongue sought entry into her mouth and succeeded. His loins collided with hers.

Her restraint cracked and she lashed out at him, shoving him as hard backwards as she possibly could. She lifted her hand to strike him across the face but he caught her wrist.

"Don't do it, if you know what's good for you," he warned.

"Then let me go." Her command was equally threatening.

"I don't really think you mean that, Maggie."

She found herself being pressed backward step by step until the cot met the back of her knees and brought her up short. Sackett put one knee on the bed and leaned into her, forcing her down. She tried with all her strength to remain standing but was easily maneuvered beneath his weight until the pillow found her head and shoulders. He pulled her arms up over her head, stretching her out vulnerably beneath the searing length of his solid body. His chest was hot and hard pressed against her bosom, and she felt with mature knowledge the growing hardness in his loins pressed brazenly against hers. She feared what he would do next, and even though she didn't want to beg, she couldn't help the sharp command that snapped from her lips.

"Let me up, damn you."

"Why, Maggie? Isn't this what you came for? Didn't you feel you could get me to say yes by making love to me? I'm only obliging, making it easier for you."

She tried to get her wrists free of his grip; tried to move out from under him, but all the attempts succeeded in doing was driving his body harder against her own. His lips were alarmingly close again and she turned her head to the side. But she felt their gentle caress move along her cheek and to the sensitive flesh of her neck. A peculiar blaze of fear and desire ignited inside her and roared through her like an uncontrollable prairie fire, leaving her wanting more but simultaneously ashamed and angry at her body for secretly responding to his touch.

"Do you think all women do deals with their bodies, Sackett?" She ground out the words angrily between clenched teeth.

"All the ones I've ever known have," he replied smoothly. "Even virgin girls know how to coerce a man with sex, Maggie. And you're an experienced woman. Don't tell me you never softened your late husband's stance just a little by seducing him in the soft glow of bedroom candlelight? And I'll bet your skin is beautiful in candlelight. Even the strongest man would succumb to your every wish or whim."

"Damn you."

"Sorry, it's already been done, honey. Plenty of times."

His lips moved past her neck to her collarbone and to the swell of her bosom, leaving a scorching path even through the barrier of her cotton shirtwaist and chemise. His lips paused on the curve of her bosom above her heart and she knew he could gauge with his lips the ferocious pounding of her pulse, the telltale beat of her fear and frustration, as well as the forbidden, traitorous feelings unfurling inside her.

"How long's it been since you had a man, Maggie?" he murmured, his lips still against her thumping heart. She sensed his eyes lifted to her face, watching her emotions, but she kept her gaze averted. "A long time?" he continued. "Well, it's been a long time since I had a woman as pretty and sweet-smelling as you. And who knows, maybe I'll change my mind about your job offer come morning. That is, if you treat me real sweet tonight."

She could refrain no longer to his abusive invasion of her privacy. "Go to hell, you bastard. If you want me you'll have to take me by force. I would never submit to the likes of you. I don't know why you thought I came here, but it wasn't to be sweet."

Suddenly he laughed, a low-throated rumble that didn't reach beyond the walls of the building. He pressed another kiss through the cloth covering her bosom, this one almost directly onto her nipple. "No, I don't suppose you *did* come here to be sweet. I can see that now."

He came to his feet, bringing her with him. She found herself caught up against his lean, hard body again. Amusement lurked on the edge of his lips, but it didn't reach his eyes. Their coldness penetrated her, like a northern wind that finds its way through the thickest wall and through the most tightly woven sweater.

"Our little encounter will have to end here then, won't it?" he said regrettably. "Because if you wanted me to force myself on you—to ease your own conscience—I just can't oblige."

"How dare you suggest—"

He overrode her objection. "You see, I like my women to submit to me willingly, Maggie. I like them compliant and soft beneath me with their arms and legs open for me. I want to hear them whispering in my ear just how much they want me to pleasure them."

Maggie lost her objection in the velvet caress of his words that were wickedly making love to her even as his lips had done before with the undeniable power of persuasion. She felt fire rise to her cheeks and knew that Sackett did not miss one leaping flame of it. But if he was satisfied at her humiliation, he gave no indication.

"I like them to tell me how much they love me, Maggie," he continued, "even if I know they'll pretend they don't know me the next day."

As he spoke, bitterness and a trace of cynicism edged into his voice, deepening until Maggie wondered if he would choke on them both. She had the peculiar feeling that he harbored a deep contempt not toward her, or even toward the world, but rather toward himself. And that his light, mocking attitude was only a cover up for a darkness inside his own soul.

He released her, and oddly enough she felt more vulnerable away from his body than she had when pressed against it. Something in her still craved the masculine part of him that had stirred her, reminding her of pleasures she had not felt since Trent's death and would probably never feel again.

Her wrists stung but she refrained from rubbing them. She'd be damned before she'd give him the satisfaction of knowing he'd hurt her. She stepped past him and to the door. She wasn't running from him; she was running to hide her disgrace that a killer's lips had actually stirred her womanly passions. Her body had betrayed her, surprising her with the disturbing realization that she could too easily be one of those shameless women he spoke of. But maybe the women shouldn't be completely to blame; maybe Sackett just had a way of drawing out the dark side of desire.

"I guess this means our business deal has fallen completely through?"

His taunting remark brought her to a halt with her hand still on the doorknob. "You can leave in the morning, Sackett. You may think all women will prostitute themselves for what they want, but I'm not one of them. I'll find somebody else who will accept a thousand dollars and expect no strings attached."

"And if you don't?"

"Then I'll die fighting."

His low chuckle made her burn inside with even deeper indignation. She had the urge again to slap his arrogant face, but if she did, she knew she would land back in his arms and she considered that a danger worse than any to date.

"When a woman comes to a man's room in the middle of night, Maggie," he added indifferently, shrugging his shoulders, "there's usually only one reason. What did you expect me to think you were offering at nearly one in the morning?"

"You can think any damn thing you like, Sackett. And now you can go to Hell, too."

Seth watched her storm from the building but suddenly decided he wasn't ready for her to go just yet. The tack building was cleaner and more comfortable than a lot of bunkhouses he'd been in—at least there were no lice—but Maggie's presence had given it a vital color of life that was otherwise absent. Or maybe it was just the lingering memory of her sweet-smelling skin that made him go after her. She'd started an unexpected blaze inside him that needed either more fuel or complete extermination.

At the sound of the door creaking on its hinges again, he saw her pause in the shaft of light that stretched out from the building's doorway. But suddenly she moved into the safety of the darkness, and Seth understood why she had done it. The last thing a respectable woman like her would want is for some night owl over at the bunkhouse to see her with him in the middle of the night. He'd ruined a lot of reputations, even if he'd done it unintentionally. When a woman became his lover, sometimes she had to be willing to suffer the consequences of association. And it seemed Mrs. Cayton wasn't willing to do either . . . yet.

He expected her to flee, but she waited with what he perceived to be an impatient stance until he had stopped a few feet away. She had courage; he had to hand her that. Most men wouldn't have stood up to him. And most women—well, all they wanted to do was get under him. Then they discarded him, or he discarded them.

"What do you want now, Sackett?" she snapped. "It had better be good because you've worn out your welcome."

"Did I ever have one?"

An amused smirk moved her lips. "How perceptive of you to notice that."

He leaned against the hitching rail. "You know, Maggie, my father wouldn't have liked you. But I do. So I've reconsidered, and I'll take that money you have in your hand."

She lifted a brow. Suspicion glittered in her eyes. "No you won't, Sackett. Unless you plan on staying and doing your job—and leaving me alone."

His chuckle drifted lightly into the quiet night, hiding, he hoped, the old emptiness that had sprang up unexpectedly inside him once again. She was the wrong kind of woman for him. She was the sort a man could lose his heart to, and frequently did—in vain. He'd be wise to leave while the path of departure was clearly set out before him. If he'd known she was so desirable he would never have come here in the first place. But, as was often the plan of God, temptation had been placed before him, and never had it looked so good.

His gaze slid to her bosom. His lips remembered the feel of her softness; his nose the scent of freshly washed skin. "I'll stay," he said, "but I won't promise to leave you alone. I'd be willing to bet that wad of money in your hand that before I leave here, you and I will be lovers."

Her back stiffened. "It'll be a cold day in Hell first."

"Hell is where you make it, Maggie."

She scrutinized him with obvious disdain, but he waited patiently for her ultimate decision. He didn't need her money, or her war. He could have found an easy way out, so why was he standing here asking for the job back?—outside of the fact that she was entirely too enticing to willingly walk away from.

"I don't know that I can trust you to stay and not ride out at first light with the money," she added stubbornly.

"You weren't worried about it a few hours ago. Or even a few minutes ago when you came to my room."

She gave him a cool perusal but could offer no denial.

"The way I see it," he continued, "you have no choice. It's either me or Ben Tate."

At last they'd come full circle to the bottom line, and he saw how quickly she was sobered by reality. She drew in a long, deep breath and handed him the money.

"I hope you're good at taking orders, Sackett," she said, elevating her head in that haughty, authoritative way he found most annoying, and yet appealing too. "Because your first order is to quit calling me Maggie. To you, and all the other ranch hands, I'm Mrs. Cayton."

So, she was determined about not letting him get too close? Would she have been so adamant if he hadn't kissed her? He supposed if he were in her shoes, he would do the same thing. After all, what good, upstanding woman of the community wants a piece of trash making an eyesore of her respectability? It was natural for a woman like her to think of that sort of thing, but he knew he could wear her down eventually.

He forced himself to find a bit of humor in her command. "If I recall, your foreman, Sonny Haig, referred to you as Maggie quite frequently in the conversation we had over in Deadwood. Doesn't the rule apply to him? Or maybe he's already filling your late husband's side of the bed?"

Her face tightened with anger again, but she didn't lift a hand to him a second time. That was another plus for her; she learned quickly. "My personal life is none of your business, Sackett."

He pulled a cigarette from his vest pocket and lit it, blowing a stream of smoke to the crystal clear night sky. "You're absolutely right. Your personal life isn't any of my business. But if I'm to do my job to the best of my ability and earn all that money you're paying me, I'll need to know about the people closest to you."

"I don't see why that's necessary. All you need to do is stop Tate."

"I'm here to protect you, Maggie, to fight your battles and to win your war . . . as is the nature of all good-hearted soldiers of fortune. If I'm to be successful, you need to do as I say."

He saw her mind at work, considering his demand. For all her attempts at bravado, he'd seen the fear in her eyes earlier when he'd pinned her beneath him on the cot. She was positive he was a killer, and now she was probably not fully convinced that his crimes did not also include being a rapist. But she surprised him, nevertheless, by conceding to his terms.

"All right, Sackett," she said. "There's nothing between Sonny and me. He's just worked here for a long time, that's all. Now, what else would you like to know?"

A breeze drifted down from the Big Horns. It felt good and cool to him, but he saw her shiver. If she had been more receptive, he would have found a pleasant way to keep her warm.

"Nothing else right now," he said. "But I do have a word of advice."

She waited, her lips pursed. She clearly didn't like getting advice and he wondered for the first time if her husband had had a time keeping her under control. But she would have at least made life interesting. And lively. Personally, he wouldn't want a passive woman. Everything in life was better if it contained a little fire.

"Leave your gun at home from here on out," he said, mincing no words. "Wearing it will only buy you a bullet—the same way it did your husband."

"Well, maybe it will bring me a bullet," she replied arrogantly, "but not wearing it can do the same thing."

He remained outside until she had disappeared inside her fancy, white frame house. She was certainly a high-toned, sharp-tongued, stubborn woman who thought she was better than he was— and she was—but he couldn't help but feel a certain kinship with her just the same. She was a fighter, a prideful fighter, and that alone was enough to put him on her side of the line.

It was too bad he'd never be able to introduce her to Ezra Sackett. She would never be the sort to turn the other cheek to that fire and brimstone preacher, and it would have been a battle worth sitting in on. But battles with his pa were over, even if the cause of them had been left disturbingly unsettled.

He finally sauntered back to his new quarters and closed the door behind him. He put the money in his saddlebags and stretched out on his cot, thinking of Maggie's body and mouth so soft and irresistible. He couldn't make her like him—no, that would be too much to ask—but his pride might be soothed by knowing he could make her want him.

He grabbed the pillow to fluff it, and the forgotten Bible beneath it tumbled out onto the floor, falling open. A well-known verse leaped out at him before he gathered the book with care and put it back in his saddlebags. It had been his mother's Bible, her gift to him just before she had died. But the verse had ironically been one of his father's favorites, and Seth didn't need to read it to know what it said. The words of Jeremiah 49:16 rang out loud and clear in Ezra Sackett's shrill, condemning voice:

Thy terribleness hath deceived thee, and the pride of thine heart. . . . though thou shouldest make thy nest as high as the eagle, I will bring thee down from there, saith the Lord.

Chapter Three

Seth Sackett was no stranger to the calculating scrutiny of ranch hands. When he joined the other hands for breakfast in the cookshack it didn't surprise him that no one offered a greeting. They recognized him for what he was—or for what they perceived him to be—and nothing but time could change their minds. And sometimes, not even that, because there were those instances when what they perceived him to be was exactly what he was. Some held contempt for him, others were afraid of him. He could tell the difference easily enough. The former openly glared at him; the latter evaded his eyes altogether, probably believing that if they paid him no mind he wouldn't find a cause to shoot one of them.

As he held out his tin plate for the cook to fill it with his portion of bacon, ham, eggs, and biscuits, he was bitterly amused by it all. There were some things in life that never changed. But it was just as well that no one wanted to like him. He was successful at what he did because he was feared. A man couldn't have friends and fear, too. If a man like him ever allowed anybody to get too close he would lose his edge and his effectiveness as a gunman. Their knowledge of his inner scars would make him vulnerable, and only death awaited the vulnerable man.

He set his plate on the end of the wooden table and went the few feet to the stove to pour himself a cup of coffee from the oversized coffee pot. A leather glove was nearby, provided as a hot pad, and he draped it around the handle.

"You might as well leave, Sackett," came a cocksure voice behind him. "You ain't goin' to get to kill nobody here at the White Raven . . . unless you do it in cold blood. And I hear you're real good at that."

A hush fell over the room. No one moved. They barely breathed. Seth had continued to fill his cup while the man spoke from behind him. He was highly aware of everyone in the room, of their precise positions. From the moment he'd entered the cookshack he had instinctively separated the harmless ones from the ones who might pose a threat to him. They probably didn't know it, but he'd been covertly watching them and listening to their small talk. Even now he knew who had spoken simply from the tone of the voice. It was the kid; the one who'd been watching him ever since he'd come from the tack building; the one who'd tried to get his attention by donning a perpetual sneer. He was just a boy. He *might* be twenty, but Seth sincerely doubted it. At any rate, his senses had been alerted by the young voice and now they were honed to every sound the kid made, every nuance of his stance, his breathing, the rustle of his clothing.

Very purposefully, Seth placed the big pot back on the hot plate and set the leather glove aside. He turned slowly, both hands cupping the gray mug. He barely noticed the heat emanating through the heavy glass to his fingers. The boy's hands were free, and his right hand hovered over his gun. Sometimes Seth grew weary of it all, but in every place he went there was always one who had to challenge him. It was like being the new kid in town. You always had to bloody at least one nose before the others would cut you a wide swath.

"What's your name?" Seth asked, keeping his tone level.

A flash of confusion and then anger crossed the kid's face. "What's it to you?"

Seth shrugged. "I just like to know the names of the men I work with."

The kid shifted nervously. His challenge was going unanswered and that was embarrassing him in front of the others. Seth knew it; God knows he'd seen it all dozens of times before. He knew every thought that was racing through the kid's head, and he wasn't surprised by the flush of red creeping up into the sunburned cheeks, spreading even more humiliation. The kid was plainly getting desperate because things weren't going the way he'd envisioned them at all.

"Ain't you going to deny what I said and stand up for yourself like a man, Sackett?" he blurted.

"No sense in denying the truth, kid."

"I ain't a kid!" The boy's hand inched closer to his gun.

"Then tell me who you are so I can call you by your name."

"Name's Forster!"

"Forster. What's your first name?"

The boy's hands started visibly shaking. "Don't you care that I called you a cold-blooded killer? You got a yellow stripe down your back or something, Sackett?"

He'd made what he considered an adequate challenge, and Seth knew he was expecting to be drawn on any second. No doubt he'd been practicing on tin cans and now wanted to put his quickdrawing expertise to the ultimate test. Beads of perspiration had popped out on the sides of his face beneath his big wide-brimmed hat, and it began to trickle down his lightly stubbled cheeks. He lifted a skinny shoulder to wipe it away. Like tiny spiders inching from his hair, it was distracting his concentration.

Seth sipped at the hot coffee, remaining very careful to keep both hands around the mug. He kept his peripheral vision on the rest of the room's occupants, anticipating a move from one of them in an attempt to protect the kid.

"It's kind of hard for a man to see his own back," Seth replied nonchalantly, "but I've never had any of my lady friends tell me I had a yellow stripe. Have you got yourself a lady, Forster?"

The boy's composure was clearly on the verge of collapse. He spread his legs into a wider stance, bracing himself for the draw he wasn't sure was coming. Seth saw his thoughts as plain as the freckles dotting his face, and he knew Forster was reaching a dangerous point of no return.

"Yeah, I got a woman," the kid's lip curled into a snarl. "I can get any amount I want to in town."

"No, I don't mean whores, Forster. We can all get whores. Even me. I want to know if you have a young lady who's sweet on you."

"Yeah, I got me one of those, too. Plenty of 'em." By now his upper lip was quivering and he had a hard time holding it in the snarl.

"Want to see any of them Saturday night, or maybe Sunday after church? Take one of them on a picnic?"

Forster shifted uncertainly, obviously confused by the direction of the questioning. "Sure, why not, Sackett?"

"Well then, you'd better go back to your table and eat your breakfast. I'm sure those young ladies would rather kiss you than bury you."

The kid's eyes skittered nervously across the faces of his fellow cowboys who watched him with solemn disapproval. He was, after all, interrupting what had promised to be a good meal. He'd made a fool of himself and he knew it. Now, he had to try and figure a graceful way out of it. But there wasn't one, at least not for Forster. The wild, panicky look in his eyes deepened. Seth knew the precise moment when the kid decided to save face and go for his gun—and Seth's Peacemaker was in his palm before Forster's old revolver had even cleared leather. Seth's shot rang out, snapping the gun from the kid's hand and sending it clattering across the plank floor. The cup of coffee in Seth's other hand didn't lose one drop of liquid.

Nobody moved. Frozen, they waited to see what would happen next. A few seconds later, the door of the cookshack burst open and another young man of about sixteen rushed in. Seth braced himself for an outside attack, but quickly saw there was no cause for alarm. The new arrival took one look at Forster, and at Seth's smoking gun, and he didn't need any explanations. He gathered up Forster's gun which he had spotted on the floor in front of him.

"Sackett's on our side, Milo, so why don't you let him eat in peace. And the rest of you—your eggs are probably already cold."

Seth waited until everyone had edged back to the table and gone back to eating before he dropped his gun back into the holster. Forster stalked out the door, and the dark-haired young man who had intervened joined Seth, offering his hand in an open, friendly shake.

"My name's Lance Cayton," he said. "You're Sackett, I guess."

"You must be Mrs. Cayton's son."

The boy nodded, seeming proud of that fact.

A reserved smile touched the corners of Seth's lips. Lance Cayton may not have had his mother's auburn hair, but he looked a lot like her, and he took after her in personality—courageous, authoritative, and driven. He was still a boy in age, but he was a man in form. Because he treated Seth the same as he would have anyone else, he managed to win Seth's instant respect without even trying.

Lance rested his hands on his narrow hips and glanced at the men at the other end of the room. "I'm sorry for what happened, Sackett. There was no call for Milo to make trouble. But sometimes he just doesn't use good sense. Don't worry, I won't give him back the gun."

"He might need it for protection out on the range."

"Aren't you worried about him back-shootin' you?" Lance asked, amazed.

"No," Seth chuckled. "I think he'll leave me alone from here on out. But thanks for breaking things up. Everybody's food was getting cold, and there's nothing worse than a fried egg that's gone cold."

Lance chuckled, looking over at the men. When he spoke again he lowered his voice so it would be easily muffled by Cookie's clattering pots and pans and the talk that had started up among the men. "I guess maybe I shouldn't have interfered. It isn't my place, but Sonny wasn't doing anything and he's the damn foreman."

Seth saw it was a great source of annoyance to Lance, and he sensed it wasn't the first time Haig had shirked his duties. "He shouldn't care. There was no harm done."

"No, but he gets mad when I assume authority. Anyway, I need to go. Ma likes me to eat at the big house. I'll be talking to you later."

Seth watched Lance Cayton leave. The men were watching him, too, but none of them seemed to have minded his interference, except Haig who followed his exit with a dark scowl. Yes, there was plainly some resentment there. But was it because Lance had assumed authority? Or because he had broken up the gun battle?

Seth set his coffee aside and had Cookie fill up another plate. The bewhiskered, cranky old man eyed him irritably but didn't ask why he needed another. Seth sauntered outside with it and saw Forster sitting on the top pole of the horse corral, sulking just as he figured he would be.

"Better eat up," Seth said, handing the plate of food up to him. "It's a long time til noon."

"I ain't hungry, you sonofabitch," Forster growled.

Seth studied the belligerent young face, knowing Forster didn't really mean it, at least not the part about being hungry. "No, I don't reckon you are at the moment, but you will be."

"If I was hungry I'd go in there and eat. You ain't stoppin' me from it."

"I didn't figure I was, but those old boys in there can be a mite intimidating. I can tell you one thing, they'll have a lot more respect for you if you accept your defeat like a man. They sure won't hold it against you for losing the draw."

Forster's glare turned to sorrowful regret and confusion, but his tone was still combative. "I suppose you think I ought to be grateful you didn't shoot me."

"No, not at all. If you want to die that's your business. But I wasn't real sure that's what you wanted. Next time I'll be more than happy to oblige. A man who wants to die isn't any good to have around anyway."

Forster angrily grabbed the plate in a gesture of pure appeasement. "Okay, Sackett, I'll take the damn food, but this ain't going to make me like you."

Seth latched his thumbs in his gun belt and gave the kid a cool measure of consideration. "Well, you wouldn't be much of a man if it did."

Leaving the angry young man, Seth returned to the cookshack and ate his cold breakfast—everything except the eggs. He ignored the curious and silent appraisals of the men as each glanced his way now and then. He didn't care what they thought of him for trying to make peace with Forster. It was none of their damn business anyway. He just figured he'd have enough opposition from Tate and his men, he didn't need trouble in his own camp, too.

He lifted his gaze only once during the course of his meal and that was when he felt Haig watching him. When their eyes locked for a curious moment, Haig quickly went back to eating. Like Lance Cayton had said, it was a little perplexing that Haig hadn't stopped Forster before things got out of hand. How could Haig have been sure Seth wouldn't have killed the kid?

But then again, maybe he hadn't been.

"Mama! Mama!" Nine-year-old Alison burst into the family dining room. "That man you've been waiting for is out in the tack building and Sonny says he's a hired gun!"

She slid onto her chair next to her mother, apparently oblivious to the silence that had suddenly descended over the breakfast table.

"You're late," Maggie managed, feeling her own mother's questioning eyes from across the table. She had really hoped to keep her mother in the dark about Sackett, or at least break the news to her a bit more gently. "Go wash your hands, Alison, and then you can eat. The rest of us are nearly done. Except you and Lance. Have you seen him?"

"No. He's probably upstairs fussin' with his hair like he does every morning after he's done with his chores."

"All right. Go wash your hands," Maggie reminded.

"But I didn't get them dirty, Mama."

"She did, too," came an accusing voice from the doorway. Lance sauntered in, pulling out a chair. As Alison had suggested, his dark hair was freshly combed, swooped back from his forehead. It did look like he'd been working on it for quite a while to get it to lay so perfectly. He sat down and reached for the pot of coffee in the center of the table. "Don't believe her, Mom. She was out there playing with Mimi's new batch of kittens."

"I was not!"

"You were, too. I saw you from my window plain as the cat hair all over your dress."

"O-o-oh, I hate you, Lance. You think you're so dang smart just because you're a boy and because you're the oldest. Well, you're not any smarter than anybody else in this family. And your hair looks dumb with that stinky tonic all over it. You're going to meet Cecilia again today, aren't you?"

"Shut up, you little rodent." Lance started out of his chair but Maggie caught his arm.

"Children—*please*. Must you quarrel constantly?"

"She's a brat," Lance said defensively. "Why don't you tan her hide? I'd gladly do it for you if you'd just give me the word."

Alison looked from Lance to her mother. "He's a big bully, Mama. If anybody deserves a lickin', it's him. He's getting too big for his breeches ever since he turned sixteen. He's always hanging around with the cowboys and—"

Maggie held up her hands. "Enough. Or I'll take a switch to both of you. And don't think you're too big and too old for it, Lance." She gave him a stern look. But the truth was, the boy *was* too big for it. He had already reached the six foot mark. Of course, Maggie would keep him thinking that his backside was physically vulnerable to retribution for as long as she possibly could.

But what was this nonsense about him meeting Cecilia Wagner? Maggie didn't like that girl one bit. She was three years older than Lance and she was looking for a husband. Maggie was afraid she'd get one, too, by hook or by crook. Even if it meant playing on the innocence of a sixteen-year-old boy. Maggie glanced sharply at Lance. Surely he'd have enough sense not to be taken in by an older woman?

"Is it true what Alison says?" Natalie spoke up. "Is that man really a gunslinger, Mother? You told us he was going to be the new wrangler. If he can't break horses then I'm never going to be able to ride my mare. I'll have to break her myself."

"You will not! That mare is too spirited for you to handle, young lady. You might be a good rider but I'll sell that mare if I catch you out there trying to break her yourself."

"Well, is this man a wrangler or a gunslinger?" Natalie persisted, ignoring her mother's threat.

Catherine Marshall leaned forward across her plate toward her daughter. "Yes, Margaret. Do tell us about this new man you've hired."

Her eyes held a peculiarly delighted gleam that surprised Maggie. She would have thought her mother would have been upset at her for hiring Sackett. Instead she actually acted like she found the entire discussion greatly amusing. Well, she'd change her mind quickly enough when she met Sackett face to face. He'd scare her mother right back up to her room and to her sleeping draught!

Maggie was satisfied and greatly encouraged that her mother had stayed away from the draught since the night of the fire. Her mother had been very upset that she had slept through the entire thing, and Maggie could only assume that the older woman had decided then and there that the drug was indeed habit-forming and dangerous—in more ways than one—and that it was time to quit being dependent upon it. Catherine had discarded what remained of the draught and had since taken to drinking warm milk and reading before she went to bed. She had selected a huge volume from the library, a book whose "Frenchy-sounding" title and complicated content she could never name nor discuss, but which she said aided enormously in creating drowsiness.

To have Catherine interested in something at long last was a tremendous milestone. Maggie just wished her mother's curiosity had been piqued by something other than Sackett.

"Very well," Maggie began, feeling the pressure of four sets of eyes upon her. "I didn't want to alarm any of you, but I felt we needed protection after what happened. A man of Sackett's calibre could make Tate think twice before coming in here again and burning any more buildings. Next time it could be the house."

Catherine dropped her fork. It landed on her plate with a loud clatter. "Oh, dear. We can't have that. I think you're absolutely right, Maggie. But do you think this man could bring more trouble than he can deter?"

"I've thought about that, Mother. And believe me, if he doesn't work out, I'll send him on his way."

"He's nice," Alison spoke up defensively, tossing her chestnut-colored braids over her shoulder. "I was in there riding on the saddles when he came back from breakfast. He didn't even get mad at me—and it was *his* saddle I was on!"

Maggie's eyes sharpened on her youngest child. "From now on you leave Mr. Sackett alone, Alison. He isn't the sort of man to want to be pestered by children. And stay off the saddles. You've been told before."

Alison abandoned her breakfast and began digging in her dress pocket while she spoke. "You're wrong, Mama. He said I could visit him any time. He said saddles were meant for sitting on, and he even gave me this." She finally found the object she was searching for and displayed it in the palm of her hand. "It's a marble."

"We can see that, stupid," Lance interjected.

"Oh, you shut up!" Alison glared at him. "Mr. Sackett said it was his lucky marble. He's had it since he was my age. Isn't it pretty?" She stared almost entranced at the orange and white orb, as if it did indeed contain magical qualities. "He said it would bring me luck the way it has him."

Lance snorted. "And you believe that malarky? If it's so lucky why'd he give it to you? You're so dumb, Alison. You couldn't drive nails in a snow-bank."

Alison came off her chair, clenching her fist around the marble. "It is too lucky! He said so and I believe him. You're just jealous 'cause he didn't give it to you!"

Maggie anticipated her youngest daughter's flight and caught her arm as she tried to make her hasty, tear-blurred departure. "Come back and eat, Ali," she said gently. "If Mr. Sackett said it's a lucky marble then I'm sure it is."

Alison's shoulders shook from the onslaught of tears, and Maggie drew her into her arms. From over her daughter's shoulder she gave Lance a re-proachful look that finally made him realize she would tolerate no more bickering.

They finished the meal in silence with the only sound being the clattering of utensils against plates. But Maggie never believed for a moment that the subject of Seth Sackett was closed.

Chapter Four

Maggie positioned the leather holster on her skirted hips and checked the load in the Starr, belligerently defying Sackett's order to leave it home. She was going into town to check on the lumber she'd ordered for a new barn, and she simply didn't feel safe without the gun anymore.

She went to the head of the stairs. "Natalie!" she called. "Are you ready yet? If you don't hurry I'm going to leave without you!"

"I'll be there in a *minute*, Mother! For heaven's sake!"

Maggie sighed and tugged her hat down onto her forehead. A total of thirty minutes had passed since her daughter had last said that. The girl had overheard Maggie telling her mother that she was going to town. Immediately Natalie had invited herself, despite Maggie's argument of possible danger in light of the recent developments with Tate. But Natalie had simply said, "Then you should have someone with you, Mother. If one of us gets shot, the other will have to get the body back to the ranch and send out the posse."

"You take this very lightly, Natalie."

"It's boring here, Mother. The cowboys are all out working and you don't want me out there with them, or riding alone. Lance isn't even around to go riding with me. He *says* he's going to check the south fence, but you know he's really gone to meet that deplorable Cecilia Wagoner. She's such a priss. What do the men see in her? The only thing she has worth looking at is her bosom."

"Natalie, is that any way to talk?"

"It's the truth, Mother. Anyway, it'll only take me a minute to change into my riding clothes."

"Yes, thirty of them," grumbled Maggie again. Of course Natalie wasn't so sneaky herself, and Maggie wasn't naive. She knew her daughter wanted to go into town in hopes of seeing Andy Dray, the new young man in town who'd taken a job over at the smithy's. Maggie didn't like the idea of Natalie seeing too much of him. Andy was too old for her, by about seven years. But Natalie had always had the eye for the older ones. She claimed the ones her own age were stupid, silly, and skinny. And she wouldn't listen to her mother who repeatedly reminded her that girls develop faster than boys but that the boys would catch up when the time was right. In a few years when Natalie was of a marriageable age, then a more mature man would be welcomed, but right now it could lead to nothing but trouble. Maggie preferred her daughter to keep company with boys who were content to sit on the porch swing and do nothing more than hold hands, and who were still inexperienced enough to blush just doing that.

Maggie glanced at the clock in the foyer again. If they didn't get away soon they'd be in the dark getting home, or they would have to stay over in town.

Frustrated, and wondering if she'd ever live through raising her children by herself, she left the house and started for the corral. She could at least get the horses saddled by the time Natalie was ready.

She searched the sky for storm clouds and checked the direction of the wind. The air was calm, sultry in fact, and if the heat should bring on another sudden storm she was satisfied it wouldn't occur until they could at least make it to town.

The cowboys had already gone to do their various jobs about the ranch; checking watering holes, fences, searching for sick or injured cattle. The spring roundup was over, along with its strenuous weeks of branding, de-horning, and castrating, so except for the building of the barn, things would take a slower, relaxed pace now until the fall roundup began in September.

Some of the hired hands weren't skilled with horses and lariats but had been hired specifically for ranch yard duty. Their work consisted of fixing corrals, building new ones, repairing wagons, roofs, harnesses, gathering firewood, and cutting hay for the winter months. Right now, they were busy clearing the burned barn timber so when the lumber came in they could start construction immediately.

It would be a big project and it needed to be completed before winter set in.

She had put Otto Putnam in charge of the construction. Married to Maggie's house cook, Dorothy, the couple had been employed on the ranch for a decade. They were both in their fifties and had never had children. They'd made the White Raven their home and lived in a small cabin outside the main yard. Trent had built several cabins because occasionally a good cowboy came along who also had a wife and children. Trent had always supplied the family men with their own cabin. One of the women, Essie Freeman, had come to the ranch seven years ago with her husband. While he had taken a job as a wrangler, Maggie had hired Essie as a school teacher because she had credentials and experience. In the school room in the main house, Essie taught her own children, Maggie's, and any others who happened to be on the ranch. Essie's oldest daughter was a year younger than Alison and they were good friends.

Before Essie had arrived, Maggie had conducted the school classes herself for Lance and Natalie because it was impractical for them to go to school in town every day because of the distance, and she had never wanted to board her children out.

Church had always been conducted the same way, at home with Maggie or Trent reading the Bible. Occasionally a traveling preacher joined them for Sunday dinner and he would conduct a broader sermon to them as well as everyone else on the ranch who cared enough to gather around.

Maggie remembered those early years being such

a struggle, and all the nights she had gone to bed completely exhausted. But she had only had to stand by Trent then, she hadn't had to take his place. Now, all the decisions were on her shoulders.

Tugging at her hat brim just a bit more to protect her eyes from the bright morning sun, Maggie started across the yard to the horse corral. To her dismay, she found not all the cowboys were at work after all. Sackett was sitting atop the pole corral, smoking and looking bored. In the corral itself, swishing their tails against a hoard of early morning flies, were two saddled horses—Sackett's bay and her own sorrel gelding.

She didn't know what she had expected, but she had honestly hoped Sonny would have sent Sackett out this morning to get familiar with the ranch or something. Anything so she wouldn't have to be alone with him again—or face him so soon after last night's disturbing episode in the tack building. As it was, she had dark circles from tossing and turning until three in the morning. Her mind had insisted on dwelling on his brazen lips taking unfair advantage of hers, drawing from deep within her a physical desire she never thought she would feel again, or even want to feel again. Just thinking of another man besides Trent holding her and kissing her had made her feel ashamed and guilty, as if she had somehow betrayed Trent. Sackett was such a perceptive man, she didn't doubt for a minute he would take one look at those dark circles and know exactly what had caused them. She pulled her hat down farther on her forehead, clear to her eyebrows. If he hadn't already seen her, she would have hurried back to the house and waited for Natalie.

He slid down off the pole corral and had the gate open for her when she got there. "Mornin', Maggie. Sleep well?"

His mocking smile was proof he knew darned well she hadn't. Plus, the use of her first name made her bristle even more. He was simply trying to be an irritant and she wasn't going to give him the satisfaction of succeeding. After all, Sonny and some of the men who had been on the ranch for years did call her by her first name, or referred to her as Miss Maggie, a form of politeness. It was just easier to let Sackett have his way on this one.

"Good morning," she replied tightly, responding only to his greeting, not his question. Giving him a polite nod, she did her best to avoid the mesmerizing but dangerous glow in his gray eyes—eyes that were, once again, probing the inner soul of her like some dastardly worm drilling its way to the center of the earth for no other reason than to see what was there.

"It seems you've made a friend already," she said conversationally, bringing up the first topic that came to mind. "Alison loves the marble, but I told her not to bother you anymore."

"She wasn't bothering me. She's a pleasant child."

Maggie wondered if Sackett was being honest in his compliment. She could gauge nothing from his expression, although she didn't think he would be the sort to say something he didn't mean. So far he had proven to be brutally honest.

"Yes, Alison is an agreeable child," she replied. "But I'm sure you won't want her making a pest of herself. I'll tell her not to come to your quarters again."

Sackett's eyes sharpened to a piercing point. She had touched his ire, but she was ignorant as to why. "What are you really worried about, Maggie? Her bothering me? Or me bothering her?" His tone deepened with anger. "Well, don't worry about the latter. I've done a lot of unsavory things in my life, but I've never had a fancy for little girls."

Maggie was stunned. "I wasn't implying—"

He had already started toward the horses and she knew she had insulted him without intending to. The thought had never occurred to her that he would bother Alison in a sexual way. Why would she even *think* such an abominable thing?

"Sackett. Wait."

He turned, spearing her with eyes that had turned cold and stormy.

"I just don't know you very well," she said lamely. "I was afraid you might get annoyed with a child intruding on your privacy. Heaven knows she chatters a great deal and could get on a person's nerves if they didn't like children. . . ." She drifted off, feeling it was an inadequate explanation, but she saw the steel in his eyes soften in slow degrees as he gripped his temper and accepted her apology.

"It's all right, Maggie. I think I understand. If she was my daughter, I'd want to protect her. And I have nothing against children."

Unexpectedly Maggie saw a human side to Sackett. A man with needs. A man who might have a wife, a child. Did he? She hadn't bothered to ask. She hadn't even considered that he might. A man like him didn't seem the sort who would need or even want love and a family.

He proceeded to the horses and she quickly changed the subject, speaking to his back. "How did you know I was going to town?"

"I didn't," he said, tightening both saddle cinches. "I figured you'd want to show me around the White Raven today and then take a ride over to get a perspective on Tate's spread."

"Well, yes, I'd like you to do that, naturally. But didn't Sonny give you the orders to go ahead and look around on your own?"

He lowered the fender on her saddle and faced her again. "I didn't hire on to take orders from your foreman, Maggie. I take orders only from you. I saddled your horse because I expect you to go with me. If you want me to settle this mess in the minimum length of time, you've got to show me where you've had trouble. I can find poisoned water holes and dammed-up creeks. I can find all the dead cows there are out there, but I can find them a lot faster and easier if you just take me to them."

She didn't want to be alone with him again. He probably knew it and was pressing the point just to be annoying. "I'm afraid I need to ride into town today and check on the lumber I ordered for the barn. They said it might be in and I need to get it as soon as possible."

"Then I'll ride with you. With your husband gone, you'll more than likely be the next target."

Maggie had preferred not to think about that or

it might make her so frightened she would never dare step foot outside the house again. "It won't be necessary, Sackett. Go about your business."

She swung onto her gelding, consciously aware that Sackett watched her with the eyes of a hawk. He truly reminded her of that sharp-eyed bird, circling the world far below him with the aloof air of not truly being a part of it even if he was temporarily and unwillingly involved with its pettiness.

"My business is your business, Maggie," he said, undeterred by her excuses.

"But I told Sonny to send one of the men with you," she insisted. "Didn't you have breakfast at the cookshack with the others?"

Seth remembered the thirty minutes in the company of the other men. Thirty tense minutes. "Yeh, I did, but like I said, I don't like taking orders from your foreman. How do I know he isn't in on this plot to run you off the White Raven?"

Maggie laughed. "Don't be ridiculous, Sackett."

"Your enemies can be anywhere, Maggie. Sometimes in your own camp. Sometimes even in your bed. You'll live longer if you keep that in mind. I'll be observing all the hired hands, and probably asking you a lot of questions about them. Today would be a good time to get started. You show me the ranch and tell me everything that's happened and when. The sooner I can get started, the sooner I can leave. That last thought should appeal to you," he concluded sardonically.

"It'll take days to show you the entire ranch."

"Then we'd better get started."

"I need to check on the lumber in town."

He gathered his horse's reins and swung into the saddle with the ease of a man who called it his second home. "Then we'll go to town. It'll be a good opportunity for people to see us together. Word will spread quickly that I'm here. And Tate can start worrying."

Maggie pursed her lips. She might as well get this initial phase of the relationship over with. There was truly no way to avoid discussing matters with him and setting a course of action. She couldn't merely turn it over to him and wash her hands of it, no matter how much she'd like to. And he was obviously not going to let her go anywhere by herself as long as it was outside this ranch yard.

"Very well," she said. "Let's go."

Suddenly the loud bang of a slamming door drew their attention. Maggie looked up to see Natalie dash from the house, trying to pull on her gloves and hat both at the same time.

"Wait, Mother! Wait! Don't leave without me."

Maggie saw Sackett's gaze shift questioningly from her daughter to her. If her perceptions were accurate there was the hint of annoyance in his hooded eyes and in the set to his lips. He was clearly not happy to see her daughter. But Maggie was suddenly very relieved that Natalie had insisted on going to town with her.

"Oh, I forgot to tell you," she said blithely. "Natalie wanted to go into town with me today. She's my middle child. She's fourteen. It's such a lovely age."

"It's not safe," Sackett replied in a gruff voice, allowing no argument.

Maggie just shrugged her shoulders. "That's what I tried to tell her, but she wouldn't listen."

"Can't you control her? She's your daughter."

"I take it you've never raised a child, Mr. Sackett."

"No, I've never had that particular experience," he replied impatiently, apparently seeing no sense in the direction of the conversation.

"Well, if you had, then you would know that children usually always listen to their fathers, but seldom their mothers." She said with a smile, "I believe it's just that children aren't usually afraid of their mothers. Were you afraid of your mother?"

He was glaring by now, and it deepened noticeably. "No, I wasn't, but I listened to her. I obeyed her."

"My, then you were an exceptional child."

Sackett's expression settled into definite irritation as he watched the perky young girl trotting toward them. After a moment he sighed and stepped down from his bay.

"Where are you going?" Maggie had the delicious urge to bite back a smile.

"To saddle her horse," he grumbled. "What else?"

En route to town, Seth kept Maggie busy telling him everything Tate had done since her husband had been murdered. How Tate had offered to buy the White Raven and then how the trouble had started when she'd refused his offer. She told Seth about every incident of fence-cutting, rustling, every time a creek had been blocked off, an animal shot, and finally the burning of the barn and the loss of Trent's stallion. The latter she had been unable to relate without tears.

The tears changed everything about her. She was no longer the high-handed, sharp-tongued authoritarian he had confronted last night, but a sensitive and compassionate woman protecting her home and her children. A woman who would die fighting for them. A woman he shouldn't have treated like a whore.

Unexpectedly he was riddled by guilt, self-loathing, and the memory of his father's words: *Just who do you think you are, boy? Well, I'll tell you who you are. You're nobody. You're just a piece of worthless coal that God has put in my trust to try to shape into a diamond. I'll make something out of you, I will, whether you fight me every step of the way or not. It's your choice. But you will never accomplish anything on your own because the devil's in you, and it's my purpose to drive him out. Someday you'll thank me.*

"What about you, Maggie?" he asked, trying to block out the unpleasant memory of his father and the sobering revelation about Maggie. "Have you retaliated in any way toward Tate?"

The anger caused from Tate's transgressions turned to bitterness. "I felt I'd be no better than him if I did to the Broken Arrow what he's done to the White Raven," she replied. "Oh, believe me, I wanted to—plenty of times. But in the end I haven't been able to. The closest I came was when Trent was killed. I headed over there with gun in hand, ready to shoot Tate in cold blood. In the end I realized I could never do something like that, and even if I had been able to, I didn't have the proof that it was him or one of his men. I only had my suspicions. It's been hard keeping some of the men under control. They've wanted to fight."

"Which men?"

"Oh . . . Barker and Clements mainly. They've been the most hot-headed and have tried to instigate the rest of the men to follow them. But they've been with the White Raven the longest. They're loyal to the brand. They consider this place their home and they don't want it destroyed anymore than I do. They don't like to see injustices served toward me either."

Seth remembered the two men she mentioned from the cookshack this morning. Both were leery; neither had been friendly. They'd made no bones that they didn't like having him around. Clements had been the only one to actually speak to him, and he'd said, in front of everyone: "You might as well leave, Sackett. You ain't going to get to kill nobody unless you do it in cold blood. Mrs. Cayton ain't going to ask you to pull that trigger. I don't know why she even hired you. She'll have you crawling just like she's got the rest of us."

"Then why don't you leave?" Seth had countered. "It doesn't sound like you're doing her any good anyway."

"What do you mean by that?"

"If you can't stand behind her, or beside her, then the best place for you is over the fence."

"You mean go over to Tate's side?"

"Yeah. Sounds like to me he could satisfy your hunger for fighting and killing."

"You bastard. You think that just 'cause you've got that gun on your hip you can do and say anything."

Seth had merely turned his back on him and walked away. He'd expected Clements to draw on him when his back was turned, and he knew he had angered the man enough that it had occurred to him. But Sonny had interceded and told Clements to saddle his horse and get to work.

Seth could read most men fairly well, and he felt quite confident that neither man was a spy for Tate. Clements had been too insulted by Seth's suggestion to turn traitor. Barker was just an opinionated, middle-aged cowboy who figured his years in the saddle, which outnumbered everybody else's, should give him the right to authority and respect.

The remainder of the ride into town was spent listening to Natalie talk about her mare. "Look, Sackett, I know you're a gunfighter," she said, "but mother says you can break horses. Is that true?"

He'd given Maggie a curious glance but she'd just shrugged her shoulders helplessly, and he realized she had given him an "honest" profession, whether he wanted one or not.

"Yeah," he had replied dryly. "I can break horses."

The girl had continued to monopolize the conversation, and she was in a good position to do so. Maggie had allowed her to ride in the middle, and Seth guessed it was because Maggie hadn't wanted to ride next to him anymore than she had wanted to ride into town with him. After what he'd done last night, she was probably afraid he'd assault her again while they were alone on the range and she would have no sanctuary for escape. Did her attitude stem from fear, repulsion, or did she just hate him because of what he was?

Last night he had been angry with her attitude toward him and he had retaliated, but she had still won the battle. He had succeeded only in taunting his own desire, tormenting himself with his own weaknesses. His male instincts sought her feminine surrender in its entirety, regardless of her personal opinion of him. It didn't matter what happened after he seduced her because he didn't want anything to happen. He didn't want to love her. He didn't even want to like her. Maggie Cayton had a dangerous purity about her. If she got too close and saw his weaknesses, his black soul, she would dislike him even more than she did now. She would compare him to the perfection of her husband and he would fall miserably short. No one, except possibly his mother, would ever truly understand why he had done what he'd done all those years ago in order to escape from Hell.

But had he escaped? Or had Hell merely followed him?

All he knew for certain about life was that friends were the perfect tools for betrayal and that love was the potion of a heart's destruction. So he made no friends, and he didn't look far into the future with any of his romantic relationships. If the women he bedded were whores, they took his money and looked forward to the next time. If they were ladies they pretended they didn't know him when they saw him on the street. It wasn't until they grew hungry again for the satisfaction they couldn't get from their husbands that they would send messengers with notes, requesting him to meet them. Sometimes he obliged. Sometimes he just saddled up and rode away to the next town, the next job.

And sometimes, like now, the old battle began inside him again. The battle between right and wrong. Between Satan and God, both struggling inside him for dominion. Sometimes God won out. Most of the time the victory went to Satan. But he often wondered if either understood that he only did what he did for the sake of survival.

The sun was at it's mid-morning high when they walked their horses down the center of Buffalo's main street. Seth had to admit that even though Natalie was a pleasant-enough young girl, she could certainly wear a person's ear out. He was relieved when she hurried off to see friends, promising to meet them at two o'clock in front of the General Store. Seth escorted Maggie to the lumber yard only to find that the lumber order had not yet been filled. The owner promised Maggie he would deliver it, free of charge, by the beginning of the week.

Before heading back to the ranch, Seth and Maggie stopped in at Maggie's favorite restaurant. It seemed to be the place where men caught up on news and the women caught up on gossip, or vice-versa. His presence created the stir he'd wanted. There was no doubt in his mind that before nightfall

Ben Tate would know he was on the White Raven.

Their meal was interrupted repeatedly by people inquiring after Maggie's health. How was she doing since Trent's death? How were the children? Did she need help? Was she going to sell out and come into town where things would be easier for her? Would she be attending Dugan's barn dance on the Fourth of July? And who was the man she had with her? A new hired hand?

She introduced him as White Raven's new wrangler. The men recognized his name and quickly gave him a wide, polite berth, knowing good and well why he'd really been hired. The women were unaware of his notoriety with a gun and merely seemed to look upon him as a new topic for gossip. Lissa Dugan, whom Maggie clearly did not like, expressed the obvious thoughts of all when she'd said, "Mr. Sackett, what a pleasure to meet you. I didn't know Maggie needed a new wrangler . . . but then I guess she would. Her husband's been dead for nearly a year. A woman can't break her own horses now, can she?"

The insinuation that Maggie had taken Seth as a lover had not been implied so much by words, but rather by the nuance of the woman's voice and the suggestiveness in her eyes. None of it slipped past Seth. Nor had the tightening of Maggie's lips and the cold glare she'd given the woman. Regardless of what Maggie thought of the idea, Seth found it more appealing with every passing hour. He had envisioned her in his arms all night. His stay on the White Raven might very well turn into a lengthy one, and a man needed more than dreams to get him through the long, lonely nights.

While Maggie continued to deal with the over-bearing woman and her nosey questions, Seth kept his eyes on the door and the windows that faced the street. He'd positioned himself, as always, with his back to the wall. It was the only safe way for a man who lived by the gun to keep from dying by it too. There were plenty of men, enemies and rival gun-fighters, who would want to put a bullet in his un-suspecting back and claim the notoriety of being the man who shot Seth Sackett.

Because of his position, Seth was the first to see the big man heading across the street with an au-thoritative swagger. He was followed by three henchmen, one of whom Seth recognized instantly as Max Morrell, a man who had the reputation of being one of the fastest guns in the West. He also had the reputation for being a cold-blooded killer.

When the men entered the restaurant a hush fell over the room. Some of the people hastily gathered their hats and their handbags and scurried from the restaurant, leaving their meals unfinished. Hearing the hush and the sudden scraping of numerous chairs against the hardwood floor, Maggie turned her head. The color drained from her face, only to return in an angry red rush. Seth didn't need to be told that the craggy-faced, white-haired man who had just come in was none other than Big Ben Tate.

Maggie started to rise, her face burning with the blind fury that would propel her into battle, abso-lutely no match physically for the grizzled rancher. Seth laid his hand over hers, snapping her blazing eyes back to his. He said nothing, just gave her the look that said, "Stay seated."

She shot him a questioning glance but reluctantly obeyed his silent command.

Tate saw her immediately and pushed his barrel-chested body past the tables and chairs that seemed to be the size of children's furniture when placed in the shadow of his giant frame. He halted in front of their table, snagging his thumbs on his low-slung gun belt. His dark brown eyes looked like the devil's own with the fires of hell dancing in their reflection.

"So you're determined to start a war, Maggie Cayton," Tate said, his voice booming throughout the dining room. "I used to think you were a gentle woman, but I can see I was wrong." His gaze slid to Seth and held there in an accusatory silence.

"You're the one who started a war," Maggie countered hotly. "You started it when you killed Trent. If you think I'll roll over and let you drive me off the White Raven the way you've driven other ranchers from their property, you're dead wrong."

"I don't know what it's going to take to make you believe that I didn't kill Trent," Tate replied. "And I didn't *have* him killed either."

Maggie's fiery gaze shifted to the three men Tate had brought with him, halting on the shifty-eyed gunslinger. It was clear to Seth that a hatred burned deep inside her. No doubt she suspected Morrell as the one who had killed her husband. Seth sensed it was only with a great deal of willpower that she didn't light into him with her bare hands.

"And I suppose you hired Morrell to gather firewood for the winter?" she added derisively. "Don't insult my intelligence, Ben."

Tate's eyes locked momentarily with Seth's. "I hired Morrell for the same reason you hired Sackett. To protect my interests. You want to play men's games, Maggie, I'll sure enough oblige."

"Men's games? Killing and barn-burning? Is that what you mean?"

"I didn't burn your barn anymore than I killed your husband. But I just came from the undertaker's. Turned over the body of Wendell Pensy. Remember him, Maggie? He was the man who played fiddle at your tenth wedding anniversary. He's been with me since I came to Wyoming twenty years ago. He was bushwhacked shortly after midnight last night while he was riding back from town with a couple of other hands. Seems kinda coincidental that he shows up dead and then Sackett shows up with you."

His eyes, like gleaming black arrowheads, pierced Seth, demanding an answer. Seth leaned back in his chair. He knew Morrell wouldn't need an excuse to go for his gun so he moved slowly. Even now Morrell reminded him of a weasel with his skinny body, his long yellow hair, his close-set eyes eagerly gleaming while he awaited the precise moment to leap on his prey. Morrell would force Seth's hand some day if given the chance—something Seth did not intend to do. Morrell wanted Seth's reputation, and from the impudence smeared on his ugly face, he was positive he would win. But Seth had learned many years ago that over-confidence, not swiftness, was oftentimes the killer when one gun went up against another.

"You give me too much credit, Tate," Seth replied. "I just got in last night."

"So I hear. But what were you doing just after midnight?"

Out of the corner of his eye, Seth saw Maggie tense, but he didn't look her way, didn't meet her eyes because that might cause his own to reveal tell-tale signs that they had been together. Tate might not be able to break Maggie by killing her cattle, but Seth didn't know her well enough yet to know if she would crumble under character defamation.

He continued coolly, never batting an eyelash. "I was sleeping. The rooster crows early at the White Raven."

"Can anybody attest to that?" Tate demanded, his eyes narrowing with growing suspicion.

The blood coursed in a hot stream through Seth's veins, but his opponents would never know. He had trained his voice, even his eyes, to be as cool as a frozen lake beneath a cloudy November sky.

"Nobody has to attest to it," he replied calmly. "I was where I said I was. Maybe instead of randomly accusing people, you ought to check the calibre of the bullet that killed your hired man to see if there's anything unique about it."

Tate's ominous visage darkened even more. He reached into his vest pocket and pulled out a cartridge, dropping it on the tablecloth in front of Seth. "Found it on a rocky knoll overlooking the line shack where Pensy was staying."

Seth picked up the cartridge and rolled it over a

few times in his fingers. It was a standard .44-40, used by practically every Winchester and Colt in the territory. It was a worthless lead and he told Tate so, then tossed it back to him. Tate caught it in a big hand that resembled a paw more than a hand.

"I'd say whoever shot him must have been pretty good to hit his target at midnight with only the moonlight and starlight to see by," Seth said.

"Yeah," Tate's eyes narrowed with a satisfied gleam. "He would have had to be good, Sackett. *Real* good—like you."

"Or like Morrell."

Morrell reacted as if he'd been kicked in the groin. Almost instantly his hand dropped to his gun, but Tate grabbed his arm, capping his explosive temper. Nevertheless, Seth's accusation didn't sit well with the big man either.

"You'd better be careful what you're saying, Sackett."

Seth's eyes held a grip on Tate's for several long seconds. "I'm always careful. Are you?"

Tate was the first to look away, appearing momentarily disconcerted by Seth's suggestion that Morrell was straddling both sides of the fence. He turned to Maggie again. "I don't know what you're expectin' to come of all this, Maggie, but I can tell you true, it ain't gonna end pretty."

"Then call off your dogs, starting with Morrell."

"Not until you do."

"You started it, Ben. Only you can finish it."

Tate's eyes narrowed to mere slits, as if the sun had come out in blazing force. He turned on his heel and stalked out of the restaurant.

Chapter Five

Seth watched Maggie calmly remove the napkin from her lap and set it on the table. The only indication that Tate's visit had upset her was a shaking hand and forced control to her voice.

"I need to find Natalie," she said, scooting her chair back. "It's getting late."

She didn't wait for him but started for the door. Plucking a toothpick from the decanter on the table, Seth followed. He didn't worry about the bill. The restaurant could charge it to the White Raven.

Outside, Maggie started across the street toward the livery. Seth put a hand on her lower back, directing her around a slow-moving wagon loaded to the top of the side boards with sacks of grain. But once past the wagon, her tightly held composure suddenly crumbled. Bursting into tears, she broke away from him and ran down the street, past riders, wagons, and curious pedestrians until she finally disappeared inside the livery.

Seth made his way much slower, knowing it wasn't his company she wanted. At the livery, the mid-day sun cast its light only a few feet through the big double doors. The remainder of the barn faded into hushed shadows filled with smells of straw, hay, manure, horses, dank earth, and leather tack. The only sounds came from one or two horses shifting in their stalls, a swallow fluttering in the eaves, and the soft sobs of feminine crying.

He followed the last sound to the rear of the livery, to an empty stall that had been recently cleaned out and lined with fresh mounds of fluffy straw. Maggie was sitting in the middle of it, her back to him. He shuffled through the straw and went to his haunches behind her.

"Don't let Tate get to you, Maggie," he said. "It's what he wants."

He placed his hands on her shoulders in an attempt to comfort her, but she leaped to her feet and scrambled into the corner, her back to the wall, her eyes blazing at him through scalding tears.

"Don't touch me!" she warned. "Just stay away from me. I'm sick to death of the sight of men and guns. Trent is dead because of a man just like you! So . . . please . . . just stay away."

She closed her eyes and leaned her head back against the wall. Tears streamed from her eyes, down her face, and dripped off her chin onto her breasts, leaving splotches on her white shirtwaist. "Leave me alone," she reiterated, never opening her eyes, as if she truly hated the sight of him and held him responsible for her dilemma.

Seth doubted he would ever forget the picture of Maggie's vulnerability in that moment. Nor would he forget the powerful urge to take her in his arms and comfort her. But there was nothing he could do to help a woman who wanted no help. He tossed his toothpick into the straw. "I'll go find Natalie."

When his footsteps faded from the livery, Maggie crumpled to the straw again. How she needed Trent! But he was gone. Forever gone. Seeing Tate and Morrell had brought it all home again.

Even Sackett's presence made the fact weigh heavily and more clearly on her mind than it ever had before. He was there, a substitute for Trent offering comfort, but he was anything but comforting. He was just another agonizing obstacle to torment her heart. Every time he was near he made her remember just how alone she was now. How alone she would be for the rest of her life. His embrace was only a wicked power that taunted her senses and her better judgment.

She wrapped her arms around herself, holding onto the memories while trying to block out the pain of loss and the bitter truth. She tried to remember how Trent's arms had felt around her. How his lips had felt. She tried to remember the sound of his voice caressing her softly in the dark; the unique scent that had been his alone. But her mind refused to dwell on her wishes. The only lips and arms, the only voice and scent she could remember now were Sackett's!

Seth found Natalie twenty minutes later at the blacksmith's shop talking to Andy Dray. They met Maggie on the street shortly after, seemingly recovered from her private ordeal. Natalie didn't notice her mother's red eyes, but Maggie deftly kept her hat brim tilted downward and her head averted.

By the time they finally rode away from town it was later than they had planned to get away. They were forced to ride harder, too, if they wanted to reach the ranch before dark.

They had only gone a few miles when Seth began to have the uneasy feeling they were being followed. He didn't want to alarm the women when all he had to go on was his honed sixth sense for trouble. He intensified his visual examination of the hills they were riding through. He wished Natalie would stop chattering about the dress she wanted Maggie to help her sew for the Dugan's Fourth of July barn dance. It solicited a response from Maggie that propelled the women into a disagreement.

"You're not going anywhere with Andy Dray," Maggie said with a stubborn set to her jaw. "He's twenty-one years old! He shouldn't even be looking at you. You're much too young for a man his age. Why in the world isn't he interested in a girl closer to his own age? I think he's taking advantage of your innocence."

"Daddy was six years older than you, Mother," Natalie countered.

"Yes, but I was also eighteen when I married. I will not allow you to get married at your age, young lady."

"We're not getting married, Mother. We're only going to a dance."

"Dances lead to other things, Natalie, which I'm sure you are very well aware of. You may not be ready to get married, but I daresay Andy is."

"You can chaperone me every step of the way."

"It would be the *only* way I would ever consent for you to be courted by Andy Dray."

Seth cupped his ear in an effort to hear beyond their squabbling. Maggie had told Tate that only he could end the trouble between them. The hair on the back of Seth's neck prickled. This would be an ideal time to do it, and it was difficult terrain to scout. The grassy hills that tumbled down from the Big Horn Mountains reminded Seth of a jumble of knuckles whose lovely green valleys could hide more than peacefully grazing cattle.

Suddenly from his peripheral vision, and almost behind them, Seth caught the faint glint of sun against metal. He grabbed for Maggie, yanking her to the side. Almost simultaneously the crack of a rifle report echoed through the valley. Natalie screamed and Maggie released a startled cry of surprise.

"Dismount!" Seth yelled. "Head for cover!"

Natalie didn't need to be told twice. In another second her feet hit the ground. Seth leaped from the saddle, taking Maggie with him. Another bullet zinged past and they hit the ground together with Seth covering Maggie's body protectively with his. The horses wheeled in confusion and Natalie screamed again, covering her head with her hands while scurrying behind a large boulder. A third bullet hit the dirt just above Seth's and Maggie's heads.

"Maggie, make a run for that fallen cottonwood. Now!"

As she scrambled for better cover, Seth rolled to his back and fired off a few rounds from his revolver to cover her. When she was safe, he dove for the log himself, rolling to his final position next to her. Another shot took a chunk of bark out of the tree, pinging it past their heads.

Then all was silent.

Seth quickly reloaded his revolver, knowing it was virtually useless to him in his present situation. Whoever wanted them dead was using a rifle and was out of his revolver's range, but it would be suicide to go for the rifle in his saddle scabbard.

"Seth."

Maggie's weak voice and the use of his first name, startled him. She was lying on her back so close to him he could feel her leg pressed against his. But she was oddly still and the fear in her eyes was of the sort that sent warning signals racing through him. A sick dread closed over him.

"Maggie, what is it?"

She moved her hand from where it had been resting on her shoulder. Her fingers came away covered with blood.

From her position a few yards away, Natalie saw the blood and began to scream. "Momma! My God, Momma!" She leaped to her feet, sprinting across the distance between them like a jackrabbit. She fell to her knees next to her mother and tried to lift her into her arms. "My God, Momma, you've been hit!"

Seth grabbed Natalie and shoved her down next to Maggie. "Damn it, girl! You're going to get your head blown off! Stay down!"

"She's my mother! Don't tell me what to do,

damn you! Just stop that maniac out there! You're supposed to be a gunfighter!"

Maggie turned her head toward her frightened, hysterical daughter. "Be quiet, Natalie—for just once in your life. Mr. Sackett can't do anymore than he's already doing."

Amazingly enough the girl heard the edge of steel in her mother's voice and finally cowered back down behind the cottonwood alongside Maggie.

Seth pulled his bandana from around his throat and pressed it to Maggie's shoulder. "Hold this tight to the wound."

"Is she going to be all right?" Natalie demanded fearfully.

"I think so. But I want you to be perfectly quiet for a few minutes, Natalie," Seth said. His tone and the glint in his eyes were dangerously demanding, allowing no room for argument. "Hold your breath if you have to. I've got to be able to listen."

"For what?"

"Natalie, just do as he says!" Maggie inserted impatiently.

This time the girl obeyed. They all listened, although the women didn't know what they were listening for. After a time Seth heard it.

"They're leaving," he said. "I hear one horse galloping back toward town."

He waited to see if it was followed by more but was finally satisfied that the assailant had acted alone. He figured the attacker had come from town and had returned to town. Whomever it was had probably seen their arrival in town then ridden out here to lay in wait. Was it Tate, or one of his trained monkeys?

Cautiously, Seth came to his feet, but no more shots were fired.

Natalie helped Maggie to her feet. "We'll get you to a doctor, Mother."

Maggie nodded, reaching for her head. "Maybe I should sit . . . back down."

"Mother, are you all right?"

"I—"

"Sackett! Something's wrong!"

Seth whirled just in time to catch Maggie as she fainted into his arms. She was losing a considerable amount of blood and he was afraid she was receding into shock. All the color had drained from her face.

"Get the horses, Natalie," he said. "And make it quick."

The afternoon sun had just dropped behind the Big Horn Mountains when Seth, carrying Maggie, strode into the doctor's office startling both the doctor and a female patient he was talking to. One look at the blood staining Maggie's white shirtwaist and the physician was out of his chair.

"What's happened to Maggie? Bring her into my operating room." He led the way, not waiting for an answer to his question. His previous patient quietly left the office, but Seth recognized the excited gleam in her eyes and knew she'd have the news all over town before dark.

He carefully laid Maggie on the examining table.

She stirred, as if trying to regain consciousness, but then she drifted away again.

"She's been shot, Dr. Clifford," Natalie said, tears choking her words. "Somebody tried to kill her. Please don't let her die like Daddy did. Please."

Dr. Clifford, a thin, bald man, gave her an understanding glance. "I'll do what I can, Natalie. That's all I can promise." He moved rapidly, taking inventory of Maggie's wound, her pulse, the loss of blood. "Nothing vital has been damaged," he concluded. "But I've got to remove the bullet and get the bleeding stopped. It'll go easier and quicker if I have some help. Can you help me?" He looked at Natalie from over the top of his spectacles.

She paled. "I . . . don't know. I—" Suddenly she crumpled into a nearby chair, losing herself to great, wrenching sobs.

"I can help you," Seth said. "Let's get started."

Seth watched Natalie pacing the floor of the doctor's office two hours later. The surgery had gone well and Clifford assured them that Maggie should recuperate with no complications. It would take a while for the ether to wear off and he had asked them to remain with her while he went home for a while. He'd been up the night before delivering a first child and he needed some rest badly.

"Why don't you try to get some sleep, Natalie?" Seth suggested from his chair next to Maggie. After the surgery Clifford had instructed him to move her to the bed in the corner of his small operating room where she could rest more comfortably. "Your mother won't wake up for awhile."

Seth saw the weariness in Natalie's blue eyes. Eyes that she had apparently inherited from her father. She went to the cot and sat down, burying her face in her hands.

"You probably think I'm a real coward, don't you, Mr. Sackett?"

Seth ran a hand through his hair. No wonder old Doc Clifford was exhausted. Surgery took a lot out of a person, even an assistant. He really didn't feel like talking. "Why would you say that?" he offered off-handedly.

"Because of the way I acted," she admitted. "I'm sorry I got so hysterical. I'm sorry I couldn't help the doctor. I—"

"Don't worry about it, Natalie. She's your mother and you're close to her. Why would I fault you for that? I was close to my mother, too."

She lifted her head, her eyes round with surprise. "You mean you—"

"—had a mother?" He chuckled.

"Well, no, that's not what I was going to—" Her face flushed noticeably.

"My mother was a good woman," he said, remembering for a moment just how much truth was in those words. "She had a lot of patience and strength, just like your mother."

"Is she still alive? Your mother?"

Seth looked away to the darkened window where old ghostly images unexpectedly appeared in the reflection.

You quit protecting that boy, Grace. Hiding him

behind your skirt ain't going to save him from me or God. Only a good thrashing and asking for God's forgiveness for his sins can save him from eternal damnation.

He didn't do anything that calls for the razor strop, Ezra. He's just a boy. Boys do things. They're not perfect.

The poison of asps is under his lips—Romans 3:13. Now, move aside, Grace.

No. I won't let you beat him over this. All he did was—

Seth started, jarred by the memory of his mother being flung sideways across the room. Falling. The blood on her head . . .

The images on the dark glass vanished. All that remained was the reflection of his own haunted face. And Natalie's, waiting for his answer. His mind searched for the question she had asked, searched for the answer.

"No," he replied softly. "She died about a year back. Now, why don't you try to get some sleep on the sofa out there in the waiting room. I'll keep an eye on your mother."

Natalie settled on the horsehair sofa with one of the doctor's wool blankets over her. Soon her breathing indicated she had fallen asleep. Seth returned his attention to Maggie and to the job that had quickly escalated into the position of bodyguard.

Even though he had half expected this to happen, he was nonetheless troubled that Maggie had become the assailant's target. Tate must want the White Raven badly to commit murder and at-

tempted murder, especially murder of a woman.
But why? What did the White Raven have that
would lead Tate to such destructive desperation?
Was the land worth that much to him? Why did he
need it so badly? If he had lost a large percentage of
his herd in the blizzards of '86 and '87, and was in
financial straights like many of the other ranchers,
then he wouldn't have the cattle to fill that much
land anyway. Unless he was rustling.

Seth picked up Maggie's hand, small and fragile
in his, yet contradictorily strong and capable. Earlier, while he'd held her in front of him in the saddle,
she'd felt cold and lifeless; the heat had gone from
her body and the color from her face. He had been
stirred by an emotion that returned to him now.
He'd been with her less than twenty-four hours, but
he felt he already knew her. He understood her
cause and understood why she would fight for what
she had. She fought not for herself, but for her
children, for her mother, and for the men she employed. And, if for no other reason, she fought because she was simply a proud woman who would
not let bullies like Tate push her around. He didn't
mind helping a person who would fight. He admired
strength and pride, and he hated to see anyone as
strong-willed and determined as Maggie Cayton
brought down by the cowardly bullet of a back-
shooter. There was injustice in that, and if Tate was
behind it, Seth would see that he faced his transgressions.

*For the mystery of iniquity doth already work; only
he who now hindereth will continue to hinder until he
be taken out of the way.* 2 Thessalonians 2:7.

Suddenly the main door to the doctor's office opened. Seth's hand went automatically to his revolver, thinking that the assailant might have heard he had failed and had come back to finish the job. Through the open door of the examining room Seth saw a light-complected man of average height and build, wearing a tailored suit and a bowler hat. He sported a heavy blond mustache and sideburns streaked with gray. He glanced at Natalie, still asleep on the waiting room sofa, then spotted Seth rising to his feet next to Maggie in the inner room. He hurried to join them, a deep etching of concern on a face that had weathered at least forty-five years.

He gave Seth only a cursory glance, as if he considered him not important enough to acknowledge. He went directly to the opposite side of the bed, taking Maggie's hand in his and trying to wake her. "Maggie, it's me, Cleve."

Seth felt the rise of inexplicable disdain for the man. There was arrogance in his bearing and in the pale blue eyes that were set too far apart. One glance into those eyes, though, was enough for Seth to recognize a man of power and position, and a man who was used to wielding both to get what he wanted. He might look like a dandy, but there was nothing frivolous or soft about his mind.

"She's had ether," Seth said coolly. "You won't be able to wake her up until she's good and ready."

"I'm Cleve Williams, a friend of hers and the family's. What happened here?"

Seth didn't like the superior, demanding tone of voice that reminded him of a general interrogating a private. "I suspect you already know that, or you wouldn't be here."

The lines around Williams' eyes tightened in retaliation. "Don't fool with me, mister. I want an explanation."

"No, I figure what you want is a description," Seth replied. "All I'll tell you is that somebody tried to kill her. You seem to know her quite well. Maybe you have some idea as to who would want to do a thing like that."

"No, I have no idea. Were *you* with her?"

Seth bristled at Williams' accusatory tone. It gave him the notion to pick the man up by the seat of his pants and the back of his coat collar and toss him outside like a side of stinking, rotten meat.

"Natalie and I were with her," he finally said, clenching and unclenching his jaw.

"And you saw no one?"

"She was back shot. If I'd seen who it was I'd have the sheriff after him."

Williams silently considered that information, seeming to tuck it away for future use. He gave his attention back to Maggie. "Well, this is no place for her. I'm taking her home with me."

Seth's hand caught Williams' coat lapel just as he was bending down to pick Maggie up. "She stays right where she is."

Williams' pale blue eyes turned almost white with fury. He straightened and faced Seth from across the bed. "You're just a hired hand. A hired *gun* from the looks of you. You have no right to be assuming authority over Maggie Cayton."

"As far as I'm concerned, neither do you," Seth

replied levelly. "Only Maggie can make the decision whether she stays here or goes with you. And, as you can see, it'll be a while before she can do that."

"Then I'll discuss it with Natalie."

Seth moved to a position that would force Williams to go around him to get to the door. "Natalie's too young to be making that kind of a decision."

"Maggie will be more comfortable at my place," Williams continued stubbornly. "Why don't you go back to the ranch and tell them what's happened? I'm sure you have work to do there. I'll bring her home in my carriage when she's recuperated. She'll be perfectly safe with me."

"She'll be the one to decide. Her and Doc Clifford, and he won't be back until tomorrow morning."

"Just who in the hell are you anyway?" Williams' light complexion was taking on the appearance of a sunburn. "You can't order me around."

"No? Well, I have a Peacemaker that says I can do any damn thing I feel like doing."

Williams' attention suddenly became riveted to the Colt .45 that had miraculously appeared, seemingly from nowhere, and was making a distinct and memorable impression against the base of his throat, just about where his jugular suddenly began to heave with noticeable rhythm.

"Let's talk rights again, Mr. Williams. My name is Seth Sackett, and I'm acting as Maggie's bodyguard. Now, do you still want to take her out of here?"

Williams' eyes lifted from the gun and filled

quickly now not with irritable impatience as they had before, but with the cold calculation of recognition. The initial fear for his life had already passed. "So you're Sackett?" His top lip lifted into a sneer. "Somehow you fall short of the shadow cast by your legend."

"Clear out, Williams. I've seen about all of your face I care to see for one night."

Williams' subsequent perusal held Seth in even stronger contempt now that he knew who he was. "We could discuss this matter like gentlemen, Sackett. The gun isn't necessary."

"I've never before been confused with a gentleman," Seth replied. "Don't humor me."

Williams' scowl deepened as his last civilized attempt failed, but instead of arguing further, he gave Maggie one last glance and left the building.

Seth moved to the darkened window and watched Williams' departure, lit by the street lamps, until he disappeared around a corner. It was only then that Seth reholstered his weapon. There was something about Williams he not only didn't like, but didn't trust. The man reminded him a lot of the old cur that used to worship his father—the one who only bit when your back was turned.

Chapter Six

"Trent? Where are you?"

At the sound of Maggie's mumbled, almost incoherent words, Seth left his chair and worked his way through the darkness to her bedside. He had doused the lamp earlier, hoping to get some sleep, but he hadn't been able to rest in the chair. It wasn't all due to the chair either. Somewhere out there was the person who had tried to kill Maggie, and Seth was afraid he would keep trying until he had accomplished his mission.

She was still heavily under the influence of the ether, and he knew from experience it could be hours before she was completely free of its drugging effects. He struck a match on his belt buckle and saw her tossing her head back and forth on the pillow, apparently in the throes of a bad dream. She was clothed only in her camisole now and the blanket had slipped down below her breasts. The dark pink nipples showed through the thin cotton cloth and the creamy fullness that rose above the edge of lace tempted his touch. Her flawless skin seemed the color of warm honey in the flickering glow of the match flame, and he wondered if it would taste as sweet.

"Trent?"

He gave the match a flick of his wrist and the flame was vanquished, plunging the room into darkness again. He set the burned match in an ash tray where a pile of others had previously been placed by Dr. Clifford. Maggie was beginning to whimper and he wondered what sort of dream made her so restless. He touched her hand.

"It's all right, Maggie. You're safe. Go back to sleep."

Her hand closed around his. "Don't leave me, Trent. I need you."

Seth was suddenly confronted with a decision, but it was a relatively easy decision for him to make because, as his father had always said, his soul had been blistered by the fires of Hell, probably even before he was born. So Seth made the choice to lie down with her, with Maggie Cayton who despised him and who loved another man. He would let her believe, for the space of a few hours, that he was the man she loved and needed. He was used to taking the place of those men whom women loved but couldn't have. It was the first time he'd filled in for a dead man, but he supposed there was a first time for everything.

He removed his boots and gun belt, his hat, and slipped beneath the covers, lying on his side next to her. He put an arm across her, feeling unusually protective. She relaxed, succumbing again to the effects of the ether. She was warm against him, soft, utterly feminine with the swell of her breast just above where his arm rested, the curve of her hip against his loins. Her thick auburn hair touching his face on the pillow reminded him of silk scented with the perfume of flowers. She didn't have the suffocating smell of a whore; of whiskey, smoke, facial cosmetics, cheap perfume . . . other men.

He lay awake for awhile, listening to her steady breathing and to the noises of the town. After midnight the town finally became quiet. Only then, when the world was at peace, was he able to relax his vigilance and allow sleep to come at last. But it had always been that way for Seth Sackett.

It seemed Maggie fought to return to consciousness for days, but maybe it was only hours. In a neverending nightmare, her mind kept repeating the scene of the ambush. When she finally awoke, feeling almost lucid, she saw dawn lighting the curtains at the window. She also felt the solid warmth of a body next to hers. Disoriented, she turned her head on the pillow. Her first thought was of Trent, but through the cloudy haze of her mind she remembered she'd lost Trent, and almost instantaneously she recognized Sackett. She tried to struggle up from the bedding but his arm was like a dead weight pinning her. A piercing pain shot through her shoulder at the attempt and she aborted it, falling back to the pillows. Sackett stirred. When the pain subsided and she opened her eyes again, he was propped up on one elbow, gazing down at her. His hair was tousled but otherwise there was no evidence in his alert eyes that he had ever been asleep. A slow smile moved his lips beneath the black moustache.

"You didn't believe me, did you, Maggie, when I said we'd become lovers?"

His whisper sent shivers through her, and she became intensely aware of his hand, hot and big, branding her near-bare midriff. "Get out, Sackett, you brazen sonofabitch."

His dark brows lifted, expressing feigned innocence. "I'm only here because you were asking for me last night."

"I was not."

"Well, you were sedated. Maybe you don't remember."

She placed her hand on his and tried to lift his arm away. Pain shot through her shoulder again. She couldn't use her other arm either because it was pinned against his hard, immovable body.

"I'm not sedated now. Nor am I suffering from narcotic induced delusions. I don't want you in bed with me. Where's Natalie?"

"In the other room, asleep."

Maggie's eyes ovaled in alarm. "She could wake up any minute and come in here and see us!"

Sackett smiled mockingly and placed a kiss to the corner of her lips. "Or any second." But chuckling then, he left her side.

She watched with a peculiar fascination as he pulled his boots back on and strapped his revolver to his lean hips. The place he'd occupied in the bed was warm but cooled quickly, leaving her with an extremely empty feeling.

"You had a visitor last night," he said nonchalantly, running a hand through his hair in an attempt to smooth it before returning his hat to his head.

Maggie once again tried to sit up, this time succeeding in propping herself on her good elbow to rearrange her pillows against the headboard. "Oh? Who was it? How could anyone know I was here?"

"News travels fast it would seem. Your visitor was a man by the name of Cleve Williams. He wanted to take you home with him, but I frankly couldn't imagine any sensible woman—and you are a sensible woman, Maggie—wanting to do such a distasteful thing. So I told him what I was sure you would have told him." He leaned indolently on his hip, latching his thumbs in his gun belt.

"And what did you tell him?" Maggie asked cautiously.

"Basically? To take a train to California and not come back. Of course, he ignored me. He wanted to hear it from your lips, so he'll be back this morning for further verbal abuse."

"Oh, dear." Maggie was unexpectedly overcome with an incredible wave of nausea and suddenly she feared she was going to lose the contents of her stomach right in front of Sackett. "I'm afraid I'm going to be sick." She slid down, flat on her back in the bed, and barely noticed Seth getting a basin and placing it in her hands.

"Don't feel bad, Maggie. Williams turned my stomach, too."

Maggie flashed him an annoyed look. "I'm not sick because of Cleve. It's the ether."

"Whatever." He shrugged indifferently. "Will

you be going with him? Or do you want me to stick around and rent a buggy to take you home?"

Maggie gripped the nausea with all her willpower, refusing to vomit in front of him. She saw him glance at the clock on the wall. She didn't need to look at it to know the sun would be up soon. He seemed restless, probably tired of playing nursemaid. He walked to the door separating the small infirmary from the waiting room and propped himself up against the door frame.

"Well? Which will it be, Maggie? Me or Williams?"

Maggie didn't miss the sexual suggestiveness in the question, as she was sure he had intended. It brought her mind back to the way he'd felt next to her in bed. Very nice, as a matter of fact. But how brazen of him to simply assume the position of her lover.

She side-stepped his question. "I'm sure I'll rest better in my own bed and I certainly don't want Cleve's bevy of English maids hovering over me. Not that they're not nice; but they remind me of busy bees trying to collect all their pollen in one day."

Maggie looked beyond him and saw her daughter asleep on the horsehair sofa. It was a great relief knowing Natalie hadn't been hurt in the ambush. But what if she had? Suddenly the cold sweat of fear joined the nausea and the pain. What if Tate started picking the Caytons off, one by one, starting with her children? Worry knotted her stomach. What were Lance and Alison doing this very minute? Her mother? Yes, she certainly needed to get home, and the sooner the better.

The grip she'd had on her stomach finally failed. Knowing she could hold it no longer, she struggled up on one elbow, bringing the basin to her mouth with a shaking hand. "Would you please leave, Sackett? I'm going to be—"

Instead of obeying her order, Seth strode to her side just as she released the contents of her stomach and then fell weakly back to the pillows. She felt the basin being removed from her hands, felt a damp cloth on her lips, dabbing gently, felt the heat of his hand brush the blazing humiliation of her face. She would never be able to look at him again; she was sure of it. He slipped a hand beneath her neck and lifted her head.

"Here, have some of this."

She opened her eyes enough to see the glass of water he held to her lips. She took several sips before he lowered her back to the pillows.

"I . . . I'm sorry," she said, turning her head away from him and keeping her eyes closed. Even the room's pre-dawn grayness couldn't conceal a face she knew was as scarlet as a whore's satin dress.

"No need to be," he replied, his voice containing none of the earlier facetiousness. "Coming out of ether tends to do that to a person. I've been in that position a time or two myself."

Maggie couldn't envision Sackett being ill. He simply seemed too invincible for such weakness. She glanced down at her shoulder where the throbbing was beginning to take precedence again now that the nausea had temporarily ceased. She saw the bulky, blood-stained bandage but she also saw, to her horror, that her bosom was covered only with her camisole, a garment made of fine muslin that was practically transparent. Quickly she pulled the blanket up to her chin. A new blaze of embarrassment scorched her cheeks. How much of her body had Sackett seen? Had he assisted with the surgery? They were both questions she didn't want to know the answers to.

"Cold?"

His huskily spoken question jarred her. He was still there, hovering over her, taking care of her. Why couldn't he just leave and go do whatever it was gunfighters did first thing in the morning and leave her to her own devices?

"I'd like my clothes," she said, forcing herself to look at him again with a confidence she certainly didn't feel. She saw nothing in his eyes that indicated the shameful upheaval of her stomach had bothered him in the least.

"You don't have to put them on for my benefit, Maggie. And you'll be more comfortable without them. The doctor said you should stay in bed at least until tomorrow. By the way, who is this Cleve Williams?"

He found another blanket at the foot of the bed and spread it over her. She felt his hands skim the naked flesh of her shoulder. The familiar rush of awareness unexpectedly surpassed the gnawing pain pulsating from her shoulder.

"He's a friend. He was Trent's friend."

"And yours?"

"He's become more my friend since Trent died."

"I see. What does he do for a living?"

Maggie decided Seth Sackett *saw* entirely too much. He somehow knew Cleve was interested in her and had been taking her out on occasion. What had the two of them discussed last night while she had been asleep? Her relationship with Cleve hadn't exactly escalated into courting; it was all done under the pretense of Cleve stopping in at the ranch to check on Trent's widow, or to take her to lunch when she came to town. But Maggie knew—and apparently Sackett did, too—that Cleve was interested in her in a romantic way. His perception had also been keen enough to pick up immediately on the fact that Sonny had become a suitor, too, in his own shy way.

"Cleve's something of an entrepreneur. He owns Williams & Co., a merchandise chain, which consists of stores that sell everything from clothing to groceries. He has established them in every major city and town from Montana to New Mexico. He's also into construction and land development."

"A man of means."

Maggie noticed the way he said it with mocking disapproval. Then, without another word, he went into the waiting room and woke Natalie up. "I'm going to go over and get some breakfast for you and your mother," he told the girl. "Stay here and don't open the door to anyone but Doc Clifford. Understood?"

Natalie, still half asleep, nodded her head and locked the door after he'd departed. Then she hurried to her mother's side. Maggie was feeling better. The nausea was gone, at least for now. But Sackett wasn't. The imprint of his body still branded hers in the most unsettling way.

Maggie pushed herself to recovery because she wanted to go home. Doc Clifford came in early and told her to rest up in the infirmary at least until tomorrow. That suited Maggie because she was terribly weak, but she knew she wouldn't regain her strength lying around either. She forced herself to sit up, which made her dizzy at first, but soon her head cleared and she felt much better, except for the pain in her shoulder.

Seth returned from the restaurant with breakfast for her and Natalie. Natalie received a healthy plate of bacon and eggs and fresh baking powder biscuits, but Maggie had to settle for toast and broth. Seth made coffee in the doc's coffee pot for himself, but he gave Maggie a glass of water and a sardonic smile.

"Wouldn't want you losing it all again, Maggie."

She looked away, the blood-red petals of embarrassment blossoming out onto her cheeks again. Despite his apparent amusement at her traitorous stomach, Seth took good care of her in his rough, off-handed way. By noon he brought her some soup with noodles and a fresh-baked roll. She had nearly finished the meal, enjoying it immensely, when Cleve walked in. He strode through the waiting room and into the infirmary. At Maggie's bedside, he tossed his hat to the foot of the bed and scooped her hand up in both of his.

"Cleve, what a . . . surprise," she managed, preferring a less ostentatious display of affection.

"I was here last night. Didn't Sackett tell you?"

"Yes, but somehow I expected you to be tied up with business today."

"You're more important than business, Maggie." His immense concern for her brought deep furrows to his brow. Maggie thought she also detected a hint of irritation in his demeanor, which was verified when he finally spoke again. "Maggie, Maggie . . ." he shook his head in disappointment, like one would do to a child who has undertaken something entirely foolish. "If you would have only listened to me and given up this crazy fight with Tate, none of this would have happened. Maybe this will change your mind and you'll consider what I said before."

Seth sauntered into the room at that moment and settled himself in the only chair, propping one foot on the opposite knee. He picked up a newspaper and pretended total absorption in its contents. But Maggie sensed Sackett wasn't missing one single word or nuance of their conversation. She wouldn't be surprised if he had joined them specifically to eavesdrop. She could have told him to leave, but somehow she felt that with him present Cleve wouldn't be able to pressure her into going to his mansion to recuperate. It was a lovely place and Cleve was always the perfect host and gentleman, but she just wanted to go home and be with her family.

"I truly appreciate your concern, Cleve, as always," she said, feeling very ill at ease with his attentions. "But if I gave up the fight, I'd be giving up the ranch, and what would I do in town? All I know is cattle, horses, and land. How would I support my children, my mother?"

"From the proceeds of selling the ranch, of course."

"For a man who has your experience in business and real estate, you should know that the money, unless re-invested, wouldn't last but a handful of years."

"Then invest it in other things. Buy and sell land, Maggie. I could teach you how. You could become a rich woman by doing that. Perhaps you'd like to open up a store? And if you still felt financially insecure, I could make you the manager of one of my new ladies' dress shops."

Maggie couldn't think of anything more boring than to be stuck indoors, day after day, arranging dresses on racks and hats on shelves, and waiting for someone to come in and buy something; to never again ride the range again on a hot summer's day with the scent of leather and horses and grass filling her nostrils, or to never again ride hellbent for cover from a sudden, encroaching thunder shower.

"I turn over thousands of dollars every year in cattle and horses, Cleve," she countered. "Can you afford to pay that sort of salary to a female store manager?" She didn't give him the opportunity to respond. She was tired of his ideas and methods of trying to persuade her to do something she didn't want to do and wasn't cut out to do. "Let's discuss it later, Cleve. I'm just not ready to leave my home. And right now, I'm too tired to think about it."

Cleve stood up. His congenial attempt at coercion had shifted to tight-lipped irritability. "If that's how you want it, Maggie. But if you change your mind let me know and I'll help you with anything I can. I'm only concerned about your welfare."

He kissed her cheek, donned his hat, and left the room, giving Sackett a departing glare. Seth set the newspaper aside and uncoiled from the chair. He sauntered over to the window next to Maggie's bed and looked out over the busy street.

"I'll rent that buggy for first thing in the morning. Will you be ready to go?"

Maggie settled deeper beneath the covers, suddenly feeling very exhausted and very relieved that Cleve was gone. *"More* than ready."

Seemingly pleased with her decision, he started for the door. "Then I'll get things moving."

"Seth." Her voice caught him just before he exited. Was she a complete fool, or out of line, to confide in him? After all, he was only a hired man. Maybe she was totally wrong to turn to him for answers.

"Is something wrong, Maggie?" he prompted.

"No," she said hastily. "No, it's just that—well, just that everybody seems to have an opinion on what I should do. Everyone but you."

His silence was long and contemplative. When he spoke he was dead serious. "Well, Maggie, I rode a fair piece from Deadwood to do a job and make some money. See some action. Now, personally, I'd be right disappointed if you stepped aside so Big Ben Tate could take over the White Raven. But don't listen to me, or anybody else. There's always two sides to every coin. Do what your heart tells you to do. That's the only sure way not to regret things later."

With Natalie's help Maggie got dressed the next morning. She was weaker than she cared to admit and had to repeatedly lie back on the pillows to keep from passing out.

"Mother, maybe going back home isn't such a good idea," Natalie said with a wrinkle of concern in her young brow. "Maybe you should just have Sackett take you to the hotel. Or maybe you *should* go to Cleve's."

Maggie wouldn't tell her daughter she was worried for the safety of her, her siblings, and her grandmother. Nothing would be gained by giving her fear to the girl.

"I'll be fine, dear. Really."

Natalie's skeptical expression hadn't changed when Seth returned.

"Buggy's out front," he announced. "Ready and waiting. "The livery rented me their best light buggy, a slat-bottom road wagon, so you'll be as comfortable as if you were in a rocking chair."

"I think she should stay here," Natalie proclaimed. "She isn't up to this. And what if we're attacked again?"

"Staying here will be your mother's decision." Seth's gaze shifted expectantly to Maggie. "But I sent a messenger to the ranch first thing yesterday morning and requested that Sonny send a couple of outriders to go back with us. They got into town last night just before dark. Two of the ranch's best men with a rifle."

"Pierce and Stokes?" Maggie asked.

Seth nodded, noticing the flash of relief that crossed her face. "So I can drive the buggy and they can keep a lookout."

"That won't be necessary, Mr. Sackett," Maggie said, suddenly realizing that if he drove she would have to sit next to him the entire way home. "Natalie can drive."

Seth shook his head and walked across the room toward her. "No, she can ride."

Maggie wasn't happy but didn't really have the strength to debate the point further, and she did notice the relief on Natalie's face. The girl never had liked driving buggies or wagons if she could ride.

Seth motioned for Maggie to give him her hand. "Come on. I'll help you out to the buggy."

She accepted his strong arm, although she would have liked to refuse it. Even with his assistance, she had gone only a few feet toward the door when she began to feel lightheaded again. Her grip tightened on his arm as her vision suddenly blurred. In the next instant she felt herself being lifted into his arms.

"I'm fine," she protested.

"I'm sure," he countered derisively. "Fine enough to keel over."

Natalie saw what had happened and came rushing back. "Is she all right?"

"Just weak," Sackett replied matter-of-factly.

Maggie had no choice but to put her arms around

his neck to help hold herself upright. He shifted her in his arms to a more comfortable position.

"Isn't this better than walking?" he quipped.

"I would prefer walking, Mr. Sackett."

His smile mocked her, as did his eyes. But he said nothing more and she knew he was enjoying the feel of her breasts against his rock hard chest as much as she was enjoying them being there. She knew the thoughts he harbored—probably every single one—because she was no stranger to mens' thoughts. He hadn't changed his mind about making her his lover, and he was determined not to let her forget it either. He carried her outside with great ease, as if her hundred and ten pounds were a mere quarter of that. She was hotly aware of his arms; one beneath her knees; the other across her back, both leaving the imprint of him on her memory and her flesh, like a firebrand pressed into soft leather. She tried to take his touch and translate it into Trent's. Tried to tell herself it reminded her of Trent's and that was why the flush of heat and the sexual awareness of him came tumbling over her in brazen waves that threatened to suffocate her stability. But, try as she might, she could not correlate the touch to Trent's in any way. All she felt was the burning, shameful feel of Sackett's erotic and forbidden intimacy. Possibly worst of all, she was positive he sensed her reaction to him.

He placed her carefully in the buggy to keep from bumping her shoulder, then spread a newly purchased wool blanket over her knees. She closed her eyes against the morning sun and leaned her head back against the tufted leather seat. The buggy dipped beneath his weight as he climbed in next to her. With her eyes closed she was doubly aware of his body in the tight quarters touching hers from shoulder to thigh.

"Put your head on my shoulder," he whispered. "No need to be shy."

Her eyes snapped open, flashing at him, but his merely gleamed with amusement. "I know what you're trying to do, Sackett," she whispered back, glancing at Natalie and the outriders to be certain they weren't within earshot. "And it won't work."

"You're dedicated to your husband's memory? Is that it?" He offered when she didn't explain herself further.

"That's right."

"A memory won't keep you warm at night, Maggie, or scratch that itch that even ladies get on occasion."

"You're vulgar, Sackett."

He chuckled and snapped the reins over the horse's back. "Giddup horse. Let's get the lady home."

Maggie turned her head so she was looking away from him, and she tried not to allow her thoughts to dwell on the warm contact of his body, so alive and virile. She tried to convince herself it wasn't just a man she needed, but Trent. Only Trent could ever fully fill the cavity of emptiness in her heart. She tried not to think of what Sackett's shoulder would feel like beneath her head, even when the movement of the buggy began to lull her to sleep and her head began to nod and droop against her will. But when she woke up at the ranch, hours later, she came awake to the feel of that exact shoulder beneath her cheek.

She sat up self-consciously and refused to look at Seth, but he wasn't going to let her off the hook without at least one taunting remark.

"It's truly an abomination, isn't it, Maggie, when a killer's shoulder can serve the same function as the shoulder of God-fearing man? Sometimes I wonder why God didn't make renegades with warts so ladies wouldn't be tempted by us. But maybe he made men like me to tempt women like you and to test your willpower, as well as mine. Like he did Eve and the apple. Do you know that story, Maggie?"

Maggie's self-consciousness was forgotten during the course of Sackett's peculiar dissertation. She'd never heard him speak with so much carelessness. It seemed he was constantly insinuating a sexual attraction for her, but it was done with a sort of flippancy, almost as if he believed she would never respond to his advances and therefore he had decided to amuse himself by making her uncomfortable and feeling foolish. He was a complex man whose real self he kept hidden behind a great and mighty wall of pride that wore the faces of arrogance and cynicism and self-mockery.

"Did anybody ever tell you you talk too much?" she snapped.

His mouth lifted into a wry half-smile. "No, but it seems to be something I only do when I'm with you."

She removed the blanket from her legs and sat up, preparing to disembark from the buggy, with or without assistance. "Well, put a lid on it, Sackett.

Your shoulder is more appealing than your philoso-
phizing."

"This sounds as if we're making progress in our
relationship, Maggie."

"I wouldn't go so far as to say that. Let's just say
we're like two jackasses that have been tied with the
same rope. We have no choice but to share the same
pile of hay if we don't want to starve. It doesn't
mean we can't bite each other once in a while if we
feel like it."

"I prefer nipping."

Her patience was wearing thin. Did the man al-
ways make sexual innuendoes to everything?
"You're always with the last word, aren't you,
Sackett?"

"It's just one of my many flaws, Maggie."

Any further retort Maggie might have chosen
was cut off by the bang of the screen door, the
thunder of feet, and the rabble of voices. Everyone
rushed out to meet her and fire a barrage of questions. Maggie found Sackett taking charge, bun-
dling her up in his arms again and answering the
questions for her. He politely pushed his way
through the gathering crowd of family and hired
hands and followed Maggie's mother as she led the
way to Maggie's bedroom. She wondered how he
could know she was exhausted, but she was grateful
for his interference and gladly welcomed her bed
when he at last laid her upon it with the same gentleness he had used earlier to place her in the buggy.

Lance, Alison, and her mother fretted over her
for the next few minutes. Over the tops of their
heads, Maggie saw Sackett quietly standing in the

corner, watching, still assuming duty as her protector, standing guard against danger and intrusion of her privacy.

Unexpectedly a stark and painful expression flashed across his face. It was so totally different from the jesting, reckless attitude he'd had in the buggy that it startled Maggie. But before she could put a name to it, it was gone. And so was Seth, slipping quietly from the room.

Sometime later, after everyone had gone, the empty look that had shadowed his handsome face returned to haunt Maggie. But it wasn't until she woke up in the middle of the night to the silence of her dark room and the loneliness of her bed that she fully understood what he had been feeling in that fleeting moment of self exposure.

Chapter Seven

Seth was halfway across the yard when he heard the front door open and heard his name being called. He turned and saw Catherine Marshall, skirts hiked up to her ankles, hurrying toward him with a distinct purpose to her step. She had been very kind to him since he'd arrived at the White Raven and she had made him feel comfortable and welcome. She didn't seem to hold the same ill sentiments toward him as Maggie did. A slender, pretty woman, she'd grown mature without losing her youthful vivacity, and he suspected Maggie would be the same way when she was that age. But where Maggie was bold and adventuresome, getting actively involved in the ranch, her mother was more the gentle woman, preferring to leave that sort of labor to the men so she might dally in the gentler aspects of her life, such as sewing and working in her flower garden.

She caught up to him, holding a dainty hand over her heart. "Oh, dear," she said with a smile and a slightly out-of-breath voice. "I'm not used to hurrying so."

"Is Maggie all right?" he asked, wondering what brought her out in the heat of the day without her bonnet.

"She's as well as can be expected, Mr. Sackett." Her lovely face darkened with worry. "This is all so upsetting. I can't imagine Ben Tate stooping so low. But I suppose he has left us no choice but to accept his true colors.

"Anyway, talking about Tate is not why I came out here. Actually, I wanted to thank you for protecting Maggie and saving her life. She told me that if you hadn't grabbed her when you did, the bullet would have more than likely hit her dead center."

Seth considered for a moment the fact that Maggie herself hadn't thanked him for saving her life. He supposed he understood why. Feeling the way she did about him, she was probably too proud to be beholden to him in any way. If he had any good qualities she was averse to accepting them, much in the same way his father had always been blind to everything but those things he considered evil or wrong.

"I was just doing my job, Mrs. Marshall."

"Well, I'm certainly glad you were. I just wish Ben would talk to Maggie and get this mess straightened out in a civilized way."

"Mrs. Marshall, if Tate murdered Trent, or even hired him to be murdered, he needs to be brought to trial. I think this situation has gone beyond discussion."

"You're right, of course," she hastily agreed. "But how can we take him to trial when we can't even prove he's done anything wrong?"

"I'll be riding out to keep an eye on things," Seth replied, hoping to ease her mind. "Watching the borders between the ranches and the hired men—on both ranches. I'll see if I can catch somebody red-handed. That's about the only way we'll bring an end to this."

Resignation settled heavily on her face and momentarily stole the illusion of youth. She wasn't as tough as Maggie, and he sensed she just wished they could sweep it all under the rug like so many dust balls and get on with normal living again.

"I guess I'll head out to the cookshack," he said as way of ending the conversation, which he felt could go nowhere else.

As he turned to walk away she placed a hand on his arm. The worry lifted from her face for a moment and was replaced with a smile. "We would enjoy having your company at dinner with us tonight, Mr. Sackett, if you would consider it. We're all very grateful for the way you've looked out after Maggie."

Numerous thoughts rushed through Seth's head. The first being the picture of Maggie in her big bed with all her family gathered around her. He hadn't belonged in the scene. He hadn't even belonged in the room. He had wanted to make love to her from the first moment he'd set eyes on her, but there was more to it now, something rather crazy and elusive. It wasn't just sexual fulfillment he sought from her now, but something that would penetrate the emptiness in him and fill the awful, lonely void. But he feared the consequences of allowing her to get too close to him. She would ask questions about who he was and where he came from and about his family—his father. What would she do when she knew the truth about him and saw his black soul? And even if she didn't ask questions, Mrs. Marshall would for the sake of conversation if nothing else.

He would surely like to see Maggie again. He'd even like to get to know her mother and children better, but Maggie had made it more than clear she didn't want him in her house, associating with her family. He needed to get his job done here and move on. Already he was becoming too emotionally involved with Maggie Cayton and that was the biggest and most foolhardy mistake he could ever make.

"Well, ma'am," he finally replied, meeting Mrs. Marshall's hopeful eyes while at the same time pulling the shutters on his own feelings. "I really need to go talk to Sonny."

"Oh, that's perfectly all right, Mr. Sackett. We'll wait for you. Supper won't be ready for an hour anyway. I'll tell Dorothy, our cook, to set you a place."

Before he could object with another excuse or a lie, Mrs. Marshall had once again gathered her skirts and was scurrying back to the house.

He muttered an oath at himself for not being more firm with her. But it was done now, and truthfully he found himself actually anxious to join them.

A few minutes later, he waylaid Sonny on his way to the cookshack. While Sonny piled up his plate with beefsteak, potatoes, gravy, and biscuits, Seth poured himself a cup of coffee and took a place at the end of the long wooden table to wait for the foreman to join him.

Everyone was all ears tonight, Seth noticed, wanting to hear his and Sonny's exchange. From the men's conversations, he knew they were all concerned and sorrowed about what had happened to Maggie. She was well-liked among them. They seemed to have accepted her taking over Trent's position without resentment of any sort. It said a lot for the new boss of the White Raven.

"I can't figure Tate wanting to kill Maggie," Sonny said around a mouthful of mashed potatoes. "I suppose we all understood killing Trent because Tate knew he'd never get him out of the way any other way. But a man just doesn't play that dirty with a woman opponent."

"Why not?" Seth asked evenly, hiding his own feelings on the matter, but wanting to see theirs. "Tate has apparently tried to force her out by other means and she's proven as tough as her husband was. If Tate is cold-blooded enough to kill Trent Cayton, I don't see why he should hesitate to kill Maggie. Just because she's a woman doesn't mean she still isn't an obstacle."

Forster interjected his unwanted opinion into the conversation. "Hey, Sackett. Did it ever occur to you or anybody else in here that maybe Tate wasn't after Mrs. Cayton? Maybe that bullet was meant for you."

A deeper hush settled over the room and the long wooden table. Cookie was even quiet for a change, standing by his pots and pans without so much as stirring a spoon in the gravy. Forster was clearly egging Seth on and everyone wanted to see if he would tolerate it a second time.

"It's possible, Milo," Seth finally replied. "And it would make more sense. But if that bullet had been meant for me, then whoever was staring down the barrel of that rifle must have had pretty poor eyesight. I figure it was Max Morrell, and we all know he hits what he aims at. Maggie's alive only because I saw a flash of sun on metal and pulled her to the side."

No more was said. Everyone returned to their meal and finished it in silence, unable to argue with Seth's reasoning.

Later Sonny walked outside with Seth. They stood by the hitching rail, talking and smoking. Sonny kept glancing at the house, at the second story window that belonged to Maggie. It was becoming more and more clear that he was in love with her.

"I don't know how you have so much patience with Forster," Sonny said, his tone laced with contempt. "I'm afraid I'd take him down and knock some of that shit out of his craw if it was me he kept needling."

Seth took a drag on his cigarette, wondering why Haig was so much as encouraging him to do something violent to the kid. "Oh, somebody will, sooner or later, Haig. But I don't see the need for it to be me. He's just a kid who hasn't gotten life all straightened out in his mind yet."

"Well, Tate's gone too far this time." Sonny shifted the conversation back to the main matter at hand, all the while keeping his eyes trained on Maggie's window. "What are your plans to stop him? Has Maggie given you some direction?"

Seth pointedly ignored Sonny's question. He had no intention of keeping Haig—or anyone—informed of his plans. "Tate says one of his men was killed," Seth said instead, watching Sonny's expression. "Maggie swears she didn't order it. I guess you wouldn't know anything about that?"

Sonny was plainly caught off guard by the question. For the first time Seth saw how swift his temper could be ignited. "Are you implying that *I* killed him?"

"No," Seth replied. "But I am beginning to wonder if someone on the White Raven isn't acting on his own. Or maybe Tate has a man working both sides of the fence. Clements was mad because Maggie wouldn't let him fight. Would he be the sort to go off alone and take matters into his own hands?"

"It's possible. He's hot-headed, but he's been with me most of the time."

Hot-headed like you? But again Seth didn't say what was on his mind. "Well, keep an eye on him. Keep an eye on all of the men."

"And what will you be doing while I'm watching everyone, Sackett?" Again there was the faint hint of a contemptuous curl to his top lip.

Seth dropped his cigarette into the dirt and smashed it out with the toe of his boot. He lifted his gaze pointedly to Haig. "Why, I'll be watching you."

* * *

Seth stretched out on his cot, enthusiastic about getting started on *Antigone,* the book Mrs. Marshall had loaned him from the family's small library. Over dessert, they'd gotten on the subject of the book Mrs. Marshall was reading and the moment she discovered he enjoyed reading, too, she had taken him to the library and let him take his pick of books. He'd felt like a child in a candy store, not knowing which one to take. He usually didn't have access to anything but the Bible. It wasn't that he didn't enjoy the Bible; it just reminded him too much of his father and brought back too many disturbing memories. He had taken up reading it when his mother had given him her copy and said, "Make it speak to you, Seth." And it had. He'd learned quickly that the quotes his father had used so frequently over the years to lay guilt or shame on his family and congregation had been used out of context and had been given the meaning he had chosen for them, instead of that actually intended.

But he had thoroughly enjoyed the dinner with Mrs. Marshall and her grandchildren. Maggie had stayed in her room and Seth wondered if it was because of him or if she simply hadn't felt up to coming to the table. Although Natalie wasn't overly pleased to see him at the table, Alison and Lance seemed glad to have him there, had treated him with great deference, and carried on a lively conversation.

He had found it unusually easy to give Mrs. Marshall satisfactory answers to her questions. She had been the perfect hostess and had never pried too deeply, although Alison had asked some pointed questions about why he wasn't married and why didn't he have children, for which she had been quickly reprimanded for by Mrs. Marshall. Seth hadn't answered Alison's questions even though he'd wanted to, but he found the answers had been too complicated and he doubted a child of nine would have understood the full complexity of his life. There were those skeletons in his closet that he couldn't tell her about. Without the whole truth it was oftentimes hard to tell anything at all.

Savoring the family atmosphere of the evening, he opened his borrowed book and began reading. He had barely read a paragraph, though, when a knock sounded at the door. His first thought was of Maggie, but just as quickly he realized she wouldn't be the one visiting him this time. And it was too late for Alison to be out.

Warily, he uncurled from his prone position, pulling his gun from the holster. He walked across the small room and moved off to the side of the door. A man in his occupation never knew when an old enemy would start blasting .44's right through the door.

"Who is it?"

The voice that came back to him made him relax instantly. "It's me, Mr. Sackett. Lance. I'd like to talk to you—if you don't mind."

Seth holstered his gun and opened the door, *Antigone* still in hand. Lance sidled in, his hands in his back pockets. He noticed the book. "I guess I'm bothering you."

Seth closed the door behind him. "No, I hadn't gotten into it yet. What's on your mind?"

Lance moved farther into the room and stood next to a saddle tree, fingering the saddle draped over it. He was uncommonly nervous, not his usual confident self.

"Is something wrong, Lance?" Seth prodded. "Your mother is still all right, isn't she?"

Lance jerked his head up, startled by the question. "Oh, yes. Yes. Grandma says she's sleeping." Seriousness suddenly settled over his young face. "But she's the reason I'm here, Mr. Sackett. It's about my mother being . . . shot. I. . . ."

Seth waited, seeing a turmoil of emotions roiling over Lance's young face. The predominant emotion was fear, followed by a lifting of his chin that Seth interpreted as defiance, as if he was about to ask something for which he was certain he would receive a negative response.

"I've come to ask a favor of you, Mr. Sackett."

"I'm listening."

Lance took a deep breath and blurted out everything in one fast gush. "I want you to help me learn to use a gun the way you do. I want to be good enough so I can protect my mother and sisters and my grandmother."

Seth felt as if he'd been hit in the side of the face with a brick, but he didn't let the boy know how the question had unsettled him. It was an enormous favor; a dangerous thing young Lance Cayton was asking.

He sauntered to the cot and set *Antigone* at the foot. When he faced Lance again, the boy's face still registered fear and defiance, but there was hope there as well.

"I doubt your mother would want me to teach you anything, Lance. Especially how to draw a gun. Your mother doesn't think too highly of me, in case you didn't know."

"Well, I know she didn't want to hire a gun, but she hasn't said anything personally against you, Mr. Sackett. And you're probably right about her not wanting you to teach me how to handle a gun the way you do. But if you don't teach me, I'll just keep practicing on my own. I've been going out ever since Dad was killed."

Seth's eyes narrowed suspiciously. "The girls said you were sneaking out to see some young lady."

Lance shifted to the other foot. His slender fingers—fingers that Seth noted would be good with a gun—gripped the saddle in front of him until his knuckles turned white. "I've seen her a few times, but I've mostly been practicing my quick draw."

"Loaded or unloaded?"

"Sir?" His face screwed up in confusion.

"Have you been practicing with a loaded gun or an unloaded gun?"

Sheepishness washed over Lance's expression like hot sauce over cold pudding. "Loaded," he mumbled, looking at the floor.

Seth sat down on the cot and leaned against the wall, propping one foot up on the edge of the bed. "I guess you just figured out the first thing you're doing wrong."

His voice rose in a knowing question. "It's a good way to shoot myself in the leg?"

"You've got it. After you have your motion down, *then* you add the shells."

Lance looked up again, undeterred by his own stupidity. "That just goes to show you how much I need your guidance, Mr. Sackett."

Seth acknowledged that the boy certainly did need guidance. He thought back to Captain Jagger who had given him his most important pointers on firearms and quick-drawing. The man had been a rebel captain in the War Between the States, a drover on some of the first cattle drives north from Texas, and finally he'd taken a job as a lawman in one cattle town after another as each sprung up and his services were needed. Jagger hadn't been the fastest man around, but he never missed what he aimed at.

Seth would have more than likely learned without him because he'd always used rifles and pistols to hunt game to keep food on the table. But Captain Jagger had kept him from learning the hard way and making mistakes that could have been deadly. Of course, that was after Seth had been on his own for several years already, hiring out his gun so he could make money and support his mother. He'd been a soldier, a mercenary, and later a hired gun on ranches. Even though he hadn't been with his mother during those years except for occasional visits, he had been her provider, making certain she had a comfortable home and money to have the things she needed.

He draped his arm over his knee and studied Lance who waited anxiously for his answer. He knew it had taken a bit of courage for the boy to ask in the first place, and if the boy was determined to learn. . . .

"All right, Lance," he finally capitulated. "But what about telling your mother?"

"Well, I don't think I will, Sir." He looked Seth right in the eye, stating his opinion boldly even though he knew it was likely to meet with opposition. "She wouldn't let me do it. And I need to be able to do this. But she wouldn't understand. She'd say she could protect herself."

"And if she finds out?"

"I'll take full responsibility. I wouldn't let her fire you."

Seth wasn't worried about being fired. There were always other jobs. But the bottom line was that Lance Cayton was going to learn to use that gun on his hip for more than just drawing once in a while to kill a rattlesnake, or a horse with a broken leg. He might learn some bad habits in the process of self-teaching, bad habits that could get him killed.

"How does starting tomorrow sound?"

Lance clipped off a yelp of elation. His smile was as wide as a singletree. For a second Seth thought he was going to come around the saddle and hug him. He stood up just as Lance picked up his hand and proceeded to give him a happy, pump-handle handshake.

"Thank you, Mr. Sackett. You don't know how much this means to me."

"Don't tell the men, Lance," Seth warned. "Don't tell anybody. If people find out I'm teaching you, every gun for a thousand miles will be wanting you to prove your worth. A man doesn't need a reputation, especially if he wants to live out his life, so don't even go lookin' for notoriety."

Lance's enthusiasm couldn't be dampened by anything, and especially something as sobering as reality. "Oh, don't worry, I won't."

"And don't call me Mister anymore. My friends call me Seth."

Lance grinned, obviously pleased to be considered a friend. Little did he know that Seth appreciated his friendship just as much, maybe more. Men like Seth seldom established emotional bonds with other men, mainly out of fear of betrayal. But he knew he could trust Lance Cayton to never double-cross him on anything.

Filled with anticipatory excitement, Lance hurried to the door, said a quick "See you tomorrow," and was gone.

Seth returned to his cot and picked up the copy of *Antigone.* He opened it and began to read, but the oft-heard words of the Bible crowded out those on the page and began ringing as clearly and insistently in his ears as the trumpets at Jericho.

. . . *in heart ye work wickedness . . . weigh the violence of your hands . . .*

Seth closed the book and lifted his gun hand, but it wasn't his own hand he saw in that moment. Instead he saw the innocent hand of a sixteen-year-old boy who didn't understand that the price of manhood could sometimes be high. Very high. It was a price that could easily go beyond blood, beyond pain, beyond death. It was a price that could go to a man's heart. A price he could very easily have to pay for for the rest of his life.

Chapter Eight

"Darn it!" Maggie unwound the hairbrush from her long hair. Instead of smoothing tangles she seemed to be making them. She simply wasn't handy with her left hand, but her shoulder hurt too much to allow use of her right hand.

A light knock sounded at the door. "Momma? May I come in?"

Maggie's spirits brightened at the voice of her youngest child. "Certainly, Alison. Please do."

The door opened and Alison burst in. It seemed the only way the child could enter a room, but her presence lit the darkest of spirits on the darkest of days. She slid next to Maggie on the vanity bench, cuddling in close and putting her arms around Maggie's waist.

"Grandma says dinner will be on the table in a few minutes, Momma. Are you ready to come down?"

"Not quite. I can't get the tangles out of my hair. Do you think you could help me?"

Alison leaped eagerly to her feet, and her eyes

grew as round and shiny as new silver dollars. "Oh, *could* I? I'll be careful. I promise."

Maggie handed her the brush, and with great enthusiasm, Alison set to the task. Smiling, Maggie returned her gaze to the mirror. But when she did, she found a man's reflection staring back at her from the open doorway of her bedroom.

Alison saw her mother's startled reaction to the visitor and hastened to explain. "Oh, I forgot to tell you, Momma. Mr. Sackett is having dinner with us again and Grandma sent him up with me to help you down the stairs."

Maggie's eyes locked with Sackett's in the mirror. *"Again?"*

From the half smile playing beneath the black moustache, it was obvious that Sackett was very aware of her disapproval of him not only being in her room, but being invited to her table. However, he seemed to be finding her irritation at the situation very entertaining.

"Apparently your mother likes me," he said. "We have something in common."

"I find that hard to believe, Mr. Sackett. My mother has never liked guns or killing."

"I would be surprised if she did. She's a gentle woman. But she *does* like books. And so do I."

To say Maggie was surprised that Sackett had ever cracked a book, let alone read one, would have been an understatement. She wondered if he was only playing on her mother's gullibility so he would have the opportunity to annoy Maggie with his presence. His intent to make her his lover was still more than clear. It gleamed in his eyes perpetually, like the steady sparkle of light in a diamond, and he was just waiting for her to say yes.

Well, he would be stoking the fires in Hell long before she would ever give him what he wanted. She would have challenged her mother's impetuous invitation to dinner right now if Alison hadn't been present. She would tell him to return to the cookshack and eat with the other hired hands where he belonged. She didn't want him in her house, didn't want him helping her with anything but what was required to set Tate in his place. Having him here was allowing him to get too close to her and her family—the one thing she definitely didn't want. She knew next to nothing about him, and still wasn't sure she could fully trust him to be dedicated to the cause of the White Raven, even if he had saved her life.

And yet . . . his presence in the room brought an excitement she hadn't felt for years and years, ever since she'd been a young girl and had first set eyes on Trent Cayton. Seth Sackett, damn his black heart, seemed to be having the same effect on her now. Perhaps it *would* be a change from the ordinary dinner doldrums to have him at the table. Of course, she must never allow the slightest indication of that particular desire to be conveyed to him. He would become more confident than he was now, which would probably make him totally unbearable.

"I'm glad to hear my mother finally found someone with whom she could discuss all those boring classics," Maggie finally said. "Personally, I never could get past the first few pages in any of them."

"There's much to be learned from them, Maggie, although it does take time and patience."

"Perhaps that's my problem then. I've never had either. As for you helping me down the stairs, I do appreciate your assistance but it really isn't necessary. I'm feeling fine and Alison will be here to help me."

"Alison can't stop a fall if you faint."

"I'm not going to faint."

Alison snagged a tangle and Maggie winced. "Oh, I'm sorry, Momma."

Maggie's eyes never lifted from Seth's, locked in the reflection of the glass. "It's all right, Alison."

Sackett remained at the door's threshold. "Your mother was afraid you'd be lightheaded," he continued. "She said they've been bringing your meals to the room and you haven't been on your feet very much."

"I'll be fine," she assured him.

"I'll stay around just to be sure. If I left you and you tumbled down those stairs head first, then I doubt your mother would ever invite me back to dinner again. I'd hate to see that happen. I've grown rather fond of your library, your family's company, and your cook's cuisine. It's so much better than Cookie's."

Movement at the window drew everyone's attention. One of Alison's kittens had managed somehow to get on the porch roof and had just leaped onto the sill of the second-story window.

"Oh, no!" Alison cried. "How did you get up here, Inky? I'll have to take you back outside."

Before Maggie could respond, Alison had rushed

to Seth and shoved the hairbrush into his unsuspecting hand. "Here, Mr. Sackett, will you brush Momma's hair? I'll be right back."

Alison, moving like a swallow in flight, swooped to the kitten, slowing down just in time to keep from frightening the poor thing back out onto the roof. She drew the kitten up against her and soothed it with kind words and long even strokes over its black fur. Then she hurried past Seth and out of the room.

Maggie and Seth were both caught off-guard by the intimate situation Alison had innocently thrust upon them, but Seth was the first to recuperate. He started across the room, hairbrush in hand. Maggie quickly recovered, too, and reached for a tortoise-shell comb on the vanity. "I'll just put this comb in. It'll be fine."

Seth stopped behind her. His hand closed over hers and the comb. "It won't do at all, Maggie. You've got a nasty-looking tangle back here. I think Alison put it there, if you want the truth, but sit still like a good girl and I'll fix it for you."

Maggie had the choice of obeying or simply getting up and moving beyond his reach, but his nearness and the touch of his hand on her shoulder somehow thwarted her better judgment. The brush began to glide through her hair. She should have taken this private moment to tell him she didn't want him inserting himself in her family's lives. Instead she found herself relaxing, succumbing to the vaguely sensual magic of his touch and the strokes of the brush. She closed her eyes. She didn't want him to see the way his hands were working wicked magic on every nerve in her body.

Seth studied Maggie's reflection in the mirror. God, how beautiful she was! Her face glowed with serenity. Seeing her in her blue day dress—a soft creation of cotton, lace, ruffles, and ribbons—with her long auburn hair draped out over her shoulders, made that big gap in his life yawn even bigger. The need to fill it with her presence, her touch, became almost overwhelming.

The voice of temptation began whispering:

Do it, Sackett. Bury your hands in her hair. Lift the silky strands to your lips. Inhale the perfume. And remember. Remember it all, because for men like you, memories are all you'll ever have. Do it, Sackett. Do it.

He made a mental note of her hair's texture and thickness; the way it waved as if she'd had it recently braided; the way the sunlight made the red strands flicker and crackle like fire as the brush passed over them.

Turn her into your arms, you fool. Carry her to the bed.

He kept brushing until her hair shone and no tangles remained. Alison would be back soon. Dinner was waiting.

Do it, Sackett. Do it.

He lifted the length of hair away from her neck. The shapely column was soft, slender, and irresistible. He had no control over his actions. Driven by desire, his lips touched that tender, scented flesh, and absorbed the heat of it to the very marrow of his bones.

She stiffened, but didn't move.

He heard footsteps in the hall and lowered the mane of hair back to its proper place.

Alison burst into the room. "I'm back. I hope that stupid cat doesn't get on the roof again. He's going to get himself killed. Oh, Mr. Sackett, you did a *good* job on Momma's hair!"

Seth's eyes lured Maggie's once again to his in the reflection of the mirror. If he wasn't mistaken, hers appeared smokey, not quite focused, even a bit dreamy. There was no anger there, just what appeared to be a silent question.

"We'd better get going," Alison said, dancing anxiously now from foot to foot. "Grandma is going to be upset if the food gets cold."

Maggie couldn't pull her eyes away from Seth's, probing as always into her thoughts and into her reaction to his outrageous behavior. She wondered, as she had before, if he held some sort of magical influence over her. "I'll just put a couple of combs in my hair first, Ali," she heard herself say. "Run and tell Grandma we'll be right down."

The child hurried off again. Maggie waited until her footsteps were halfway down the stairs before she said, "Why did you do that, Seth? You know how I feel about you."

Despite that spark in her eyes, Seth had the feeling Maggie was being as duplicitous as he was—saying one thing while feeling another. He might be wrong, but he believed she'd enjoyed receiving his kiss as much as he'd enjoyed giving it. "You'll have to forgive me, Maggie," he said softly. "The devil and I have crossed paths many times, and he never fails to throw temptation at my feet. I hate to say it, but so far I've never been able to step around it without picking it up first."

She returned her attention to her hair. He watched her slender hands expertly slide the jeweled, tortoise-shell combs into place. "In the future, Seth, stay out of my bedroom."

"I'll only come by invitation."

She stood up and gave her hair one last look. "The invitation will never be mine."

He shrugged. "Everyone's good intentions fall by the wayside once in a while, Maggie. To quote my father—and the Bible, *'The spirit is ready, but the flesh is weak.'*" He held out his arm to her. "Shall we?"

She brushed past him, ignoring his offer of assistance, but before she'd reached the dining table, her arm had slid through his and she was leaning heavily against him.

"As I said, Maggie," he whispered so only she could hear. "The flesh is weak. Even yours."

"He's not going to sit in Daddy's place," Natalie said from the dining room. "I don't care if one of us has to sit on the floor."

"You're being stupid about this," Lance replied just as hotly as his sister. "There are only six places at the table without adding a leaf, so somebody will *have* to sit in Dad's place."

"Then we'll add a leaf," she replied stubbornly.

"Don't you think that would be a little obvious, Natalie? It would make it look like we had a shrine to Dad or something. Besides, Dad wouldn't care if

Sackett sat in his place. He might even be honored."

"Honored? Ha! Sackett's a killer."

"He is not."

"He is too. He's no better than that creep Max Morrell who tags around Ben Tate like a dog on a leash. Let Grandma sit there, or you, or Mom. But not him. It's bad enough that Grandma keeps asking him to eat with us, but the next thing you know he'll be trying to *act* like our father and he'll be bossing us around."

"He isn't like that."

"How would you know?"

"I've been around him a lot here lately. I go out riding with him nearly every day. That's how I know. We'll ask Grandma what she thinks."

"It's her fault he's here. She *likes* him. I'm sure she'll *want* him to sit in Daddy's place."

"We all like him, Natalie. You're the only one who doesn't."

"Mother doesn't."

Maggie stopped short in the hallway that led to the dining room. She was appalled by the heated exchange she and Seth had just inadvertently eavesdropped on. For as much as she had tried to make Sackett think she wasn't attracted to him and didn't like him, it was most annoying and embarrassing to hear it coming so callously from her daughter. Maggie actually found herself wanting to defend Seth to the girl, and to tell Seth she didn't feel that way at all. But to deny dislike for him would certainly be exactly what he wanted to hear. Still, hearing it spoken from her own daughter's lips brought high color to her face. She couldn't even look at Seth. She was no longer comfortable using him for support and began to pull her arm free of his, but he seemed to sense her humiliation and caught her hand, holding it fast.

"I guess I came to dinner one time too many," he whispered lightly in her ear. "It wasn't a problem before."

"I don't know why Natalie said that. We never discuss you, one way or the other," she insisted lamely, hoping he would believe her, but knowing her guilt was entirely too evident.

"You don't know why she dislikes me?"

His careless tone made Maggie tilt her head to meet the amusement in his eyes. "No, I'm afraid I don't."

"It's easy enough to see," he continued casually. "Natalie's frightened. She thinks you're going to fall in love with me and we'll get married and I'll be her new father."

If he had intended humor in the remark, it was lost on Maggie. Her lips tightened in disgust. "That's the most ridiculous thing I've ever heard."

Seth laughed, loud enough for the children in the next room to hear. If Maggie didn't know better she'd think he'd done it intentionally to warn them to cease their discussion. It worked. The dining room became deathly quiet, not even disrupted by the clatter of a dish or the creak of a floor board.

Holding onto her arm, Seth directed her to the door. "You're absolutely right, Maggie," he replied, still in that flippant, self-mocking way. "It is ridiculous. A man like me wouldn't be good at any of those things."

His words somehow prompted the memory of the stark look she'd seen in his eyes the day he'd brought her home from town. Suddenly she felt as if she needed to make a clarification. It was bad enough that Natalie was being a brat; she shouldn't behave like one, too.

"I didn't say it would be impossible for some woman—"

"You don't need to explain, Maggie. I understand."

The children were indeed red-faced when Seth and Maggie entered the room. Seth pretended he hadn't heard the argument. Maggie rectified the seating situation by taking her usual place at one end of the table. Lance, following Maggie's instructions, took his father's chair at the opposite end with his grandmother on his left and Seth on his right. Natalie and Alison sat to the right and left of Maggie, respectively.

Catherine, ignorant to the undercurrents that had gone on before she'd arrived, chattered gaily through the entire meal, almost like a giddy young girl. Since she was directly across from Seth, she spent considerable time discussing *Antigone* with him, which he hadn't yet finished. Maggie was actually thankful for her mother because she wasn't sure how she could have kept a conversation going with Sackett the entire time. She also intended, however, to have a little talk with her mother after the meal. She didn't want Sackett being invited again.

Alison tried to insert herself into the conversation

by relaying to everyone who didn't know that Inky had climbed onto the porch roof and into her mother's bedroom. Natalie picked up on it immediately. "Yes, and your stupid cat was in my window, too. It came into my room and walked all over my bed with dirt on its feet! You're lucky I didn't toss it out the window on its head."

"Oh, you're so mean, Natalie," Alison shot back. "How would you like it if someone tossed you out the second-story window on your head!"

"Girls, please don't fight—and especially at the table." Maggie turned apologetic eyes to Seth. "I'm really sorry, Mr. Sackett. I'd like to say they don't usually do this, but I'm afraid they do. Of course, they never did when their father was here." She gave the girls a scathing glance, and, sufficiently shamed in front of company, they went quietly back to eating.

Every time Seth had come to supper, he had been surprised by the way the three Cayton children bickered and voiced their opinions on all sorts of matters. If he and his brother had said one word without being spoken to, they'd have felt the razor strop or the bruising lash of their father's hand across their face. The Cayton children were vocal, but they also had enough respect for their mother and grandmother that when they *were* told to behave, they acquiesced to the authority. He found them quite delightful, and he wondered what it would have been like to grow up so free in a household that was a little crazy like this one.

The way he'd lived hadn't been normal. This was normal, to observe the imperfections of human nature; to gently mold undesirable behavior while accepting it as normal; and to deal with it not by physical and verbal abuse but with tolerance, understanding, and forgiveness. These people loved and respected each other. Here there was no fear and loathing. Here one could eat a meal and savor the taste of it then walk away from the table feeling happy and content.

Seth remembered how his stomach had always knotted at mealtimes until he could barely eat. His father would in turn cuss him for not eating and tell him not to waste food. He'd choke down his meal, afraid of being dragged from his seat and beaten before the meal was over because his father seemed to pick that time of day to correct all their transgressions and imperfections. Seth had learned to take small portions so he could get them down quickly and be excused. Sometimes after he'd eaten and left the table to the relative safety of the outdoors, he would throw up his supper because of the fear and tension under which he'd consumed it.

I told you to haul wood last night, Seth.

I did, Pa.

Yes, a few measly sticks.

I hauled what you told me to haul. Six armloads.

One stick per load?

No, as much as I could carry.

Seth, ye are of your father the devil, and the lusts of your father ye will do—John 8:44. Now, stand up and precede me outside and accept your punishment.

Ezra, is that really necessary? There's plenty of firewood.

Be quiet, woman! It's not the question. The boy is

disobedient. He lies. He's lazy. For that he must be punished. Come outside and take off your shirt, Seth.

"Mr. Sackett?"

Seth started. Catherine had asked him a question. "I'm sorry, Mrs. Marshall. What did you say?"

"Would you care for more dessert?"

He glanced around the table, realizing that the meal was winding down and nearly everyone was done eating. Maggie was watching him with a strange look on her face, and for the first time he couldn't meet her scrutiny, her silent questions about who he was and what he was, and why he was behaving so odd at the moment.

He wiped his mouth on his napkin and pushed his chair back. "It was a wonderful meal, Mrs. Marshall, but I honestly couldn't eat another bite. If you'll excuse me, I just realized I need to go out and talk to Sonny about something."

Before Catherine could extend another dinner invitation or suggest a friendly chat in the library, he had left the room and departed the house on long strides. He went directly to the tack shed, but outside the door he stopped and lit a cigarette. He didn't need to talk to Sonny. He had just needed to get away, to get back to the reality of who he was. He had enjoyed the companionship of the Caytons the last few days, and had enjoyed seeing how normal people lived. But he was what he was, and that could never be changed.

No matter how he hated to admit it, Natalie was right. He had no business sitting at the head of a family like Maggie Cayton's, even temporarily. He, a man who had sinned in every possible way, would never be worthy of that eminent position.

On the chaise lounge by her bedroom window, Maggie had a clear view of Seth Sackett down in the yard. He didn't seem to be in a hurry to talk to Sonny, even though he'd sited that reason for leaving so abruptly. He had positioned himself on the top pole of the horse corral, and he was smoking. His hat shaded the upper portion of his face, and the slump of his shoulders indicated a brooding mood. He took one last drag on his cigarette and flicked the butt into the deep, soft dirt of the corral. He remained there, his forearms resting on his knees while he hung his head and stared at the ground some eight feet below.

"Hasn't he left the ranch to do anything since I came back from Doc's?" she asked her mother.

Catherine, who had assisted Maggie back to her room, took a seat at the foot of the chaise lounge. Following the direction of Maggie's interest, she saw Seth. "No, I don't believe so," she replied, smoothing her skirt in a habitual gesture. "From what he's said, I believe he felt it was more important to keep an eye on you than on Tate and his men. We nearly lost you, and he's very worried even if he hasn't come right out and said so. But I can see it in his eyes when he speaks of you and the accident."

"He's just afraid that if I die, he won't get the rest of his money," Maggie quipped, secretly hoping even as she said it that it wasn't true. She didn't like to admit it, but the man was getting under her skin and into her mind more and more often.

"I don't believe that's true at all, Maggie," Catherine retorted defensively, as if she herself had been insulted. "I believe he is genuinely concerned about you."

"I doubt if Sackett is capable of caring about *any*one, Mother. He uses people when it suits his purposes. He's a gunslinger, in case you've allowed him to charm you out of remembering that."

Suddenly Maggie sat up straighter. Lance had come from the house and had joined Sackett. They talked for a few minutes then left the corral, got on their horses and rode off.

Maggie had pondered for days how she, Seth, and Natalie had been so easily set up for ambush. The only logical explanation was that Tate, having seen them in town, had sent Morrell to follow them. Sackett was right in being cautious, but what was he thinking to ride out with Lance at this time of the evening? Anybody riding in Sackett's company was ultimately in danger, and surely he knew it.

"Don't worry about him," Catherine said. "At least he's not meeting Cecilia."

Maggie glanced at her mother who had also watched the two ride away. "How did you know I was thinking of Lance?"

"I gave birth to you, girl. I raised you. A mother can read her children's minds. You might be grown, but I'm still pretty good at reading you. So what are you really afraid of?"

Maggie returned her gaze to the window even

though Lance and Seth were no longer in sight. "What do you mean?"

"I know you're worried about Lance's safety, but I have the feeling there's more to it."

Maggie didn't know if her second concern for her son was petty or legitimate, but she'd always respected her mother's opinion and always confided in her when she had a problem. "I don't like Lance getting too close to Sackett," she admitted. "He can't be a good influence on a boy. He's a killer. And he's brazen as hell."

"I hate it when you swear, Maggie."

"Mother, please. I'm not going to change what I am at this late date anymore than you are."

"You've been swearing since you were ten."

"My point exactly."

"Talk about bad influences. I always knew I shouldn't have let you spend so much time with your father. The man couldn't think without coloring it with profanity, except when he thought I was listening, of course," she said with a wry grin.

"It's hardly the same as Lance being influenced by a killer."

"Seth carries a gun on his hip like every other man in the West, Maggie, but it's not the gun that makes a man dangerous, or makes him a killer. It's what's in his heart and how he chooses to use that gun. Trent wore a gun, too, if *you'll* remember. Did you know Seth's father was a preacher?"

Maggie thought about the words Seth had spoken earlier, quoting his father and talking about the weakness of the flesh. But he could have heard that phrase anywhere. "Just because he tells you something doesn't mean you have to believe it, Mother. What preacher's son would become a man who lives by the gun? Honestly, how could you be so gullible? I'm beginning to think Sackett has you wrapped around his little finger and he knows it."

Catherine wasn't troubled by her daughter's bluntness. She and Maggie had always spoken their mind to each other. She had missed their talks dearly during those years after Maggie had married and left the ranch in Denver to move up here with Trent. Then Maggie's father had died, and Catherine had been all alone. The other children, two sons, had gone to California to build an empire in oranges. Catherine had never had anything to do with the ranch, didn't know how to run it, and hadn't wanted to. So she had sold out and moved into town. But Maggie had hated to see her all alone, and had convinced her, quite easily as a matter of fact, to come and live at the White Raven. It had truly helped her to cope with the loss of her husband. And then Trent had been killed, and she had been here for Maggie. They had grown closer than ever before.

"Preachers' sons are usually always the kind who rebel, my dear," Catherine finally replied. "Surely you knew that? Their strict upbringing tends to stifle them."

"Does it normally turn them into killers, too?"

"Seth isn't anymore a killer than Trent was. But I certainly do see him as a defender of justice. And he wasn't lying when he told me his father was a preacher. I went out to strip the bedding off his bunk for washing and I saw a Bible under his pillow. A very *worn* Bible, I might add."

Maggie smirked. "He probably sleeps on it to help clear his conscience and keep evil spirits away."

"Whatever works."

"You're beginning to sound like Alison and Lance. They think he walks on water. I hardly believe the man is Jesus incarnate. The only one who isn't singing his praises is Natalie. At least she's got good judgment."

"Believe what you want, but I don't doubt his word for a second. He's very honest. I can see it in those incredible gray eyes of his. Oh, I suspect he's hiding some things—aren't we all?—but the boy isn't a liar."

"Neither is he a boy."

Catherine broke into a grin. "I'm glad you noticed. I was beginning to wonder if you had gone blind."

Maggie gave her a scathing look, but Catherine ignored it. "I daresay Seth is nearly as old as you, dear. But to a sixty-year-old woman such as myself, thirty-eight seems young." She looked outside again dreamily. "If I was your age I'd surely be smiling at him a lot more than you do. Come to think of it, I don't believe I have ever seen you smile at him. Have you?"

Maggie rose from the chaise lounge, no longer interested in the scenery from the window since Seth had become missing from it. "Why exactly have you been inviting Seth to the house for meals, Mother?

You haven't invited any of the other hired hands to eat with the family."

Catherine chuckled. "You evaded my question rather nicely, dear, but to answer yours, I've invited him because he's a nice young man."

"So you said."

"And he's handsome."

"So you said."

"He's a good conversationalist. It's not very often a man comes along who can discuss books and things of that nature with a woman. He's educated, smart, and well-mannered."

"Anything else?"

"He's lonely, and—"

"And what?" It was Maggie's turn to smile. Her mother's extensive defense of Seth was becoming quite amusing. She was beginning to think her mother was mildly lovestruck by him. Why else would she become so totally blind to the man's faults?

Catherine rose from the chaise lounge. She lifted the curtain as if something outside had her attention, but Maggie knew it was just an action, something to be doing with her hands. "He's interested in you."

Maggie laughed, shaking her head in disbelief and delight at her mother's observations. At the same time she wondered if her mother might know something she didn't. Did he honestly like her, or did he just find her attractive enough to take to bed? She removed the combs from her hair and placed them on the vanity, remembering for a moment the way his lips on the back of her neck had sent an electrifying rush throughout her body. She shook the memory aside, preferring not to think about the dormant fires stirred by his intimacy.

"It sounds as if you're trying to play matchmaker, Mother. Do you honestly want me involved with a man like him? You know he wouldn't settle down. He would just take whatever I'd be foolish enough to give and then he'd be gone. For heaven's sake, I'm too old for romances and love affairs. I've been married. My children are nearly grown. I can't believe we're even talking about this, much less that you seem to be encouraging me to have a relationship with him."

"I think you need to take a closer look at Seth, my dear. I've talked with him extensively since you were wounded and I'm beginning to know him quite well. I honestly think he would like nothing better than to have a wife and a family."

"A readymade family?" Maggie's brows lifted in a dubious reaction.

"You're not too old to give a man a child."

"No, but I don't know that I'd want to be pregnant again. Good Lord, I don't believe we're discussing this! And with Sackett in mind as the father no less! Enough, Mother. Enough. Nothing's been stopping Sackett from having a family so far. Nothing except Sackett. He likes what he does. Why would he want to settle down to honest physical labor when he can blow off a few heads once in a while and make a thousand dollars."

"Maggie! I can't believe you said that."

"Believe it. And believe something else, too. I'm not interested in another man. I still love Trent. I am *not* looking for a husband. I don't know what gave you the idea marriage was even a topic on the agenda."

"You'll always love Trent, Maggie. He was your first. But you still have a life to live. I can certainly tell you one thing, a man doesn't have to wear a three-piece suit and a bowler hat to be a gentleman."

"Oh, so we're back to Cleve."

"I'd rather see you married to Seth Sackett, gunslinger or not, than I would to see you hitched up with Cleve Williams or Sonny Haig."

Maggie gave her a quizzical look. "What makes you think Sonny is interested in me?"

"Good heavens, Maggie. I do believe I'll have Seth drive you to town and have your eyes examined! Anybody who's not stone blind can tell that Sonny is hopelessly in love with you. As for Cleve . . . well, the man reminds me of a weasel. Not in his looks, mind you, but more of something fluttering around in his eyes. Something skittish, evasive. And I know, as surely as I know my own name, that Cleve wouldn't stay on the White Raven. He'd want you to move into that mansion in town. I daresay he'd send me packing, too. As for Sonny, that young man really doesn't have what it takes to run a place the size of the White Raven. He isn't smart enough, and he's not the type who would want your advice. Nor would he listen to it if it was offered. He'd end up losing the ranch, and probably in the space of five years or less."

Maggie suddenly burst out laughing.

Catherine's lips formed a pout. "What is so amusing, Margaret?"

Maggie managed to get her laughter under control but her eyes still twinkled. "I see a little self-interest here, Mother. You want me to marry someone who will keep the White Raven and who will let you stay here, too."

"Well, any decent man would do both out of consideration for not only you, but for your mother and children as well. A decent man wouldn't think only of himself. I can tell you that Cleve Williams is a man who only thinks of himself. And Sonny, too, to a lesser degree."

Maggie held up her hands in surrender. "All right. I believe you've made your point. You don't like any of the men who are interested in me, except for the one I'm not interested in. So, I guess we'll just have to remain merry widows, you and me, and continue to run the White Raven by ourselves. But there is one other alternative we haven't discussed."

It was Catherine's turn to look suspicious. "What is that, dear?"

"Well, perhaps *you* should go out and find someone to marry."

The subject put Catherine on the defensive again. "I loved your father dearly, had his children, and gave him nearly forty years of my life. But if a handsome man my age came along and looked at me the way Seth Sackett looks at you, I certainly wouldn't be hanging around causing problems for my daughter."

Maggie rose from the vanity and went to the window. She put an arm around her mother and gave her a squeeze. "You're never a problem for me, Mother. Don't ever think that. I don't know what I would have done without you the past year."

Catherine met her daughter's eyes, the same color as her own. "I don't know what we'd have done without each other, Maggie. But with everything that's going on, I guess I just feel you need someone to watch over you. Someone like Sackett. Don't be so hard on him. And don't be so hard on me for enjoying his company. He's quite refreshing, and the poor man seems to like having someone to talk to, even if it is an old eccentric woman. He's so alone in his, um, profession, and he's all drawn up inside himself. He has a lot of wisdom and ideas to share. There's good in him, and he sees good in others. You just have to be willing to look for it the same as he does."

Maggie wondered if her mother was right. Wondered if she had completely misjudged Seth because of her preconceived notion of what he was. But she wasn't willing to give up that notion entirely. It was safer to keep him at a distance. She wasn't ready to become involved with another man. She wasn't sure she ever would be. And if she did, it wouldn't be with a man like Sackett anyway. A man who was entirely too dangerous to a woman's heart.

"All right, Mother. I'll try to have a more open mind where Seth is concerned. But that's *all* I'll promise."

Catherine patted Maggie's cheek. "I would never ask you to do more than that, dear."

Chapter Nine

Seth watched Natalie lead her two-year-old mare around the corral. In the three weeks since Maggie had been home recuperating, Seth had been meeting with Lance and helping him with his draw. He'd also taken the time to help Natalie with her horse. There was no doubt in Seth's mind the girl would have attempted to break the horse herself, which was fine, but she needed to know a few basic do's and don'ts before she did. Working with him would give her that knowledge so she would be able to break her next horse by herself if she chose to do so.

The mare, which Natalie had named Shadow Dancer, was coming along fine. It learned quickly and strived hard to please. It was spirited but not so much that it would be a dangerous mount for the girl.

In actuality, Seth had had to handle Natalie more carefully than he had the horse. He didn't know much about teenaged girls, except they had moody flights of fancy and could get upset at virtually nothing. Likewise they could find humor in things that weren't humorous at all, like the time when Shadow Dancer had plopped her foot on Seth's toe and refused to do anything but lean her entire nine hundred pounds into it.

Natalie had been tense the first few days. Seth attributed it to her not knowing whether he had overheard her remarks that day in the dining room. He'd never let on that he had. She hadn't been confident in his horsemanship ability in the beginning either and had constantly made references to her father and how he would have done it. Seth had seen her change her mind quickly enough though when her horse responded favorably to his more gentler techniques. Soon she was asking his advice and listening intently when he explained something to her. He was pleased to see her attitude toward him soften.

Seth hadn't minded staying around the ranch. He'd told the men and Sonny he was afraid Maggie's assailant would return when everyone was out working. There was truth in it, but it was also a good excuse to stay close to her.

Partly because of Natalie's opinion of him, and partly because he felt he didn't belong, he hadn't accepted any more of Catherine's dinner invitations—until this morning when she'd caught him and asked him to join them on Sunday. Fried chicken and apple pie were on the menu, she'd said, as way of enticement. He'd accepted because he feared that any more flimsy excuses would hurt her feelings. He enjoyed her company and found her a very pleasant woman. He didn't want her to think he didn't like her.

Although the apple pie, fried chicken, and Catherine's lively conversations had been an enticement, the real reason he'd accepted was because he had wanted to see Maggie again. She'd stayed inside and given ranch orders through Sonny, seldom appearing outside herself. He found himself constantly looking toward the house, hoping for a glimpse of her. Occasionally he spotted her walking in the yard or sitting in the porch swing taking some sun. She was devastatingly beautiful with the sunlight setting her auburn hair ablaze. In the afternoons when the sun was the hottest, she wore a large, floppy-brimmed hat to protect her face, but even that couldn't cover the full glory of the auburn mane of hair.

All in all, he'd been so distracted he hadn't been able to even concentrate on the newest book Catherine had loaned him for thinking about Maggie and the sweet taste of her skin against his lips. Regardless of how foolish or hopeless it might be, he wanted to experience the ecstasy of that fragile pleasure again.

He glanced at the house for the hundredth time in the past thirty minutes. Doc Clifford had come to check on Maggie's progress and Seth expected his departure any time now. Besides Doc, Maggie had had a constant stream of visitors since she'd returned home. Cleve Williams had come twice, rendering roses. Neighboring ladies had converged on the ranch loaded down with homemade pies and cakes, jellies and preserves. The local preacher, Reverend Baker, had come offering prayers, philosophies, and caution. The hired hands had filed in one at a time with their hats in their hands expressing in timid and abstract ways their genuine and deep concern for her life. The only person who hadn't come by offering condolences for her misfortune was Big Ben Tate. His absence seemed to cinch his guilt.

The screen door gave out its familiar screech and Doc Clifford emerged, black bag in hand. He saw Seth and headed toward the corral on the quick pace of a man who could not afford to tarry. Seth handed Shadow Dancer's reins to Natalie. "We're done for the day," he said. "I'm going to talk to Doc Clifford before he leaves."

He met the doctor halfway between the house and the corral. The man promptly turned around and started back toward his buggy and his next patient, glancing back at Natalie in an anxious, nervous manner as if he wanted to say something not intended for her ears.

"What is it, Doc?" Seth prodded, keeping stride at his side and feeling an unexpected knot of fear form in his stomach. "Maggie hasn't developed complications, has she?"

Concern cut deep furrows in Clifford's wizened brow. "No. The wound is healing nicely. I told her not to use her arm on anything extremely heavy for another week, then to ease back into her work load as she sees fit." He gave a heavy sigh. "Actually, it's her mental state I'm worried about. You see, she isn't afraid of dying, but she *is* afraid of losing one of her children or her mother to Tate's hired gun. Now, they all understand the dangers of this "war" but if Maggie doesn't scare them witless so that they jump at every sound, I'm afraid she'll turn this ranch into a prison. Then I'm afraid the Cayton children will rebel. They are not accustomed to having boundaries and may not realize how dangerous things really are. They may get careless. With Tate as an enemy, Maggie has every right to fear for their lives."

They had reached the buggy and Clifford climbed in, gathering the reins of the horse that had been standing in his harness, dozing, as if he was very accustomed to long waits. "I hope for everyone's sake that you can try to initiate a settlement of the battle between her and Tate. Even if it means convincing her to sell. This ranch is not worth her life."

Clifford had said all he intended to and slapped the reins over the horse's rump. Seth made no comment to the man's request. He bid Clifford good day, watching him turn the buggy around and head back to town. He continued to watch until the buggy rounded a bend in the road and disappeared behind a sloping hill. It disturbed him that everybody wanted Maggie to quit, to take the easy way out. Their reasoning was justified in some regards, but how could she continue to hold on when no one was on her side? Why didn't all these people who claimed to be so concerned about her health and welfare do something besides give advice and pity? Why didn't they help her find proof of Tate's guilt and bring him to justice?

Natalie called from the corral, curry comb in hand. "What did he say about Mother?"

"She's fine!" he called back. "I'm going in to talk to her."

Natalie nodded and went back to her job. Seth

headed up the steps to the house. It was Alison who answered his knock, looking extremely glum.

"Mom's in the conservatory, Mr. Sackett," she said, then slipped past him on her way outside. She had been quiet all week and Seth supposed it was natural for her to be worried about her mother.

The house was quiet except for a distant rattle of pots and pans back in the kitchen at the rear of the house. He hadn't had a formal tour, but he knew approximately where the conservatory was and he walked down the silent hall that split the house into two wings. At the end of the hall, he turned left, passed through a small storage room and finally came to the conservatory. It was actually an enclosed porch that held an abundance of potted plants, rustic furniture, and the beautiful Maggie Cayton. Seated in a cushioned rocker with her feet propped on a footstool, she was gazing out the window at the garden where her mother, Lance, and Essie Freeman and her two children were preparing rows for the seeds to be planted in. Maggie's elaborate emerald-colored tea gown, trimmed with lace and ribbon, was the perfect contrast to the burgundy-colored fabric on the cushions and to the auburn mantle of hair cascading over her shoulders.

The sun's rays came through the screened area and fingered every red and golden strand in her head before slanting across her length where it then warmed the graceful curve of her dainty ankle and slippered foot exposed below the hem of her gown.

She didn't appear surprised to see him, and, if he wasn't mistaken, her eyes lit up ever-so-slightly.

"Come in, Seth. How's Natalie's mare coming along?"

He walked the length of the long, narrow room to where she sat. The small rugs scattered intermittently across the floor gave his footsteps an uneven sound. Stopping next to her chair, he joined her in watching the activity outside. "The mare is fine. I think it's a good choice for a young girl."

"Trent picked her as a colt. She's out of Shadow. When you go back out, would you tell Natalie to come help with the garden?"

"She won't like that," he quipped.

She lifted those exotic, hypnotizing green eyes to his. A smile flirted at the corner of her lips. "No, I'm sure she won't. Not anymore than Lance does. He seems to think that gardens are women's work and that he should be out with the men."

"He should be."

She cocked her head, an eyebrow lifting quizzically. "You men must all think alike, Seth. Trent would have said the same thing."

The sound of Seth's name on her lips stirred feverish desires, even when said in the same breath as her deceased husband's. He wanted her more than ever; wanted her to want him. But he wasn't sure now that he would be satisfied with only one night. Lately that initial dream of lust had changed into a haunting desire to take her in his arms and keep her there forever.

He nearly smiled at his own foolishness. Desires and dreams, that's all they were. Maggie wanted him no more now than she had the first night she'd met him. She despised him, as well she should. He wasn't a man worthy of her love.

"Men have their pride, Maggie," he replied. "It's probably the biggest flaw we all carry, but I also believe a woman shouldn't have to do all the work involved in keeping a household running. Children are young and strong and more capable than they'd like you to know when it comes to work. It won't hurt them to help."

"Well, children certainly believe they should be exempt from work."

She returned her gaze to her family. Seth wondered if she wanted them all out there in one spot so she could keep an eye on them.

"Doc says you're nearly mended enough to go back to your normal routine," he added.

"Yes, sooner than he thinks."

"Gunshot wounds shouldn't be taken lightly, Maggie," he cautioned. "You'd better listen to him."

"He's overly cautious." Maggie shrugged off Doc's advice as well as Seth's, but she wasn't as successful in focusing her thoughts away from Seth. Even when she trained her eyes elsewhere, all her senses were alert to his commanding presence. He'd been a perfect gentleman the past two weeks and had made no more overtures to them becoming lovers. Little did he know that when her mind rested for a time from its concerns about Tate and the danger to her family, it was immediately haunted by sharp remembrances of his kisses and lying with him at the doctor's. Had she honestly asked for him, as he'd said? She remembered how it had felt to be in his arms—safe, secure, and full of desire. The memory of the kiss he'd placed on the back of her neck still sent shivers to her toes. And then there was the way he'd lingered in the background, watching over her, when she'd had company. He had studied each person as if he didn't trust any of them to be what they claimed to be. At times he seemed to possess a sagacity no one else could lay claim to, as if he could see a person's weaknesses and sins even before they were committed.

Maggie couldn't understand the way he haunted her, both day and night. She couldn't wait to be away from him, and then when she was she kept hoping to see him. Or she would catch herself listening, thinking she had heard the sound of his approach. Her body betrayed her and she found herself yearning for his touch again, all the while fearing it. But she knew now that it wasn't his touch she actually feared, but her own reaction to it.

"Doc Clifford wants me to talk you into selling," he said nonchalantly. "Want me to try?"

The remark surprised her, coming out of the blue as it had. Was he serious? Or jesting? Why could she never tell? "Somehow I get the feeling you're mocking me, Seth, and everything I'm trying to accomplish."

"Not at all. I just find it entertaining that all these people who have known you for years don't really know you at all."

"And you do?"

Tiny fires flickered across the surface of his eyes like campfires at night on the open range. His bold perusal had the same effect as a physical caress.

"I understand you, Maggie," he said softly. "I know the kind of person you are, and I would never suggest to you to quit."

"Because *you* would never quit?"

"No, because you shouldn't have to quit. But you do have to think about the ramifications of fighting Tate. And you need to take precautionary measures. But you're not in this alone. Talk to your children—at least the two oldest ones—and tell them the dangers they're facing. Ask them if they stand behind you in your decision. Decide what you can all do to better protect yourselves. Don't carry the weight of this. Lance and Natalie are old enough to know what they're facing. I don't think either one of them would want to give into Tate anymore than you do."

What he said was true, but if Maggie lost any of her children or her mother because she had chosen to stand and fight she would never be able to forgive herself. The thought had tormented her ever since she'd woke up in Doc's office in Seth's arms. Even in her dreams, the fear escalated into frightening nightmares that brought her awake crying out in the darkness.

"Have there been any more incidents of foul play this week?" she asked.

"I've stayed pretty close to the ranch since you were hurt," Seth confessed, "but the men found some cut wire on the fence line by Black Mountain. Some of Tate's cattle were on your range. They drove them off and fixed the fence."

"Had the wire been cut?"

"Slick as a whistle."

"Anything else?"

"No. Everything seems fine for the moment."

In a slow, leonine movement that sent warning signals flashing through her, Seth lowered himself to his haunches next to her and gave her his full attention. She shifted uncomfortably in the rocker, sensing a subtle change in his demeanor. His hand closed over hers and gathered it up in both of his. She would have pulled away except that there was something magically hypnotic about the way his eyes searched hers, about the calloused heat of his palms, and about the sensual circles his thumb began tracing on the back of her hand. The aura of danger she'd seen around him the first time surrounded him again, as darkly as ever, and just as mysteriously. She feared him, yet ambivalently yearned for his nearness. He was like a flame, mesmerizing her, taunting her with promises of warmth. Somehow calling out for her to come closer . . . closer.

She pulled her hand free of his as if she had truly been burned. His lips curved into a half smile, and his eyes told her that he guessed every thought in her head and knew the way his touch had affected her.

"I'm going out tomorrow to look around," he said, still balancing on the balls of his feet next to her chair. It was hard to concentrate on what he said because his voice was low and sounded more as if he spoke poetic words of seduction than business. "Catching someone red-handed will be the only way we'll ever be able to get the law to take the case to trial. How about if Lance goes with me?"

The magical spell he had cast was instantly broken. Maggie left her chair and went to the window where she watched her family. "No, I don't want him going away from the ranch."

Seth moved to a position behind her. She could feel the heat of his body and feel the puff of his breath on the back of her head.

"He'll be okay, Maggie," he said in that same calm, persuasive voice. "Nobody knows where I'll be going. I'll wait until everyone's gone. That way we won't be followed and we won't have someone waiting in ambush for us at our destination."

Her heart didn't believe him and hammered out of fear for her son, and because of the alluring danger of being so close to Sackett. "Is there someone on the White Raven you don't trust, Seth?"

"I don't trust anybody at this point, Maggie, except your children and your mother. You would be wise to do the same."

"But I have to trust you," she countered, glancing over her shoulder at him.

"Never trust anyone. Least of all me."

He started for the conservatory door but her words stopped him. "I don't want Lance going with you, Seth."

Her steadfast gaze left no room for negotiation. She was scared—of a lot of things. She was scared of Lance getting killed. He figured she was probably scared, too, that some of his evil ways would rub off on the boy. And maybe they would. As his father used to quote from Proverbs 16:29: *"A violent man enticeth his neighbor, and leadeth him into the way that is not good."* It was true. Evil and violence had a way of spreading, consuming everything like a cloud of hungry grasshoppers.

"All right, Maggie," Seth conceded. "Whatever you say."

He left the house through the back door. At the corrals he relayed the message to Natalie that she was to help with the garden. Then he headed for his quarters, more than ready to clean up and get some chow at the cookshack. But when he opened the door to the tack building, he saw Alison sitting on the edge of his cot, staring at something in her hand. There was a terribly solemn set to her little heart-shaped lips.

He tossed his hat on the bed and sat down next to her. Almost immediately he wondered if he should move to the other cot nearby.

It was all a pack of lies, Grace. I didn't touch that girl.

Ezra—

I'm a man of God, Grace. I've been your husband for twenty years. How could you believe I'd mess with a child?

I didn't say I—

You didn't have to, woman. I see it in your eyes. You're no better than the others with their evil minds, thinking evil thoughts.

Seth turned the unexpected memory over and closed the cover on it. He wasn't guilty for that crime. He had to remember that. He hadn't done the things his father had done, and he never would. He might have the devil's blood, but he hadn't acquired all of his perversities.

"What's wrong, Alison?" he asked gently, remaining by her side. Her childish innocence, and fragile vulnerability, made him feel very protective of her.

Sorrowful eyes met his. She picked up his hand, and, turning it over, transferred the item in her hand to his. It was the marble he'd given her.

"You can have it back," she said. "I've done a lot of thinking and I decided I don't want it anymore."

"But why? I gave it to you to keep."

"I found out it isn't lucky after all."

"You did? Why did you decide that?"

"Because if it was lucky my mom wouldn't have got shot."

She stood up and started for the door. He caught her hand, so tiny and fragile in his. "Maybe you're not looking at things in the proper perspective," he said, humoring her with a smile.

"What do you mean?"

"Well, your mother was hurt, but she didn't die. She's getting better. Don't you think that's lucky?"

Her eyes brightened for a second, but almost immediately darkened again. "If it was truly lucky it wouldn't have happened at all."

Seth drew her to his knee. She was as light as a feather and smelled of kittens and straw and the outdoors. "Alison, life isn't always without mishaps, or without bad things happening to good people like your mother and to you. Sometimes we really feel as if we've been dealt a bad hand. But eventually things turn around, the sun comes out from behind the clouds, and we see that even bad things, even really sad things, brought something good to us in the end."

"I've heard that. Reverend Franklin, our traveling preacher, is always saying that God has our path set and some things have to happen before other things can happen."

"He's right. It's all God's plan."

She shyly stared at her hands resting on her knees. "I wasn't snooping, Mr. Sackett. Honest. I was just resting on your bed and I felt something under your pillow. I guess you know about God if you read the Bible, don't you?"

Seth looked into her confused eyes and knew she wanted to believe him. What could he tell her that wouldn't be a complete lie? She was looking to him for guidance. How could he tell her he was as lost and confused as she was? More so? What was it his mother used to say that always managed to turn his father's self-righteous words around and sooth the shattered hearts and broken spirits of her two sons?

"We have to trust that God knows what He's doing," Seth repeated the words as best he could remember them. "We all have different destinies, different purposes. Some of us have a harder row to hoe, but in the end, we emerge with the stronger back and the best fruits for our labors. God has reasons for what He does, even if we don't understand them."

"I'm afraid," she admitted, looking down at her hands again.

"Of what?"

"Afraid I'll lose my momma like I did my dad. I miss him. I just don't know what I'd do if something happened to Momma, too."

He turned her hand over and returned the marble

to it. "Your dad must have been a very good and kind man."

She said nothing, but he saw her lower lip quiver.

"Cherish your memories of him, Alison. Keep them close to your heart and never forget just how much he loved you. Take that love into your own relationships. Give it to your family, your friends."

Unexpectedly she threw her arms around his neck and gave him a quick squeeze. "You're a nice man, too, Mr. Sackett. I'm glad my Momma hired you. You'll take care of her, won't you? Just like my daddy used to?"

Her eyes held a waiting hope that she had not overestimated his ability. "I'll try, Alison. I surely will try."

Clutching the lucky marble in her fist, Alison ran out, calling "thank you" and "see you tomorrow."

Seth sat back on the cot and leaned against the wall. He reached under the pillow for the Bible and turned to Jeremiah 49:11. *Leave thy fatherless children; I will preserve them alive; and let thy widows trust in me.*

Then he turned to Timothy 1:9. *The law is not made for a righteous man but for the lawless and disobedient, for the ungodly and for sinners, for unholy and profane, for murderers of fathers and murderers of mothers, for manslayers. . . .*

He closed the book and leaned his head back against the wall. The strange emptiness yawned inside him, ready to swallow him whole again, as it had threatened to do thousands of times before. He stood at the edge of the frightening black hole that dropped directly into Hell. As always, he was desperately trying not to fall in.

And he wondered if he should tell the Caytons they were putting their faith in the hands of the wrong man.

Chapter Ten

"I don't see why I should have to help plant the garden again tomorrow," Lance said, angrily pouting at the parlor window. "I should be out helping the men."

"If he doesn't have to help, then I shouldn't have to either." Natalie looked up long enough from the new dress she was working on to proclaim her position on the matter. "It just freezes half the time anyway if we forget to cover it."

Maggie was feeling weary. If Trent were here there wouldn't be an argument. The children might go off in private and complain, but none of them would have uttered a word to Trent's face.

"We need the vegetables, children."

"I hate vegetables." Natalie stabbed her needle into the cloth as if it was a cabbage, a squash, or worse—a plate of green beans.

Maggie sighed. "You're not the only one in the family, Natalie, need I remind you again. And there are those of us who enjoy fresh vegetables. Even the hired hands look forward to harvest time."

"Do you want to get scurvy or something?" Alison piped up, coming to her mother's defense.

"What do you know about scurvy?" Natalie gave her a sour face. "Or anything else for that matter?"

Alison returned Natalie's sour face with one of her own, along with an extended tongue, then she went to Maggie's side and gave her a hug. "I'll help you, Momma. I like planting seeds and watching things grow."

"Thank you, Ali." Maggie put an arm around her. "But Natalie and Lance are going to have to help, too."

There was mutual groaning from the two older children. Natalie irritably tossed her dress aside and came to her feet. "I'm going to bed. I want to be all rested up so I can be sure and do a good job throwing dirt over those seeds tomorrow," she concluded facetiously.

"Throwing temper tantrums won't change my mind, Natalie," Maggie responded. "You should know that by now."

Natalie tried one last time—this time a plea that strongly resembled begging. "Do we *have* to have a garden, Mother? I mean, is it really necessary?"

"The hardest part is already done. Why quit now?"

Lance's stance suddenly stiffened, drawing everyone's attention. He yanked the curtain back and peered out into the gathering dusk.

"What is it?" Maggie immediately left the sofa and joined him at the window.

"Sackett's riding in," he replied. "Looks like he ran into trouble."

He didn't need to say more. Maggie saw for herself that Seth wasn't alone. He was leading another horse, and over the saddle was draped the body of a man.

"My God," Lance whispered. "That's Milo's horse."

They started for the door simultaneously, followed by Natalie and Alison. Maggie told Alison to get back inside, but she had already seen the body. Natalie's face paled. Not wanting to see more of it herself, she grabbed her little sister by the shoulders and shoved her back into the house, following close on her heels.

"Who is it?" Alison demanded, trying to see over her shoulder and past Natalie.

"None of your dang business, you nosey little pest!" Natalie responded just before slamming the door, sequestering herself and Alison safely inside.

Seth pulled rein in front of the house and stepped to the ground just as Maggie and Lance hurried down the steps to join him. His arrival had also drawn the attention of a couple of cowboys who in turn had spread the word until all of the men were converging on the scene, firing questions left and right.

Seth said nothing while untying the body and gently laying it out on the ground. It was Milo Forster all right. He had been shot dead center in the heart.

Clements shoved his way through the semi-circle of men. When his eyes lifted from Forster's body, they settled accusingly on Seth. "So you finally got even, did you, Sackett? I suppose you're going to tell us that he went for his gun first and forced you to draw on him? Or maybe you just shot him in cold blood, like I hear you're fond of doing. You know, I'm beginning to wonder what kind of man you'd be without that gun on your hip." His lip curled into a challenging snarl.

Seth's eyes darkened ominously, reminding Maggie of a thundercloud gathering over the mountains, gaining momentum and ferocity as it grew larger and larger. One hand reached down and released the leather lace around his thigh that held his holster down while the other hand started on the buckle at his waist. He had the rig off in seconds and was handing it to Lance. "You want to know, Clements? Let's find out."

Maggie stepped forward, wondering in a whirl of confusion what had brought on the animosity between the two men. "Enough," she commanded. "I want you both to stop this foolishness right now."

But neither man seemed to hear. Nor did the men standing on the sidelines, looking hungry for blood, as long as it wasn't their own. Clements shed his gun belt and with eyes gleaming with the lust to do battle, he raised his bare fists and began to circle Seth, who in turn circled him. The other men fell back, forming a loose ring around the combatants.

"Get him, Clements!" one shouted.

"Yeah," yelled another. "Show him that gun doesn't make the man!"

Lance grabbed Maggie's arm and pulled her back away from the milling men. "There isn't anything you can do, Mom," he said. "They've got to have it out once and for all and get it out of their craws."

Maggie had seen men fight before, plenty of times, but she had never understood the primitive, animalistic nature that seemed to demand that they show through strength who was the most powerful, who would be the leader.

Clements struck first. Seth ducked and came back with an upper cut that cracked against Clements' jaw and sent him sprawling backward onto his back in the dust. He was only temporarily stunned and was up again, punching Seth with brute determination. He managed to lay some powerful blows to Seth's face before he was knocked down again. Maggie watched Seth grab Clements and haul him up to his feet only to knock him down with a slamming fist to his mid-section. Clements rose to a crouch and charged Seth head on, like a rangy Longhorn bull, knocking him off his feet. They both fell to the ground in a tangle of clashing fists that cracked and popped and thudded against bone and flesh. Blood sprang from their faces, their knuckles, their noses, their lips. The men on the sidelines hooted and hollered, swinging their own fists, their eyes alight with the thrill of the battle, yelling orders to Clements to get up and knock Seth down to size.

Maggie couldn't understand their extreme hostility toward Seth; he'd done nothing to any of them. He minded his own business. He was here fighting on their side, and yet she feared by the look in many of their eyes that any second they might gang up on him and do their best to finish him off. They reminded her of a pack of wild dogs working themselves into a frenzy. Only Sonny stood off to the side, his face strangely passive.

Seeing his complacency triggered a new anger. She reached over and pulled Seth's gun from the holster Lance had draped over his arm. The boy was so engrossed in the fight he didn't even notice. She did notice, however, that he was the only one rooting for Seth, and suddenly she was very proud of him.

She raised the revolver skyward and fired off three shots in rapid succession, nearly frightening the men out of their boots. By now Seth was on top of Clements and the latter seemed too weak to attempt further attack. At the sound of the gunfire, Seth's arm halted, drawn back and ready to plunge another fist into Clements' face. Both men were covered with dust, mud, blood, and sweat. They could barely breathe from the physical exertion.

"Stop it!" Maggie ordered. "Stop it *now!* Sonny, you and Lance separate them."

Several of the men also helped break up the fight, then they held Clements' and Seth's arms behind their backs to keep them from lighting into each other again.

Maggie stepped in front of Clements. "I'm going to tell you something," she said with steel in her eyes, "and I want you to listen real good because I won't repeat it. I'm as upset as the rest of you that Milo Forster is dead, but Seth Sackett did not kill him. If you can't abide by that then you can pack up your gear and head out. You've been with the White Raven a long time and I appreciate your loyalty over the years to Trent and me, but I won't have you making accusations against one of our own men without some solid proof that you know what

you're talking about. In case you've all forgotten,
Sackett is on *our* side. You don't have to like it, but
you'd damn well better get used to it."

Clements, always argumentative, immediately retaliated. "That all might be well and true, Mrs.
Cayton, but I wouldn't be a bit surprised if Sackett's
working for Tate and he's come here to kill us all,
one by one."

Maggie clenched her jaw and ignored him.
"Sonny, take Clements to the bunkhouse and get
him cleaned up and doctored. Johnson and Messenger, I want you to help Lance take care of Milo's
body. Sackett, I want to talk to you in my office."

Maggie waited until the men had dispersed, then
she led the way to the house. Seth followed, using
his shirt sleeve to wipe at the blood seeping from his
nose and a split upper lip. In the foyer, Natalie,
Alison, and Catherine blocked the two of them with
a bombardment of questions. Maggie merely took
Seth by the arm, out of her mother's doting reach,
and directed him toward the kitchen. "I'll explain it
all later, Mother," she said. "Right now I need to
talk to Seth privately."

In the kitchen she closed the door and told Seth
to take a seat. She went to the cupboard and
removed the box of medical supplies.

"I thought you wanted to see me in your office."
As always his tone took a sardonic edge.

"I'm glad you're able to take this so lightly," she
replied. "But if some of those men—the ones who
don't particularly like you—had thought I was
bringing you in here to help you, they might have

decided to skin and quarter us both. And then where would the White Raven be?"

He wiped at the blood on his lip again. "I reckon you'd be sunk, darlin'."

"This is no time for jokes, Seth." With a disgusted click of her tongue, she spread out the medical supplies on the table in front of him.

"I see you've tossed your sling," he said. "Doc's orders?"

"Forget about me. You could have gotten yourself killed out there. Clements wasn't the only one who wanted your blood."

He chuckled. "I'm used to people wanting me dead, Maggie. The only way to survive the hatred is to not think about it anymore than at least once a day."

"And when *will* you think about it, Seth?"

He shrugged. "Maybe tonight."

She forced her eyes back to the bandages and medicines spread out on the table. "All right, let's attend to your wounds."

Even as she said it she realized her folly. In order to tend Sackett's wounds, she would have to touch him, and his watching eyes told her he was more than aware of that fact. With the hint of a knowing smile, he waited.

"If you would rather tend to your own cuts," she said, suddenly fussing nervously with the items on the table, "there's a mirror in the bathroom just on the other side of the kitchen. Through that door and at the end of the back porch." She pointed but his eyes remained fixed on hers.

"No, I would rather you did it, Maggie. There's

nothing more soothing to a man's rattled nerves than a woman's gentle hand."

There was, once again, the hint of sexual suggestion in his tone and in his eyes, but she would never let him know she was acutely aware of it.

"All right." She braced herself for the predicament she'd unwittingly led herself into. "Let's take a look at the damage."

Gently she took his chin between her thumb and forefinger and lifted it slightly, turning his head this way and that while examining the cuts and bruises springing out now in ugly multi-colored splotches on every part of his craggy face. One eyelid was swelling badly, and the gash slicing across it had dripped blood down the side of his face. Concentrating on his condition, however, became difficult because visual perception was blurred by the fiery tactile sensation of his firm jaw covered with a day's growth of prickly black stubble. The contact sizzled through her with the power of a lightning bolt. She wanted to release him but was afraid if she did he would know the hungry thoughts of desire that tempted her body and tormented her mind.

Finally she made her assessment of the damage. "I suppose you can get by without stitches if you don't mind a few minor scars."

"A few more won't matter. Now," he continued, "did you want to talk to me about Forster? Or did you just want to be alone with me?"

Her hand curled around the neck of a bottle of whiskey she had intended to use as disinfectant. But she suddenly considered breaking it over his head instead. Her eyes flashed, but her tongue seemed tied in a thousand knots.

He tried to smile around his cut lip. "Well, are you going to salve my wounds? Or give me some more?"

"I'm seriously considering the latter."

He laughed but said no more, apparently satisfied by her reaction to his flirtations. She returned her attention to the matter at hand. After wetting a piece of gauze with the whiskey, she gently began cleaning his facial cuts.

"So what did you do to make an enemy of everyone on the ranch?" she asked, dabbing at the cut on his eyelid.

"It seems I don't have to do anything but show up."

A guilty flush crept onto her cheeks. Indeed. How could she fault the men for the way they were behaving when she had behaved no better toward him herself? She had hated him from the beginning, not giving him a chance to prove himself. She had hated him for what he was, not who he was. She had, like the men, even overlooked the fact that he was here fighting on their side, for her, for Trent, for the children. He was risking his life for a cause that wasn't his. And she had asked him to do it. Because of that he deserved respect for services rendered. She'd seen the evil in Max Morrell's eyes, and she'd known without a shadow of a doubt that he was a killer. But evil wasn't present in Sackett's eyes. She didn't know exactly who he was, for he hid his true self exceedingly well. Until she did know, it was unfair to make judgments. She realized that now.

"I believe I'm here because you wanted to talk about Forster," he prodded. "Isn't that why you really brought me in here? I know you don't care about all these cuts and bruises."

Maggie had to catch herself from denying that. She *did* care about him being hurt. It had distressed her greatly to see Clements abusing him, even if he was doing equal or greater damage to the other man. She found it a startling realization when just a few weeks ago she had told him she didn't care if he lived or died just as long as he performed the job he was being paid for.

"Yes, tell me about Forster," she replied, tilting his head to better get at the cut over his eye.

"I found him this afternoon face down in the middle of Medicine Creek," he said. "Ouch. Be careful."

"Sorry."

When she proceeded more gently, he continued. "My guess is he was shot first thing this morning. I saw tracks on both sides of the creek. It looked as if two riders had met and were facing each other from across the creek." Unable to move freely because of the way she had his head tilted back, he fumbled in his vest pocket, pulled out a spent cartridge, and tossed it on the table along with the medicines and bandages. "I found this slug on the ground just under the second set of horse's tracks."

Maggie put down her piece of gauze and picked up the bullet. "A .44–.40. The same that killed Pensy."

Seth nodded.

Maggie considered all he said while applying

salve to the clean cuts. "I wonder why Milo was out there alone," she said. "I gave Sonny orders right after Trent's death that the men ride in pairs, no matter the job or the location on the ranch."

"Since he was obviously talking to someone from across the creek, I wonder if he knew the person."

"But did Sonny send him out there alone?"

"I don't know. I've been leaving the ranch either before everyone else, or after. That's a question you'll have to ask Sonny."

Yes, and she certainly would, as soon as she had Seth taken care of. Meanwhile, many other questions tumbled through her mind. Who could have possibly known Milo was headed to Medicine Creek except men from the White Raven? And, if one of them hadn't shot Forster, had they sent word to Tate's men that he would be out there alone? It was possible, but she doubted there would have been time to get that sort of message over to the Broken Arrow and then time for someone to get back and kill Forster in the morning of the same day. Unless someone had known yesterday that Forster was going to be going over there. Was one of her own men a spy, an accomplice of Tate's, undermining her operation from the inside? Or had one of Tate's men been watching the ranch, following the men, choosing one that had headed out alone?

There was one other possibility she didn't want to consider, and yet she had to. Could Sackett be working for Tate as Clements claimed? Was he truly on her side or only pretending to be? If he was working for Tate, the most logical thing for him to do was to kill her. He could have done that plenty of times in the past few weeks. But of course he hadn't.

He stood up. She felt his nearness only six inches away. Why did she have the crazy yearning that he would touch her, turn her around, and draw her into his arms? She had felt that way with no man since Trent. Not Cleve, not Sonny. Why did she seek the caress of a dangerous man like Sackett whom she couldn't fully trust? Was it safer in the end? Safer because she knew he would ride away and she wouldn't have to commit her heart or her life to him, and because her memories and her devotion to Trent and Trent's children would continue unthreatened?

"Here." She handed him a small tin of salve. "You might want to take this with you and apply it to your cuts for the next few days. And tell Sonny I need to talk to him."

His fingers brushed hers when he accepted the medicine. His eyes lifted indolently, challenging her again to deny the feelings his touch incited. Finally he pulled his hat down onto his forehead and turned to the back door just off the kitchen.

"Where do you think you'll be headed in the morning?" She heard herself asking, wondering even as she said it why she was detaining him. Wouldn't it better to have him gone? Yet she persisted. "And what time will you be leaving?"

He paused with his hand on the doorknob. His face was in the shadows now, but she felt the penetration of his eyes as always. She felt so very disappointed that he was leaving when she should have been relieved.

"I'll be heading out before daybreak," he replied. "If you want to know where I'm headed, you'll have to come with me."

A shiver of excitement raced through her. The inflection in his voice suggested it wasn't just an offer to ride with him, but a challenge to be alone with him. Surely he couldn't think she would be so foolish? They both knew what would happen if they were alone together. There was an undeniable energy between them that if joined would become volatile. He would never attempt to curb the resulting explosion; the responsibility would be hers, and she wasn't sure she had the strength. Being near him was beginning to set her thoughts straying from what was right to only what she desired.

His cut lip lifted in that disarming smile that once again suggested he knew the battle she waged with her conscience. "Sleep on it, Maggie. Lonely beds sometimes have a way of helping people make hard decisions." He touched the brim of his hat in a gesture of farewell. Before she could say more, he was gone.

Sonny arrived at the house within ten minutes of Seth telling him Maggie needed to talk to him. He settled himself in Trent's horsehair chair by the fireplace in the family parlor, the main parlor. It was a bigger room than the front parlor. It was where the family gathered for informal evenings together, playing games, reading, or just talking. It was the room Trent had always used for his cattlemen's meetings, where the men could go to smoke their cigars and drink their whiskey.

The furniture was rugged, even rough-looking compared to the brocades and satins of the front parlor. This was a man's room with its Western paintings and its set of Longhorns mounted over the fireplace, its hardwood floors covered with braided rugs, its chairs and sofas of durable horsehair. It was a comfortable room and Maggie came here when she wanted to be close to Trent.

Tonight, after experiencing the crazy feelings she'd had for Sackett, she had to remind herself that she was a widow with three children, a mature woman of thirty-eight who needed to mind her reputation and her personal actions for the sake of her children. She had to set a good example. This room brought her position in life back into sharp focus.

She forced her attention back to Sonny's waiting face and suddenly wondered if she should have moved Trent's favorite chair to her bedroom. It was a totally selfish thought, but if she did, then Sonny wouldn't be able to sit in it anymore. He wouldn't be able to try and assume Trent's position for even a few minutes. She wasn't sure that's what he was doing, but she wondered sometimes, and it annoyed her. She sensed he would like to move into the position Trent vacated, into everything—his ownership of the ranch, his chair, his bed. . . .

Sonny pushed his ten-gallon hat to the back of his head. He seldom took it off completely, probably because without it his height was reduced dramatically. A strand of unruly brown hair fell down onto his high forehead. So many of the men wore moustaches, or bushy sideburns, as was the style, but Sonny was always clean-shaven, his sideburns short. The only facial hair was thick, dark eyebrows rising above deep-set, intense brown eyes that seemed to take the world and everyone in it much too seriously. Trent always said he had a "Napoleon complex." Because he was short, he had to try to do things that would give him stature in the eyes of others. Consequently, he was often angry or disappointed in those around him when their actions and behavior fell short of the strict expectations he placed not only on himself, but on others as well. Despite his lack of height, he was wiry, and, without his shirt, extremely muscular.

Maggie often wondered what it was Sonny really wanted in life. Was he content to be the foreman of the White Raven and nothing else? But she'd never been able to find out because Sonny was not one to talk about himself. He was not handsome, but he wasn't homely either, and she wondered why he hadn't gotten married, why he didn't seem to even want a steady girlfriend. She had always been, as she was now, uncomfortable in his presence. She had always sensed his infatuation for her, even though she was older than him by six years. It troubled her greatly that she was the object of his adulation. He was nice and she liked him, but she knew she could never think of him as anything more than a friend or a hired hand.

She walked to the sideboard and poured him a shot of whiskey, as Trent would have done. "Let's get right down to the matter of Forster." She handed him the drink. "Who knew he was headed out to Medicine Creek this morning?"

Sonny held the whiskey glass in his fingers for a moment, contemplating her question before tossing the amber liquid down his throat. When the fire had cleared from his insides he looked up at her. "I guess we all did, except Sackett. But he could have easily waited and followed Milo."

"Then you agree with Clements that their differences—which Lance already told me about—was motive enough for Sackett to kill Forster in cold blood?"

"I wouldn't put it past him. He's a cold sonofa—" He caught himself. His face reddened and he shifted uneasily in his chair. "He's cold, Maggie. That's all I'll say."

The description, the perception of Sackett, struck Maggie as peculiar. She'd felt a lot of things in Seth Sackett, mainly danger, but she had never felt coldness. If anything Seth was a man of fiery passion held in check by a very disciplined wall of reserve. Perhaps Sackett was hiding who he really was, but she couldn't perceive he was a totally heartless man like his counterpart, Max Morrell.

Maggie began to pace back and forth across the braided rug. "All right, Sonny, you and Clements have your opinion about Sackett. Some of you even think he could be working for Tate, is that true?"

Sonny nodded, getting excited by that idea. He was about to offer an additional opinion but Maggie intercepted, not wanting to hear any more derogatory remarks about Seth.

"Personally, I can't agree to that notion, Sonny.

After all, Sackett saved my life. So, for now, let's look at some other possibilities. Why did you send Milo out there alone?"

Sonny shifted uneasily again. Maggie decided he looked like a little boy, dwarfed by the massiveness of Trent's chair. To avoid her eyes, he focused on one of the paintings on the wall and answered sheepishly, "Well, Maggie, the area hadn't been checked for several weeks and I wanted to make sure Tate hadn't damned off the water farther up. If he would have, we'd be left dry on that side of the range. It's something he's bound to do, sooner or later. I've been short a man since Jessop quit and I didn't have enough work for two men over at Medicine Creek. I was going to go out there myself, but Milo insisted on going. It's so far from Tate's borders that I just didn't think the kid would run into any trouble out there. I honestly figured he'd be okay."

Maggie couldn't fault him for the decision he'd made. She might have made it herself under the circumstances. "Sackett says that whoever shot Milo was just on the other side of the creek from him," she added. "They were only a few feet apart, their horses facing each other. It sounds almost as if Milo might have been talking to someone he knew."

"Someone from the White Raven?"

Maggie shrugged. "Who knows? It could have even been a drifter."

"Unless he knows someone from the Broken Arrow."

"I don't like to think it, Sonny, but I suppose it's

possible that Tate has planted someone here to keep him informed of what I'm doing. Maybe you'd better keep an eye on the men, especially those I've hired since this trouble began.'' What she didn't mention was that maybe Milo had been Tate's man and Tate had had him killed for some reason.

She rubbed her shoulder—it was hurting tonight—and she was tired, both mentally and physically. "Keep an eye on things for me," she added. "It's about all we can do at this point. Now, if you'll excuse me, I believe I'll retire."

Sonny rose, using one foot to unconsciously pull down the leg of his pants that had ridden up to the top of his boot. His gaze shifted to her wounded shoulder. "Are you all right now, Maggie?"

She looked away, disturbed again by the warmth in his eyes, the warmth that told too much of his feelings. What was she going to do about that? She couldn't send him away. He had been the foreman for years and was a top hand. She wouldn't want to put any of the other men in his place, and yet she wasn't sure she could continue on as always, knowing how he felt about her. When Trent had been alive he had served as a buffer, and she had always figured that Sonny would give up his infatuation with her and find a nice girl. Now, though, he seemed more intense, and it bothered her. If he cared for her—which she was sure he did—why didn't he make some move in that direction? She could then tell him no, and he could forget about her and get on with his life. It was as if he knew that by not asking he couldn't be told no. Maybe she was all wrong and he merely thought it was too soon to approach her after Trent's death. If that was the case, she could appreciate the respect he was giving her.

She smiled and lifted her shoulder, rotating it to ease the stiffness. "It's healing well, according to Doc."

Sonny nodded but anxiety laced his tone and tightened the crow's feet faintly visible around his eyes. "We've all been worried about you, Maggie. Real worried. The men don't want to lose their jobs, but I know none of them would hold it against you if you gave up this fight with Tate and just sold out."

Maggie had surmised she'd been the frequent topic of conversation in the bunkhouse since Trent's death, but it bothered her just the same to have her suspicions verified. "Is that your opinion, too, Sonny?"

He looked at the toe of his boot. "Well . . . I don't want to see you end up like Forster, but I wouldn't want to tell you what to do either. I know how much the White Raven means to you."

"I won't sell to Tate."

"There's others. Cleve Williams would buy it."

"I'm sure he would, but I won't sell to him either."

Sonny tugged at his earlobe. "Most men just hate to see you out here alone, Maggie, and especially with trouble brewing."

"I'm not alone." The discussion of her leaving made her angry and she couldn't conceal it. "As for trouble—it's part of ranching."

Sonny had no rejoinder, although his eyes continued to silently question her judgment. She saw him to the door, thankful when he was gone. Then she closed herself in her office where she stood at the window, pensively staring out over the backyard.

Should she sell? Was she doing the wrong thing by holding on, jeopardizing the lives of her family and innocent men like Milo Forster? She'd told the men months ago that they were free to leave, but they had all elected to stay. They had accepted her battle as theirs, risking their lives right along with her for the preservation of pride and the White Raven. But was she wrong in even giving the men that choice? Many needed the work badly and had been here for years. It was home to them. They didn't want to go somewhere else, some other ranch that might be hundreds of miles from here. It was possible they felt they had no choice but to join the fight or lose their jobs. Things were changing in the West. The open range was giving way to cities and farms, to rules and regulations made by people who believed ranchers had had the lion's share of the land for too long, even though in reality the land was good for little else and even though it had been a cattle kingdom for less than three decades.

By the time the clock struck ten, Maggie had come no closer to a solution to her problem. She could hear the girls in the family parlor with her mother, playing a game of some sort. Lance had probably gone to the bunkhouse to be with the men and play cards. Since she had left the kitchen with Seth, Dorothy had returned and was still rattling pots and pans, probably cleaning up or preparing something special for tomorrow, as she often did.

Wearily, Maggie left her office through the back door and went into the conservatory. She gathered the wool shawl from the hook near the back door, lit the metal kerosene lantern that was also on a shelf nearby, and slipped quietly into the backyard.

A worn path wound through the trees and flower beds, past the vegetable garden, and to the rear gate. Beyond the gate, the path curved over the top of a rocky pinnacle, twisted down an incline and rose again onto a sagebrush-covered knoll. On the knoll, a white picket fence enclosed the graves of the two babies she'd lost. Next to them was the tall headstone that marked Trent's grave.

Maggie opened the gate to the family cemetery and stepped inside. Her first baby, Robert, had been born before Lance. He had died shortly after birth. He had been a healthy, happy baby, and then one morning she had gone to get him from his crib only to find he had stopped breathing some time in the night. She remembered the wrenching pain that had made her wish her own heart would stop, too. But she had had no choice but to continue fighting, and living. If Robert had lived, he would have been eighteen now, and she often wondered what sort of a young man he would have become.

The second baby, Samuel, had been born prematurely when Natalie was two years old. She'd never really known him. He had never been alive in her arms nor suckled at her breast. Still, the loss had been tremendous. The only thing that had eased it at all was the fact that she had still had Lance and Natalie.

She and Trent had decided after Alison not to

have anymore children and they had been successful in preventing pregnancy by methods Doc Clifford had shared with them.

She set the lantern on the ground at the foot of the graves and pulled her shawl closer around her shoulders. The evenings here on the plains just east of the Big Horn Mountains were nearly always cool, except during the hottest weeks of summer. The cool air tonight made her shoulder hurt, but she wasn't ready to go inside.

As always when she came here, the loss of the babies was felt with severe intensity. Even greater pain came now from the absence of Trent in her life. She had often been alone in her married life when Trent had been gone on trips back East to cattlemen's conventions, or had gone on cattle-buying trips and cattle drives from as far away as Texas and Oregon.

In those days she had worried about his safety, fearing in the back of her mind that something disastrous might happen to him. But he had always returned to her side, unscathed, until as the years rolled by she had come to believe that no ill wind would ever take him from her. She had honestly believed that she and Trent Cayton, her first love, would grow old together.

She had been totally unprepared the day Sonny and a couple of other men had brought Trent home across his saddle, just as Sackett had brought Forster home today. It was as if the ground had fallen out from under her. She had refused to believe he was dead. She'd tried desperately to revive him in any way she could think of. She'd had no time to adjust to it happening, to see it coming, to tell him she loved him, to let him go, to say good-bye. . . .

Hot tears scalded her cheeks. Automatically she reached up to wipe them away.

"Is everything all right, Maggie?"

She whirled at the sound of the male voice behind her. For a moment it had sounded so much like Trent it had nearly made her heart stop, but it was Sackett she saw standing a few yards away, barely discernible in the darkness. The house lights were not visible from here and he stood beyond the circle of light cast by the lantern. The red stub of a cigarette glowed between the fingers of his left hand. His right hand was free, as always, to reach for his gun if necessary.

"What are you doing out here?" she demanded, angry at him for intruding on such a private moment and for sneaking up so quietly she hadn't heard him.

"I was outside and saw a light down here. I was afraid it was one of Tate's men up to no good."

She relaxed somewhat by his explanation. "No, it's just me. You may go back. I'd actually like to be alone, but thank you for your concern."

He seemed to focus on her tears which insisted on continuing in a steady trickle down her cheeks despite her repeated attempts to wipe them away. Instead of leaving, he stepped closer to the enclosure and leaned against the gate's supports. The lantern light lined the planes and angles of his face but darkened the hollows of his cheeks and the area around his eyes. His gaze traveled over the headstones. She knew he was reading the names, the dates, collecting the statistical information of the people he hadn't known, people who meant nothing to him.

"I had a brother named Samuel," he said.

A distant look entered the gray, enigmatic depths of his eyes and even the darkness couldn't conceal the sorrow in his whispered comment. Suddenly Maggie was reminded once again that Sackett was not merely a man with a gun, but a person who had a life beyond that gun and beyond her tack building. He had parents, a brother. Where were they? Why had he taken a road away from them to become a loner fighting for other people's causes?

Her curiosity about him mounted until it could no longer be contained. Momentarily she put aside her own loneliness, pain, and grief to satisfy some of that sudden curiosity.

"What happened to him?" she whispered, not wanting her voice to carry beyond the cemetery. "Your brother?"

His eyes remained on her son's grave. "He died. Same as your son."

She tried to gauge by the tone of his voice if he preferred not to discuss it. But she felt in him only that which she felt in herself: a quiet pensiveness when one remembers that which is gone forever.

"How old was he when he died?" she probed, thinking that at any second he would drop the curtain on her questions. Sackett had always seemed the sort to think he could delve into other people's minds, but the privilege was not to be reversed. And he did appear as if he was silently debating whether to continue the subject.

But finally he said, "He was twelve."

"And how did he die?"

Seth released what sounded very much like a weary sigh and cast his unsmoked cigarette to the ground, snubbing it out with the toe of his boot.

"There was a goodness about Samuel that I never possessed," he said gruffly with a peculiar catch in his voice. "I held him in my arms when he pulled his last breath. He was killed so senselessly—murdered like your husband. Not by a gun, though, but by the bare hands of a man whose heart was filled with hatred and anger."

His blunt admission pierced her heart like the swift rush of a penetrating arrow, and suddenly he slammed the door on the past and on the memories. He took her by the arm. "It's late, Maggie, and you shouldn't be out here alone. Let me walk you back to the house."

Moved by his story, Maggie allowed him to act as her escort. Later in her room, it wasn't Trent and the babies that occupied her thoughts until well past midnight, but rather the many questions circling the gunslinger, Seth Sackett.

Chapter Eleven

At daybreak Maggie dressed in her riding clothes, strapped on her gun belt, and headed outside to join Seth. She hadn't told him she was going with him, but she had made her decision sometime during the night. If she was going to get the trouble straightened out with Tate, she was going to have to start working closely with Seth whether she wanted to or not. But more than anything, she was still being bit by curiosity. It might get her killed, just like it had the proverbial cat, but Seth was a mystery she found herself wanting very much to solve.

The sun hadn't risen but was close enough to the horizon to give the eastern sky a golden glow. Despite the early hour, she found she had just missed the gunslinger. She spotted him disappearing over the skyline, heading north toward the Broken Arrow.

She decided to saddle up and follow him. It would be the perfect opportunity to find out if Clements' accusation was true.

She could hear the cowboys in the bunkhouse

beginning to stir. Smells of bacon and eggs were already drifting from the cookshack. Because she didn't want Sonny or any of the other hands to see her leave, she quickly caught and saddled her horse. In ten minutes she was on Seth's trail.

She rode for two hours successfully keeping him in sight, and then suddenly both he and his tracks vanished into thin air. After scouring the area she rode to a rocky knoll, but there was still no sign of him. Discouraged, and finally feeling the heat of the day, she stepped from her saddle, removed her jacket, and tied it behind the saddle. She wasn't far now from the border of the Broken Arrow.

The silence of the open country began to settle over her. It had probably been foolish to come out here alone. She rubbed at the pain in her shoulder, wondering if whoever had wanted her dead would try again. She'd left a note for her mother, telling her she'd planned to go with Seth this morning, but other than that no one knew she was out here, unless Seth had spotted her following him.

She gathered her reins and swung back in the saddle. Maybe it would be wise to head home, but she nudged her horse into an easy lope. She would look just a little longer.

Her perseverance paid off. At the base of the next hill, she saw him, relaxing on a pile of rocks. He saw her immediately and motioned her to join him. She knew then that he'd been waiting for her.

She stopped her horse a few feet from him, but remained in the saddle, feeling she could deal more effectively with him if she had the horse between them.

"So you decided to join me after all?" His knife-sharp gaze unsettled her. Gone was the taunting gleam she had nearly learned to deal with. The Seth Sackett she saw now was the same man who had ridden onto the ranch that first stormy day, the man who had given no quarter and asked none.

"I intended on joining you this morning," she was quick to explain, "but you left before I could catch you."

"Are you sure, Maggie? Or did Clements get you to wondering about my credibility?"

The saddle leather squeaked beneath her as she shifted uneasily, realizing even as she did so that the action itself gave away her true thoughts. He knew for certain now she didn't trust him, even though she had defended him to the men.

He came to his feet and sauntered over to her, refusing to keep the distance she so desperately desired. He placed a hand on her knee, unsettling her further by the way its heat flowed through the heavy cloth of her riding skirt to scorch the flesh beneath.

"Why are you following me, Maggie?" His eyes, for all their indiscernibility, made her feel peculiarly guilty, as if she had betrayed his trust and hurt him deeply. But she had every right to question his credibility, even if he didn't think so.

"If I recall, you invited me to join you today," she replied as evenly as she could without giving away her own emotions. "As I said, when I came out this morning, you had already gone. I was only trying to catch up with you."

"Lying doesn't become you. I know a person who's following, and one who's trying to catch up, and you weren't trying to catch up. If you had wanted to join me, why didn't you just tell me so last night? I would have been more than happy to ride with you. It's not often I get the chance to ride with a beautiful woman."

Why couldn't his hand remain motionless on her knee? Why did he have to move it in that slight way that reminded her so very much of a caress. It scattered her thoughts, made her forget why she was out here. It even made her forget that he was a man she'd be foolish to trust in any way, although she was beginning to do so more and more every day.

"Because," she replied, "by the time I had decided to take you up on your invitation it was too late to disturb you."

"The lateness of the hour didn't stop you from coming to my quarters once before."

The velvet quality of his voice was dangerously provocative. The intenseness in his eyes deepened. She shifted again, but this time from wariness, knowing full well the sexual direction his thoughts—and hers—had taken.

"I believe you laid the ground rules on that, Seth. I was only abiding by them."

He took a casual stance, leaning against her horse. In the process he put one arm along the ridge of the cantle, brushing his hand against her hip and gun belt. The other hand remained on her knee. His chest touched her thigh. There was no escaping the man, and his nearness once again created a magical turmoil she hoped he couldn't detect. But when his gaze lifted hypnotically to hers, she nearly laughed at her own folly. Sackett would never be blind to sinful thoughts that were identical to his own. If anyone could bring her downfall, it would be him, simply because he knew too well the weaknesses of human nature, and knew how to play on those weaknesses.

She decided, based on the insistent chant of desire throbbing through every inch of her, that truth—or at least partial truth—would be her only salvation, so she plunged into confession. "All right, Seth, I did follow you out here. But that wasn't my original intention. When you had already gone, it was then that I decided to see where you went, what you did."

Her admission came as no revelation. "Smart woman. You're always thinking aren't you, Maggie? But I'm not working for Tate. You appear to be the underdog in this range war so far, and I've always felt an uncontrollable need to protect underdogs. Especially pretty ones."

She fell helplessly into the entrancing depths of his fathomless gray eyes. Surely he was a powerful wizard disguised in nineteenth-century garb, using a magic potion for which she knew no antidote.

"Checking up on me is all good and well, Maggie." His hand slid from her knee to her thigh. "I like a woman who is smart and cautious. But I think another reason you came out here was because you wanted to be alone with me." The hand draped over the back of the saddle glided to her waist, sending chills racing down her spine.

"I came out here to check fence lines and water sources," she heard herself deny. But it was hard to focus on her denial when her thoughts were being pulled to the hypnotic play of his hands on her flesh. "Don't make more of it than that, Seth."

"I'll bet your husband died hard, didn't he, Maggie?"

Her eyes snapped to his. "What do you mean by that?" she demanded, unable to fully conceal her wariness of him and the line of questioning he had embarked upon.

"Well," he drawled, "if I'd been your husband, I'd have died hard knowing you would eventually turn to the arms of another man, and probably forget me in the process."

The agony of desire, and of her body's betrayal to her husband's memory, came out in an angry burst. She put her heels to her horse until it moved forward and took her beyond the reach of his wandering hands.

"I don't want to talk about my husband," she said. "Let's get on with our work."

"Do you still love him?"

"Of course!" She cried, tears suddenly glistening in her eyes. "And I always will."

Seth went to his horse and swung into the saddle. "Love and desire are two separate things, Maggie. I doubt even your husband would have denied himself the latter if you had been the first to die. It might be one more thing for you to think about in your bed alone at night."

"I believe you're under the delusion that I could desire a man like you, Sackett."

"And you're under the delusion that you couldn't."

He leaned forward in the saddle and his horse

broke into a lope. She watched him move farther and farther away. It was only after serious consideration that she finally went after him.

When she caught up to him, he accepted her presence without question. They slowed their horses and followed Crow Creek northward for several miles, covering the distance in silence. He acted as if she wasn't there, and Maggie didn't know what irritated her the most—his sexual advances or his silence.

The vultures were what finally drew her mind away from her handsome but annoying companion. There had to be dozens of the ugly, gawky birds hopping around on the ground in the meadow up ahead. Sackett drew rein and Maggie stopped next to him.

"Looks like Tate's been at it again," he said.

With heart sinking, Maggie surveyed the distant humps of dead cattle lining the creek banks. She couldn't count the numbers at this distance, but she knew it was another tremendous loss.

Anger surged anew. With Seth right behind her, she nudged her horse forward to make a visual inspection and a determination of the cause of death.

"Tate must have sent a bunch of men down here and then waited until the cattle came in to drink and then shot them," she said when they arrived at the first group of carcasses.

Seth stepped to the ground and walked around the dead animals, assessing them with alert eyes. "I don't think they've been shot, Maggie," he replied after a moment. "I don't see any bullet wounds. I'd bet it was poison that's killed them."

Maggie dismounted too. Upstream, beyond the next set of low hills, was Larkspur reservoir, a major source of water for this section of White Raven range. She and Trent had hired a crew of men to build it when they'd first settled here. It was designed to collect winter run-off and aid in the stock water supply. If the water in the creek was poisoned, as the carcasses suggested, then the poisoning had probably originated in the reservoir.

"Has it been poisoned?" she asked, turning again to Seth and dreading his response.

"From all indications, I would say so."

"Then we'd better check Larkspur reservoir. There might be more cattle over there."

Seth hadn't been to this part of the ranch and wasn't familiar with it, so Maggie led the way. When they topped the hill overlooking the reservoir, the scene was a continuation of the one they'd left behind. There were dead, bloated carcasses everywhere. Maggie feared she'd lost at least two hundred head.

It was too much to see the years of toil turn to this senseless slaughter, not to mention the suffering the cattle must have experienced until the poison had finally killed them.

"I'm going to end this," she suddenly announced. "Ben Tate is going to get his chance to deny this, and right now."

She kicked her horse into a gallop, straight for the Broken Arrow. She didn't know what she was going to say to Ben Tate, but fury drove her. All she could think about was to light into him with her claws bared.

Thunder pounded in her brain. The thunder of her horse's hooves. The thunder of her rage. The wind beat at her face and bent the brim of her hat back, and still she rode on, blinded by her own determination and fury. It took a moment for the second set of hooves to register in her brain. She saw movement just as she realized Seth was riding up alongside her.

"Pull up, Maggie!"

She leaned out farther over her horse's neck, urging the animal on even faster. Seth wouldn't stop her. By damn, he wouldn't! This mess was going to get settled even if both she and Tate ended up dead in a pool of blood.

"Damn it, Maggie! I said pull up!" He reached over for her reins but she out-manuevered him and veered her horse away. He stayed with her, keeping his horse neck and neck with hers. Before she realized what was taking place, his arm had circled her waist. In the next instant she was jerked from the saddle and hauled to a position in front of him.

"Let me go!" She struggled against his arm, but it was like a band of steel she couldn't weaken regardless of the blows she laid to it.

He pulled his mount to a stop. "What in the hell do you think you're doing, Maggie! You can't go over there in a rage. You don't even have any proof Tate did this!"

"I know he did it! Who else wants me off the White Raven!"

"I don't know, but you hired me to find out. Now why don't you let me do my job!"

"You haven't done a damn thing yet!"

His eyes shot fire. "Yes, but because I was camped out at the ranch trying to keep you from getting shot up again!"

He was right, even if she didn't want to admit it.

Energy spent, she conceded the battle and gave up her struggle. She became intensely aware of his nearness. His thighs and loins pressed against her buttocks. His arm pressed into her bosom. Everywhere he touched her he branded her with the impression of his body, and she feared it was an impression that would never fade away.

"Let me down," she demanded.

"So you can jump on that horse again and go tearing off like you're trying to outrun a prairie fire? Not on your life, woman."

He stepped from the saddle, taking her with him. When her feet touched ground again, she tried to bolt but found herself fast in the embrace of not just one arm now, but two. To her dismay he pulled her even closer, molding her body the entire length of his. He was a brazen sonofabitch, but the security of his arms seemed exactly what she needed, and she found herself leaning into him, laying her dust-streaked face against his brawny chest. But she wouldn't put her arms around him. She refused to do that! Instead, she balled her fists and pressed them against him. It was safer, should he overstep his bounds and need to be pushed away.

"Something's got to be done, Seth," she said,

feeling very weary now. "If Tate keeps going, I'll have to sell out and file bankruptcy."

Seth Sackett found his mind dramatically deviating from the business of hand to the soft and enticing curves of Maggie Cayton's body. God, it was almost more than he could bear, holding her so near when the fire inside himself blazed hotter and more ferocious than it had for any other woman he could summon to memory. He wanted her in a desperate way he had never felt before. He hardly understood it himself, except that the feeling seemed to go beyond the mere act of taking her to his bed. He wanted to do more than fill her with his need. He wanted to fill a gaping cavern that had opened up inside him at the first sight of her. It had gotten bigger each time he had seen her, each time he had touched her or stood next to her, each time he had even so much as stood in the doorway of the tack shed and looked out across the yard at the big house that kept her safe from the likes of him. It was a consuming, desperate need that cried out for more than physical fulfillment.

Her hat had fallen from her head when he'd dismounted with her in his arms. Her mass of hair was twisted into a thick braid that arrowed down the center of her back, almost to her waist. Strands of the coarse hair had fallen free and lay in wavy wisps along the sides of her face. He smoothed them away, memorizing the silkiness against his fingertips and the palm of his hand. He felt her body tense and guessed that any second she would bolt for freedom like a skittish filly unwilling to give up her independence. But Maggie was no inexperienced young girl.

She was a woman who knew the ways of men, and who probably knew what his thoughts were at this very moment. It only made him want her that much more. The pain began in his loins, throbbing insistently. She was a woman who would know how to satisfy him if she would only make up her mind to do it.

But he couldn't lay her back in the grass and make love to her in the sweet heat of the sunshine as he longed to do. He had to think of why they were here. He had to think of her pain and agony, not his.

"You don't have proof that Tate did this," he said gently, stroking the stiff curve of her back. To his amazement he felt her spine relax, if only a degree.

"But he did," she insisted. "He's done everything, even if he never leaves proof. Who else would want to run me out?"

Seth leaned into her, lowering his head to the top of hers, unable to resist placing his lips to the perfumed strands of auburn hair. His loins ached with a powerful, incessant throb, and he thought he might have to have her here and now, regardless of anything else.

"Then we'll have to search harder," he whispered. "Find proof."

She turned her head ever-so-slightly until she was looking up at him. Her lips were only mere inches from his and they were pleasing lips. Full, but not too full. Soft. Like her breasts touching his chest. Full, but not too full. Soft . . .

He lowered his head, falling into a dream whose

focus seemed to be deep in her green eyes. He expected her to pull away. Expected it any second. And he couldn't let that happen.

Suddenly he claimed her lips with the full force of his desperate need for her. She must have felt some of that desperation because she met the grinding force of his mouth with an urgency of her own. Her lips parted beneath his and her tongue met his in a wild and reckless mating dance. Her fists, balled against his chest had soon curled into his vest, gripping him to her with a ferocious need.

That she would want him with the same passion he felt for her, caused a moan of pleasure to tumble from his throat. He couldn't hold it back, couldn't keep from letting her know his sinful desire that might send her running away, hating him more than she did now. But she had that desire, too. How could she deny it?

His arms tightened around her and he began to lean into her, to lean her back and down toward the grass.

"No, Seth. . . ."

It was a stifled moan, a sound that said she didn't want the kiss to end but knew it must before it went any farther. He could have easily held her but he allowed her to escape. His need for her was too powerful, and he had been on the very edge of succumbing to it.

She scooped her hat up from the ground, caught her horse and swung into the saddle, straightening her riding skirt over her knees with jerky movements. "If we need proof," she said, "then let's go back to Larkspur reservoir and see if we can find it."

A pain knifed through Seth's heart. How could she pretend the kiss had never happened? But at the same time, Seth knew that was the only thing she could do. The only thing either of them could do.

So he straddled his horse and rode with her, his thoughts having been scattered far away from Ben Tate. Something dramatic had happened between him and Maggie; something had changed. She still might not like what he was, but at least she had loosened the hold on her hatred.

Chapter Twelve

Seth walked around the reservoir, stepping over and around the carcasses. There were a few cattle still suffering from the poison. When he came across them, his gunshots, putting them out of their misery, echoed across the wide valley. Maggie remained on horseback, too heartsick to get down and walk among the animals, most of which she and Trent had raised from calves.

Seth lowered himself to his haunches next to the reservoir's edge and plucked something out of the water. With his back to her, Maggie couldn't identify the object. All she could see was the expanse of his back and the way the muscles flexed beneath the tan-colored shirt and black vest. It was too easy to visualize herself in his arms again. She could vividly feel and taste his lips even now in her memory, and she found herself irrevocably drawn to him. Had she misjudged him as her mother had suggested? Was he, like Trent, a protector of property and a defender of justice? A man who killed only when he had to? Or was she softening towards him, seeing goodness in him where it didn't belong, and justifying the gun on his hip because he was capable of making her want to love him?

She tried not to look at his hands; hard hands, yet soft. Proficient at everything from fist-fighting to exquisitely tender lovemaking. Were they proficient at murder?

"What have you found?" She forced her thoughts back to the matter at hand.

He came to his feet and held the object up for her to see. "Just an old stogie somebody threw in here. It doesn't help us much. A lot of men smoke cigars. Do you know if Tate does?"

Maggie observed the soaked cigar butt he held carefully between a tanned thumb and forefinger. "All I've seen Tate smoke are hand-rolled cigarettes."

"This could have been dropped by anybody, even a drifter. But from the condition it's in, I'd guess it was tossed in here yesterday, along with the poison. Do you know if anybody from the White Raven was over here recently?"

"Not by my orders, but I'll ask Sonny if he sent anyone over."

Seth rolled the stogie up in his bandana and tucked it in his saddlebags, keeping it as evidence, of a sort. "Cattle will be coming in soon for their afternoon water," he said. "We'll have to drive as many away from here as possible. I'm going to drop the wire and push them all over onto Tate's side. It's the only way to keep them from drinking the water until we can get it fenced off. I'll ride over to Tate's tomorrow and tell him what I've done."

Fear immediately gripped Maggie at the thought of Seth riding onto the Broken Arrow. What if Tate's men, or Tate himself, shot him on the spot? Max Morrell surely wouldn't need an excuse. But Seth was right. Unless the cattle had a fence between them and the reservoir it wouldn't matter if they were driven ten miles away. They would return to the water and die like the others. She had hired Seth to do a job. It was clearly becoming time for her to let him do it.

"All right," she said. "Let's get busy."

As quickly as the cattle came in for their afternoon and evening water, Seth and Maggie moved them onto Tate's property. When it looked as if no more would come in for the night, Seth repaired the fence with the omnipresent hammer and staples in Maggie's saddlebags, equipment a rancher seldom left behind when he, or she, went out on the range.

By the time they were back in the saddle and headed toward the White Raven, clouds covered the sky, blocking any starlight that might have guided their way. The range was home to Maggie; she knew her way well. But at night, without even the North Star to use as a guide, it became a jumble of identical hills and valleys with definite landmarks lost to darkness. She watched the sky, hoping the clouds would break up, but the air was stagnant and heavy and smelled of rain.

A furrow creased Seth's brow. "I'm sure you know the dangers of riding in the dark, Maggie," he said lightly. "A horse could step in a badger hole and break a leg. And, by the looks of those clouds, we could get wet. You didn't bring your slicker so

I'd be obliged to give you mine, and then *I'd* get wet—unless, of course, you were inclined to want to ride double and share. If not, maybe we should make our way to that line shack that isn't too far from here."

Maggie refused to even consider spending the night with Sackett or sharing a slicker—both were tempting but ultimately too dangerous. "I need to get back to the ranch," she said adamantly. "Everyone will wonder where we are. After what happened before they'll probably think we've been attacked by Tate's men and then they'll come looking for us."

"They might, but I doubt they'd have any luck when none of them saw which direction we went," he pointed out. "I should think they'd make the sensible decision to wait until morning. And we should do the sensible thing by holing up in that line shack."

"We can get home." She set her jaw in a stubborn line and refused to allow her horse to slow its pace.

"I don't think it's fear of the men coming looking for you that has you troubled, Maggie. I think it's the fear that they won't, and you'll be in that line shack all night with me. You're afraid my prophecy about us becoming lovers just might come true tonight."

She tossed him a withering glare. "You can stop a bullet as easily as the next man, Seth. And if you touch me that's exactly what you'll be doing."

"I'm beginning to like you more every day, Maggie." He gave her a taunting half smile. "I'm truly convinced you don't like me, but I don't believe you when you deny liking how I make you feel. You enjoyed that kiss today as much as I did."

Maggie had hoped he would forget about that. Or at least have the decency not to mention it. "Don't flatter yourself. It caught me by surprise, that's all."

"Some of the best things in life are surprises. Why don't you learn to go with your feelings? Live for today and quit worrying about a yesterday and a man you can't bring back."

"Why don't you get the notion out of your head that I would ever want to make love to you?" She glared at him this time. "If you want a whore, then go into town. I'll even give you a few days off so you can get it all out of your system."

"A whore wouldn't get anything out of my system. She'd just make me want a woman like you that much more. No, Maggie, sometimes it's a challenge for a man to ride a horse that he's had to coax to saddle."

"I'm not a wild mustang that needs to be broken." She was clearly insulted. "And it thoroughly irritates me that you men insist on using that disgusting correlation."

"Well, if it fits, why not? But I wouldn't want to break you, Maggie. I'd want all that spirit intact. Makes for a better ride. I'd just want to gain your trust so you'd come willingly and eat all the sugar I had in my pocket."

"Always dreaming, aren't you?"

"Sometimes for a man like me, that's about all there is to do. Now, even though I like the direction of the conversation and would like to continue it, I think you've gotten a little off track."

"Me!"

His smile was infuriating, but he so much as ignored her outburst. "You may not want to spend the night with me, but I'm not worried about spending the night with you. I *am* worried about wandering around out here in the dark for hours and getting lost or breaking my horse's leg—or getting soaked in a rainstorm. If you want to make love to me, I'll surely oblige. But if you don't, then just tell me to go to hell and let's quit this bickering and get to some shelter before it's too late."

The first drops of rain hit Maggie's face. She tried to muster as much contempt for him as she possibly could, but it wasn't nearly as easy as it had been a few weeks ago. Seeing no sensible alternative, she turned her horse toward the line shack.

"Go to hell, Sackett."

Laughing, he followed.

They reached the line shack just before the sky opened. They split duties. Since Seth had a slicker he tended to the horses, unsaddling them and turning them loose in the small corral behind the line shack. Maggie went inside and started a fire with the dry wood that had been stacked in the box by the previous occupant. Not only did they need the fire for cooking, but if it continued to rain there would be a chill in the cabin by morning.

Seth came in with rain dripping from his slicker and the brim of his hat. His boots were clumped with mud. He removed the wet gear and hung it on a small set of deer antlers that had been attached to the log walls for that specific purpose. He shed the boots, leaving them on a worn rug by the door. The cabin was squat and small, measuring only about twenty feet by thirty, and it was made even smaller by Seth's height and the expanse of his chest that seemed broader than usual in the cramped surroundings.

In his stocking feet he washed up and helped her prepare a meal of canned meat and vegetables from the cabin's stock, along with coffee and fried soda biscuits. She insisted he didn't have to assist her, but he insisted he would.

"You can round up cattle as good as any hand on the White Raven, Maggie," he said. "Now, I may not be able to cook as well as your Dorothy, but I can stir up about the best fried soda biscuits you'll ever eat."

She was uneasy at first, working alongside him in what was traditionally a woman's role, but when the meal was laid out she had to admit that what he'd said about the biscuits was true. Smeared with some honey from the cupboard, they were so light and fluffy they nearly melted in her mouth.

They ate in relative silence and after things were once again cleaned up, he rolled his bedroll out on one of the cots, immediately stretched out on it, and gave Maggie a yawn and a mumbled "see ya in the morning."

In one way Maggie was relieved he was ignoring her. In another, she was irritated. After removing her boots and gun belt, she curled up in her own blankets on the cot opposite Seth's. It was going to be a long, uncomfortable night. Already she missed her big bed and soft sheets. But lying in the darkness, in the crude surroundings, brought back memories of the nights in her younger years when she and Trent had been forced to sleep in worse conditions. Once while she and Trent had been looking for strays in October, they had slept on the ground. They'd woke up in the middle of the night in each other's arms, and with an inch of snow on their bedding. They hadn't noticed the cold or the hard ground. Love had always diminished life's hardships, making them more bearable.

She pulled her blanket tighter and looked over at Sackett's broad back. The fire from the stove gave out enough light that she could easily see his form. She tried to imagine him as being Trent, but no matter how hard she tried, Sackett remained Sackett. His own charisma was too powerful to be overshadowed by blurred images of another man.

She closed her eyes, sinking back into her memories as far as she could. She didn't want to release them, and it disturbed her that Sackett's presence always reminded her that some day she would no longer be able to content herself with memories of the times she and Trent had shared. Sackett made her think of today, of tomorrow, and most of all, of tonight.

You won't do it, boy. You'll never pull that trigger.
I will if you don't leave her alone.
Put it down. She disobeyed and she needs to be punished, same as you.
And you?

That's enough of your smart mouth. Now, put it down.

Don't come any closer. If you do, I swear I'll—

Seth came awake with a start, surrounded by darkness and silence. It took a minute for him to remember he was in the line shack with Maggie. He wasn't in that cheap hotel room all those years ago, facing down the devil in what proved to be the final showdown.

He ran a shaking hand through his hair and glanced at the cot where Maggie slept. There was enough firelight slipping out from around the door of the stove to enable him to see the curve of her hip and the mass of long hair spread out over the pillow.

He sat up slowly, quietly placing his feet on the rough, plank floor. The silence pounding in his ears told him the storm was over. Barefooted he tiptoed to the door and carefully pulled it open. It creaked, but not too loud. Settling on the stoop, he drank of the silence and the night. He needed to feel the freedom that existed beyond the confinement of the shack; to smell the rain-washed earth and the wet sagebrush; to absorb the peacefulness of the unmolested land. It was the only way he'd ever found he could fully clear his mind of the demons.

Maggie wasn't sure if it was the cool breeze that woke her, or the shirtless man sitting in the open door. But so melancholy was his posture that it took her a moment to realize it was Seth and that something was wrong with him.

The rain had stopped and a patch of stars peeked out just overhead through the disintegrating cloud cover. It allowed her to see his rugged facial contours, his body's muscular silhouette, and a crisscross of white ugly scars across his back. She blinked, probing the moonlight and wondering if the light was playing tricks on her. Apparently not. The scars remained.

She wasn't looking at the dangerous gunfighter now, nor the arrogant playboy. No, both of those men seemed to have vanished inside the man in the doorway, who seemed to have vanished inside himself. She was reminded of a small boy, lost and alone and vulnerable in a strange land where everyone was his enemy. In him she saw utter hopelessness.

He didn't hear the rustle of her blankets or her bare feet across the floor. Her hand on his shoulder startled him, but on seeing her, he immediately relaxed. He also changed. The vulnerability vanished so swiftly she wondered if she had imagined it. The slump in his shoulders disappeared. A mocking smile lifted his lips. A gleam edged the dullness out of his eyes and he caught her hand.

"Get lonely for me, Maggie?"

Suddenly irritated that she'd felt one shred of compassion for him, she pulled her hand free of his grip. "Do you always overestimate your effect on women?" she snapped.

"Not usually."

His arrogant smile was maddening. She wondered why he persisted in tormenting her when he knew good and well how she felt about him. Or did he? Did he actually see beyond what she told him? Could he see into her mind and somehow know that she very much wanted to feel his arms and his lips again, as shameless as that might be?

"I came over here to see what was wrong. Quit playing me for a fool."

She started back to her bed, but she had barely turned away when he caught her hand again. Coming to his feet, he towered over her. Her natural defenses went up, as well as her hands against his brawny chest in an attempt to ward off his brazen, and yet strangely exciting advances. She felt the heat and life of his body pulsing into her fingertips, through her hands, and on into every fiber of her being. His heart thumped directly beneath her palm, and the patch of hair on his chest did nothing to buffer its steady rhythm so like the last drops of rain running off the shack's tin roof and plopping into puddles beneath the eaves.

The cynicism in his whisper made her shiver. "Nothing's wrong that you can fix, Maggie . . . unless you can fix the past. But I do have a current affliction you might be able to take care of."

"I'm serious, Seth."

"So am I."

So it was the past that haunted him? Somehow that didn't surprise her. A man like Sackett was sure to have had a lively—and deadly—roster of events with which to fill his memory and his diary. She couldn't help but wonder what those events were that he guarded so closely, even to the point of denial.

"You may pretend you want to make love to

me," she said, "and I'm sure you would if I consented. But you feel nothing in your heart for me. You don't even like me."

"From what I can tell, the feeling is mutual."

"I don't like what you represent, Seth, but if there is a man other than a killer behind your gun, you're making sure I don't like him either. You don't know how to treat a woman."

His arms tightened around her. Her breasts were pressed firmly against his chest. Only one arm held her, the other sent tingles running through her body as his fingertips glided upward along her throat. She might have been able to break free, but she found herself mesmerized by the tantalizing touch. The hardness in his eyes gave way in slow degrees to a muted passion, as soft as the pastels in a spring sunrise. Odd how she had once thought he might be less dangerous without his gun. She had been dead wrong.

"Show me how a woman like you wants a man to treat her, Maggie," he said in a husky whisper. "I'm always willing to learn new things."

"No." It was a faint denial as she tried to look away from his captivating eyes, sparkling in the light of the moon. She tried to break free, refusing to be the one to initiate any kind of lovemaking with him.

"Show me," he insisted softly. His hand slid beneath the heavy mass of her long hair at the base of her neck. The movement was so gentle it caused a chill to race down her spine.

Feelings of need began to make themselves known inside her. How could he stir those coals that had gone out when Trent had died? How could any man ever make her feel desire again? And yet, it was happening.

"No, Seth."

He lowered his head. His lips grazed her throat. "Is this the way to make you like me, Maggie?"

Emotions as powerful as lightning, bolted through her body. She gripped his arms, not sure if she was trying to free herself from him, or trying to hold on tighter.

His lips continued their exploration of her throat. She wanted to cry out with the torment of their exquisite touch.

"Let me go, Seth."

His tender, feather light kisses found her cheek, her forehead, her eyelids, the tip of her nose. She sank helplessly into the sensations, away from the stubborn idea that she had to deny herself the pleasure he gave.

"Is this the way, Maggie?" he whispered.

"Yes . . ."

"And this?"

His lips halted just a fraction of an inch over hers. She waited for what seemed an eternity. Her eyelids fluttered open to find him watching her with a tortured heat in his eyes so hot it frightened her. Then suddenly, with a deep groan in his throat, his lips swooped down, taking hers in a possessive and demanding kiss that drew from her every need she had hoped to deny. She longed for him. Hungered for him. Needed him in a way that was utterly insane. She clung to him on the verge of giving all, taking all.

Then she was stumbling backward, breaking away from the insanity, only to be caught short by the open door. She felt as if she'd been running, but realized it was only from herself she fled.

He pulled her against him again, but there was no kiss forthcoming, only anger. "When are you going to admit you want me as much as you wanted your late husband—maybe more. Why can't you quit hating me just because I live by my gun?"

She tried to break free of his grip but to no avail. "Stop it, Seth. Just stop it."

"You never thought you would betray your husband, did you?"

"I've told you before I don't want to make love to you! When are you going to accept that?"

"When you can fully convince me you mean it."

"I do mean it."

"I don't think so." His eyes searched hers intently, seeking the answers he wanted to hear but that she wouldn't give. "You could have just gone back to sleep when you saw me sitting here, but you didn't."

"I wanted to see if something was wrong with you. If you were sick."

"Then you don't hate me as much as you say. Be careful about caring, Maggie. It can cause all sorts of problems."

"And you never allow yourself that particular emotion, do you?"

"All the time, that's why I know so much about it."

She didn't want to hear this. Didn't want to know how he hurt. And she knew he hurt deeply from something that had happened long ago. Something that had to do with the scars. If she knew about him, she *would* care, and he was right, it would torment her to see his pain. It would make her feel compassion for him. Maybe she just didn't want to face the truth that Sackett was human; a man with intensely deep feelings standing silently behind the gun.

"Why do you want me to care about you? To go to bed with you? Why are you *doing* it, Seth? Does it give you a perverse pleasure to get women to your bed so you can use them and then discard them? Or are you just afraid of your own heart, that you might actually find *yourself* caring for someone, so you make damn sure you just use them? Maybe you're afraid that someone might make demands of you that would interfere with your freedom. Or maybe you just have some sort of contempt for women in general."

"Quite to the contrary, Maggie. God had a good day when he made Eve. Women have always been good to me, and I try to be good to them, insofar as I can. But a woman who gets involved with me is too likely to be the target of my enemies. It's something always in the back of my mind. A man like me needs a woman like you, because right now you have as many enemies as I do.

"But that's not what you want to hear, is it? You want to know why I want to make love to you, but why I'm not asking you to marry me."

She tried to break away again, disgusted with the direction of the conversation. "Don't be ridiculous."

"I'm not. Don't you know that women don't want to marry men like me unless they can change us, tame us?"

"Then maybe you're around all the wrong women."

"What would you do, Maggie? Would you want to tame me? To take my gun away and make me go to church every Sunday?"

She laughed at the absurdity of it. "Only a foolish woman would ask that of a man like you."

"And what exactly is a man like me, Maggie?"

Since he had quite pointedly asked for her opinion, she openly perused him. For all her attempts to answer his question, though, she couldn't.

In the ensuing silence she became acutely aware of his hard, muscular body pressing the length of hers, from her bosom to her knees. Through her clothing she felt the rock hardness of his chest and the bulge of his manhood. He'd read her too accurately. He knew all her secrets, whereas she knew none of his. She wanted to make love to him, here and now, as he had intuitively guessed. She yearned for the taste of his lips on hers and the gentle caress of his hands on her body. It didn't matter at the moment what else he was; Seth Sackett could satisfy her as no other man she knew possibly could.

"You can't answer my question because you don't know the kind of man I am, do you?" he finally said. "But if you did, you would hate me worse than you do."

Abruptly he released her, his eyes as piercing as an Indian's lance. She stood in the open doorway while he strode back to his bed. Sitting on the edge, he rustled around in his saddlebags until he found his cigarettes and matches. The match scraped across the cabin's crude log wall and the reflection of its flame cast his rugged features in a haunting red light.

"I know you've killed men," she said. "What could be worse?"

It wasn't until he had taken several drags on the cigarette that he replied. "I'll tell you what's worse than killing men, Maggie. It's living with it. But you know how that feels. You've killed men, too, haven't you? Indians, bandits, renegades."

She closed the door, obliterating the only source of light except for the red glow at the end of Seth's cigarette. But then she heard his match strike the wall again and she returned to her cot while he lit the kerosene lamp.

She was troubled by the words they'd exchanged. She didn't want to fight with him. She wanted to hold him, soothe him. Have him soothe her. "Yes, Seth," she admitted. "I've killed men, but only in self-defense."

"It's still hard to live with, though, isn't it?"

"Yes."

"You think about it once in a while, don't you?"

"Yes."

"At night."

"Yes."

"Well, so do I."

Maggie dropped to her cot and crawled back beneath the blankets, both relieved and disappointed that he had released her. She didn't like the bitterness that was suddenly consuming him. She preferred his arrogance.

"Does who you are and what you're hiding have something to do with the scars on your back?" she asked with her back to him.

Seth wondered why he had opened the door to his past so she could go probing in. Was it because he wanted her to know? Wanted to just get it out in the open with her and get it all over with? His nightmare and his memories had been successfully banished by the shocking touch of her hand on his shoulder, a touch that seemed branded on his flesh forever, and certainly on his mind forever. Even now he could feel it although she was feet away. Was she aware of the effect of her touch on his tortured soul? Was she aware of how good it felt to a dying man?

And he was dying, bit by lonely bit. How could he live with his sins without forgiveness, and yet how could he ask for forgiveness when he didn't regret what he had done? He didn't even feel remorse. He had asked God to forgive him for his crime, but there was nothing he could do beyond that. He had never felt any remorse for the day he'd pulled that trigger. He'd only felt a tremendous rush of freedom and of relief that at last it was over. At times he had felt guilty for never regretting it, but he'd never felt guilty for doing it.

If Maggie knew. . . . Oh, if she knew, she'd hate him worse than she did now. She wouldn't have touched him so intimately. She would never have consented to stay in this small cabin with him on a cot only a few short feet away from his.

Maybe he would never tell her. Maybe it was one of those things she would never need to know. And yet some foolishness in him wanted her to know it all, wanted to see her reaction, wanted her to understand and forgive him.

"Seth?"

Her whisper jarred him from his agonizing reverie. God, even his name whispered from her lips was torture to his heart. He could just tell her to leave him alone, that it was none of her business. If she'd been any other woman he might have. But there was something about Maggie Cayton that stirred his blood and his desires, his dreams, and he had to tell her something. He didn't want her to hate him. He didn't know why he persisted in torturing himself with impossibilities. He wasn't good enough for her. It was just better to tell her the truth and end it all now. Get it over with and get on with his job.

He snuffed out his cigarette in the ash tray by the bed. His eyes lifted to her dark form, the curve of her body beneath the blankets. Suddenly the frustration of his life boiled over inside him and he came off the bed, pacing the floor. He was barely aware of the rough planks against his bare feet. The truth was like the frustration, clawing to get out of him.

He turned to face her. "A French whore had a wicked knife. I think she figured it was easier to stab me in the back and steal *all* my money, than to work for just a few dollars of it."

Maggie wasn't appeased by his explanation. "That can't account for all the scars, Seth, unless you were terribly slow in reacting to her attack."

He faced the night instead of her and added flippantly. "I also had a father with a heavy disciplinary hand."

"Is that why you went into this line of work? Was it an act of defiance?"

He lit another cigarette and smoked it nervously, feeling as if he was on trial, but also feeling he had to tell her. "It was the foolishness of a poor boy, Maggie, and it was my only salvation. I could shoot and that's all I could do. I needed some shoes; my mother needed things."

She was silent for a few moments. "Have you ever regretted taking the path you ultimately chose?"

He blew smoke to the heavy beams in the squat log cabin. "No. I still need boots. And I've found out that women like men who have money in their pockets."

"Why not use your talent with the gun as a lawman?"

"It doesn't pay well enough."

"The real reason, Seth."

Silence hung heavily in the darkness for a few minutes and then suddenly he chuckled. "Maybe I was wrong about you. Maybe you *do* know me. You certainly seem to know when I'm lying."

She smiled too. "What *is* the real reason, Seth?"

The lightheartedness that had sparked his eyes lasted only a moment before quickly being shadowed once again by seriousness. "I'm a lot of things, Maggie, but a hypocrite isn't one of them. I never thought it was proper for one killer to be slapping on a badge and going after another. I walk a thin line between the lawful and the lawless. And sometimes I step over it, both ways. It's just the way it has to be."

"Will you ever take the guns off?"

"I did once," he admitted. "A friend and I tried to take up ranching in Colorado. But another gunslinger who had heard about me, wanted to go up against me. He came to our place and killed my friend in cold blood, then he shot me. He made sure he didn't put the bullet where it would kill me. He wanted me to see my friend die. If I'd had my gun on, it wouldn't have been my friend who had died. I've never taken it off since.

"No, Maggie. Until the wolves are gone, the gun stays."

Their eyes locked for a moment in keen understanding. This was still a country where the only difference sometimes between life and death was a six-shooter.

He left the cabin then and Maggie let him go, sensing he wanted to be alone. He would come back a little later and if she was still awake she would pretend to be asleep, because that was the safest thing to do. But at least she knew Seth Sackett a little better now, and she felt a kinship with him she hadn't felt before. She also knew he'd done something with her he'd never done with any other woman.

He had revealed his heart, if only a small portion.

Chapter Thirteen

Maggie should have been relieved to see Sonny and three hired hands meet them on their way back to the ranch the next morning, but she wasn't. The men rode up on a gallop, halting in a cloud of dust. Their eyes were full of questions about why she and Seth had spent the night together, and suspicions as to what had happened between them. Sonny was especially on edge, and the contempt he felt for Seth was clear. But neither he nor the other men voiced their thoughts. The reason was also clear: they were afraid of Seth.

Owing them no explanation about the night in the line shack, Maggie told them only what had happened yesterday at Larkspur reservoir. "I'd like you to assign several men to get our cattle off Tate's land and drive them—as well as anything else in this section—to the south and southwest sections of the ranch."

"But that'll put some real strain on the feed over there," Sonny argued.

"I don't have a choice, Sonny. Until that poison

has a chance to clear out of the water we can't put cattle in the northeast section."

"Yeah, and if we put all our manpower over here, what's to stop him from hitting us somewhere else?" Sonny continued belligerently, as if he thought her ideas were foolish.

"We'll have to put guards on all the major water sources."

"We don't have the manpower for that."

"Then get it," she said impatiently. "Hire as many men as the job takes. It may pinch the purse strings, but I can't afford to lose any more cattle either, or you'll all be packing your saddlebags."

She started for the ranch again and the men obediently followed. Seth rode up next to her. "Now that you've got an escort back to the ranch," he said, "I'm going over to Tate's to have that little chat."

Their eyes locked. Hers were filled with worry and concern. "Be careful, Seth. I don't trust Morrell."

"It pays not to, but killing me won't gain them anything. Killing you might, so you're the one who needs to be careful."

She nodded. "I will."

He touched the brim of his hat in a gesture of farewell and rode away. Maggie watched him, immediately forming a picture in her mind of Tate's men gunning him down the minute he rode onto the Broken Arrow. Damn it, she should be going with him!

Sonny seemed to read her mind. "Let him go," he said caustically, watching Seth getting smaller and smaller in the distance. "It's about time he earned his keep."

Maggie reluctantly continued on toward the ranch. She was met by her mother and Natalie and Alison, all of whom wanted an immediate explanation for her all-night absence. Once satisfied, the girls departed. Thankfully Natalie hadn't made any pointed comments about her having spent it with Seth.

Maggie went to her room to get clean clothes and prepare for a bath. Her mother followed on her heels and closed the door behind them. She said nothing, but her silence and silly smile soon grated on Maggie's nerves.

Pulling some underwear from the top drawer of her bureau, she flashed her mother an annoyed look. "You look like the cat that just ate the cream, Mother. Is there something you want to tell me?"

Catherine went to the chaise lounge, smoothing her cotton dress as she reclined on it to watch her daughter. "So you spent the night with him, did you?"

Maggie glared. "We had no choice, Mother. It was either stay together in the line shack or get drenched trying to get home in the rain. It was dark, too."

"Oh, I'm sure nothing happened, but of course everyone with a brain in his head thinks it did."

"Well, it didn't! Seth was the perfect gentleman."

"Much to your chagrin."

"Mother!"

"Come now, Maggie, all women would like a man to be a little aggressive when they're alone together. You know, a few kisses. That sort of thing."

Maggie tossed the clean underthings on the bed and went to her closet. "I hate to inform you, Mother, but if you're going to kiss Seth Sackett you might as well plan on going to bed with him. The man is as . . . as . . . ."

"As what, dear?" She purred innocently.

"As horny as an old Longhorn bull! That's what. He's not a man you can tease and expect to walk away from with your undies still in place!"

Catherine was trying to muffle a giggle. "Oh, really?"

"Yes, really!"

"Well, what a pity. I would think that either kissing him, or going to bed with him, would be quite nice then. Virile men are always so exciting."

Maggie's glare deepened. "Have you been reading those sordid romance novels again, Mother?"

"Oh, heaven's no! Well, just *Romeo and Juliet,* but it's really quite a wonderful story. I wonder if Seth would enjoy it?" she added in a musing sort of way.

Maggie rolled her eyes, scooped up her clothes, and headed for the bathroom downstairs with Catherine hastening to keep up. "Keep his mind on the *Iliad and the Odyssey,* please."

"Has he been making advances, Maggie?"

"That's none of your business, Mother."

"Ah . . . so he has. Well, it's a relief to know he finds you attractive even if you haven't yet admitted that you find him attractive. You know, the dance is coming up. Who will you be going with?"

"I have no intention of going to Lissa Dugan's barn dance unless it would be to burn the place down. I detest that woman. Besides, I have a ranch to run."

"All right, but let's just assume you might change your mind. Then what?"

"Mother, the dance is the farthest thing from my mind! I just lost two hundred head of cattle!"

"And I'm very upset to hear that, Maggie. Don't misunderstand me. If you end up out in the street, I'll be right there with you and I'm simply too old to be sleeping on the ground. This is just a hypothetical question."

Maggie clicked her tongue impatiently. "Oh, all right. If you insist on an answer, I suspect Cleve will extend an invitation before it's all over with."

"You don't sound too happy about that possibility."

Maggie's step faltered, shaken by her mother's ability to read every little inflection in her voice. But it was the absolute truth. She wasn't looking forward to going with Cleve.

"Why not ask Seth?"

"You've got to be kidding, Mother." Maggie glanced at her mother from over her shoulder, not knowing whether to be appalled or amused.

"I'm really quite serious, dear."

Maggie had reached the bathroom downstairs. "For some reason I can't see Seth Sackett dancing. Unless it would be to the tune of bullets falling at his feet. Now, I'd like to take my bath in peace—and in private—if you don't mind, Mother."

"Of course, dear. We'll talk later. And do try to

calm down. You really seem quite agitated. But I expect when Seth gets back from Tate's you'll feel much better . . . knowing he's all right."

Catherine smiled and departed, humming to herself as she went on her way. Maggie released a weary sigh and locked the door behind her. It was amazing how her mother always knew exactly what was on her mind.

Seth rode on a cautious walk toward Tate's house, a looming two-story, white mansion on a knoll overlooking the rest of the ranch. The rain-damp earth muffled the sound of his horse's hooves, and his approach seemed to go completely unnoticed, even by the flock of loose chickens who automatically cleared from his path while single-mindedly continuing their search for food.

Seth never believed for a minute he wasn't being watched. As he rode past the barn and corrals, he sensed eyes on his back. He wondered, as he always did, if those eyes were looking at him from down the barrel of a rifle. A flash of sunlight off metal reaffirmed his suspicion, but before he could react a rifle boomed. The bullet kicked up dust just a few yards in front of his horse, making the animal scramble backwards in surprise and fear.

"Stop right where you are, Sackett," a voice yelled from the hay loft. "Or the next bullet will end your thinking."

Seth reined his horse until he was facing the hay loft. He didn't recognize the man staring down his gun sites at him. At least it wasn't Morrell. If it had been, Seth guessed he would have found himself face down in the dirt with a bullet in his head.

"I came to see Tate!" he yelled back.

"He's at the house. But don't try nothing stupid because I'll be here when you come out."

Seth turned his back once again on the barn loft sentinel and trotted his horse up to the picket fence that enclosed the house. The gunshot had surely informed Tate that he had an uninvited visitor, but Seth's knock at the door brought a smartly starched maid who left him in the parlor while she went after her employer. While he waited, he found a position by the window where he could see activity in the yard. It was quiet. The men, except for the guard, were apparently all out on the range. But where was Morrell? That little snake didn't work.

He turned at the sound of Tate's boot heels clomping down the hardwood hall, accompanied by the rhythmic ringing of his spurs. His step alone told Seth that he was not in the most congenial of moods. The big man stopped in the doorway, his shoulders filling the space. He looked like a bull, head slightly down and ready to charge.

"What are you doing here, Sackett? I don't recall giving you an invite."

"Then your recollection serves you well. But I'm used to not getting invitations, Tate. Most people don't look forward to my visits."

Tate moved into the room and took a seat. He motioned with a wave of his big hand to the chair opposite him. "Sit down, Sackett. Get on with your business. I reckon this *is* business and not a social visit."

Seth settled in the horsehair chair. It was a big chair, but then all the furniture was big. It had to be to accommodate Big Ben Tate.

"Maggie and I were over to Larkspur reservoir yesterday," he said. "What we found didn't settle too well with us."

Tate's eyes narrowed as suspicions and questions entered. "Well, go on. What's that got to do with me?"

"We found about two hundred head of dead cattle, Tate. They were poisoned. Now do you know what I'm talking about?"

Tate snorted belligerently. "No, I don't know what you're talking about. How were they poisoned?"

"Through the water. The whole reservoir is ruined until that water runs out of there and cleans itself out. I just wanted to let you know that we put our cattle over on your range last night. We'll have them out today."

"What!" Tate leaped to his feet. "My range can't support Cayton cattle!"

Seth watched him pace the floor, running a hand through his silver hair. "I figured it was the least you could do after poisoning that water."

Tate looked for certain like he was going to charge with his head down and roaring, like a buffalo on the fight. He took steps toward Seth, fists clenching. "I've done some things in retaliation for what's she's done to me, but I didn't poison no water and I didn't order it done! Goddamned if I know what's going on, but you tell Maggie I didn't do it. I didn't burn that damn barn of hers either."

"So you say."

"So I say is right!"

Seth studied the raging bull. Unless Tate was a darn good actor, Seth didn't believe he was lying. Something was wrong here, terribly wrong. "Sit down, Tate. I think we've got some things to discuss. I'm beginning to think you and Maggie should have talked about this a long time ago, except that you're both too damned hot-headed to do anything but kill each other with your bare hands."

Tate settled heavily back in his chair. "That little woman couldn't kill a flea."

"Don't underestimate her," Seth warned. "She's got more backbone than most men I know."

Tate made a rare concession. "She is a hard-headed one, that's for sure. Doesn't behave the way a woman should."

"You mean she hasn't backed down to you?"

He shot Seth a nasty look. "Listen Sackett, when Trent died, Maggie should have packed up and got the hell into town where she belongs."

"That's what you wanted her to do?"

"No, that's just what she should do. Wouldn't have got herself nearly killed if she had."

"And you had nothing to do with that either, I suppose?"

"Your welcome is wearing mighty thin, Sackett."

"It usually does. Like I said, most people don't look forward to my company. But let's get back to the matter at hand, Tate. You insist you're not killing Maggie's cattle, and Maggie insists she isn't killing yours. Now, if neither one of you is behind all this, just who is? And why?"

Tate rubbed a hand over his jaw and studied Seth as if debating whether he could trust him to tell the truth. "You're sure she isn't behind any of it?"

"I'm sure."

"But what about some of her men?"

"I can't be sure of that. But then, can you be sure your men aren't doing things behind your back right this minute? For starters, where's Morrell? We both know he isn't out helping fix fence or brand late calves."

Tate was silent. "All right, Sackett, so I don't know where every man is every second of the day. And I don't know where Morrell is, except that he said he was going to town. But there's no reason for my men to do the things you're accusing them of, not without my orders. And I didn't give no orders of that nature."

"It would seem that if both you and Maggie are as innocent as newborn babes, then you're both being set up."

This was clearly something Tate hadn't considered before. "But why? And by whom?"

"Put two and two together, Tate. You and Maggie go at each other, kill each other, and what have you got? You've got two prime pieces of land up for grabs. And intimidation can easily take care of the women and children left behind on both spreads. Your wife would do exactly what you think Maggie should do. She'd pack up her bags and high-tail it to town. Catherine Marshall would probably do the same."

"You're saying someone is trying to get us off the land so they can take it?"

"It's a possibility worth considering," he said deliberately. "But what's so special about the Broken Arrow and the White Raven to make someone want to commit numerous murders in order to get them?"

Tate's eyes flashed. "Why it's some of the best damn grazing land around, that's why!"

"And land is getting harder to find. It's mostly taken up now. I guess if a person wanted some, they'd go for the best. Which brings up another question."

Tate clearly didn't like all this thinking. He was a man of hot-headed action. He just wanted to do battle and get it over with. He wanted things cut and dried, black or white.

Seth continued. "The cattle market hasn't been so good the last few years since the blizzards of '86 and '87. It would be a good time to get into cattle, the prices are low. On the other hand, why would anyone really want to with things being depressed the way they are? A lot of old ranchers have gone under because of the droughts and the blizzards. If someone wanted land, why not just buy up those guys who were selling out anyway?"

"Beats the hell out of me, Sackett."

"Yeah, I guess it does me, too, Tate." He came to his feet. "But I'm beginning to think there's a third party involved who's trying to pit you and Maggie against each other for his own gain."

Tate didn't say anything more, but Seth saw he wasn't convinced, nor was he willing to budge too far from his belligerent stance in believing Maggie was behind all the damage he was experiencing. And Maggie was just as stubborn.

Tate showed Seth from the house. Seth knew it was going to take some doing to forestall a range war between Maggie and Tate. Tate would listen to reason, as would Maggie, but they were both going to have to be given proof before either would give up on the notion that the other wasn't an adversary.

He left the Broken Arrow and began by riding the border between the two ranches. Miles of shiny barbed wire, angling over hills and down into valleys, kept land lines clearly defined. It wasn't until Cayton property came in contact with Wagner land that he finally saw something beneath a clump of poplar trees that made him draw rein. He didn't know exactly what he'd been hoping to find, but it hadn't been a young man by the name of Lance Cayton drowning in yards of some girl's yellow skirt with flounces and lace.

His first thought was that Lance was playing with fire, in more ways than one. Seth's biggest concern was that the kid had come out here alone when he wasn't supposed to go anywhere by himself. He was the heir to the White Raven, and because of it, he was in as precarious a position as Maggie was.

He debated whether to approach the two young lovers and break up their shenanigans, or just bypass them. But bypassing them would take him farther out of his way than he wanted to go. The problem was solved when Lance's gelding looked up, saw Seth's bay, and let out a deep, rolling whinny.

In the next instant, the two lovers were scrambling away from each other, hastily straightening clothes, and trying their damndest to look as if they hadn't been doing anything more serious than taking fresh cookies from the jar. Seth figured if he had come along fifteen minutes later, he'd have found them both as naked as newborn babes.

The girl didn't stick around to face the intruder. She leaped on her horse and fled back toward Wagner property. Lance, however, waited under the poplars like a man, having recognized Seth and knowing he would have to face him sooner or later.

Seth had a hard time keeping a straight face when he stopped his horse next to Lance. On the other hand, the boy's face was as red as if he'd been riding all day in the sun without his hat.

"Thought Sonny assigned you to keep an eye on the fence," Seth said.

Lance glanced at the fence. "I was."

Seth nodded. "I see you were—in a manner of speaking."

Lance's gaze dropped sheepishly to his boot toes.

"I didn't think Sonny was supposed to send anybody out alone," Seth continued. "But then, I guess you weren't alone."

Lance clearly didn't know what to say in his defense. Seth finally felt sorry for him, mainly because he remembered what it had been like to be sixteen and just learning about the opposite sex.

"Get your horse," he finally said. "You can ride back to the ranch with me."

Lance welcomed the reprieve from the interrogation and gladly obeyed. They started back to the ranch on a leisurely walk. Lance kept his eyes straight ahead and his hat pulled down low on his forehead to further shadow the embarrassment still lurking in his eyes.

"So . . . wedding bells are going to be ringing pretty soon." Seth looked out across the rolling hills. "You know, I don't think I've ever been to a wedding. I saw one once, but I wasn't invited."

Lance's head came up with a snap, as if it had been attached to a puppeteer's string. His expression was clearly panicstricken. "There isn't going to be a wedding, Sackett. I'm too young to get married."

Seth shrugged. "Maybe you are, but from what I saw of that girl, she isn't. Shapely young woman. Yes, indeed."

Lance looked sheepishly back to his horse's ears. "She's three years older than me. So I reckon she does want to get married. At least she talks about it a lot."

"To you?"

"You mean marrying me?"

Seth nodded.

"Yeah," Lance replied quietly. "To me."

"But you're not ready?"

"No, not really. I'd like to wait a couple of years."

"Lance." Seth's tone took on a serious note. "I would think you've been around cows and bulls enough in your young life to know how calves come about."

"Well, of course." Lance was clearly insulted that his intelligence about the birds and the bees would be questioned.

"I hate to have to be the one to tell you this," Seth continued, "but it sort of works the same way with people."

"I know that." Again Lance was clearly insulted.

"Just thought I'd clarify it because you looked to be getting real close to making yourself a father."

"Don't tell me you ain't fooled around," Lance's tone turned defensive.

"Sure. A lot. But not with women who ever wanted to marry me, or even expected me to. And certainly not with pretty young girls with stars in their eyes. And never with a woman whose daddy would have come after me with the shotgun."

"Then who did you do it with?"

"Whores mostly."

"Oh."

"Course, now, maybe you'd be perfectly happy spending your life with that girl." Seth shrugged again as if it really didn't make any difference to him. "I wouldn't want to interfere with that."

Lance was quiet, his eyes evasive.

"Sometimes a man doesn't really know if what he's found is what he truly wants to keep," Seth added. "I wouldn't have recognized quality, or even true love, when I was your age. A pretty face, a tender touch, and some sweet words are all it takes to blind a man, especially an inexperienced man. You have to ask yourself if she's a woman you'd want to wake up facing every morning for the rest of your life. A woman you would be able to talk to and not just make love to.

"And you shouldn't take a good woman lightly," he continued. "If you get her in the family way, you'd better be prepared to honor your responsibility to her and your baby. It's a hard row in this world for women and babies. They depend a lot on men since most can't get decent jobs to support themselves."

"Well, she doesn't tell me no."

"Why should she? Women like making love just as much as men. She probably just assumes that if she gets with child, you'll do the honorable thing by marrying her."

"I see your point, Sackett," Lance said quietly. "Maybe I'd better slow down a bit. Just see her at dances and things like that."

"Might not be a bad idea. By the way, have you been practicing what I taught you so far with that gun?"

Lance's face brightened. "Sure have. Want to see?"

Seth pulled rein. "Here's as good a place as any."

Lance jumped to the ground with the agility of youth. Seth smiled, figuring the Wagner girl had pretty much been forgotten for the moment. As for himself, his own thoughts drifted to Maggie and all those words of advice he'd just spouted off to her son. It was ironic how advice was never quite as sound when it involved your own heart.

Chapter Fourteen

From the looks of the two long tables, spread with white tablecloths and food, Maggie was turning Sunday dinner into a camp meeting. And, of course, all the heathens had been invited. Including him.

Seth sat on a block of wood outside the tack building and put the last few dabs of polish on his boots. He'd had enough preaching to last a lifetime, but he couldn't gracefully get out of this one. All the hands were invited and planned on going. Most figured they could suffer through a dose of religion if it meant getting a chance at somebody's cooking besides Cookie's. Already the smells of fried chicken were drifting out across the yard, making the men hurry over to the lawn in front of the big house.

Seth put his shoe polish away and pulled his boots on. His stomach knotted. He wanted to see Maggie, be close to her again. He had done nothing but think about the time spent alone with her in the line shack and dreaming it had gone further than it had. If it wasn't for Maggie, he would have just forked his horse and rode out on the range alone. He would have had his own talk with God. He never had been one who felt like he had to go through some sanctimonious interpreter who thought that just because he had elected to shout words from the Bible he was somehow closer to a crown of jewels than anybody else. Besides, once the preacher found out who and what Seth was, he'd drop anything else he had planned and set out on a one-man, one-hour crusade to save Seth Sackett.

But Seth could deal with preachers. Mainly because he knew there weren't any of them who weren't without sin themselves. No, the person it had irritated him even more to see pull up in his fancy rig an hour ago wasn't the preacher, but Cleve Williams. He'd been inside with Maggie all this while. When he wasn't there, he was dogging her steps, helping her carry plates, glasses, cups, utensils, and food out to the tables. Seth had overhead him talking to the children, trying to make them think he liked them, but the kids weren't fooled, and neither was Seth. Williams had no time for Maggie Cayton's children. It was something he wondered if the lady rancher was aware of.

She hadn't seemed to mind Cleve's constant companionship, and Seth wondered if she had invited the lily-livered pantywaist or if he'd just shown up. One way or the other, Maggie had had a smile for him every time she'd looked at him. Her laughter had trilled gaily across the yard, reaching Seth's ears and making him wonder what it would be like to see that smile on her face for him. She was dressed to the nines, too. Gone were the plain cotton shirtwaist, the riding skirt, the high-heeled riding boots, the wide-brimmed hat, and the gun. Her hair was piled high on her head with ringlets dangling down the back and curls around her ears and on her forehead, softening the dramatic angles of her face. She wore dainty white, lace-up boots with narrow, angular heels. Her flowered, peach-colored dress was of some sort of gauzelike material that seemed to float around her when she walked. The long sleeves were full. The bodice conformed perfectly to her bosom and swept up to her throat. Her waist looked like the center of an hour glass.

He stood up and looked down at his boots.

"Got 'em shined enough yet, Sackett?" Sonny's taunting voice came from behind him. "No use bothering. Williams is here today. She won't be looking at you."

"Or you, I reckon."

Sonny's humor faded. He apparently liked dishing it out, but didn't like taking it. His gaze traveled to Maggie as she fussed with the corner of the tablecloth that the wind insisted on picking up and tossing over a bowl of rolls.

"You're right about that, Sackett," Sonny continued. "I hate to see her marry that boardwalk stroller. He doesn't care about the White Raven, just how much money he could make off it if it were his."

So Sonny cared about the White Raven. He wasn't a man of emotions and hadn't revealed much about the way he felt on things. "Who says Maggie will marry him? He doesn't really look her type."

"Nobody says so yet, but Williams wants her and

he's working on her, playing the perfect gentle-man."

"You mean he isn't?" Seth had his own opinion of Williams, but he wanted to know Sonny's.

Sonny scoffed. "Williams a gentleman? Hell, no. He's nothing but a snake in the grass. Course Maggie don't know it."

"Maybe you should tell her."

"She wouldn't listen to me. But she'll get tired of running this ranch pretty soon, and what woman could pass up a fancy place in town and a life of leisure?"

"I think you've underestimated Maggie Cayton."

Sonny suddenly seemed to realize he'd spoken quite freely with Seth, and raised his defenses. The foreman's eyes narrowed. "Are you suggesting you know her better than I do? What really went on out in that line shack, Sackett?"

Seth met Sonny's imperious demand without so much as a blink of the eye. "I know for certain now that you don't know Maggie. If you did, you wouldn't jump to the conclusion that just because we were alone she made love to me. She's not that kind of woman, Haig. Much to my regret. And yours, no doubt."

Sonny said nothing, but angry sparks in his eyes, and the clenching of his jaw, told his reaction better than words. And amid the sparks, his jealousy was highly evident. "We might as well get to it," he snapped. "This only happens a few times in the summer—these picnics with the preacher. They're worth it for the vittles. Old man Putnam's wife makes the best fried chicken and biscuits this side of the Rockies."

Sonny started for the front yard on a stride that would make one think he was bracing himself for a brawl in the local saloon. Seth pulled his hat down on his forehead and followed. He had much the same feeling himself.

The preacher was a man by the name of Reverend Mark Franklin. Seth had overheard the men say that he didn't have a congregation. He had started out as a circuit preacher years ago, and he still preached that way. More than just tall and slender, he resembled a willow permanently bent by the force of a continual, unforgiving wind. Seth guessed he spent more time in the saddle than he ever did at dinner tables. But for as frail as he appeared, his eyes revealed inner strength. They were alive with the lust for living, and for giving of the Lord's word. There was one thing missing from those eyes, though. Reverend Franklin had the fire, but the brimstone was missing. The stubborn inclination to stamp out the sin and pride of mankind seemed to be absent. Instead, a light of peace glowed gently around him like a steady flame that never flickers even under the harshest wind.

Maggie seemed almost giddy as she stopped in front of Seth with her arm linked to the Reverend's. "Seth, I'd like you to meet Reverend Franklin. Reverend, Seth Sackett, our newest addition to the ranch."

They exchanged a handshake. There was nothing

soft or gentle about the Reverend's. Seth searched the old man's eyes, as he in turn searched Seth's. They sized each other up in those quick seconds and Seth couldn't help but wonder if the hand clasped in his had beat more than his Bible. The thought had no sooner crossed his mind, though, when it left. Reverend Franklin probably didn't even beat his Bible.

"Mr. Sackett," he was the first to speak. "It's a pleasure to meet you. Maggie tells me your father was a preacher."

Seth suddenly wished he hadn't told Catherine who in turn had told Maggie. Some things were better left alone. Some memories were better left in the past. Seth only nodded to the inquiry, unable to elaborate.

The Reverend seemed to sense the subject was not open for discussion. Gracefully he bridged the uneasy silence. "I certainly hope you'll be able to forestall any more violence in the valley. Your role as peacemaker is very important to Maggie, and I know Trent would have appreciated what you're doing to protect his family and to preserve the home he spent twenty years building. I was very distressed to hear someone had tried to harm Maggie." He looked down at her fondly, like a father would his daughter, patting her hand that still lay resting on his arm. "I presided over Maggie and Trent's marriage and I've blessed all their children. They're like family to me, and I'm very glad you're here to help them in their time of need."

His greeting wasn't what Seth had expected to hear, and he found himself short on a rejoinder. But

Franklin didn't seem to notice. He merely shook Seth's hand again and then left to talk to the others, each in turn. As Seth watched him walk away, on a bit of a limp, he wondered where the private sermon was telling him he was wrong to be wearing a gun on Sunday, wrong to be killing people—even if it was to protect other people. Where was that pious look in his eyes that implied Seth was a lost soul bent for damnation if he didn't repent?

Seth watched Maggie walk away, too, arm in arm with the preacher, being the perfect hostess. Shortly she deposited the Reverend next to Cleve and started back to the house for something else with which to grace the already burgeoning tables.

He sauntered over to the punch bowl and filled one of the fragile, cut-glass cups. There were several of the other hands hanging nervously around the liquid, having nothing better to do. Clements was one of them. The perpetual sneer on his ugly face deepened when he turned his attention to Seth.

"So you've decided to come out of your hole long enough to get some spiritual enlightenment, Sackett? Somehow that comes as a real surprise."

Seth downed the punch and nearly gagged. It was awful. When a man was used to whiskey, watered-down punch came as hard as a blow below the belt. But he supposed glorified dishwater was what one served when the preacher came calling. He wiped his mouth with the back of his hand, hoping to wipe away some of the taste along with it.

"No, Clements," he replied when he was able to speak again. "I came for the food. The Reverend will have his work cut out trying to save you. I doubt he'll even get around to me today."

Clements' face turned red and for a second Seth thought he was going to come over the table at his throat. But suddenly something behind Seth caught Clements' eye and he stalked off, followed by the other two men. Seth turned, empty cup in hand, and saw Maggie approaching, carrying a huge platter heaped with more chicken. Her arms seemed to be straining under the load and she was holding it away from her to avoid touching her dress. He hastened to assist her, and she gratefully relinquished the platter to his strong hands.

"Why, thank you, Seth," she said, slightly out of breath. "It was heavier than it looked."

Indeed it must have been, for he noticed how her bosom, well-defined in the tight-fitting dress bodice, rose and fell from the exertion. "You must have half a dozen chickens piled on this platter, Maggie," he said. "Is the Reverend going to put some away for a rainy day?"

"He always takes some with him," she admitted. "But I don't mind. The poor man doesn't think about his stomach until his big intestines start gnawing on his little ones. He has a tendency to wait for God to provide."

Seth chuckled. "Yes, and God always provides. I remember as a boy hearing His voice booming from the heavens, saying, 'Seth Sackett, your father is away spreading the Word. If you want to eat, you'll have to go out in the woods and kill a rabbit.' My mother was always abundantly grateful and she'd cook it up with some potatoes she'd grown, or maybe some other vegetable. Then the old man would come in and sit down, bow his head and thank God for putting the food there. He never thanked me, never thanked my mother. He only thanked God. And it looks as if Reverend Franklin can say thanks to God, too, in his roundabout way, via the generosity of Maggie Cayton."

Maggie laughed. The sparkle in her eyes made Seth slightly weak in the knees. Only moments before he'd wished she would look at him the way she had Williams, and miraculously his wish had come true.

"Maybe Franklin's right after all," Seth said softly. "Maybe God does provide—in His round-about way."

He set the platter on the table, aware of several of the men watching them, including Haig, Williams, and Clements.

But Maggie didn't seem to notice, or if she did, she didn't care. "Thank you for joining us today, Seth."

"Did you think I wouldn't?"

Her smile slipped a fraction of an inch, but it was her eyes that changed the most. They probed his much too deeply, in a pondering sort of way. They were the most beautiful eyes he'd ever seen. "No, I guess I didn't, Seth," she said. "After what you said about your father . . ."

She looked away, the topic reminding them both of the small confessions he had shared with her during those tense moments in the line shack.

"Sometimes you can't have the pearl without the sand," he said so softly that only she could hear.

"When I saw you in that dress, I knew that's the way it was going to be for me today."

Color rose in her cheeks, giving her a flushed, girlish look that was very becoming.

"I like your hair that way, too, Maggie," he whispered.

She self-consciously reached up to touch it. "Mother fixed it."

"Talented lady, your mother."

She glanced away, almost like a shy young girl might do when receiving her first compliment from a man. Then, remembering her purpose, or perhaps merely wishing to end the intimate direction of their conversation, she pivoted to the others. "It's time to eat now," she announced. "Please, come and help yourselves."

Maggie's children had set out a few chairs, but most everyone preferred to settle on the lawn, the porch steps, or even the railing around the veranda. Maggie found a place near a huge lilac bush and was quickly joined by Cleve, who, with a flourish, spread a blanket on the ground. It annoyed Seth that Williams was monopolizing her. But there was enough room on that blanket for three, and he would enjoy being a thorn in Williams' side.

He finished filling his plate and was headed to the blanket when he saw Alison sitting by herself beneath the big cottonwood. It was a peculiar tree. It came out of the ground with only the standard trunk but about two feet up it branched out into four separate trunks, leaving an almost flat spot in the middle where she liked to play with her dolls, her cats, and Essie Freeman's children.

She looked so beautifully forlorn in her fancy blue dress with all the layers of ruffles and lace, and he suddenly knew she needed a friend worse than Maggie needed a second suitor.

"Why aren't you in your tree?" he asked, sitting down next to her in the shade.

Her chestnut hair was pulled back from her face and caught at the crown with a ribbon. It fell down to her waist in a mass of gleaming ringlets. When she leaned forward, one wayward ringlet slipped off her shoulder and dangled down into her plate. She didn't seem to notice that the ends were brushing her potato salad like a paintbrush in paint. Glancing at her mother, she said glumly, "I'm not supposed to climb up there with my good dress on. Mother said I'd probably rip it."

"Well, your mother might be right," Seth replied, gently lifting the ringlet out of her food, wiping off the end, and placing it back over her shoulder. "I'll bet she knows from experience."

Alison gave him a bemused look. "Do you think my mother used to climb trees?"

Her innocence delighted him. "I would bet my horse on it. She probably climbs them now and again when nobody's looking."

Alison, not sure whether she should believe such a tall tale, studied her mother from the distance. After a time, she said, "Why does she have to sit with Mr. Williams?"

Maggie wore a wide-brimmed straw hat that concealed most of her face, except the smile she gave to Williams. "If you want to sit by her, Alison, then just go over there."

Alison's face scrunched up with distaste. "I don't like Mr. Williams. He pretends to be nice to me when Mama's nearby, but when she isn't, he grouches at me. He really doesn't like me. I wish he would quit coming around."

Seth picked up a chicken leg even though looking at Maggie with Williams killed any desire for eating. He'd never felt possessive of any woman before he'd met her. If he could get one to his bed that's all he'd ever cared about. Where she went afterwards, and with whom, had never concerned him. But Maggie Cayton was different.

"That makes two of us, Alison."

"You don't like him either?" she looked up at him with surprise in her eyes.

He grinned at her. "He grouches at me, too."

She laughed and seemed to feel a lot better after that. She dove into her food with renewed gusto.

"Do you mind if I join you and Alison, Mr. Sackett?"

Seth looked up to see Reverend Franklin, standing hunch-shouldered over him with a friendly and expectant look on his face. So the preacher had pin-pointed the sinner in the crowd was now going to take on the impossible task of soul-saving? Seth supposed it should have irritated him, but it didn't. His image of the preacher would have been shattered if he had done anything else. And, in all honesty, there was something about the old man that made it difficult to dislike him. But despite it, Seth couldn't quite keep the cynicism from his voice.

"Be our guest, Reverend. Where else can you find innocence and iniquity both in one place?"

The Reverend shot him a surprised, almost puzzled look, but he said nothing. He folded his long skinny legs and lowered himself to the ground, his joints creaking and popping as he did.

"The ground's hard, Reverend," Seth pointed out. "Maybe you should have pulled up a chair."

Franklin shook his head vigorously. "Oh, no. No, I'm more comfortable in the place where I spend most of my time."

Then he bowed his head and said a silent prayer over his plate of food. He spent the next few minutes engulfing what was on the plate, commenting only that Mrs. Putnam was an excellent cook and if he didn't watch himself, he could much too easily become a worshipper of her cuisine.

Alison finished her meal and hurried away, bored with sitting in one place too long. Seth had hoped she would have stayed. He hadn't wanted to give the Reverend any opportunity to open up on him with his sanctimonious recriminations. He could leave, too, of course, but at the same time he had a curiosity about Franklin. He wanted to see what made him different than Ezra Sackett, or if his kindness was merely an illusion.

Finally the Reverend's fork slowed and he lifted his eyes from his plate. The distant Big Horn Mountains, still snow-capped, caught his attention. "I would hate to see Maggie lose this place," he said pensively. "I really hope you can prevent it from happening."

Franklin was constantly spewing words that were

the least expected. But he was a man Seth soon found he could talk to, as if there was a silent understanding between them. "Funny you would say that, Reverend. You're the only one who hasn't asked me to talk her into selling. I'm surprised you'd condone a battle of any sort. I figured you had come over here to preach to me about the sins of my profession."

Reverend's eyes lifted to his. "Why? Because I'm a man of God? What *is* a man of God, Seth?"

"I don't know, Reverend. I've tried to figure that one out for years," he said solemnly.

"Well, I'll tell you what I think. If it's a man who goes to church every Sunday, then I'm not. I haven't been in a church for years. The sky is my stainglassed chapel. I'm closer to God right here on this good earth. And it keeps me from getting too righteous when I have to brush dirt off the seat of my pants and wring my clothes out after getting drenched in a rainstorm. It puts me a lot closer to God, and the closer I am to Him, the farther I am from the ways of people who can sometimes get pious in their thinking.

"Now, this war with Ben Tate has me perplexed, though," he changed the subject with barely taking a breath, as if there was a correlation between topics. "Tate's a hard man and he can be unyielding, but I just find it difficult to believe he would resort to violence. I believe even less that he killed Trent. They were actually quite good friends in years past."

"People are oftentimes not what they appear to be, Reverend."

Franklin studied him with keen perception. "Do *you* think he's guilty?"

Seth stirred the baked beans around on his plate. "I don't believe Ben Tate is a ruthless man, but I do know that sometimes people will do things they normally wouldn't if they're put in a bad situation."

The old man's eyes lifted and locked with Seth's in a deep, understanding way. "Yes, you're right. Sometimes a man—or a woman—has to do battle to protect themselves and their families, their beliefs. And I realize that sometimes it means taking another life. I remember one time I ran into a small group of renegade Blackfeet Indians that wanted my scalp. I don't know how I survived, but I did. I killed them all.

"Now, I'm a god-fearing man, Seth, but I'm also a realist. It's not for me to condemn another person's actions, or what drove him to do an ungodly thing. It's only for me to show him the way to the Lord so he can ask forgiveness and be able to live in peace. But then, I'm sure you know that, your father being a preacher and all."

Seth released a bitter laugh. "Forgiveness was never a topic of my father's sermons. And I heard them, every one, every Sunday for seventeen years. I would have slept through a few of them, but he had a voice that carried all the way to heaven—or to hell—and it was impossible to get much rest. I even tried crawling under the church pews when I was real little, but I always paid for it when we got home."

Franklin gave him a quizzical look, but almost instantly seemed to understand the bitterness that had laced his words and turned his eyes cold. He looked over at the mountains again in a contemplative way. Then he shook aside his musings and started to rise. His bones creaked again. When he was to his feet, he shook Seth's hand again.

"I don't profess to have all the answers, Seth, but I do know one thing," he added. "God has his way of righting wrongs. Now . . . I guess I'll mingle." He grinned, as if that idea amused him. "Take care of Maggie. Maybe I'll see you the next time I come around."

Seth shook Franklin's proffered hand. Their gazes locked with unspoken understanding. Franklin's beliefs took on a balance of right and wrong, and like life, there were shades of gray. It was a concept Ezra Sackett had never been able to see in his demand for perfection.

Seth watched the Reverend walk away, stopping and talking with the other hands. Just chatting, dropping words of wisdom and bits of God's message as he went. He was a little like Jesus, Seth supposed, telling parables, only using situations that a bunch of rough-necked cowboys could relate to. Perhaps that was his secret to success. Whatever it was, he had left Seth feeling strangely at peace, a feeling he never had when he had been around his father.

Shortly Dorothy Putnam, the cook, brought a big pot of coffee from the house. Seth sauntered over with some of the other men, having long since given up on the punch.

"I see the Reverend tried to reform you, Sackett. Did he have any luck?"

Seth turned to face Cleve Williams. The business-man had joined the hired hands for a cup of coffee. Maggie was still sitting on the blanket, helping Alison with what appeared to be a knot that had formed in her doll's pinafore.

"And I see you're still trying to reform Maggie," he countered. "Any luck?"

Williams didn't like the correlation, or how Seth had so easily turned the tables to him. "Maggie is a friend, Sackett. I won't deny I'm interested in her. It's been a year since Trent was killed, it's time she got out and started having fun again, started thinking about marriage again."

They watched Maggie hand the doll back to Alison, giving her a kiss and a hug as she did. The girl skipped away and Maggie rose to her feet, starting toward him and Cleve. He felt his heart begin to hammer. "A woman like Maggie doesn't need to marry for the sake of marrying, Williams. And she surely doesn't need to have a man take care of her. If she remarries, it'll be for love. I suspect that'll leave you out of the running."

"What makes you so sure of that, Sackett?"

"I'm getting to know Maggie quite well, living here with her," he said, trying to goad Williams with the potentially intimate arrangement. "She's being polite to you, that's all."

Williams' face tightened, but Maggie joined them at that moment, cutting off any retort he had hoped to make. He turned to Maggie, forcing a smile despite his irritation at Seth. "Can I get you something? Some more punch perhaps?"

Maggie shifted uneasily when Cleve's arm went

around her waist. She stepped closer to the table, beyond his reach. Gathering up the punch ladle, she stirred the bowl's contents as if suddenly very interested in it. "Oh, I don't think so, Cleve," she replied. "It seems a little weak. Natalie made it and I suppose I should have supervised her closer."

"Nonsense!" Cleve exclaimed. "It's wonderful. Tell Natalie she'll make some young man a fine wife someday."

"I'm sure she'll love to hear that, since marriage and the upcoming barn dance are all she seems to think about."

"Speaking of the dance, Maggie," Cleve put in with the most convincing smile he could muster. "I had hoped you would do me the honor of allowing me to be your escort."

Seth didn't miss Maggie's hesitation, nor the faint look of desperation that leaped into her eyes, that look of a woman groping for an excuse to say no. Williams had been completely without manners to ask her in front of everyone, unless he'd done it intentionally to put her on the spot.

"Come now, Maggie." Cleve saw her hesitation and hastened on. "Trent's been gone a year. You really should get out and start living again."

"I believe that's not the reason for Maggie's reluctance in giving you an answer," Seth cut in. "I'm sure she intended to tell you eventually, but she has already arranged for me to be her escort."

Williams looked as if he'd been struck. There was a heavy silence for several seconds before he managed to recover from his shock, but he quickly tried to pretend it didn't bother him overly much that she had accepted an invitation from someone other than himself. "I see. Well, I'm glad to hear you at least have decided to go. That's a step in the right direction to getting on with your life. You will save me a dance or two?"

"Oh, of course."

"Good. Now, if you'll excuse me, I need to pay my respects to the Reverend before I go."

As soon as Cleve was gone, Maggie casually took Seth by the arm and escorted him beyond the earshot of the men. But when she turned to him, it was with a choked whisper of dismay. "How dare you put me in such a position, Seth Sackett!"

He placed a hand on his chest in mock innocence. "Me? I think it was Williams who put you on the spot. Besides, I didn't hear you denying it."

"I was too . . . stunned."

"I was only trying to give you an easy way out of a situation that you clearly didn't want to get into," he expounded. "I thought I was saving you from a fate worse than death."

"By going with you?"

"Well, every man has his own idea of what could be worse than death. Besides, you wouldn't want Williams to take you for granted, would you? An easy quest is usually an empty quest. He'd take advantage of you and then probably decide you'd been too easy and then he'd go looking elsewhere after he'd tarnished your halo."

"And you would never dream of doing a thing like that, would you?" Her lips curved facetiously.

He shrugged. "The difference between me and Williams is that you know I would, but you probably think he wouldn't—him being a 'gentleman' and all."

Humoring him now, Maggie merely shook her head and started to walk away.

"By the way," he called after her.

She looked over her shoulder at him with eyes as green as an Ireland pasture, and the anger had gone from them, even though she still pretended to be irritated. "What now, Mr. Sackett?"

He grinned. "Despite what Williams says, the punch tastes like dishwater. Just thought you ought to know."

Chapter Fifteen

The house had been quiet for over an hour and still Maggie couldn't sleep. Tired of tossing and turning, she had finally resorted to pacing the braided rug. It was the day's events that had kept her wound up— that and Seth Sackett's assuming declaration that he was going to be her escort to the barn dance. Why hadn't she just laughed in his face and shamed him in front of everybody? What had ever possessed her to go along with it? As it was, Cleve hadn't spoken to her again until it had been time for him to go. Then he'd given her a rather curt goodbye. Not that she was overly troubled to have fallen out of favor with him. She had begun to dread his attentions. Was that the real reason why she had gone along with Seth? Or was there more to it than that?

She moved to the window and lifted the curtain. The light still shone in the tack building. She could envision him lying on his cot, shirt unbuttoned, reading another of her mother's novels. She could also envision herself in his arms, dancing.

She released the curtain and resumed pacing.

Eventually she found herself in front of the armoire, pulling the doors open. What did she have that she could possibly wear to the dance? It was only two weeks away. She didn't have time to have something sewn, although she was sure her mother could whip up a creation if she asked her to. Her mother was as nimble with the needle as a leprechaun was with an Irish trick. But did she want to draw attention to the fact that she was going with Seth? Make it look as if she were a giddy young girl, like Natalie, who had to have the perfect dress to impress her beau?

She pulled first one dress out and then another. The pink one was too tight in the bodice, the green too large in the hips, the silk plum too fancy, the red unbecoming with her complexion, the blue—ah, the blue. It was beautiful, and it had been Trent's favorite. He had given it to her just weeks before he'd died. She had never even worn it.

Immediately she placed it back in the armoire. It reminded her too much of Trent. Reminded her that she shouldn't feel this excitement about going to the dance with Seth, about being in his arms for a waltz, or two.

She pulled her wrapper over her nightgown. With lamp in hand, she left her room. A cup of hot milk might help to settle her jitters so she could sleep. She'd add a little chocolate to it, and in no time at all she would forget about Seth and the dance and what she was going to wear. She would just wear the same thing she wore today. The peach-colored dress. She didn't need something new to impress him with. Besides, he had said he liked it.

In the kitchen, she put some more dry wood in the cookstove and soon had the few remaining coals blazing. She sat at the table while the milk heated. She tried to think of other things; of the cattle, the ranch, the poisoned water. Of Trent and what they had shared. They had often come into the kitchen at night together and shared a late-night snack. Then they'd returned to their room and made gentle but passionate love.

A tap at the back door put her heart in her throat. Who, besides herself, could be up at this time of night? Was it one of Tate's men here to try to kill her again?

She gathered up a knife from off the counter and cautiously moved to the door. "Who is it?"

A husky male voice replied, "Just me, Maggie. Seth."

She had barely breathed a sigh of relief, when her heart began hammering again. Why was he here?

As if he'd read her mind, he spoke from the other side of the door again. "I saw the light. I hoped it might be you. I need to talk to you. May I come in?"

"Can't it wait until morning, Seth? I . . . I'm in my nightclothes."

There was a lengthy silence, then, "I don't mind that you're in your nightclothes."

No, she supposed a man like Seth Sackett wouldn't mind at all. He'd probably seen women in every form of dress and undress imaginable. "Perhaps you don't mind, Seth, but I do."

"Well, I guess it'll wait until morning. Night, Maggie."

Suddenly she panicked. She hadn't thought he

would back down so easily. She didn't want him to leave. She didn't want to be left alone to think about him. Better to have him with her in the flesh. It was more dangerous, true, but infinitely better.

Hastily she unlocked the door and pulled it open. The light from the kitchen barely spilled out into the darkness, but it was enough for her to fully appreciate his tall silhouette swathed in undeniable virility.

"Seth . . . wait."

He turned back, but by the way his gaze slid over her, as if enraptured, she suddenly realized the light behind her had outlined her body beneath the flowing wrapper and thin gown. She stepped in front of the door and pulled it partially closed to block off the light.

"Change your mind?" he asked softly.

"We might as well talk," she added as explanation. "It seems neither of us can sleep. Please, come in. I was just making some warm milk. Would you like some? It's supposed to help make a person drowsy."

He paused on the stoop. "Oh, I'll pass. But I'd make myself a hot toddy if you had some whiskey."

"I . . . think I could find some."

Maggie allowed him to come in, all the while wondering at her own foolishness. She found the bottle of whiskey in the cupboard where Trent had kept it. No one had touched it since his death and it had collected a glaze of dust. Maggie couldn't reach it because it was on the top shelf, but Seth reached over her head and easily plucked it from its perch. For a moment his nearness was like a liquor all its own, sweetly intoxicating. Her gaze slid to his lips, and his to hers. The clock chimed noisily from the distant foyer, sounding loudly in the quiet house, jarring their wayward thoughts.

"Got a glass?" he whispered, as if he didn't want to disturb the quietness or possibly wake the house's sleeping occupants.

Maggie opened another cupboard door and allowed him to take his pick. Her milk was warm so she mixed cocoa and sugar with it while he poured his whiskey.

"I thought you were going to have a toddy," she said, eyeing the amber liquid in the bottom of the glass just before he tossed it down his throat, as if he needed it badly. That puzzled her, because Seth Sackett wasn't a drinking man.

"I decided it was too much trouble," he replied.

He watched her pour the cocoa mixture from the pan to her cup. "There was something you wanted to talk to me about?" she prodded.

He leaned back in the chair and folded his arms over his chest, suddenly looking unusually uneasy. "Well, yeah. There was one minor little thing I forgot to mention when I asked you to Dugan's barn dance."

Her guard came up, along with an inquisitive eyebrow. "Oh, and what was that?"

His right shoulder lifted in a feeble shrug and he avoided meeting her probing gaze. "It's nothing too major, Maggie. It's just that I . . . well, I don't know how to dance."

For a moment she wasn't sure she'd heard correctly. Then she had the sudden urge to burst out laughing. He'd asked her to the dance and he didn't even know how? What had he thought he was going to do? Drop bullets at people's feet to get them to step higher during the Virginia reel? But the look on his face was so serious that she knew if she even so much as chuckled at the mess he'd gotten himself into it would undoubtedly shatter his pride. And Seth Sackett had a lot of pride. Judging from his almost sheepish behavior, it had probably taken considerable nerve just to come to her tonight and admit the truth.

"Well, I'm glad you told me about this before the dance, Seth." She managed to keep a straight face. "You know I won't hold you to going if you don't want to."

He had been looking at the ceiling and leaning back on his chair with the front legs off the floor, but suddenly he lowered the chair back to the floor and looked her directly in the eye.

"Why, so you can go with Williams?"

She was taken aback by his sudden irritation. "No, the thought hadn't entered my mind. I just thought you were here to tell me you had changed your mind . . . in light of the circumstances."

"I haven't changed my mind, Maggie. I still intend on going to the dance—with you. Dancing can't be all that hard. You can teach me."

She stared at him in dismay. "Teach you?"

He nodded.

"But I don't have any music, Seth."

"Sing a song." He started to rise.

"Do you mean, right now?"

"Why not? We're alone. Nobody will see us."

"I can't sing."

"Can you hum?"

"Can you?"

"I'm afraid I don't know any songs."

Maggie was faced with a challenge quite unlike any she had ever had before. Here was Seth Sackett, one of the country's most notorious gunfighters, and he wanted her to teach him how to dance, overnight. Literally overnight. She felt a twinge of pity for him that he was thirty-five, had never danced, and didn't even know the tune to any songs. But, sympathy or not, if word got out about a clandestine midnight dancing lesson—with her in her nightclothes, no less—her reputation would be ruined forever, maybe even longer.

"I can't, Seth." She went to the door and pulled it open, blatantly showing him the way out. "Perhaps we could meet tomorrow night, say about eight?"

He closed the distance separating them. His hand circled her wrist and he drew her toward him, so close in fact she could feel the heat of his body through her thin cotton gown and wrapper.

"If I come tomorrow night at eight," he whispered close to her ear. "I'd have an audience, and I don't want an audience. A man has his pride, Maggie. Teach me now. Tonight."

He placed his arm at her waist and gathered her hand in his, drawing her into the dance position. He was uncomfortably out of his element, and yet he seemed determined to make himself as proficient at dancing as he was at drawing a gun.

His eyes, the color of pewter clouds on a calm winter day, drifted down to meet hers like lazy, mesmerizing snowflakes. And they were almost pleading. She had asked a lot of him when she'd hired him, and he had given a lot of himself during her convalescence. Now he wanted just one small favor in return. Could she turn him down? And could she truly deny the overwhelming need to be in his arms, to be with him just a little while longer? Surely no one would find out. How could they?

Ultimately, she capitulated. "All right, but let's go to the family parlor. There's more floor space there."

It seemed he released her with some reluctance, almost as if he thought she might change her mind once free of his arms. But she gathered the lamp and led the way into the other room. She deposited their only light source on a small round table in the corner. The pale golden glow gave the room an undeniably romantic atmosphere, or possibly it was only her own mind that made it so.

With heart hammering almost loud enough to hear, she turned once again to Seth. Her gaze fell critically on the Peacemaker at his hip.

"Is something wrong, Maggie?" he asked.

She lifted her eyes to his. "Oh, nothing, really. I guess I just thought you might want to remove your gun."

It was his turn to hesitate, and she saw the thoughts running through his mind. She knew he felt vulnerable without the gun, even while safely indoors. Truly not keen on the idea, he nevertheless reached down and undid it. In another moment it was on the table next to the lamp.

"Am I ready now?" He was certainly trying to

please her, but for a moment his eyes looked as starkly naked as the hips that had held the gun.

She nodded.

Self-consciously she placed her hand on his shoulder and slid her right hand into his left. He drew her into the dance position. It was only the second time she had willingly touched him, and the fact that he was fully clothed this time did little to diminish the firestorm his nearness created.

"All right. We'll start with a waltz. That's three-quarter time," she glanced up at him to see if he understood. "One, two, three. One, two, three . . ."

He nodded, gravely absorbing it all. She wanted to smile at his seriousness, but to do so might offend him and send him stalking back to his quarters. She didn't want that. Now that she had him in her arms, it felt too good to risk losing him. Besides, he was trusting her, and she couldn't let him down.

"Since you're the man," she continued, "you'll lead—just as soon as you know how. You will start with your right foot—no, your left. I start with my right. Here is the pattern to be followed."

Standing as far from Seth as she possibly could and still remain in dance form, Maggie showed him the foot pattern to be followed, counting slowly as she moved each foot.

"Now, join in."

Time slid away while they counted together and watched their feet move to the three-quarter beat. Seth relaxed. He was none too graceful at first and Maggie's slippered feet took the brunt of his boot toes until, laughing at his clumsiness now, he called an intermission to cast off the offending footgear. In his stocking feet he proceeded more gracefully. After a time he was able to guide her with impressive expertise and even without looking at his feet. His eyes locked with hers in full concentration, and Maggie began to hum her favorite waltz, "Over the Waves."

Natalie didn't know what had woke her, but as she lay in her room, listening, she thought she detected laughter—distant, low-throated male and female laughter. She was momentarily reminded of her father, for she couldn't recall having heard such husky laughter in the middle of the night since her father had died. The memory of it haunted her now, making her realize just how much she missed him. But not only him. She missed the joy he had once brought to the house and the smiles he brought to her mother's face. She hadn't seen her mother smile like that for a year.

She tossed her covers back and pulled on her dressing gown. With lamp in hand, she crept down the stairs to the lower back hall. From there she could see faint light spilling out from the family parlor. The voices of the man and woman were more prominent now, even though spoken in low tones. She couldn't understand the words they said to each other, but she recognized the female voice as definitely that of her mother. And the tones were light. It was not business that was being discussed.

She blew out the light and inched forward. Flattening her back against the wall, she moved closer to the door. It was almost totally dark in the parlor. The only light was the overspill from one lamp on a corner table.

"I'll never be any good at this, Maggie," the man said. "I feel like a walrus out of water."

"You're doing fine. It just takes practice."

Natalie recognized the male voice as Sackett's, but there was something different about it. It was lighter, somehow, sounding younger and not so harsh.

What in the world was her mother doing with Seth Sackett in the parlor in the middle of the night? She peeked her head around the open door to see.

"Now, come on, Seth. You're making great progress. Let's try it again."

"I'm beginning to think this was a stupid idea."

"It was your idea, remember?"

"Yeah, I remember," he remarked dryly.

But Seth would be damned before he would back out of the dance. If he did, then Maggie would go with someone else, probably Cleve. He'd wear blisters on his feet trying to waltz before he'd willingly hand her over to that jackass. And especially not when he'd finally finagled her into his arms. She had relaxed completely and was enjoying herself. Her smile was disarming; her laughter titillating. She was so beautiful, but she was more so when she was happy.

He repositioned his hand on her waist. He could feel her body swaying slightly as she held to the beat she'd been counting. He knew she wore nothing

beneath her nightclothes but a few skimpy underthings, and the erotic thought of it made him instinctively pull her closer.

She stiffened. "Seth, is something wrong?"

Her eyes were expectant when they met his. They
were also his undoing. He fell into their jade green
depths, drowning like a common fool. Lost was the
man who had taken control of his life at the age of
seventeen and who had kept control ever since.

"Yes, Maggie. Everything's wrong. You're here
with me and you shouldn't be."

Maggie sensed his need and started to back away,
but he caught her closer in an embrace of exquisite
tenderness that was almost as persuasive as the tender light in his eyes.

"Don't run from me, Maggie. Not again."

"Let me go, Seth."

Her response was a whisper no louder than his.
He heard but didn't heed. His lips closed over hers
in a hungry kiss, demanding to quench that deep
inner, aching need. And suddenly she felt that need,
too. Her arms went around his neck and she held
him tightly to her. Swept into a whirlwind of passion and desire, her lips parted beneath his. His
tongue darted inside, sating only for a moment that
initial need, then driving it to a higher ecstasy. He
molded her body more fully to his, splaying his
hand on her lower back, drawing her hips to the
urgency pounding in his loins. She could almost feel
it and knew it matched her own.

She knew she should end the madness, the magic,
but she couldn't. She drank fully of his intoxicating
kiss, allowed her hands to explore and memorize the

hard contours of his back, his slim waist, his flat buttocks. His body was wonderfully unfamiliar and yet sinfully comfortable. Then his lips moved from her mouth and grazed the column of her neck, setting a whole new fire coursing through her.

"Stop, Seth. Stop." It was a tortured moan.

"Say it like you mean it, Maggie," he whispered. "And then I will."

But she couldn't.

Natalie gripped the door frame in horror. The figures were nearly lost in the darkness of the parlor corner, but she saw enough. Enough. How could her mother betray her father? And with that scum of a gunfighter, no less? How could she preach to Natalie about morals and then succumb to sin herself?

Blinded by tears and rage, Natalie quietly but quickly raced back to her room. She would never forgive her mother for this. Never.

Maggie's breast was deliciously soft beneath Seth's hands even through the obstructive layers of clothing. She strained toward him, pulling him to her. At last he had succeeded in his objective. He had been the one to touch the dormant embers of her desire, and he would be the one to see those embers fanned to flames before he properly put them out. He would make her want him again and again, not just tonight, but until it was time for him to leave. He was good enough for this purpose in her life. That was all he could expect, all he could ask.

He held her lips in a hungry kiss while releasing the buttons down the front of her gown. When his hand moved over her breast again, he heard and felt her sharp intake of air and her fingers digging urgently into his back. He released more buttons and followed the advancing opening with his lips, past her neck and collarbone, to the valley of her cleavage, until at last his mouth closed over the honeyed pertness of a nipple.

With his other hand he lifted the hem of her gown, feeling the heat of her thigh brand his palm. She pressed closer. He sensed she was like dynamite, ready to explode.

He reached down to release the buttons on his pants. It was only then that she stumbled from the wonderful dream they had both fallen into, crying denial and pushing him away. "No, Seth. We . . . can't."

He considered continuing regardless of her words, for he sensed her words were not her true wishes. With persuasion he would have her back where he wanted her. But was this truly where he wanted her, on the fancy Oriental rug in the parlor? No, it wasn't the proper place for his union with Maggie Cayton.

He released the breath he'd been holding and ran a hand through his hair. In the faint light he saw her hastily button her gown with shaking hands. The hem had already fallen back to the floor without his hand to hold it up past her shapely thighs.

"I'm sorry," she managed. "I shouldn't have led you on. I . . . don't love you."

He leaned against an unidentified piece of furniture. He wasn't surprised that she didn't love him. But he *did* love her. Crazy fool that he was, he'd allowed himself to lose his heart for the first time in his life, and to a woman who would never see him as anything more than a vindicator. He hadn't expected it to happen, but his heart had taken its own course and he had had no choice but to follow.

She seemed to think she needed to give him a further explanation as she fumbled with the last button on her gown, the one up high beneath her chin. "I can't do this with a man I'm not married to, Seth."

"And you'd never marry a man like me, would you, Maggie? I suppose Cleve Williams would fit the bill considerably better. Or even Sonny."

Surprise, hurt, and confusion filled her eyes. She whirled away.

"I guess this means the dance lesson is over," he said, groping for level ground and finding it when he returned his gun belt to his hip.

Maggie found the corner of the table and gripped it as if to support herself. She seemed as visibly shaken as he felt. "Please, Seth, don't make this more difficult."

He walked past her to the kitchen, needing to put some distance between them. While he put his boots on, he heard her leave the parlor by the other door and take the stairs to her room.

He left the house, his heart turned completely upside down by the storm of temptation she had created. It was temptation for more than just sex; it was temptation for life and love, a family and all those things he so desperately wanted but that had eluded him all these years, and all because of who and what he was.

With an angry twist of his hand, he locked the door to the tack building. He released the gun belt from his hip and tossed it on the cot. He joined it a moment later, feeling suddenly very tired. He couldn't even manage to remove his boots a second time.

He was a fool to think he could have a woman like Maggie Cayton. He wasn't worthy of her and she knew it. Now, if he could just get it through his own thick head. When he'd met her he had thought that just making her come to his bed would be enough, but now he knew it wasn't. It was an empty goal that would only get emptier when completed. He wasn't angry at Maggie Cayton for turning him down. No, he was angry at himself for being so foolish as to think he could dream of having what other men had.

He was a man whose life and past would never be acceptable to someone like her. He couldn't even see himself settling down, so why had he made that stupid comment about marriage? He'd lived by the gun too long and it was the only way for him now. He had seen too much and done too much. She would never understand what was in his mind, or accept what was in his past.

But he had enjoyed those light-hearted moments in her arms more than he had anything he could recall. His life had been filled with struggling for survival, with one battle after another. If not a physical battle then a mental one. Maggie Cayton had, for a few moments tonight, made him forget all that. He'd forgotten for a time just who he was. He'd lost himself in something as simple as a three-quarter beat.

Chapter Sixteen

You're late, boy.

I know, Pa. Melinda's father's buggy lost a wheel and I had to fix it.

From the looks of your Sunday clothes, I see you've been down in the grass and the dirt, boy, but I daresay it wasn't to change a wheel on Brother Taylor's buggy. You had that girl down in the grass with you, didn't you? How many times have I told you that you only do that sort of thing with whores, or with your wife. The rest of the time it's the most vile sin the devil ever concocted, but he made it the most pleasurable to tempt the weakness in a man. You've got to be stronger than that, Seth. But then, how could you be, when your seed is the devil's own?

I didn't so much as kiss Melinda, Pa. All we did was touch hands while we were doing the square dance.

Dancing is evil, boy, no matter what kind you do. It's the forerunner of sexual intercourse. I've told you that before. I didn't want to let you go to that dance tonight, but I thought I would see if I could trust you.

I might of known I couldn't. Now, take off your shirt. You'll get your due now.

I didn't touch her. Why don't you ask her father tomorrow about the buggy if you don't believe me?

Because you probably told him the same thing you told me, and he's probably gullible enough to believe you. You're good at lying, boy. Sometimes even I can't tell the difference. I suppose you think you'll get that girl to marry you, won't you? Well, she's too good for the likes of you. You might be my son, but you're not worthy of a girl like that until you can stand before God without shame.

It was only a square dance, Pa. I wasn't even thinking about marrying her.

That doesn't surprise me. You just thought you'd bed her and leave her with a bastard child, didn't you? I might of known that's how your mind would work. Now, take off the shirt. Your mother put too much work into it to ruin it.

Seth came awake, upright in bed, startled from sleep as he so often was. His flesh felt vulnerable and cold as it awaited the fiery heat of the whip. He tasted the blood. With each lash that blazed across his back, splitting flesh, he had tasted the blood in his mouth from biting down so hard on his lip. Now, even in his sleep, he'd bit into his lip. He wiped it away with his hand. It was too dark to see how bad it was. He supposed it would quit soon enough.

He continued to wipe at it until it stopped, then he rummaged in the darkness in his saddlebags and, by feel alone, found the tin of salve Maggie had loaned him. He applied it to his cut lip and stretched

back out on the cot. He wondered if he would ever
be able to walk out of the shadow left by his father.
For years now he'd tried to find a balance between
right and wrong, between Heaven and Hell. When
he thought he was beginning to see things in the
proper perspective, as he had today after talking
with the Reverend Franklin, the shadow would return, bigger and deeper and darker than ever
before.

You only do that with whores, Seth.

And he had. Even the "ladies" he had bedded
were whores at heart. Who then did he think he was
to be wanting to make love to Maggie Cayton?

He fumbled in the darkness again until he found
his cigarettes on the wooden crate next to the bed.
The match briefly lit his rustic quarters, then only
the sulphur smell of it remained along with the
smoke. He inhaled deeply, relaxing and relieving his
mind of the memories. But ten minutes after the
cigarette had been snuffed out in the ashtray, he
caught another whiff of smoke. Only this time it
wasn't the smell of burning tobacco. It was wood.

He came off the bed and lit the kerosene lamp. Its
pale glow found a curl of smoke slipping in under
the rear wall of the tack building. He placed a hand
to the wall and pulled it back when he felt the heat.
Yanking on his boots and grabbing up the remainder of his belongings, he started for the door only to
find that although the handle turned, the door,
which opened outward, wouldn't budge. It behaved
as if something was blocking it from the other side.

He hastened to the window and lifted it. But this
exit too was blocked by wooden shutters that had

been closed and latched from the outside. He reached for the axe in the corner only to find it was suddenly missing.

Smoke boiled in now from the rear wall, making it difficult to breath. At this rate he wouldn't die from the fire, but rather from the smoke in his lungs.

Calculating the distance between his head and the low rafters, he lifted his arms and jumped, grabbing a beam. Getting a good grip, he drew his knees up and back then thrust out with his feet, breaking all the glass out of the window and hammering the shutters like a battering ram. One piece of wood splintered, then another and another, until finally the old, one-inch lumber gave way. With the flames eating their way through the rear wall, he threw his possessions out into the night and dove after them head first. Up on his feet in another instant, he ran to the bunkhouse and burst through the door.

"Everybody up! The tack shed's on fire! In the back! Get out there fast!"

He didn't wait for them but hurried back to the main door of the burning building. It had been barricaded with an anvil from the smithy. He was trying to drag it away when another pair of hands joined in. Clements. Between the two of them they got the anvil out of the way then hurried inside through the cloud of smoke to save what they could of the saddles and tack. The other men rushed to the rear of the building and began beating out the fire with blankets, coats, anything they could find. Shortly they had it put out. Covered with sweat and soot, they came around to the front of the building again where Seth and Clements were hauling the last of the tack into the yard.

Wearing an angry scowl, Sonny strode up to Seth. "What in the hell were you doing, Sackett? Smoking in bed?"

Clements was standing next to Seth, trying to cough the smoke out of his lungs. "He wasn't smoking, you stupid jackass," he managed with a strangled voice. "Somebody set that place on fire trying to kill him! Look at that anvil over there. It took the two of us to get it away from that door! The shutters were even nailed shut."

Sonny glanced apprehensively from the anvil, to the broken shutters, to Seth. "So somebody wants you dead?" His top lip curled disdainfully. "Well, I doubt it's the first time. But Maggie isn't going to be happy when she finds out that because of you she almost lost hundreds of dollars worth of saddles and harnesses, as well as another building. It seems your presence here might be jeopardizing all of our lives."

At that moment, they heard running feet and turned to see Maggie, Lance, and Natalie coming from the house. Maggie saw the soot-covered men, the saddles thrown haphazardly in the middle of the yard. Needing no explanation, she ran to the tack building to assess the damage. Sonny followed her.

"We saved it, Maggie," he said, gently taking her by the shoulders and turning her back to the men. "Course we wouldn't have if Sackett hadn't woke up when he did."

From the tone of his voice, and the way his eyes pierced Seth's, Maggie wasn't sure if he appreciated that fact or was irritated by it. Confused by the intense undercurrents between the two men, she took in the lacerations on Seth's bare chest, the blood angling downward toward the waistband of his pants. Her first inclination was to go to him, to comfort him for the pain he must be feeling. Instead, she held her ground, pretending she hadn't noticed. "What happened, Seth?"

His explanation was brief. When it was over she was unsettled and more than shaken to think that someone had wanted him to die in the fire. Not knowing what to say for fear too much of her heart would show, she turned away from Seth and to the men. "You can go back to bed now," she said, dismissing them.

But the men were still wound up from the excitement, and most were as disturbed as she was that somebody had tried to kill Seth. Barker voiced a concern that was slowly coming to the minds of most of the men. "If somebody wants Sackett dead, then it might not be safe for any of us around here. I, for one, don't want to see him roll out his bedroll in the bunkhouse. What's to stop somebody from boarding *that* up in the middle of the night, too, and setting fire to it?"

Several of the men echoed agreement. Others stood silent, waiting for Maggie to come up with a solution.

Maggie only had to think of the situation and her alternatives for a moment. The men were right, of course, but she still needed Seth. Tate wasn't backing down. Tate—or whoever was behind this. What if Seth's suspicions were right, and somebody on the White Raven was the guilty party?

She glanced at the anvil again, knowing it had taken the muscle of more than one man to move it. Either that, or someone had tied a rope around it and pulled it in front of the tack building door with their horse. Seth had been at the house for over an hour, so whoever had done it must have waited until he had returned from the house and then given him time to fall asleep so he wouldn't hear anything suspicious. It bothered her that someone knew Seth had been with her, being entertained at the main house. Her gaze slid over the men. She could read nothing duplicitous in any of their eyes.

"I see your concern, Barker," she finally replied. "We'll repair the tack building, but in the meantime we'll have to find a place for Seth to bunk."

She turned back to the house, giving no more information.

"But where's that going to be, Mrs. Cayton?"

She paused, turning sideways to meet Barker's demanding eyes again. "Under the circumstances, I believe it would be best if we didn't advertise the location." She glanced at Seth. "It appears as if you're in need of doctoring again. Lance, would you take care of it?"

Maggie started for the house, not leaving herself open to further discussion, nor waiting for Lance and Seth. She didn't know where she was going to put Seth, but if someone wanted him dead, then it certainly created a problem.

Natalie followed alongside her. "Where are you going to put him, Mother?" she demanded in a hoarse whisper. "You'd better not be thinking of letting him stay in the house."

Maggie was stunned by her daughter's tone of voice that sounded very much like a threat. "And why not? He's not infested with vermin."

"And I suppose you would know first hand, wouldn't you?"

Maggie stopped short. "What's that supposed to mean, young lady?"

Natalie looked at the ground, then up at her mother, belligerently. "When he first came here, you hated his guts."

Maggie supposed she was to blame for Natalie's animosity toward Seth. The girl had always emulated her, both likes and dislikes. She'd picked up on Maggie's opinion of Seth from the first moment, even though Maggie had kept those thoughts to herself.

"I didn't like him at first," she admitted. "But I've been around him enough now to know that he wasn't what I thought he was. It's not right to hate somebody without provocation and I was wrong to judge him."

Natalie's eyes narrowed in stubborn determination just before she ran away to the house. Maggie sighed. The girl was at a very obstinate age and Maggie only hoped she would come around on her own.

"What was that all about, Mother?" Lance asked, as he and Seth came up behind her.

Maggie's eyes were drawn to Seth's brawny chest streaked with blood from the cuts he'd received on the window's broken glass. In one hand he had his saddlebags and shirt. In the other, his Winchester. "Nothing. She's just upset that someone wants us off the White Raven."

She led the way to the kitchen and once again got out the medical supplies. This time, however, she turned the job of repairing Seth's wounds over to Lance and her mother. Catherine had heard the ruckus and hurried downstairs to find out what was going on. Upon her entrance in the kitchen she had taken one look at Seth's bleeding chest and had begun fussing over him like a doting mother cow with her calf. Maggie decided it was just as well. After what had transpired between her and Seth earlier, she didn't think she could touch him again without her feelings being revealed to everyone around her.

Seth and Lance discussed what had happened. Maggie listened and said little. Natalie appeared again, sullen and silent. Maggie told her to go to bed, but she persisted in staying. There was an odd sort of coldness, almost hatred, in her eyes when she looked at Seth. Once Maggie even felt that animosity directed at her. Uneasily, she decided the girl was lingering so she could find out where Seth would be bunking. She'd made no bones about not liking Seth, but since he'd been breaking her horse Maggie thought the girl had taken a softer impression of him.

When the cuts were doctored and bandaged Lance brought up the subject Maggie had been thinking about the entire time. "Well, Mother, where are we going to put Seth until the tack building's repaired?"

Seth stood up and slipped his shirt on. "I'll just sleep outside, Lance. The weather's warm."

Lance's young face filled with apprehension. "After what happened tonight, Seth, I don't think that would be a good idea. Somebody tried to kill you. How do we know it wasn't somebody right here on the White Raven? You might end up with a knife in your back while you sleep."

"Not if nobody knows where I am. I can't risk anybody's life, and Maggie can't afford to lose any more buildings to fire." He shrugged. "It's a chance I'll have to take. Besides, it's almost morning."

"It's been a busy night for you, hasn't it, Mr. Sackett?" Natalie inserted pointedly. "The fire and all."

Maggie tensed. She knew her daughter well enough to know that the behavior she was displaying was not normal. She'd never openly attacked anyone except her siblings and, on occasion, Maggie herself—but then only when engaged in the usual family tiffs. There was a vindictiveness in her eyes now that greatly disturbed Maggie.

Seth nodded, responding kindly to her despite her curtness toward him. "Yes, you could say that, Natalie."

"He'll stay in the guest room," Catherine spoke up, leaving no room for argument.

Seth refused the idea. "Thank you, Mrs. Marshall, but I couldn't do that."

"I insist."

Maggie's eyes lifted to Seth's. She didn't know if she liked the idea of him being just down the hall from her. He turned to the door, seeming to know her thoughts and what her answer would be. After all, he'd once mocked her for not having a room in the big house for him, knowing full well she wouldn't have opened her doors to hired help, especially hired guns.

Perhaps it was because he was so sure of her answer that she surprised him by saying, "I think that's a good idea, Mother. At least until we get the tack building back in order. Will you take care of it, see that he gets settled? There are extra blankets in the linen closet."

Lance volunteered to get the blankets. He left the room followed by Catherine who was always at her best when she had a cause.

Maggie felt Seth's eyes follow her own departure, but she didn't look back, didn't want to hear anything he might have to say about her change of heart, or the chance she was taking having him in the house. It was dangerous, much too dangerous.

When she was gone, Seth found himself alone in the room with Natalie. He thought it odd that she hadn't followed her mother back to bed, but she stood, unmoving, seemingly waiting for this moment when they would be alone. The contempt in her eyes was chilling.

"What is it, Natalie? Is something wrong?"

She lifted her chin defiantly. Her tone was low and threatening. "I want you to leave my mother alone, Sackett. I'm warning you, I'll kill you if you don't."

Seth was as surprised as if she had attacked him with her bare hands. "I didn't know I'd been bothering her."

"You know what I'm talking about. I saw you tonight in the parlor. You can't take my father's place, Sackett. My grandmother might have invited you into our house, but you're not welcome by everybody here. So you just get your job done and leave. Leave the White Raven."

Ugly suspicions began to gnaw inside him. "Did you set that fire tonight, Natalie?"

She gave a bitter laugh, but tears sprang to her eyes. Her bravado was weakening, her rage diminishing to tears. "No, but I wish I had, and I wish it would have killed you!" She ran from the room then like a frightened colt bolting for safety, her nightgown held high above her ankles.

Seth suddenly felt as if he hadn't slept for a month, not just a night. Weariness overwhelmed him. Weariness and defeat.

"There shall be no reward to the evil man; the lamp of the wicked shall be put out."

"Yes, Ezra," he murmured. "But what of the lonely man? What will happen to him?"

Reluctantly he left the kitchen to find his way, unguided, through the house where he was not welcome.

Maggie spent the remaining few hours before dawn in restless tossing and turning. She could think of little else but Seth in the room down the hall. When dawn broke, sunlight speared through the window and found the photo of Trent on the bureau. It had always been a serious pose of him, unsmiling, and now his eyes seemed to be looking to the very soul of her, seeing what was there in her mind; seeing her desire for another man.

It was her own guilt from her wayward thoughts, she knew, that made the photo appear the way it did, but she couldn't bear it. She took the picture and tucked it into a drawer, then she dressed hastily and left the room. Everything in the chamber was a vivid reminder enveloping her in memories of the life she had shared with Trent. A life that was no more and never would be again.

She found the dining room empty, but was immediately relieved she wouldn't have to face Seth after their romantic encounter last night. She could only hope he had gone to eat at the cookshack. And Lance, who seemed to be taking famously to Seth, had probably gone with him. But she didn't mind. Perhaps it would waylay the gossip about where Seth had spent the night.

She wandered into the parlor to see if anyone was there. In the daylight the room was as it always was, but her eyes were haunted by the shadowy images of herself succumbing to Seth's lovemaking there in the corner by the mahogany card table. Tawdry. It had been very tawdry on her part. She was a mature woman with grown children and last night she'd acted like a foolish young girl in love for the first time, sneaking into hidden and dark places to steal kisses. Or worse than that. She had behaved like a whore who had long ago forgotten propriety to satisfy her body's needs.

Hearing Dorothy in the dining room now, she returned to see a pot of coffee on the table. She took a seat and poured herself a cup. Alison came in and slid into her place next to Maggie.

"Good morning, Mama."

Maggie shook her napkin open and spread it out over her lap. "Good morning, Ali. Is it just going to be me and you for breakfast today?"

"I guess. I tried to wake Natalie, but she wouldn't answer the door between our rooms. And I didn't hear anything either. The door was even locked. Sometimes I think she hates me."

Maggie smiled and patted Alison's hand. "No. She's just at the age where she wants to be alone. I'll see if I can get her going. She's probably still sleeping. We had a rather eventful night last night."

"Oh?" Alison's eyes grew large and interested. "What happened. Why didn't anybody wake me?"

Maggie knew the girl felt immediately slighted that she had been allowed to sleep when everyone else had been included in whatever it was that had been kept secret from her. Maggie hated to tell her the disturbing news. The recent events were worrying the child more than Maggie cared to see. She had taken Trent's death very hard, and then when Maggie had been shot, the girl had withdrawn for several weeks, barely eating and saying little. She had been at her mother's beck and call, watching her a lot and never getting too far away. There was no use trying to keep anything from her though. She would learn the truth as soon as she went outside to play.

"We had another fire last night, Ali," she said gently. "But Mr. Sackett woke up in time to tell everyone, so we were able to save the building."

"Which building?" Her eyes enlarged even more.

"The tack building."

"Where Mr. Sackett stays?" Grave concern touched her words.

Maggie nodded. "But everything is all right. Mr. Sackett wasn't hurt."

A cloud seemed to descend over Alison's face. She looked at her plate.

"What is it, Ali?" Maggie said, disturbed by the girl's withdrawal.

Finally Ali looked up but it was with extreme worry in her eyes. "Is somebody going to kill him the way they did Daddy?"

"Of course not," Maggie insisted. But her response was too hasty and the girl knew it. "I hope not, Ali," she finally amended. "I surely hope not."

"So do I. I like him. I wish he could stay with us. I feel safe when he's around. The way I used to when Daddy was here."

Maggie found her mouth suddenly dry. The child had dreams that were impossible, but Maggie couldn't tell her that now. "I'll go up and see what's keeping Natalie. Go ahead and eat before everything gets cold."

Maggie found Natalie's room empty. It wasn't like her to go out before breakfast, but maybe the events of last night had upset her, as they had everyone. Maggie was about to leave the room when she noticed the armoire open. That it was open wasn't surprising. Natalie had never been very tidy. But a sudden surge of dread raced to the pit of Maggie's stomach when she noticed the traveling bag in the bottom of the armoire was missing.

She thumbed through Natalie's clothes, trying to recollect the various pieces. There were some things missing—riding skirts and several day dresses which Maggie couldn't recall her daughter having worn during the week. Another look in the bureau drawers found only a few items where once there had been many.

Maggie didn't want to believe it. With trembling knees she backed to the bed and sat down to steady herself. But no matter how she wanted to deny it, tried to deny it, the truth was there in the empty room.

Her daughter had run away.

Chapter Seventeen

"You've got the leather too low, Lance," Seth said, eyeing the gun belt slung to the boy's narrow hips. "Remember what I told you. Halfway between your wrist and your elbow is the best position I've found. Too low and you're reaching down for it. Too high and you have to pull it up to clear leather."

Seth demonstrated with his own gun. Effortlessly the big weapon was in his hand, pointing at a mound of hay. He didn't fire, but his body leaned into the action, as if he were about to. Then he straightened and dropped the gun back into the holster. It seemed to barely touch leather, skimming gently back to its place.

"Keep your feet anchored solidly to the ground," he continued, "but put fluidness in the rest of your body motion. When you draw, have your thumb on the hammer so all you have to do is pull the trigger when it clears leather. But be careful that you don't get ahead of yourself and shoot yourself in the leg."

Lance gave Seth a silly grin. "Yeah. I'll be careful of that."

Seth smiled. "You're doing fine. Just don't try to go too fast at first. Build up to speed as the gun begins to leap naturally into your hand. You've got to get your muscles built up in that arm and shoulder to handle the weight of the gun. Now, go ahead and try it."

A clatter of the wooden gate next to the loafing shed startled them both. At the sight of Maggie hurrying toward them with grave concern etched tightly in her face, Lance's heart sank. He should have known better than to practice his quick draw so close to the house. His mother had found out and now he'd have hell to pay.

"Mom, what's the matter?" he asked, hoping for a cover-up of some sort.

She rushed past both of them to the horses that were lounging in the shade at one end of the shed. "Natalie's gone. I've got to find her."

Lance noticed the bridle in her hand and leaped into step beside her. "What! What do you mean she's gone?"

Maggie slowed her pace to keep from frightening the horses. "She's gone. That's all I know. Her bag and some of her clothes are missing. She's probably run off to be with Andy. It's bad enough that I have to worry about her being with him, but if one of Tate's men sees her alone, she could be in even greater danger."

"I'm going with you," Lance announced.

"No, Lance. I need you here to stay with your grandmother and with Alison, and to be in charge of the ranch. Hopefully nothing will happen in my absence, but sometimes Sonny's decisions on matters are not what mine would be. With you here, you might be able to prevent him from doing something I wouldn't approve of."

"All right," Lance said reluctantly, "but if you won't let me go then you should take Seth. You need the protection after what happened before."

Maggie wasn't sure she wanted Seth to be with her, or to stay as far away from her as possible. The latter would certainly be the most sensible, especially after last night. "Seth might have other things planned for today," she said, slipping an arm over her horse's neck so she could put the bridle on.

"You can't go alone," Lance persisted then turned to Seth. "She's just being stubborn. Is there any reason why you can't go with her?"

Seth watched Maggie intently bridling her horse and trying to evade eye contact with him, but at Lance's question she was finally drawn to look his way. When she did, his heart fell into the green depths of her eyes, faltering in a foolish weakness that brought back last night much too vividly. Should he tell her what Natalie had said to him? He wasn't at all certain the girl had run away to be with Andy, or if it might have had something to do with her seeing him and Maggie together. If he told Maggie, though, he knew her pride, her conscience, and her guilt would work on her until she would refuse to allow him to touch her or kiss her again. She might even fire him in order to remove temptation completely. But after last night he knew one thing: she wanted him. And, being what he was—a weak man with a tormenting desire for her—he would play into her arms any way he could, whenever he could, right or wrong.

"I was going to ride out to keep an eye on any movement by Tate's men," he finally said, "but I agree with Lance. It would be dangerous for you to go into town alone, Maggie."

The sound of her name on his lips, expressing his concern for her, crumbled any resolve Maggie had hoped to cling to. Who was she fooling? She wanted Seth by her side for whatever reason he could be there. She couldn't fight her heart and the two of them, too.

"Very well." She shrugged, pretending it meant little to her one way or the other. "Let's go."

The ride into town was a quiet one. Although Maggie was very aware of Seth by her side, her focus was on her daughter. Seth sensed her preoccupation and didn't try to initiate conversation. In town, they found the streets unusually busy for a week day. Normally Maggie wouldn't have minded the bustling traffic of wagons and riders, but today it all slowed her progress and made it more difficult to search for her daughter's face in the crowd. She wouldn't expect Natalie to be bold enough to appear in town when she would logically remain hidden, but there was always that small possibility.

Maggie's first and most logical stop was the blacksmith shop and a visit with Andy Dray. But he was no help whatsoever. He told Maggie he hadn't seen Natalie, but there was something in his eyes that convinced Maggie he was lying. Instead of concern about Natalie's disappearance and her welfare, his response had been cool and calm, almost defiant. When they had departed, he'd gone back to his work without so much as offering to help search for her or even keep an eye out for her.

"He knows where she is," Maggie said to Seth as they rode back down the street.

"I had the same feeling," Seth replied. "She's told him to keep quiet. But at least you know she made it to town without Tate's men intercepting her. She's safe."

"For the moment, maybe. But if he's hiding her out, God knows what will happen. I don't care for that young man."

Seth tried to hide a smile. "Because he likes your daughter?"

Maggie shot him a look. "Because he's too *old* for my daughter. I'm afraid he'll take advantage of her. She's much too young to have good judgment about matters of the heart. And a young man his age is going to have only one thing on his mind."

In an appraising glance that Maggie missed, Seth took in the firm set to her jaw, the straight carriage that was another indication of her unbending position on Natalie's love life. Maggie was such a fiery woman herself, how could she possibly expect her daughter to be anything less?

"Is good judgment about matters of the heart a prerequisite of age, Maggie?" Seth asked quietly. "Or is age a prerequisite of good judgment?"

That he would question her stance irritated Maggie. How would he know anything about raising children? But when she met his steady gray gaze, she realized he was referring to their own relationship, not Natalie's. She had no answers for that so she reined her horse away and continued her search.

She contacted every friend of Natalie's she could think of. None of them had seen the girl. With a sinking heart Maggie turned to the last person in town who might be able to help her—Cleve Williams. She found him not at his office in town, but at his mansion.

She and Seth were admitted into the elaborate parlor by a maid in a starched uniform. Maggie had been in the room numerous times on previous visits with Trent, and a few times since his death. Despite several re-decorating projects over the years, the busyness of the room never changed. There were too many swirls and curves in the ornate Rosewood tables, mirrors, sofa, and chairs. Too many conflicting designs in the walls, the furniture, and the floor coverings. Plus, the sheers beneath the heavy, ice blue draperies were always closed to the sun. The slick brocades of the sofa and chairs never failed to make her feel in need of a heavy wool shawl.

Seth settled himself in one of the large chairs, looking out of place in the formal room with his boots, gun, cowboy hat. But he acted as much at ease as if he were in the saddle. Maggie deduced that few situations were capable of stealing his self-assurance, or if they did he was extremely adept at concealing it.

As for Maggie, she sat on the edge of the sofa, feeling as she always did when she was here—out of her element and eager to return to the casual comfort and warmth of her own home.

Unable to sit patiently waiting while precious time was slipping away, she came to her feet and began pacing back and forth in front of the sofa and Seth. He watched her but didn't comment, content to allow her to vent her frustrations as she chose.

At last Cleve arrived. At the sight of Seth his welcoming smile turned into a tight line of disapproval. The tension between the men flashed like lightning then continued to crackle like a long roll of thunder undulating through a cloud mass. Maggie braced herself for a confrontation between them. She hadn't thought of the ramifications of bringing Seth here, and she should have because she knew the men didn't like each other.

Cleve finally gave his attention to Maggie, pretending as if Sackett was invisible. He strode across the room and took her hands in his.

"How did you get my note so soon, Maggie?"

Confusion wrinkled her brow. "I haven't received a note. Cleve, Natalie's gone. She just left without a word. I've been frantic. I don't know—"

"She's here, Maggie," he said, smiling and squeezing her hands reassuringly. "She's fine."

Maggie thought her heart would stop with utter relief. "Oh, thank God."

"She came in early this morning," he continued. "She said she was having some difficulties at home and asked if she could stay with me for a while. I sent a note with a messenger to inform you so you wouldn't worry."

"Difficulties? Did she say what sort of difficulties?"

Cleve's reassuring smile deepened. "No. And I

didn't ask. I just assumed that perhaps the two of you had had an argument."

Maggie drifted away from him into the center of the huge room. "No. Not really. Just the usual disagreements on who she should court and who she should not."

Cleve laughed. "Well, that's enough for a girl her age."

"I'd like to see her, Cleve," Maggie said earnestly. "Which room is she in?"

Cleve hesitated. "Do you think it would be wise to see her right now, Maggie? Maybe you should give it some time."

"Cleve, Natalie's got to learn she can't run away from her problems. This must be faced, and the sooner the better."

Cleve acquiesced. "Very well. She's upstairs in the guest room, second door on the right. She might be asleep. I think she must have left in the middle of the night to get here as early as she did."

Maggie nodded and started for the room, then glanced back at Seth. "Do you mind waiting for me?"

His gray eyes focused on her with a trace of something not completely discernible, but it made her think of last night together and the intimacies they had shared. "Not at all, Maggie." He turned to Cleve and his tone became smoothly sardonic. "I'm sure Cleve and I will be able to find something to talk about over a drink and a cigar? Isn't that right, Cleve?"

Cleve's eyes lingered on Seth with near-malice. He didn't give the gunman the courtesy of a response. Turning to Maggie he said, "Don't try to make Natalie return home just yet. Let her stay for a few days and get things sorted out in her mind. It'll be better for both of you to have some time apart."

Maggie considered his suggestion but didn't agree with it. She felt the longer they were apart, the larger the rift between them would grow. She kept her opinion to herself, though, and left the two men to tolerate each other as best they could.

At the guest room door, Maggie's light knock was answered with, "Who's there?"

Maggie was afraid that by telling her, she would be barred entry. She turned the door knob and stepped into the room. Natalie was sitting cross-legged in the center of a massive cherry wood canopy bed. It was big enough for not just two people, but at least three. She had her skirt and petticoats pulled modestly down over her knees and ankles and in front of her was a deck of cards in the long straight columns that indicated a game of solitaire was in progress. Her expression changed from surprise to sullen anger.

"How did you find me?"

"I checked with everyone we knew, Natalie." Maggie closed the door behind her. "What's so wrong that you felt you had to leave home without telling me where you were going? I've been worried out of my mind."

Natalie sat tight-lipped, refusing to speak, but Maggie still felt the sting of the girl's impudence.

"I wish you'd come to me first," Maggie said.

"We could have talked about whatever it is that's troubling you."

"Why? I've got nothing to say to you."

Maggie felt as if she'd been struck across the face with a whiplash of contempt. Her daughter had never been so openly hostile toward her, and Maggie wasn't sure how to deal with it. She pretended her daughter's words hadn't cut her to the quick. She moved to the window and lifted the curtains aside, only to see a quiet and well-manicured yard below that did nothing to sooth the turmoil raging inside her.

"Natalie, if this is about Andy—"

Natalie's face contorted with anguish. Tears burst from her eyes and she gripped the bedspread so tightly it frightened Maggie. "It's isn't about Andy. It's about Seth Sackett! I saw the two of you last night, Mother! I saw you in the dining room, in his arms, making love to him!"

Maggie groped for the support of the nearby bureau as the strength fled her body in a wave of humiliating shock. She felt the blood drain from her face, then rise again marking her guilty of the accused sin. Natalie had seen her. My God, how could she ever face the girl again?

She turned to the window, too ashamed to look at her daughter's hateful, accusatory eyes. She felt as if she were going to be ill. When she was able to breath again, she said, "How long did you watch us, Natalie?"

"I wasn't spying, if that's what you mean!"

Maggie managed to face her again. "Don't you

have the decency not to intrude on a private moment?"

"I came to the kitchen because I heard something. I didn't stay, but I saw enough."

"And did you tell Cleve?"

Natalie released a laugh choked with tears. "Rest assured, Mother, I didn't spread news of your behavior. I simply didn't want a gentleman like Mr. Williams knowing how my mother was behaving."

Maggie had tried to hold her temper, but the girl's arrogant rudeness was more than she could take. No matter what she'd done, Natalie had no right to speak to her that way.

"We only kissed," Maggie snapped. "Making love goes well beyond that. Would you like me to explain the full complexities to you?"

The girl's face turned as scarlet as the roses out in the yard as she shook her head violently. "But you were still kissing him," Natalie reiterated, refusing to lose the battle. *"And* you were enjoying it! I can't believe you would act like that."

"Have you ever kissed Andy?"

"Yes!" The girl snapped haughtily, as if hoping to shock her mother.

"And did you enjoy it?"

"Yes. I did." There was a hint of a challenge in her tone now, as if she dared her mother to reprimand her for her behavior, knowing she couldn't do so when her own was worthy of recrimination.

"Then you know how it feels to get that little tingle of excitement when you're in Andy's arms?"

Natalie suddenly seemed to sense the direction of her mother's questioning and where it was leading.

The defiance returned. "Yes, but Andy and I will be married some day. Sackett's just a drifter, a hired hand, a . . . a killer!"

"I thought that once, too," Maggie admitted. "But I believe now that Seth never draws his gun to kill unless his life, or someone else's, is threatened."

"Then why does he hire it out? He knows he'll have to kill somebody."

"Maybe not. Maybe by him being present, he actually keeps people *from* getting killed. Innocent people."

"So you're defending him now?"

Maggie sighed. Only when Natalie was older would she probably understand what had driven Maggie to Seth's arms. Although, sometimes Maggie wasn't sure of that herself.

In a calmer voice, she said, "Even if you don't agree with what I did, it's no reason for you to run away from your home."

"I can't come home yet. Not while he's there. If you send him away then I'll come home."

Maggie tensed. She didn't like ultimatums, especially those thrust at her by a child that simply didn't understand the size of the problem they faced. But there was more to it than mere dislike. Maggie sensed there was a reason that went much deeper.

"Why, Natalie? Why do you want him to leave?"

The girl clamped her lips tightly together and looked away, refusing to speak.

"Answer me, Natalie." Maggie demanded.

Suddenly Natalie swept all the cards off the bed with one long stroke of her arm. "Because I'm afraid you'll marry him! And then he'll try to be my father! Well, I'll tell you, he can't take the place of my father and I'll never let him!"

Maggie stared at her, appalled. It was absurd. Utterly absurd. How could Natalie think that a man like Sackett would ever want to become anyone's father, to even settle down? And especially with a woman crowding forty who had three children. But, as she looked into her daughter's tortured blue eyes, she wondered if she was the one being naive, not Natalie. Was there really the possibility that Seth would crave such a life? With her? But if she told Natalie that it was a preposterous idea because Seth wasn't the marrying kind, then Natalie would want to know all the more why her mother was kissing him if she knew full good and well he had no intention of marrying her. That got into a matter Maggie wasn't prepared to discuss with the girl who simply couldn't understand the adult passions that sometimes drew people together even when there was no possible chance of love or a future.

"I'm only thirty-eight, Natalie," Maggie tried to say calmly. "Perhaps that sounds terribly old to you, but it is conceivable that I'll remarry someday. Just as you will one of these years very soon."

Natalie positioned herself right in front of Maggie, leaning toward her with ugly belligerence on her face and with her fists clenched at her sides. "You should practice what you preach, Mother. You tell me not to get too friendly with Andy and yet you were acting like a whore with Seth Sackett!"

Maggie slapped the girl's face. "I am your

mother, young lady. You will not speak to me like that."

Natalie's hand went to her cheek. She stared at Maggie in stunned silence for a moment before lashing back. "I hate you," she hissed. "I don't ever want to see you again."

Maggie had never wanted to get into such an ugly exchange. Where had all her good intentions gone, her level head? She had not suspected the reason for Natalie's flight, but even though she knew now, she wouldn't apologize for being in Seth's arms and enjoying it. Maybe it had been wrong in her daughter's eyes, but it had felt right at the time and nothing could change that.

Maggie walked to the door, wondering sadly if this rent between her and Natalie would ever be repaired. Maybe, but only if she swallowed some of her own stubborn pride and made the first mend. With forced calmness she said, "Whatever you might think, Natalie, it is not for you to decide who I should be with, who I should kiss, and who I should not. Unlike yourself, I'm not a child. I have the experience to make my own decisions. I also know all the consequences of those decisions. Sometimes a man comes along that has the ability to make a woman do things she shouldn't. Seth Sackett's that sort of man . . . and so is Andy Dray. It's not wise to hang your dreams on men like that, but sometimes we women are blinded by our own humanness.

"Natalie, I may be your mother, but I'm still a woman, the same as you."

She pulled the door open and glanced back.

"And one more thing. Since we're discussing propriety, your staying here is just the sort of thing to set people's tongues to wagging so I suggest you come home soon."

Natalie lifted her chin defiantly yet her eyes brimmed with tears. "Cleve has plenty of female servants. It's not like I'm here with him alone."

"Regardless of what you think of me," Maggie replied, "I love you and want you to come home. All I will say is that staying here with Cleve will be a mistake in the long run. It could even tarnish your name for future relationships. The decision is yours."

Chapter Eighteen

Maggie was grateful that Seth didn't ask questions about the confrontation with Natalie. He only suggested that they get rooms at the hotel since it was getting late. Maggie agreed, numbly. She was too mentally drained and too physically exhausted to ride to the ranch, even if they would have had time before dark. All day she'd been frantic over Natalie's whereabouts and her safety. Then to have her search end in such a heartrending form of frustration was almost more than she could bear. She wanted to cry, but not in front of Seth, or in front of the people of the town. A room was exactly what she needed.

Once inside her rented haven, she didn't know where Seth went or what he intended to do for the rest of the evening. Nor did she care. His presence was always disturbing and distracting in its own way and she couldn't deal with it now.

But minutes in the lonely room ticked into hours and all Maggie accomplished was wearing a futile path in the hotel rug. She refused to respond to

Natalie's demands. The girl was being unreasonable where Seth was concerned, and thinking of no one but herself, least of all the preservation of the White Raven. Maggie couldn't tell Seth to leave. She needed him to keep Tate from using all-out force to take the ranch. Besides, if the girl made a demand of this calibre, where would it end? Maggie knew Trent would have shrugged off Natalie's tantrum. He wouldn't have allowed his life and his business operation to be manipulated by a child's dislike of one of his hired hands.

But Maggie was afraid she would lose her.

What if Natalie never came home? What if she went to Andy Dray and got herself in the family way? She knew Natalie well enough to know she was a stubborn girl and wouldn't come back begging.

Maggie paced the floor.

Natalie or Seth.

Seth or Natalie.

It should have been an easy decision. Her daughter was more important than a hired gun. But it was more complicated than that. Natalie was, quite openly, telling Maggie who she could like, and whom she could or could not marry. Not that it would come to that with Seth Sackett, but if Maggie gave into her on this issue, would she, in the future, feel she could judge every man who might come into Maggie's life? It was, quite simply, one thing Maggie wouldn't tolerate, even from her daughter.

But guilt rode her hard, like a cruel wrangler determined to break the spirit of a wild horse. Hadn't she been judging Natalie's beau, Andy

Dray? Telling Natalie she didn't approve of the match?

Natalie or Seth.

Seth or Natalie.

Was there more to her indecision than merely keeping Natalie in her place and Tate in line? Was there a feeling that went deeper? Could it have something to do with the tantalizing memory of Seth's lovemaking that made her so reluctant to tell him he must leave the White Raven forever?

At last she dropped to the bed, unable to do battle with her conscience anymore. She didn't think she could sleep, but to her surprise she did, and she came awake some time later to the sound of a light knock on the door. The room was dark. It took her a moment to remember her surroundings and another moment to remember why she was here.

Then, thinking it might be Natalie at the door, she leaped to her feet. But when she pulled it open, her heart plummeted. It wasn't her daughter. Disheartened, she turned back to the room.

"I know you don't care much for my company, Maggie," Seth said, in that self-mocking way of his. "But you could try to hide your feelings a little better than that. After all, a man has his ego." He sauntered into the room, as if he had every right to, and closed the door behind him.

Maggie rubbed her aching temples. "I'm sorry, Seth. I was hoping you were Natalie."

"Well, at least you weren't hoping I was Cleve, or Sonny. Actually I thought you might be hungry.

Dinner's being served in the dining room, but only for another hour."

"Thank you, but I'm not hungry. You go without me." She ignored his remark about the other two men. It was just one more thing she didn't want to think about or deal with.

"Staying up in this room brooding isn't going to accomplish anything, Maggie. Natalie's safe, and she'll come home. Just give her time."

Maggie shook her head and went to the window, gazing down onto the lights in the street and the night activity in the saloons and dance halls. The gaiety only made her feel more despondent.

She felt Seth's hands on her shoulders, shocking her with his touch and his nearness. "Come on, Maggie," he insisted. "Locking yourself away isn't going to help matters."

"You don't understand, Seth. I slapped her face."

Seth's hands on her shoulders tightened momentarily; his entire body tensed. "Why did you slap her?" he asked quietly.

Maggie sighed. "Because she called me a whore."

The heat of his body was only a few tantalizing inches from hers and she felt him relax again. He began to knead the tension from her shoulders, releasing it in a magical way. She wanted to let go of her determination to be strong and just turn into his arms in hopes of finding comfort and sanctuary from the pain. But she didn't. She was too malleable in his embrace, too close to becoming what Natalie had accused her of. She had nearly lost her control with him before. The ice was too thin in a relationship such as theirs. There would be consequences to pay for following the call of desire, and the woman was always the one who had to pay them.

"So she's trying to keep you on the straight and narrow?" Seth said lightly. "A second conscience is just what every mature adult needs, isn't it?"

Maggie stepped away from him, suddenly angry that he could act as if the situation was only a silly grievance. "She *saw* us, Seth! She saw us in the parlor."

With her shoulders no longer within reach, Seth put one hand on the butt of his gun, the other he hung from his gun belt by a thumb. "I know."

She felt as if she herself had been slapped. "You *know?*"

He shrugged, as if it was all inconsequential. "Yeah, so what?"

"Damn you!" Her restraint snapped. In a flurry of tears she lashed out at him, pounding on his chest with her fists. "You knew and you didn't tell me! I was worried sick about her all day and you knew!"

Seth grabbed her wrists and pulled her so firmly against his chest that she had no choice but to stop her outburst. He propelled her toward the bed and she found herself being pressed into the pillows by the full length of his weight. He pulled her arms over her head to keep her from hitting him again.

"Don't strike me, Maggie. Do anything, but not that."

Maggie saw the intense pain in his eyes and heard the hint of desperation in his command, thinking it actually sounded more like a plea than anything. She didn't understand his reaction to her physical display of emotion. Didn't he realize that's all it was? But it was so powerful it made her wonder once again about the scars on his back and how they got there.

"I'm sorry, Seth," she said, truly ashamed of her behavior.

"I know you're upset," he went on to say, smoothing her hair back from her face. "But try to calm down. These things have a way of working themselves out if you'll just let them. I didn't say anything to you because Natalie just told me to leave you alone. She didn't say she was going to run away because she saw us. I would have told you what she said to me, but what was the point in making you feel ashamed? I knew you'd let her get to you and you'd do just what she wanted. You would send me packing. And I was right, wasn't I? You're going to let her convince you that I've got to go. Well, if that's what you want, I will. But I want to hear it from your lips. And I want you to mean it."

His gray eyes held hers for a long, silent moment, then shifted to her lips. A startled cry of passion and pain escaped her throat as his mouth came down over hers with insatiable desire. She felt his hips pressing into hers, felt the hot male shaft against her leg. His kisses not only claimed her lips as his own, but their searing brand was left along her cheek and jaw, then trailed along her throat, leaving fires erupting like volcanoes everywhere in their wake.

"Seth, please don't. We shouldn't. Not again."

His lips paused at the base of her throat, absorbing the staccato beat of her heart pulsing there.

"Last night was no mistake, Maggie," he whispered. "And neither is this. There's something between us. It's been there since we first set eyes on each other. Denying it won't change it."

"I can't. Don't you understand? I have to be an example for her."

"First it was Trent. You wouldn't betray his memory. Now it's Natalie. Will there always be someone between us, Maggie?"

His lips moved downward and he released her wrists, sliding his hands down the length of her arms to the buttons on her shirtwaist. His nimble fingers easily parted the cloth, exposing the swell of her breasts to the tender torment of his lips.

She moaned her denial but found her hands gripping his shoulders while her mind whirled away into the pleasure of his touch. A small part of her fought on, weakly. "You're turning me into exactly what she said I was."

He continued to disrobe her, inch by maddening inch. "Then you don't know what a whore is."

"Seth. We can't. What if I—"

His lips claimed hers again in a long and drugging kiss. He didn't want to hear the arguments of her practical mind. He only wanted to live for the moment and worry about tomorrow when it came, if it came. He didn't want to give either of them time to think of the consequences of their behavior. He only wanted to cling to the distant hope that these moments with her might go on forever, like a very pleasant dream.

"Don't be afraid, Maggie," he whispered against her lips. "I'm here to protect you, remember? I won't let anything or anybody hurt you. I mean it."

Maggie made a decision then, and he must have sensed her surrender to desire for his strong arms easily molded her body more fully to his and held her in a gentle but powerful embrace. She found his intense need for her to be an exciting aphrodisiac all in itself. No, there would be no going back this time.

Her body yielded completely to him, as did her mind. The need in the center of her womanhood opened, too, blossoming like a spring flower under the morning sun. She removed his shirt and replaced its protective warmth with the hot passion of her lips, and in turn his kisses dropped over her bare flesh like rose petals drifting to earth on a gentle breeze.

"Oh God, Maggie," he moaned against her lips. "You're driving me crazy. I don't know how long I can hold on."

She understood and rolled him to his back, helping to ease that overpowering need back into something more controllable. Taking the dominant position, she straddled him, kissing his chest while reaching down to undo his pants. She moved away from him only long enough to free him of the remaining clothing and footgear.

He was the epitome of what God must have intended man to be, and her hands and lips explored every exquisite inch of him: the broad, brawny chest with its virile covering of black hair; the wide shoulders, made strong from unseen burdens; the stomach and abdomen that grew taut at her touch; the muscled thighs and calves; the rigid shaft of his manhood. And she quickly discovered, in the course of her exploration, those areas most sensitive to her lovemaking. He responded with muffled moans of pleasure, his own hands roving her shoulders and arms, her thighs, her breasts.

"You know too well how to kindle a man's flame, Maggie," he whispered, his dark eyes meeting hers with tender passion. "Now it's my turn to do the same for you."

Still lying on his back, he lifted her up over him and took her breasts, first one and then the other, in his mouth, creating a fire storm that would soon need quenching. When she herself hovered on the edge of fulfillment, she moved down over the length of his shaft.

Memories of Trent suddenly flashed through her mind, taunting her with a wave of guilt and dismay at her wantonness. But the reality of Seth, as a man, was stronger than memories. Soon it was only Seth she saw and felt and heard. It was his touch that moved her and brought her to life again after being in a state of mental and physical dormancy for so long. It was Seth who at last brought the sunlight to the darkness of her heart.

She paused in utter stillness, felt him quiver inside her, and she cupped his face with her hands and kissed him again, wanting in a strange, desperate way for him to feel the same emotion in their union as she did. What she felt for him was intense and uncontrollable. Earlier she had told him she didn't love him, but now she wondered if she had lied. She only knew she wanted to be with him well beyond the space of this night. Possibly forever. Their love-making should bond them, but would it? Was it based on more than just physical attraction and need?

He began to move beneath her and inside her. She met his powerful strokes, riding out the storm of desire with the sheer passion of pleasure until she rose above the tumultuous clouds and burst into the sunlight. It flashed like an explosion, washing over her in hot waves to every part of her body, fanning out in golden shafts that fell down all around her and surrounded her in beauty.

Seth rolled her to her back then, showering her with more kisses. She gripped his buttocks, pulling him closer, deeper. Where he had taken her, she now took him. In a few powerful strokes, he shuddered and cried out, then fell sated in her arms. A moment later he shifted to his side, drawing her with him so she wouldn't have to bear the brunt of his weight. She nestled against his chest. They spoke no words, merely held to the magic of the world they had created, a world where for a few glorious hours they would be the sole inhabitants.

Seth lay awake in the darkness, listening to Maggie's contented breathing. He continued to hold her because he couldn't seem to get enough of her. And in the stillness and the darkness where a man's mind could become very clear, he was struck with an awesome reality. A truth. In all the years since he had first bedded a woman, he realized he had only been engaging in sexual intercourse. This was the first time he had ever made love, and Maggie was the first woman to touch him with such unbridled passion, with such feeling and concern for his needs.

Desire had never taken such an all-consuming course for him. There had been the other women, but there had been none he couldn't have, and none who hadn't wanted him—for a night or two. It was because of the very nature of those women, he supposed, that they had barely turned his head. He had satisfied his physical needs as easily and effortlessly as he had satisfied his thirst with a five-cent glass of beer. But in the end he'd walked away without quenching either his need or his thirst. The cavern inside him had only increased to monumental size until he had come to believe it could never be filled. And he had come to accept the emptiness.

But he couldn't do that any longer. Maggie had filled the emptiness when she had made love to him in her caring and sweet way, but he couldn't help but wonder if she looked at him as he had those women from his past. As someone to merely ease a need? What would happen when she was gone from his life? Would he be like a lost soul rising and falling forever in the fiery pits of hell?

How could he hold her, a man like him? Already he felt her slipping away. Not in body, but in mind. Maggie Cayton was slowly and surely convincing herself she must turn away from him, and for reasons good and just. Should he try to convince her not to go, or should he just release her and save himself the pain of her rejection which was sure to come?

He finally slept, and when he woke, the sunlight brought a new day and realities as it always did. He reached across the bed for Maggie, but she was already dressed and looking out the window with a pensiveness in her stance. He thought she was probably brooding about Natalie, or about getting back to the ranch. But when she turned to him and evasively met his eyes, he knew her thoughts had been about him and the relationship that had developed.

In that moment the truth was clear. He couldn't take Trent's place in her life. He would have no choice but to let her go.

Maggie had barely stepped through the door when the questions began. She found herself surrounded by her mother, Alison, Lance, even Dorothy the cook. Weary, and wanting nothing more than to take a warm bath and soak for awhile, Maggie simply said, "Natalie and I had a disagreement. She's staying in town with Cleve."

"She can't just go out on her own!" Lance said angrily. "She's only fourteen. Who does she thinks she is? Why don't you *make* her come home? She'll just be hanging around with that Andy Dray if she's in town. I can tell you, Mother, he's a renegade. He runs with a wild bunch."

It was all Maggie needed to hear. Her emotions were already raw over her worry for Natalie and over her growing feelings for Seth. Last night with him had been wonderful, but by morning she had felt guilty when her first thought upon waking had been of him, not of Trent, not of Natalie. She had thought about his promise to take care of her. But how foolish could she be to think it might be forever? Her need for him was making her betray not only Trent's memory, but her duty as a mother, which should be first and foremost.

"I know, Lance," she said dully, "but she won't listen to me."

"Then I'll go into town and I'll make her listen to me."

"No you won't," Maggie said sternly. "I don't want you going into town alone. It's too dangerous."

"I can take care of myself."

"You may have that gun on your hip and you may be having Seth teach you how to use it, but I don't approve, and you're not as good as Seth, so don't go getting cocky. It'll only get you killed."

She brushed past them all and headed for the bathroom in the back of the house. They all followed her. "How did you know Seth was teaching me?" Lance queried nervously.

Maggie ran a weary hand through her hair which hung loose around her shoulders. "I figured out as much yesterday when I went to get my horse."

"You didn't say anything."

"My God, Lance, I had enough problems with Natalie running away without worrying about Seth teaching you how to use a gun! But I don't approve and I intend to talk to him just as soon as—"

"I'm going to learn, Mother. I need to learn. With everything that's going on, don't you think I should know how to protect myself and you women? Besides, I'm not going to hire my services out like Seth."

Maggie had reached the bathroom. She stopped in the doorway and turned to them. They were all lined up in the narrow hall, listening to the news, not wanting to miss anything. She rubbed her forehead. She was so mentally exhausted. "Never say never, Lance. Now, if you will all excuse me, I'm going to take a much needed bath."

Maggie tried to keep her mind off the situation with Natalie, as well as the one with Seth. For the next two days she closed herself in her office to get caught up on the records and to see how badly the ranch was hurt from the recent setbacks. It was also time to pay the hands. After two hours of juggling figures, and anticipating expenses for the months ahead, minus the money lost from the dead cattle, Maggie leaned back in her chair and realized that the financial situation on the White Raven was not looking good. It wasn't desperate yet, but if they lost any more cattle she'd have to let some of the men go. She would also have to tell the family that it was time to pare down on their spending during Saturday trips to town. She had the money she owed Seth, but she refused to break into that for anything. Quite simply, things with Tate were going to have to get straightened out—and soon. But how, when there was no proof he was even behind it?

She almost welcomed the tap on the office door. It was probably one of the children needing to talk to her, or possibly her mother.

"Come in," she said, closing the books.

She was surprised to see Sonny. Using his usual deference, he left the door open and stepped inside.

She motioned to the chair opposite the desk. "Sit down, Sonny. Don't tell me we've got more problems?"

He pushed his hat to the back of his head. From the look on his face, she knew her assumption was right. Her stomach knotted and she braced herself. "How bad is it?"

"We haven't lost any more cattle, Maggie," he said. "It's Tate. Word is out he's hired three more gunmen. It looks like he's building up for a range war."

Maggie silently contemplated this latest piece of news for several seconds before finally speaking. "Do you know why he's taken this action?"

Sonny, looking almost satisfied to be importing news, even bad news, propped a booted foot on the opposite knee. "He says he found a bunch of cattle shot."

Nonplussed, Maggie left her desk and, with one hand on her hip, paced the small area in front of the window. "Is there any truth behind it?"

She glanced over her shoulder when she heard the leather squeak under Sonny's shifting body. "Well, we sure didn't do no shooting."

She tried to read something in his eyes but couldn't. Surely if he knew one of the men might be sabotaging the White Raven he would tell her?

"I know you don't want to hear this, Maggie," he continued with the tone that told her he knew he was overstepping his bounds but was going to do it anyway. "Maybe you ought to seriously consider selling out. I mean, I don't see how we can fight power like that. Some of the men are talking about quitting. They're cowboys; not gunfighters. And they don't want to get in the middle of a range war."

Maggie didn't know what she was going to do, except that she wasn't going to sell and she wasn't going to budge. If she had to sell down to every last cow to hire gunmen, then she would, but she wouldn't lose the land. She wouldn't let Tate win until she was completely whipped. And she wasn't . . . not yet.

She returned to her desk. "First of all, I'll talk to Seth to see what he thinks of the matter. He'll probably know if Tate's bluffing or if he means business."

"Oh, I nearly forgot," Sonny suddenly reached into his pocket, "Sackett told me to give you this." He handed her a folded piece of paper. "He's gone, Maggie. A little while ago he packed up everything he owned and just rode out."

Chapter Nineteen

Maggie sat back down to steady herself. How could he have left after making such promises that he would protect her? Had it been lies? Just lies so he could have his way with her?

Sonny waited for her to open the note, to read it in front of him. But she couldn't—her hands were shaking too badly and she didn't want Sonny to see the telltale reaction to Seth's unannounced departure.

"Thank you," she said in a businesslike voice of dismissal. "I'll let you know what I decide to do next."

Seeing she wasn't going to read Sackett's note as long as he was in the room, Sonny rose reluctantly and started for the door. But at the threshold, he hesitated.

"What is it?" she inquired, feeling impatient. Was he never going to leave? The note was practically burning her hand. She didn't want to read it, and yet she knew she must regardless of the painful things that might be written there.

"I just wanted to tell you that no matter what the other men do, Maggie, I'll stay here and fight. The White Raven means a lot to me, too."

She managed a smile, despite the pain knifing through her heart. "I always knew I could count on you, Sonny."

He nodded in that self-conscious way of his then tugged his hat down tightly on his forehead. In another moment he was gone.

Maggie hurried around the desk, closed the door and locked it. With her hands shaking worse than before, she opened the piece of paper that had been folded in fourths. The handwriting was a bit elongated and irregular, the hand of a man who held a gun more frequently than a pencil.

Maggie, I'll be at the line shack (you know the one). I don't want to jeopardize your family or your men by staying at the ranch any longer. You're the only one I'm telling because I don't want to wake up with a bullet in my back. Let the others think you don't know where I am. And Maggie, since I'm not there to watch over things, be careful. Seth.

Maggie collapsed into the chair Sonny had just vacated, greatly relieved that Seth hadn't left after all. She read the note over, possibly reading more into his words of concern than he had intended. But did they mean he truly cared about her, or was he just doing his job by protecting his boss?

She tucked the note into her pocket, surmising he was at the line shack by Larkspur reservoir, the one where they'd stayed together. Tomorrow she would ride out there to warn him about the three new gunmen Tate had hired. And to see, if maybe, he really did care.

She had to be certain that no one saw her leave or they might question her riding out alone. At the worst, someone like Sonny might follow her, and she didn't want to jeopardize Seth's position or his trust in her. If no one knew where he was staying then possibly the perpetrator would get brave and step out of the shadows long enough to get caught. She hadn't spoken to anyone but Sonny last night, so the men, like Sonny, might believe Seth had simply quit the White Raven. They wouldn't know otherwise until she informed them that he was merely camping away from the ranch in light of the recent threat on his life.

She waited for the men to leave then went to the kitchen to fix a lunch consisting of a small loaf of fresh bread, some dried fruit and cheese, and a chunk of roast beef left over from last night. Dorothy was there cleaning up the breakfast dishes, but she didn't question Maggie. Maggie rolled it all up in some clean muslin, placed it in the center of a towel, and tied the four corners together. On her way out, she stopped at the library and hastily selected a book from the shelf, one she thought Seth might like. She stopped at the front door only long enough to get her gun, her hat, and her jacket. She remembered Seth's words about how he liked the looks of her hips without the hardware, but she couldn't afford to be vain. The gun had to be handy so she strapped it on.

She was careful to ride the skyline only when there was no alternative. For the most part, she made her way to the line shack through the valleys. Constant vigilance made for a nerve-wracking trip, but she couldn't be too careful.

Her heart gathered speed when she stepped from the saddle and wound the reins around the hitching rail in front of the line shack. After loosening the saddle cinch, she walked to the cabin door, but her light knock brought no response from within. Suddenly fearing that someone had already discovered Seth's whereabouts, she hurried inside. But the room was vacant. His belongings were still here, though, so she knew he was just out, probably watching movement between the White Raven and the Broken Arrow.

She set the bundle of food on the table and removed the book. She would wait for him, and read while she waited.

Seth recognized the horse dozing at the hitching rail. Damn it, what was Maggie doing here? Hadn't she learned her lesson about the dangers of riding alone? And why was she here tormenting him again?

But even as his anger flashed, it was engulfed in the memory of her lovely body rising over his, bringing him the special pleasure no woman before her ever had. He'd left the ranch for several reasons, and one was because there was no hope for a future with her. He knew it was better to nip his growing feelings in the bud. But was it possible she had missed him the way he had her? Could that be the reason for her visit? And if he was to be totally honest with himself, hadn't he left her the note in hopes she would join him?

When he opened the door to the cabin, he saw her on the far side of the room, asleep on the cot where he'd rolled out his blankets. She had a book, lying open face-down on her stomach. The sun slanted through the window and across her, lighting the lower half of her body with a warm, caressing glow.

His desire crowded out the silent vow he'd made to leave her alone, to fulfill his job and get out of her life as quickly as possible. How could he have ever been so foolish as to think he was stronger than temptation, especially when it came in such a beautiful package?

His boot heels thumped on the plank floor even in his attempt to be quiet, but she was deep in the dreams of afternoon sleep and didn't hear his approach. He sat on the edge of the cot, expecting it to squeal beneath his weight, but it's solid wooden frame held the mattress firmly and soundlessly.

His kiss brought her arms around his neck, as if her dreams had been of doing that very thing. Perhaps still drugged with sleep, she nevertheless responded immediately to his hands that took their liberty with her most intimate, feminine curves.

"Did you miss me, Maggie?" he whispered against her lips.

Her only response was a pleasant, indecipherable murmur and her arms tightening around his neck, bringing him more fully into her embrace.

His kisses brought her awake, wanting him as

badly as he wanted her. In just moments, their attire was in a pile on the floor. His naked body blocked the sun from her as he rose over her.

Her hands slid up over his thighs to the flat of his stomach and finally to his extended manhood. Her caresses and her lips nearly drove him wild. He could scarcely breath for the agonizing ecstasy of her touch. But even as he enjoyed the play of her hands and lips on his body, he equally enjoyed learning every soft contour that was hers alone and seeing the way his gentle manipulations brought her to the same tumultuous heights he, too, was feeling.

She knew exactly when the time had come to end the foreplay. She drew him to her and entrapped him, a willing hostage, in the silken bondage of her long, slender legs. Their matching passions moved them in perfect, primal harmony.

When at last they snuggled in breathless fulfillment in each other's arms, Seth felt the hand of love curl even tighter around his heart, and with a grip he knew he would never be free of again, nor would ever want to be. Running from her wouldn't change the feeling. Denying it wouldn't change it. The pleasure and the pain of it danced ambivalently inside him. How foolish could he be to hope, to dream, that he might be the man who could quench her lusty desires forever and who might be suitable to share her life? Moments in time were all he could hope to share with her.

The thought made him angry. Damn her for using him like a male prostitute, if indeed that was what she was doing. Did she think he had no heart, no feelings? But still he clung to her because a starving man never tossed a crumb of bread away in fear there would be no more. He had to take what he could and enjoy it while it lasted.

She ran a hand along his cheek and he imagined love in the stroke. He caught her hand and drew her palm to his lips. Her green eyes watched him, warily. She still didn't trust him fully, but he supposed she had good reason not to. When he'd first met her he'd played the part of a perfect ass, perfectly.

"I came to talk business," she said, giving him an impish grin that flooded him with an all-new weakness.

"Well, now that we've got it out of the way, what's next?"

Her husky laughter turned him inside out. Her body, hot and soft beneath his, and their legs still entwined, made him want her again.

"Why did you leave without telling me?" A frown furrowed her brow for a fleeting moment as seriousness edged out the frivolity of the moment.

He lightly brushed the auburn hair from her face and dropped a kiss to her chin, another to her neck. "I thought it might be better if I was away. I seem to be causing you a few domestic problems."

"I can deal with them. I thought you ran out on me."

More kisses rained on her collarbone, her shoulder, her ear. Was she concerned about a job undone? Or was she concerned he might have loved her and left her? But he didn't ask, for he wasn't sure the answer would be to his liking. His response was as noncommittal as possible.

"No, I won't leave until the job's done, Maggie."

"Seth, we have to talk."

He lifted his head. "All right, but I can tell you there are things more pleasant for a man and woman to do than talk."

She smiled, warmed by his sexual innuendo that only a short while ago would have annoyed her. But she had to proceed. She had tarried long enough in his company. "I wanted to warn you that Tate has hired three more gunmen. Apparently someone shot a bunch of his cattle, and naturally he's blaming me."

Seth sighed and sat up, reaching for his clothes. Life was business. Always business. "Maybe I'll have to ride over there and talk to him."

"With three hired gunmen? Isn't that pushing the odds?"

He shrugged. "Sometimes I would rather go looking for trouble than to wait for it to come looking for me. I figure I'm less likely to get ambushed if I catch my opponents by surprise."

Maggie didn't like the idea of him up against three men who might be nearly as fast on the draw as he was, but she knew Seth Sackett would do as he pleased.

"Sonny says some of the men have talked about quitting. They're afraid of war. And so am I."

Seth pulled his boots on. "You didn't kill Tate's cattle, Maggie, but somebody did. Somebody whom I'm convinced is pitting the two of you against each other. Somebody wants you both dead—preferably by each other's bullets. I just can't figure out why."

Maggie found her own clothes and dressed, not

wanting to think about somebody killing her and possibly Seth, too. She preferred to think of his fiery passions, even if it meant admitting she had come out here seeking his lovemaking under the guise of business. It had been so terribly lonely in her room last night. She had spent sleepless hours wondering why he had left without speaking to her first. Her only consolation was that he hadn't left permanently. He would though, some day soon, because he wasn't the staying sort of man. Even that knowledge couldn't ease the powerful pull she felt toward him, nor did it quench a need only he seemed to be able to quench.

"I wonder if I should hire more guns," she said worriedly.

"No, not yet," he replied, strapping his gun belt back on. "Tate can't fight a war if there's no opposing army."

"But what if they open fire on our cowboys?"

"Tate's a hard man but he's not without scruples. I don't think he'll do that. Just as I'm beginning to think he hasn't been behind the killings and poisonings. He admitted to cutting some fences, but right now I think he's running scared and protecting his backside. He's retaliating against crimes he thinks you're committing.

"Give me some time, Maggie," he continued. "I'll go talk to him again. Now, even though I'd like to keep you here, I'd better see you back to the ranch."

But Maggie hung back.

"Is something else wrong?" he asked, amusement flirting in his eyes.

Maggie wondered if she was wrong to even bring it up when there were so many other things going on that were more important. Finally she started for the door. "Oh, it's not important, Seth."

He caught her on the threshold. Leaning his back against the door frame, he pulled her against him. "If it's bothering you, then it's important."

His gray eyes were frank, open, sincere. Even the mask of self-mockery he seemed to oftentimes hide behind was temporarily down. For the first time she felt as if she were seeing the real Seth Sackett, a man with deep concern for humankind and for her in particular.

She temporarily focused on the buttons on his shirt rather than those eyes because she feared what she had to say might upset him and she was extremely reluctant to bring up something that might spoil the special pleasure that lingered between them, even though they had been forced to discuss business.

"Maggie, tell me." He lifted her chin and forced her eyes to meet his. "I'm not going to let you go until you tell me so you might as well get on with it, unless you *want* to spend the night here."

It was truly tempting but at the same time she knew if she didn't return to the ranch a search party would come out looking for her.

"All right," she finally capitulated. "It's Lance. I'm not sure I approve of you teaching him to use a gun. It's not that I don't want him to be able to use a gun, Seth. It's necessary in this country, but having learned from you—a man of reputation—

well, I'm afraid he might become over-confident and get himself killed."

The topic didn't seem to trouble him. He pulled her hips more firmly against his. "If he doesn't know what he's doing, he'll get himself killed anyway, Maggie. He isn't a child anymore. Would you rather he play with guns, or with Cecilia Wagner?"

"That's hardly a comparison, and how do you know about Cecilia Wagner anyway?"

"I stay alive by watching and listening. That and the fact that I caught them together a while back."

That was news Maggie didn't like to hear. "What were they doing?"

"Just about everything," he grinned wickedly. "But to ease your mind, I came along before it went too far—at least this time anyway."

Feeling agitated Maggie tried to break free of him, but he held her fast. "Damn it, Seth. What's wrong with me that I don't approve of either of the people Lance and Natalie seem so totally taken with? Am I just being an overly protective mother?"

"I suspect. I also suspect they're growing up too fast and you're not ready to let them go. You're not ready to see them begin to make their own decisions and consequently their own mistakes. You don't want them to get hurt, Maggie. It's natural to feel that way. But Lance isn't a boy anymore. He's got the same things on his mind that you had at that age. And from what your mother tells me, you were only two years older than Lance when you first shared a bed with a man."

"Yes, but he was my husband!"

Seth was amused by her defiance and moved by

the thought of her in bed, even if it hadn't been with him. A lazy smile turned his lips. "I would have liked to have known you then, Maggie, but I'm sure my father would have told me to steer clear of older women—just as you're telling Lance to steer clear of Cecilia. Those older, more experienced women will surely lead a man down the treacherous path to destruction."

Maggie didn't like the mocking twinkle in his eyes. Nor did she like to be reminded that she was three years older than him, the same age difference as there was between Cecilia and Lance. But when people became adults, years became of lesser importance. Lance was still very much a boy compared to nineteen-year-old Cecilia who was a young woman and more than ready to be married.

It seemed that ever since Seth had stepped foot on the White Raven, Maggie no longer had a leg to stand on. Every argument she might have concocted to keep her children in line suddenly became useless because she found herself guilty of the same indiscretion. To judge them would be to fall into the pit of hypocrisy.

"Have you made some sort of point here, Seth?"

He shrugged. "That we're all human?"

"All right. I've seen the light." She gave him a sudden capricious smile. "Now, are you still going to escort me home?"

He kissed her on the lips and ran his hand over her bottom in a slow, caressing way. "Ah, Maggie, you know I'd rather you spend the night."

"Because you care for me, Seth? Or just because you're lonely out here?"

His hands moved up her back, eliciting a shiver from her spine that made her seriously toy with the temptation he offered. "Both, Maggie. And you? Which reason would be the one that would make you stay, if you could?"

He was getting too close to her heart, much too close. To admit her feelings would be a mistake. She was sure he would like to know he had won her heart. Men like him liked to know they had conquered, especially since he'd been so cocksure in the beginning that he would. But she was also sure the revealing of her heart and soul wouldn't make him stay.

"Both," she replied, figuring it was best to use the same safe answer as he had.

He smiled, not fooled by her tactic. "Then at least dream about me, Maggie." He kissed her again lightly. "Because I'll be dreaming about you."

He escorted her to within a half mile of the ranch before turning back to the line shack. Maggie was relieved to see that none of the men had come back from work yet. She was confident her departure from the ranch had gone unnoticed by everyone except maybe Otto, and he wasn't one for spreading information before it was asked for.

Once inside her room, Maggie changed and then took up work on the dress Natalie had started sewing before she had run away. Her mother joined her, assuming the task of attaching lace to the skirt flounces.

"I'm going to Cleve's tomorrow," Maggie announced. "I'm going to insist that Natalie come home this time. I had really hoped she would have made the decision herself but since she hasn't she leaves me no choice."

"Then I'll go with you," Catherine said positively. "I have some shopping to do, and maybe she won't be able to say no to her grandmother quite as easily as her mother."

"You surely seem to understand the children, Mother."

"Oh, they're easy enough to figure out."

"Thank you," Maggie said sincerely. "I appreciate your help, Mother, and your concern."

Catherine patted Maggie's hand; her eyes were filled with love. "Well, she's just as important to me as she is to you, dear. I've done nothing but worry about the situation and I won't quit until she's home safely. You know I don't like Cleve and I don't like her staying over there. I wouldn't put it past that weasel-eyed man to touch her."

Maggie's brow furrowed with yet another worry. "You don't really think he would, do you?"

Catherine went back to her sewing. "I don't know, Maggie. All I know is I don't trust him and I never have."

"All right, Mother. We'll leave first thing in the morning. I'll get a couple of the men to ride with us."

"That sounds fine. Oh, by the way, Maggie. Where did Seth go?" Catherine looked innocently away, reaching for a length of lace. "Word is around the ranch that he just up and left. That seems rather odd since the job isn't completed, and since he has a book of mine. I went out to the tack building to see if he'd left it there, but he hadn't. I know Seth isn't a quitter, or a thief."

For all her nonchalance, Maggie knew her mother was dying of curiosity. She also wisely guessed something was up. Knowing she couldn't keep anything from her mother permanently, Maggie told her where Seth was and why he felt it safer for them if he wasn't at the house. "He hopes he'll be able to get Tate or whoever is behind this to come out of hiding if they think he's gone or don't know where he is."

"Then we certainly must not let on where he is. Perhaps you'd better not go out there again either."

Maggie looked up from her needle at the same time her mother looked up from hers. "How did you know?"

Catherine shrugged and went back to sewing. "I just know how a woman acts when she's going off to meet a man on the sly."

"Mother!"

"Oh, not that I mind, dear. It sounds very exciting and romantic. I wish I was young enough to engage in such pleasantries myself. It's the curse of getting old so enjoy it while you can. Does this mean he won't be taking you to the dance?"

Maggie was continually dismayed by her mother's attitude toward her romantic involvement with Seth. That she would actually encourage it was astounding. But when she was a young girl, Catherine had always been as protective of her as Maggie was of Natalie. Apparently her mother now trusted her judgment.

"He didn't say," Maggie replied. "But it doesn't matter. I have more important things to worry about right now than dances."

"Oh yes, dear. Of course." Catherine nodded, much too agreeably. "I know you do. I mean, what woman could possibly look forward to a dance with the most handsome man in the state when she has a range war on her agenda? One must have her priorities. Yes, indeed."

Maggie pulled her shawl closer around her shoulders. It seemed cold in Cleve's blue parlor, even on this warm summer day. It was all she could do to keep from getting up, walking to the windows, and throwing back all the heavy drapes so that the room might just once feel the warmth of the sun. Instead, she busied herself with the tea and cookies the maid had brought. It was just the refreshment she needed after the long buggy ride from the ranch.

While she waited for Cleve, she hoped Natalie might join her, but from all appearances the house was empty, and she wondered if Natalie had gone shopping. Knowing Cleve, he would spoil the girl frightfully and probably not think twice about giving her extravagant amounts of spending money. Maggie couldn't help but wonder if the simple cotton dress she'd made for the barn dance would look as good to the girl now that she'd been surrounded by the luxury of the Williams' mansion.

At last Cleve entered the room with the forbearance of a man who knew his importance. "Maggie, what a pleasant surprise! I should keep your daughter as a houseguest more frequently if it would encourage your visits." He sat in the chair opposite her and poured himself a cup of tea.

Maggie watched him, realizing for the first time what a dandy he was. Or maybe she was just too used to seeing Seth's ruggedness. "Is Natalie here? I'd like to talk to her."

Cleve took a sip of the hot tea. "Actually, she went out this morning. She said she wanted to visit a friend."

"Was it Andy Dray?"

"The boy at the blacksmith shop?"

"The young man—yes."

"I don't believe so. At least she didn't mention his name. But then I'm sure she wouldn't have told me. Maggie, don't look so worried. There's no need. It's broad daylight and the boy is at work. I'm sure they won't do anything they shouldn't. She's a very responsible young woman. I can tell you we've all enjoyed having her here immensely. The maids especially. I do believe they get tired of seeing no face but mine or that of an occasional dinner guest. They've been fussing over her outrageously."

It was exactly what Maggie had been afraid of. If Cleve kept it up the girl might very well never return home. Maggie rose to her feet. "Well, since she's not here, I'll see if I can find her in town. Mother's shopping so maybe she's already found her."

Cleve came to his feet, moving into a position that blocked her exit from the parlor. A look of concern unfurled itself in his eyes. "Are you sure there isn't something more I can do to help you? I've heard talk that you've lost more cattle and that

Tate's even brought in more hired guns. I really fear for your life, Maggie, and for the lives of your family. Are you sure you won't change your mind and move into town where it's safe?"

"We've discussed this before, Cleve. You know how upset it makes me to even think about selling the White Raven."

She tried to get past him, but suddenly found herself against his chest in an alarmingly tight embrace that would require a struggle to free herself from. Not wanting to make more of it than necessary she remained passive, deciding it might be better to suffer it until the moment he relaxed his grip enough that she could gracefully back away.

"I just want you to know I care about your safety, Maggie," he said, his lips much too close to hers. "I doubt you've even been remotely aware over the years how much you've meant to me. Of course, with Trent being alive and such a good friend, I could never have betrayed him with those feelings. But now, knowing you're out there on that ranch and vulnerable—that you might end up the way Trent did—well, it's been more than I care to think about."

Maggie knew Cleve cared for her, but she preferred not hearing it put to words. Words made her feel trapped, just as this house made her feel like a prisoner, or a corpse in a funeral parlor. Suddenly she longed for the security of Seth's strong, masculine arms.

"Please, Cleve," she said firmly. "I know you care about me, but it's too soon for me to think of another man."

His act of romantic aggression was unusual and short-lived. Always the proper gentleman, he remembered his manners and released her, but a flash of anger in his eyes was more than a little unsettling. It actually frightened her for a split second before it vanished.

"Is that so, Maggie?" He stepped away from her by a yard or more. "Then why are you going to the barn dance with Sackett?"

Before she could throw together an explanation, he had turned on his heel and stalked away, disappearing into another room. Maggie was greatly relieved and quickly showed herself from the house. With more desperation than before, she had to find Natalie and bring her home. It simply wouldn't do to have her stay with Cleve any longer.

Seth came awake to the darkness of the line shack. It wasn't a nightmare that woke him this time. He sat up, listening. In the silence he sensed something was wrong. Sensed he wasn't alone. He heard his horse whinny from the corral. It had probably been the sound that had woke him, but the thing that was unusual about it was that the bay was not one for noise and especially in the middle of the night, unless there was another horse nearby. But he heard no other sounds. If someone was out there he was too far away for his movements to be heard from inside the cabin.

He eased out of bed and dressed with as little noise as possible. With his .45 in hand, he started for the door, avoiding the loose, squeaky plank in

the floor, four over from the cot. On quiet feet he
continued to the door, the only exit in the one-room
cabin.

Placing an ear against the door, he listened again
but heard nothing. He didn't think he was imagin-
ing things. Someone was waiting outside to kill him.
He felt it. He had laid the bait by coming here and
he was sure he had a sucker on the hook. But how
many were there? Would they fire as soon as he
opened the door? He debated the answer, then decided that whoever was out there wouldn't be prepared for him to come out before morning.

He opened the door slowly, inch by inch, so
slowly in fact it would probably go unnoticed in the
darkness beyond. One thing that would work to his
advantage was that the sky was overcast, making it
even darker. When he had the opening wide
enough, he squeezed through sideways, flattened
himself momentarily against the cabin's log wall,
and then faded into the shadows beneath the low
eaves. In another instant he slipped around the corner of the cabin and out of range of anyone who was
watching the front door.

Going to the rear of the cabin, he moved out into
the darkness and circled wide, hoping to come up
behind the person who had more than likely positioned themselves to watch the cabin's only door.
But suddenly he heard running feet in the darkness
and then a galloping horse. He caught the movement, but didn't waste a bullet on the intruder. It
had happened so fast he hadn't been able to see
much of anything. All he knew for certain was that
the horse had been of a dark color.

He returned to the cabin, but at first light he was back out searching the ground for footprints or for anything left behind. Whoever had been there had been careful. He'd dropped nothing that Seth could find. He'd left only some boot prints, prints that were unusually small for a man and had been made by boots that were old. The sole was worn on the right shoe just beneath where the big toe would have been. Seth measured his own against them, then dropped to his haunches and studied the clearest ones he could find. When he stood up again, the prints were branded in his mind. If he saw them again, he would recognize them.

Chapter Twenty

"Maggie, why can't you age gracefully? Don't you know that for every gray hair you pluck out of your head you're bound to get two back?"

Maggie leaned closer to the mirror, trying to isolate the shiny silver thread from the auburn mass so she could snare it with the tweezers. "That's fine, Mother, as long as the two that come back aren't gray."

Catherine clicked her tongue in disgust, took her daughter by the shoulders and pulled her back onto the chair. "At the very most you've only got half a dozen gray hairs in your entire head anyway. Now, let me fix your hair. Seth and Lance were ready thirty minutes ago and I'm afraid Alison will give up on being a lady and we'll have to dress her all over again. I swear, I've never seen you have such a streak of vanity since Trent came courting. If I didn't know better, I'd think you were trying to impress Seth."

Maggie flashed her a look of annoyance and handed her the tweezers. "Just pull it out, Mother."

Catherine took the tweezers but slipped them into her dress pocket. "I will not. You look very lovely. Seth has probably seen that gray hair already anyway. And he has a few himself at the temples. Very distinguished, too, I might add."

"Gray is distinguished only on men," Maggie added dryly. "On women, it's just a sign that we're getting old. And I wasn't thinking of Seth. I don't really care what he thinks of me. He finagled this date in a rather underhanded way. It's not like he's courting me."

"Really? And what would you call it? His duty that he inform Cleve you were going with him to the dance? I suppose you're going to tell everybody at the dance that he's only acting in the capacity of your bodyguard."

"It would be accurate."

"No one would believe it."

"Mother, I'm walking into Lissa Dugan's barn dance with Seth Sackett, one of the most notorious men alive. Don't you know that every head will turn and every tongue will start wagging? If I'm going to be the center of gossip and attention, I surely don't want that ungodly silver hair sticking straight up in the middle of my part for everyone to see."

Catherine laughed and removed the tweezers, poising them over the silver hair. "Of course you're absolutely right, dear. Forgive me for not being more sensitive. Lissa would surely never let you live it down that you had a hair out of place." With a tug the single hair came free from Maggie's scalp. She handed it down to Maggie, caught in the tweezers.

Maggie lifted it free of the metal instrument and stared at it. "I suppose it is rather pretty, isn't it?"

"In case you hadn't noticed, I have a head full the same color."

Maggie gave her a smile in the mirror. "Proceed with your magic, Mother. We're running late."

Maggie didn't tell her mother she was also fretting over the dress she'd chosen to wear—the blue one Trent had given her just before he had died. While her mother gathered their shawls and bags from the bed, Maggie made one last cursory glance in the full-length mirror. The delicate muslin was suitable for a picnic or a barn dance, and the dainty flowered design enhanced the feminine lines. It was actually two pieces, a skirt and matching shirtwaist. High-collared, the shirt-waist had a front and back yoke both overlaid with lace. Four ruffles, in graduated tiers, tapered down from the yoke to enhance the bosom and make her waist look exceedingly small. The long sleeves fit her arms snugly, and sported a ruffled cuff as well as two ruffled epaulettes at the puff shoulders.

At the parlor, Maggie and her mother found Lance, Alison, and Seth carrying on a lively conversation about school. Lance and Seth were trying to convince Alison that it would be well worth it for her to spend as much time at her books as she did her cats and pony.

Seth rose to his feet when the women entered the room. Lance, remembering his manners, followed Seth's example. Both men were strikingly handsome in their white shirts, string ties, vests, and black pants. But Maggie barely had a chance to run an admiring eye over Seth before Alison ran forward and threw her arms around her waist. "Oh, you look so pretty, Mama!" she stood back and eyed her with a degree of awe. "I didn't know you had that dress. You should wear it more often."

"That's what I've been trying to tell her," Catherine put in. "But when has a daughter ever listened to her mother?"

"Maybe we'll just have to take her to more dances," Seth spoke up from his position in the center of the parlor.

Maggie heard the seductive quality to his tone and lifted her gaze from Alison's sparkling green eyes to the magnetic gray of the man she'd taken as a lover. He smiled at her from behind his moustache, a smile more discernible in his eyes than his lips, but she read it easily and knew he was thinking of the times they'd been together. His eyes blatantly suggested that there would be more of those intimate moments if he had his way. Maggie secretly admitted her mother was right. She hadn't dressed to impress the people at the barn dance. She had dressed to impress Seth Sackett. And she was sure now that she had succeeded. She was very glad he had come out of hiding. But none of the men had been told where he was staying. He had just showed up at the ranch again one day, surprising them all.

He turned his attention from her to Catherine. "Your daughter is lovely, Mrs. Marshall, but I see she's had an excellent example to follow."

Catherine smiled, pleased. "Why thank you, Seth. It's always nice to have a man about who appreciates female efforts." She turned to Lance and held out her arm. "Come along and help me into the surrey."

"Yes, Grandma." The boy hastened forward to oblige.

Alison hurried after her grandmother, too. Seth sauntered across the distance to Maggie and held out his arm. "You do look lovely indeed, Maggie, but I believe you've forgotten something."

Alarmed, Maggie glanced up at him while her mind tumbled over what it could possibly be. A hat, perhaps? No, one didn't wear a hat to a barn dance.

"Your gun," he supplied, smiling.

She released a relieved sigh. "I'm sorry to disappoint you, but it really doesn't go well with this dress."

His eyes slid boldly over her, telling her without words that he approved of what he saw. "I'll have my work cut out tonight protecting you," he whispered. "How about making it easy and saving all the dances for me?"

She only laughed, tucked her arm through his, and allowed him to lead her outside.

Seth helped Maggie into the surrey, taking note of how tiny her waist was in his hands. He also noticed some cold stares from the outriders. Practically every cowboy on the ranch was going to the dance. Only a few of the older men were staying behind to keep an eye on things. Since all the trouble between the ranches and the murders, Seth had suggested they all ride to Dugan's together.

While most of the men's faces were impassive,

Seth knew they wondered about his relationship with Maggie and no doubt there were some who didn't think it fitting that he had ridden onto the place and started courting her. They considered him temporary and wanted him to remain that way. He knew they were silently thinking that if he married her, they would be answering to him. But only Sonny flashed contemptuous eyes as he turned his horse and led the way from the ranch.

The surrey was the type often referred to as a "poor man's surrey" because it didn't have a top. But the ladies didn't mind and simply opened up parasols to keep the sun from their faces. It was the Fourth of July and was about the hottest it was going to get for this far north. They would have four to eight weeks more of hot weather before the first frosts brought fall.

Seth wished he was alone with Maggie, but he also enjoyed the company of her family. They were such a cheerful, easy-going people even in the face of danger and the recent troubles they'd faced. There was hope among them. They were not down-trodden, afraid to speak for fear of a belt across their backs or a hand across their faces. Seth enjoyed being in their company. For the first time in his life he felt the chains of guilt that had held him in their cruel grasp his entire life finally begin to weaken. Even the demons were forced to slink back into their dark shadows to wait until another time to practice their tormenting games. He didn't doubt they would return some day, probably when he left the White Raven, but for now they had no choice but to find a soul less happy than his was at the moment.

A crowd of people and a tangle of wagons and horses were already at Dugan's big barn when they arrived. Seth helped the women from the wagon. Catherine hurried off with her fried chicken and rolls to add to the array of food already collecting on the long, cloth-covered tables that had been placed in the shade of a stand of cottonwoods.

The barn was huge with an open loft. Open at both ends it allowed the breeze to flow through. Great care had been taken in making it as spotless as a barn could be made, and fresh straw and sawdust had been spread—the latter to be used on the dance area in the center of the barn. While the ladies fussed at the tables of food, the men had congregated at another spot of shade by the creek to smoke and "shoot the bull," a male form of gossip. No alcoholic beverages would be served in order to keep fights from breaking out, but a bowl of spiked punch would undoubtedly show up before the night was over.

A wooden platform near the dance area had been constructed for the six musicians who were gathering to tune their instruments. Children, dogs, and cats ran wild, and Alison was promptly lost in the melee.

The men were relieved of their guns upon entering the barn. Seth didn't want to relinquish his. A gunfighter without his gun was too easy a target, and a man like Morrell wouldn't give murder a second thought. But Seth also knew that if anyone here intended to kill him, they wouldn't meet him face to face anyway to give him a fair chance. He didn't want to cause trouble and spoil things for Maggie. He had never seen her smile so much. And he'd never seen her prettier. Handing over his guns might be the death of him, but he wanted to dance with her one more time, and to real music, before he died. He watched with an empty feeling as Lissa put his rig in a clean manger along with all the rest of the hardware, and he walked away feeling naked and vulnerable.

The chords of the first song, a waltz, were struck. To ease the lost feeling of being minus his gun, Seth found Maggie, hoping that if he had her in his arms, she could fill that disturbing void of insecurity. She was standing in a spot where the sunshine came in through the loft window and scattered golden light onto her auburn hair, making it alive with fire. He could do nothing but just stare at her for a moment until she finally lifted her hand to her hair in a self-conscious way and said, "Is something wrong, Seth?"

"Nothing," he said huskily. "You just have the most beautiful hair I've ever seen."

If he wasn't mistaken she blushed, then he took her hand and led her to the dance area, not giving her a chance to deny him a dance. He drew her into his arms, knowing others were watching them and wondering about their relationship. But the wonder he felt at having her in his arms was bound to show in his eyes and he decided it was fine if it did. He didn't care if everyone in the valley knew he loved her.

It took him a minute to get the rhythm down and

get his feet moving, but once he did, the brief lesson she'd given him that night in the parlor came back. He didn't tell her he'd been doing some practicing out at the line shack with an imaginary partner.

Her smile made him forget the loss of his guns. "You remembered, Seth," she whispered. "It was such a short lesson, I didn't think you would."

"I had a good teacher."

Before the song had ended, his movements were smooth and fluid. He was proud that he'd accomplished it without stepping on her toes and summoning the ridicule of other dancers. As the songs continued, he noticed most of the men were like buffaloes on a run, a lot of thundering speed, but not much grace.

After several waltzes to loosen up the dancers, the musicians cut to a Virginia reel. Seth was afraid he would mess it up. The only dance he'd ever been to in his life was the one with the Taylor girl, the one he'd had the dream about the other night. Even back then, he'd had two left feet as he'd tried to fake his way through the various sets of square dances. But he followed Maggie and soon got the hang of things.

He missed not having her in his arms the way he had during the waltzes, but he found himself getting drunk on the lively music, the laughter, and the fact that she seemed to be enjoying his company as much as he was hers. They were growing accustomed to each other's touch, but the electricity was still there, more powerful than ever. When their eyes met he read in the reflection of hers the vivid recollection of the intimacies they'd shared. With an unspoken promise that they would share those moments again, he suddenly wanted nothing more than to take her into a dark corner, or out back somewhere and satisfy just a bit of that desire with a kiss and the hot, soft feel of her body pressed tightly to his. But he couldn't. It would have to wait until they were alone, and he sensed it would be even more satisfying, more sweet for the waiting.

He noticed when Tate's crowd arrived, but they all handed over their guns, too, and even though the gunmen hung around with squinty, hard eyes, assessing the doings with indifference, Tate took his wife by the hand and joined in with the dancing. A big bull of a man, he looked more like he was stomping out a pile of ants than doing a square dance.

After an hour, Maggie pleaded exhaustion and Seth escorted her to the punch bowl. He wouldn't admit it, but the dancing had given him quite a work out, too.

While Maggie sipped at the iced lemonade, she watched the crowd and Seth watched her and the way her lips fit so daintily over the rim of the glass cup and the way her hands held it with such grace and beauty.

"I really thought Natalie would come," she said, disappointment thick in her voice and her eyes.

Seth refilled the tiny, cut-glass cup that held only a few swallows. It was hardly the instrument for a thirsty man. "Maybe she changed her mind when she found out Andy Dray was going to be here with Cecilia Wagner."

Maggie nearly choked.

"They're over there," Seth nodded in the general direction of the two, "in the shade of those cotton-woods."

Maggie spotted them, drinking punch and conversing in the shy manner of young people getting acquainted. "Where's Lance?"

"He left right after he got here. He probably saw them together."

Maggie set her cup down and started for the horses. Seth caught her arm. "Let him go, Maggie. When a man's been jilted, he likes to be alone."

"Why didn't you tell me?"

"You were having too much fun, and there was nothing you could have done anyway. By the way, Cleve just arrived. And he's headed this way. Maybe he can tell you why Natalie didn't come."

Maggie turned and saw the entrepreneur smiling at everyone, patting people on the backs, giving brief greetings as he made his way through the crowd toward Maggie. She tensed. She didn't want to talk to him again, but he didn't act as if they'd exchanged heated words. She had so enjoyed dancing with Seth, being in his arms and his company, that she didn't want it to end. Sonny had been watching from the sidelines but he hadn't mustered the courage to cut in. Cleve wouldn't be so shy.

"Maggie! I'm so glad you turned your back on that mess at the ranch long enough to come out and have a little fun. And you look absolutely lovely." His gaze slid over her admiringly. "I hope you'll save a few dances for me."

She glanced past him, having greater concerns.

Searching the crowd, she said, "Didn't Natalie come with you?"

"Natalie?" He reached to fill a cup with punch. "Of course not. She left to go home two days ago."

Maggie paled and reached for Seth's arm to steady herself. "What do you mean, she came home?"

Cleve's face suddenly hardened with concern. "You mean she didn't?"

"No."

"Good God, Maggie. I had no idea. Where could she possibly be then?"

Maggie began to tremble. She found a bench and sat on it. Seth sat next to her, putting an arm around her shoulders.

"Maybe she's with Andy," Cleve added hopefully. "I'm sure there's an explanation for it, Maggie."

"She's not with Andy."

Maggie felt herself losing control, felt as if she were going to fly apart and into a million pieces. Things began to whirl and to blur. The noise of the laughing people and the music and the screaming children suddenly all rushed together and came down over her in a maddening whirl. Her daughter was missing and she wanted to scream. But she couldn't. She had to remain calm. Had to keep her head about her so she could think of what to do, where to look. But Maggie Cayton had never been very good at being calm in a crisis. Suddenly, driven by a mother's rage and fear, she left Seth's side with renewed strength and marched across the yard and into the barn.

"Ben Tate!"

The music stopped. Everyone turned to look at her, but all she saw was the big rancher, turning and glaring at her. Blind with fear and worry, she blocked everything from her mind but one thing. "Where's Natalie, Ben? She's missing. What have you done with her?"

She was about to fly into him with her claws bared when she was caught from behind by Seth's strong arms, holding her back, holding her up. She was crying, but she couldn't help herself. Aware of the amazed and disapproving faces of the other women, she nonetheless held her ground, her eyes piercing Tate.

Ben left the group of dancers. "I have no idea what this is about, Maggie. I haven't seen your daughter. Nor would I lay a hand on her."

"You're a liar."

Ben's face turned livid. Cleve stepped forward, trying to quickly smooth things over and calm the big man's temper that was about to erupt in retaliation. "Natalie's missing," he said. "In light of the recent developments between the White Raven and the Broken Arrow, it's natural for Maggie to think you might be behind her daughter's disappearance, Ben. Of course we all know you wouldn't do such a thing."

"You're damned right I wouldn't! I'm not a kidnapper or a murderer. *Or* a liar!" He had been joined by his wife, and he took her by the arm and started ushering her past Maggie and the crowd that had gathered. "Come on, Ethel, we're leaving."

All his hired men hurried to gather their guns and

follow. Seth took Maggie's arm and led her from
the crowd and toward the surrey. Catherine came to
help, as did Lance.

"Lance, get our guns," Seth said from over Maggie's head. "We'd better get Maggie home and start
looking for Natalie."

"What's happened to Natalie?"

"We don't know. Williams says she left his place
two days ago. Round up Alison while you're at it."

In the background, they heard the music resume
as Lissa Dugan tried to get her party back into
swing. He and Lance hitched up the team and
helped the women into the surrey. The hired men
loyally joined them. But just as Seth came around
the wagon to climb onto the driver's side, he also
came face to face with Max Morrell.

He glanced at Seth's empty hip. "A gunfighter
without a gun is usually a dead man, Sackett."

"Get out of my way, Morrell."

His lip curled into an ugly sneer. "And what are
you going to do about it?"

Before Morrell knew what had hit him, Seth
planted his knuckles square in the gunslinger's nose.
Blood shot out and he hit the ground. He went for
his gun but found the cold muzzle of another
pressed against his temple.

"Don't try it, Morrell," Lance said, holding
Seth's big Peacemaker to the man's head. "You can
just wait until things are a little more even."

Morrell daubed at his nose, which was plainly
broken. Stumbling to his feet, he glanced at Maggie.
"You shouldn't be trusting a man whose first kill
was his own father. Maybe he's the one who kid-

napped your daughter and has her somewhere, using her for his own pleasure, the same as he is you."

Gathering his hat, he stalked to his horse. Seth kept his eye on him until he'd ridden out on a fast and angry gallop. He dreaded having to look Maggie in the eye after that, and when he finally found the nerve to, he saw the shock he'd expected. Whatever else she felt, he couldn't read.

He knew now he should have been the one to tell her about his father. She had wanted to know. Now it was unlikely she would ever see the matter from his perspective. He just hoped Morrell's accusation about him kidnapping Natalie wouldn't be taken seriously.

Lance handed him his gun belt and he strapped it on. Things immediately shifted back to normal. Once again he was reminded that he couldn't hide from who he was or what he was; couldn't pretend he was worthy of Maggie Cayton; couldn't escape the hell of his fate in the strains of some lively music and in the comforting arms of a good woman. His father's words echoed piously through his mind, reminding him of all these things and making sure he never forgot them.

His bones are full of the sin of his youth, which shall lie down with him in the dust. Job 20:11.

Yes, Seth Sackett was a killer, and his sin would go with him to the grave.

Chapter Twenty-One

The journey back to the White Raven was a silent one filled with tension. Maggie sat nervously next to Seth, fearing for Natalie's life and wondering where she could possibly start looking for her. No one at the dance had come forward with any information. Not even Andy had seen the girl or heard from her. Fear wasn't Maggie's alone. Catherine, Lance, and Alison were worried, too. Occasionally, one of them would offer a suggestion as to where she might be.

Maggie had no idea what Seth's thoughts were. He'd been grimly silent the entire trip, never glancing her way as his able hands on the reins kept the team in check. He had withdrawn and once again become the stoic gunman who had first ridden onto the White Raven weeks ago. She supposed it had to do with what Morrell had said about him killing his father, and Maggie wondered if it was true. She remembered the ugly scars on Seth's back, and remembered the few times he'd spoken of his father and how the bitterness had been thick and deep.

At the ranch they dispersed from the surrey, and

Maggie gave instructions to the men. "I want you to go out in pairs and check every line shack on the White Raven for Natalie. I'll be going to town and talking to people there."

Talking about the missing girl seemed to light a spark in the men. Clements, always the hothead, was the first to speak. "I say we go over to Tate's— the bunch of us—and see if he's holding her prisoner!"

A few of the others joined in their agreement. From the looks on their faces, they were tired of sitting back and waiting for something to happen. They were ready to make it happen.

Sonny positioned his horse in front of the group. "You need to cool off in the horse trough, Clements," he said, biting back his anger and annoyance. "If we ride onto Tate's place it would give those gunmen of his the perfect excuse to open fire. We need some proof before we do something stupid like that."

"And how do you plan to get proof? Ain't none been found so far." Clements' square jaw jutted out belligerently. "Do you plan to sneak onto his place in the middle of the night and break into his house?"

"That might be the only way." It was Seth who spoke. All heads turned his direction. "But we'll go through the regular procedures of investigation first. Natalie's probably just gone off somewhere to be alone. She could have even taken a room at the hotel."

Sonny folded his hands over his saddle horn. His small eyes narrowed even more with contempt. "It seems your being here has caused Maggie more problems than it's solved, Sackett."

"What do you mean by that?" Maggie snapped, getting back into the fray.

Sonny straightened, gathering his reins as if preparing to leave. His eyes shifted from Seth to Maggie and back. "Natalie told me one day that she didn't like you, Sackett. And you're getting mighty tight with the family. It seems to me maybe you saw fit to get her out of the way so she couldn't interfere with your cozy little set-up with the boss. Maybe Morrell was right."

Before Sonny knew what had happened, Seth had him by the shirt front and was yanking him out of the saddle. He shoved him up against the saddle fender. "Maybe you'd like to retract that statement, Haig."

Maggie placed a hand on Seth's shoulder. "It's all right, Seth. Let him go." Then she turned to the others. "I hired Seth to do a job, the same as I did the rest of you. He's not here to win your adoration, nor you his. So unless you'd like to come to my office to air your grievances, or collect your severance pay, I suggest you get busy and get to work."

The men, seeing they'd ired the boss about as much as they could get away with, turned their mounts and headed for the bunkhouse to change.

Maggie waited until the men were across the yard before turning to her family. Her instructions were simple and went undisputed. She asked her mother to stay at the ranch with Alison, and she told Lance to join the men in their search because she believed that if Natalie was hiding in one of the line shacks, it might take her brother to get her to come out. Then she turned to Seth.

"I'll need you to go with me," she said simply. "How soon can you be ready to ride?"

Seth shifted to his other foot, leaning all his weight on one leg. He looked toward the mountains in a contemplative way before finally meeting her waiting gaze. He saw in the green depths of her eyes the pain and worry. He longed to pull her into his arms and comfort her, comfort himself, and get things back to the way they had been before Morrell had shattered his fantasy world with ugly reality.

"Are you sure you want me to, Maggie?" he asked softly. "It would seem I'm the reason she ran away. Maybe it's time for me to fork my bay and head back to Deadwood."

He watched her eyes and waited to read a telltale emotion of how she felt about him now that Morrell had told his secrets, but all he saw was indecision and confusion and, lastly, her typical defiance. Maggie Cayton had survived on defiance alone, and stubborn determination. He could understand that; he could understand her.

"Don't take all the credit, Seth," she said in a voice that seemed unusually strained. "And don't leave when I need you the most."

What man could possibly say no to a woman when her eyes held so much fear and so much need? Especially when that woman had somehow managed to get past the wall he'd constructed around his heart and made him care again, made him love, and who knew him so intimately she was probably the only person who had ever gotten into his mind in the least. He had honestly thought he would never care about anything again, because to care meant to be hurt. And love? He'd never loved anyone but his brother and his mother, so loving Maggie Cayton and her children and her mother was an all-new experience. He wanted to fix everything that was wrong in her life in exchange for a gentle hand that could fix everything that was wrong in his.

"We'll find her, Maggie." But even as he said it, he wasn't so sure. "I'll saddle our horses."

He was ready and waiting thirty minutes later when she came from the house, once again in her riding attire with her gun strapped to her hip. She carried a small carpetbag and a bedroll. Alison walked beside her, toting another bundle which she handed to Seth.

"Grandma made you some sandwiches because she was afraid you'd get hungry before you got to town."

Seth took the proffered bundle. "Will you thank your grandmother for me?"

She nodded and watched intently while he tied the bundle behind his saddle. "Mr. Sackett?"

He looked down into her pretty eyes, so worried and so like Maggie's. She looked very small, vulnerable, and uncertain. He finished tying the saddle strings around the bundle and lowered himself to his haunches in front of her. "Don't worry, Alison," he said. "We'll find your sister."

Suddenly she threw her arms around his neck and began sobbing against his shirt collar. "It's my fault! All my fault! We got in a fight and I told her

I wished she'd marry that stupid Andy and go away and never come back."

Seth's gaze caught Maggie's as they exchanged their silent concern for the girl. Then Seth said, "It wasn't because of you that she left. It seems your sister left because—"

"She left because she was angry with me," Maggie interjected, cutting off Seth's confession and coming around her horse to join the two of them.

Alison lifted her tear-stained face to her mother, but retained an arm across Seth's shoulder. "But why would she be mad at you, Momma?"

"Suffice it to say we didn't see eye to eye on something."

"But that's no reason for her to leave. There's lots of times people don't agree on things."

Maggie placed a hand on Alison's shoulder. "We'll find her. And don't blame yourself."

Alison considered her mother's grave words for a moment, then reached into her pocket and extracted her lucky marble. She lifted Seth's hand and placed it in his palm. "You'll need this, Mr. Sackett. And while you're gone, I'll ask God to help you find her."

Seth stared down at the marble for a minute before rising to his full height and dropping it into his shirt pocket. "I guess if God answers anybody's prayers, Alison, He'll answer yours."

"Oh, you just have to believe," she said matter-of-factly. "That's all there is to it."

Impressed by her wisdom, moved by her innocent faith, Seth kissed her cheek. He and Maggie swung into their saddles then and headed for town as swiftly as they dared push their horses.

It was dark when they left their horses at the livery. A few minutes later they signed in for rooms at the hotel, but Maggie couldn't wait until morning to look for Natalie. With Seth willingly by her side, she went first to the stage lines to see if Natalie had left town. She hadn't. They went to every business, every hotel, and every boarding house, rousting out the owners, but they found nothing. No one had seen Natalie. Maggie feared the girl might have been abducted into a brothel, or worse, might even have gone willingly for some childish reason to get back at her mother. She insisted Seth take her to the red-light district, but he refused.

"If someone's kidnapped Natalie and forced her into prostitution, they sure as hell won't tell you anything. But I could find out if I go alone. I'm going to take you back to the hotel and I want you to eat and get some rest."

Maggie resisted at first, but Seth was adamant and she finally gave in. She didn't rest, though, and she had no appetite for food. All she could manage were a few nibbles off one of the roast beef sandwiches her mother had sent. Alternately she paced the floor and stared out the window, hoping to see Seth's return. Finally she collapsed on the bed in a state of mental and physical exhaustion.

His knock on the door well toward morning brought her awake with a start. She let him in, anxious for his findings. He tossed his hat on the bed and followed it with his body, collapsing wearily on his back in the middle of its softness, still warm from Maggie's body.

"Well, you can rest assured she's not in a brothel. I went to every one and asked specifically for a young girl to entertain me. I was given my choice at every place and Natalie was not presented, nor even hinted at as being available."

Maggie flashed him an angry look and returned to the window. "At least now I know what took you so damned long."

Seth pulled himself to a sitting position on the bed, bemused by her caustic remark. But suddenly he realized the essence of her innuendo. He chuckled, successfully driving her ire even higher. "I always knew we'd be lovers, Maggie, but I never thought I would ever make you jealous."

She whirled. "I only asked you to see if Natalie was there! You didn't have to become a paying customer at every place you went into! I don't give a damn what you do, or who you do it with, but I've been pacing this floor for hours, waiting for you to get back. My daughter is out there somewhere—maybe *dead!*—and you're dropping your pants in every brothel in town."

Maggie couldn't stop the tears that spilled from her eyes. She gave him her back, too angry to look at him. His footsteps were silent across the rug. When he placed his hands on her shoulders, she rebelled.

"Leave me alone. Please." It was an agonized plea. "Just go back to your room."

Seth put his arms around her and drew her back against his chest. "I didn't drop my pants in every brothel," he whispered in her ear. "Not even in one. I'm not interested in those women, Maggie. But I'm glad to hear you want me for yourself."

"Oh, don't you pride yourself?"

Seth expected her to tell him again to leave, to tell him she didn't want to be touched by him—a man who'd killed his father. Instead, she turned into his arms and sobbed helplessly against his chest.

"I'm so confused, Seth. What am I going to do? Was it so wrong of me to . . . to need another man? So wrong that I'm being punished for it now by my own daughter?"

Seth gathered her in his arms and carried her to the bed. Numbly she sat on the edge while he removed her boots and her clothing down to her chemise. He tucked her into bed and watched her roll to her side, curling up as if clutching a great pain in the center of her being. He turned down the lantern wick until the room was black, then he added his own clothes to the pile of hers. He slid beneath the covers next to her and conformed his body to her soft, feminine curves he was becoming so familiar with.

"You're not being punished for making love to me, Maggie. Get some rest now. Something will turn up tomorrow."

While Maggie slept, Seth was once again startled awake by the nightmare hell of the past. The familiar dream was mixed with disturbing images of Natalie and Maggie frantically trying to avoid the vicious blows from Ezra Sackett's belt. But it ended the same. Always the same. With the sneering dare and the jarring boom of a .45.

He eased out of the bed and fumbled in the darkness through his pockets for a cigarette and a match. Maggie turned over, reaching for him. "Seth?" she asked sleepily. "What's wrong?"

He could barely see her. With the shade drawn on the room's only window it was too dark. But he saw something of her form beneath the sheet, and the simple fact that she had woke, asking for him, was enough to send a raging fire of desire to his loins. It wasn't just a physical desire anymore that made him want her, or a selfish need to derive satisfaction by making her want him. No, it was an emotion from deep within that drove him to bond with her forever, to comfort her and receive the same.

"It's nothing," he whispered. "I'm sorry I woke you."

She propped herself up on an elbow, her hair falling over her shoulder in a dark cascade. Her hand slid tenderly up his back, nearly crumbling his resolve not to touch her. He couldn't expect Maggie to want to make love to him when he was the cause of Natalie's disappearance, something that weighed heavily on his conscience.

"Another dream?" she whispered, sounding more awake now.

He nodded, finally finding a match in his shirt pocket. He snapped the end between his thumb and forefinger and lit the cigarette. In the flickering light, he glanced down at her provocative loveliness, soaking it into his memory before blowing out the match.

"Seth." In the darkness he could hear every little nuance in her voice. It was tentative now. "Tell me about your father, and what Morrell said."

He had known this moment would come and he would be asked to explain it all to her. And when he was done, he would lose her. Yes, he'd known. He just wished the question would have waited. He didn't want to talk about it now, in the middle of the night. The memories were always more vivid in the darkness, closer, as if it had all just happened.

He left the bed and the reach of her hand. He walked to the window and lifted the blind. Nobody could see inside the room now; there was no one on the streets at this hour. The town's occupants slept, most likely in peace and in pleasant dreams. He couldn't recall when he had.

He took a drag on the cigarette, but it tasted bitter and didn't help to ease the feelings, or to make the job of reciting the past any easier to deal with. What was the use of explaining it all? The truth was the truth, and there was no glossing it over, denying it, or making excuses.

He faced her, being able to see her better now with the pale light from outside offering some illumination to the room. She was beautiful sitting in the center of the bed in her white, fancy underthings. How could anyone have blamed him for falling hopelessly in love with her?

"I killed a man who needed killing, Maggie," he said softly. "A man by the name of Ezra Sackett. You were right when you called me a killer. I am. I shot him in cold blood."

He turned back to the window so he wouldn't

have to see her eyes and all the revulsion and contempt that was sure to surface there. He heard her move, the bedding rustle, the bed creak. So she was leaving. It was understandable.

Her hand on his back startled him as did the heat of her body pressing full length against his. He wanted to sink into the gentleness of her touch and never surface again.

"Damn it, Maggie," he said gruffly. "Go back to bed. I'll get my things and go to my own room."

"I don't believe you killed him in cold blood. I want the truth, Seth."

He felt her breasts soft against his back, and her lips grazing his scars tenderly. Perhaps it was the wonder of the sensation, and his unworthiness of it, that caused him to suddenly whirl and grab her by the shoulders. "It's the truth! I killed him. I pointed the gun at his hateful heart and I pulled the trigger! Now, get away from me. I'm not worthy of your sympathy or your compassion. I'm exactly what you said I was!"

He tried to step past her but she caught his arm. "Your back was cut to ribbons by something, Seth Sackett," she hissed angrily, "and I don't believe it was that French whore's knife that did all the fancy work. It was him, wasn't it? Your father beat you, repeatedly, and you finally took all you could take."

Seth easily pulled free of her grip and stalked to the ashtray, crushing out the cigarette. He grabbed up his clothes and started yanking them on.

"Damn it, tell me!" she insisted, leaning over him until her face was only inches from his.

He took her by the shoulders and tossed her back

onto the bed, coming down over her. His face was angry, but it was the torment of pain and grief that etched themselves more fully into a mask of pathetic misery. His eyes locked with hers for strained seconds and, as if all his energy had been drained, he released her with a tortured moan and fell onto his back beside her.

She came up on an elbow and gently stroked his cheek. "It's all right, Seth. You can tell me. I won't judge you."

"I've never told anyone." He stared bleakly at the dark ceiling.

"You'll never be free of the pain if you don't release it once and for all and just walk away from it. Whatever happened is over. Get beyond it, Seth. Don't keep living it and putting yourself through this agony."

He threw an arm up over his head, letting it flop heavily onto the bed. "I hated him, Maggie. God, how I hated him."

"Why? Tell me."

He wanted to yell, to hit something. To cry. God, maybe it *was* time to tell someone. Only his mother had known what had really happened that fateful day. Rumors had circulated of course, telling the truth of it, and he supposed it was one of those rumors that Morrell had heard.

"Because he hated me," he said gruffly, ashamed of that fact and ashamed to be admitting it to Maggie of all people. "I could do nothing right for him. But it wasn't just me. It was everyone who crossed his path.

"My father claimed to be a man of God, but he

was really kin to the devil. He did things. Things that would have been wicked in his eyes if someone else had done them, but he always pardoned himself, mostly by simply denying he'd done anything wrong. Or he would pray to God and ask forgiveness, only to turn around and do something even more vile. He was a prisoner of his own flesh, and I think he hated it so bad that he punished everyone around him for his own weaknesses."

Seth paused but only for a minute. The story was tumbling from him now like a pitcher overflowing with water. "He cheated on my mother numerous times. He abused a young girl. We found out about it, but he denied it and no charges were brought against him because he was a preacher.

"He demanded perfection of everyone but himself, and when that perfection wasn't met by his strict standards—which he believed were also God's—he offered no forgiveness. No physical repentance or mental anguish was adequate enough. No one was safe from his wrath. Not me, not my brother, not even my mother."

Seth kept his eyes on the ceiling, not wanting to see Maggie's thoughts develop more deeply and firmly against him.

"My brother—" his voice cracked and he swallowed, waiting until he had control. "My brother died because of a blow to the head. My father hit him with a piece of angle iron, but refused to believe that was the cause of death. Even though the doctor's report stated death was due to a massive blow to the head. After that my mother couldn't stay with him any longer. Yet she feared turning him in because she thought it would just be his word against hers. He was a preacher, a man of God." The words were so bitter he nearly choked on them. "He would escape being charged and then she and I would bear the brunt of her betrayal.

"Even though she had no way to support herself or me, she took me and we ran away. We went to a town in Texas. She found a job as a cook in a restaurant. I found work, too, and we rented a room. Then he found us."

Seth fell into the mire of the memory, silently reliving it. Maggie felt the pain inside him, the mental anguish. She laid a hand on his chest but he kept his eyes trained on the ceiling.

"My pa told her she would have to be punished for running away," Seth continued in a quieter voice. "He hit her. She fell. I was afraid he'd kill her like he had Samuel. I couldn't stand by and let that happen. I had my gun. I was seventeen and I had had it for only a couple of months. I pointed it at him and I told him to stop hurting her or I'd kill him. He laughed in my face and said I didn't have the guts to do it, and he came at her again."

Seth sat up, but not before Maggie caught the glint of moisture in his eyes.

After a moment he continued. "I wasn't tried for murder. My mother told the law that I had bought the gun and my pa hadn't wanted me to have it. He'd tried to take it away and it had discharged. She lied for me, and I've often wondered if she should have. I should have owned up to it, but I . . . didn't."

Suddenly a dead silence filled the room. The tragedy of his life became a smothering cloak in the darkness until Maggie felt she could barely breath. But she refused to let it end there.

"You did it in your mother's defense, Seth," she said gently but stubbornly. "And in your own defense."

"Yes, but the thing that's the hardest to live with, harder than even the killing, is the fact that I've never regretted doing it. I've tried to feel remorse, but all I ever feel is the relief of being free of him. He always told me what a worthless sinner I was and that I was evil and destined for Hell. That I was the devil's son. Well, I was. He was the devil.

He stared into nothingness. "I've often thought of turning myself in, just to ease my own conscience. But at the same time I knew it wouldn't matter because no one would care if I chose to rot in jail, or in the Hell of my own mind. Pa had no friends. We were his only family. Even his congregation seemed relieved that he wouldn't be coming back. The law didn't even care.

"It was just our battle—my pa's and mine—and I've often wondered which one of us won."

Maggie kissed his shoulder. He hadn't expected that. When he lifted his eyes to hers he saw no revulsion, no disgust, only sympathy and understanding.

"What happened to your mother, Seth?"

He watched her watching him, her eyes glittering in the dark like gems. He watched her hand glide over his chest and he felt the tenderness wash through him, weakening him in a glorious sort of way. How he had longed for such compassion, such gentleness from a lover! Her lips touched his naked shoulder again and his heart finished falling all the way to the depths of hopeless love.

"I supported her," he whispered. "With the gun. I was a soldier, a mercenary, a hired gun. She died just last year, but she found peace before she did."

Maggie knelt behind him and wondered if he would be so lucky, or if he would punish himself with guilt all the way to his grave. If only there was something she could do or say that would ease his conscience and make him realize that even for what he'd done, he wasn't an evil man, only a desperate man who had acted out of that desperation.

"Do you think God will forgive your father for what he did, Seth?" It was more of a curiosity than a question.

He looked miserable. "I've heard He'll forgive the worst sinner. That's something that amazes me. I can't find it in my heart to forgive my father, so how could He? Like I said, I don't even regret doing it."

"Seth," Maggie left a feather-light kiss to the curl of dark hair at his nape, "I don't believe you. I believe you do regret it, very much. Why else would you still be tormented by what happened? As for forgiving him, maybe you should try. As you said, your father was not only expecting you and your family to live up to impossible expectations, but he expected the same of himself. He sounds like a man who inadvertently created his own Hell and then lived in it every moment of his life."

Seth shook his head. "Yes, and he transferred his self-made Hell to me. I can't forgive him, Maggie. The bitterness is too strong, the scars too deep."

"If you refuse to forgive him," she said tentatively, wondering if she was treading on dangerous ground, "Then how will you ever forgive yourself?"

A muscle in his shoulders jumped beneath her hands. She thought he might leave her side, but he didn't. "I don't care about any of that, Maggie. I only care what you think."

She pulled him down next to her on the bed. "You know what I think, Seth. I think you did what you did because you feared for your mother's life, and you had good reason to. I don't condemn you."

Soon she was making love to him, pulling his desperate heart into her comforting embrace. This time when they joined, it was with a deeper satisfaction than ever before, a deeper bonding. Seth felt that they joined at the soul, somehow, and that she became more a part of him than ever before.

Afterwards he held her in his arms and she fell asleep. She had blocked her troubles from her mind temporarily, but he couldn't. Talking about his father had brought it all back too vividly, too painfully. And with it came words from the book of Luke that kept rolling over and over in his mind, taunting him: *Judge not, and ye shall not be judged; condemn not, and ye shall not be condemned; forgive, and ye shall be forgiven. . . .*

Could it be that Maggie had the answer he had been searching for all these years? Could it be that peace of mind was as simple as that?

Chapter Twenty-Two

Seth left the room before Maggie woke up, deciding it might be more difficult to face her in the daylight after his unsavory confession than it had been at night. The darkness accentuated some things like fears and memories, but it also dulled things like reality and good judgment.

He had the horses saddled and at the hotel hitching rail when she came down the steps pulling on her gloves. Nothing was said about last night, but the brief glance they exchanged acknowledged it.

"I don't know what else we can do, Seth," she said, swinging into the saddle and wearing a grim expression. "Everyone in town will be on the lookout for Natalie. The only place we haven't looked is the Broken Arrow."

"And you'll be courting a bullet if you go there."

"I have no choice. My daughter is out there somewhere. Call it intuition if you will, but I know she's still alive. I have to keep looking until I find her."

Seth understood the desperation in her eyes. "All

right," he replied. "We'll ride to the Broken Arrow."

They bought jerky before leaving town, as well as fresh rolls from the bakery. It was something to sustain them through the day and on the long ride across Broken Arrow land. Staying to low areas they checked as many line shacks as Maggie knew existed on the southwestern portion of the ranch which was the area closest to town. The rest of the ranch would take several days to cover. As evening neared, they turned their mounts toward home.

Angling down through the hills, Seth's trained eye was suddenly drawn to an unusual black outcropping about a quarter of a mile away. Dusk would be upon them soon, but for now the sun rested on the horizon and pointed out the spot clearly.

Curious, he loped his horse over to it and Maggie felt obliged to follow. After stepping to the ground, he lowered himself to his haunches, turning over rocks and rolling a few small pebbles between his fingers.

"What is it, Seth?" Maggie watched him from her saddle.

He studied the black smudges on his fingers. "Possibly the reason someone wants you off the White Raven."

"What?" She, too, dismounted.

He handed he a chunk of the black stuff. "Do you know what this is?"

She fingered it for a moment. "It looks like coal."

"Did you know it was here?"

"I've seen similar outcroppings around the ranch. I never paid much attention to them."

Seth's keen eyes searched the distances to the north and then the south. "From the layout of the land, the upthrust of the hills, I would say there's most likely a seam of coal under the surface. It could underlie your entire ranch and Tate's, too. There could very well be enough here for the owner of this ground to make some big money. You'd probably never have to raise another cow for as long as you lived if you could get a big company interested in getting it out."

"Then you're saying that Ben Tate knows this is here, knows its value, and that's why he's trying to get me off the White Raven so he can get it all for a fraction of what it's worth?"

"Ben . . . or somebody else. Maybe someone knows it's here, knows there's a lot more of it, and wants you *both* out of the way so he can move in, buy the grazing ground cheap, then scrape in the profits from the coal. I'm sorry, Maggie, but Ben Tate is an old cattle rancher. He doesn't strike me as the sort who would give up his cattle and land. The grass means too much to him to tear it up for coal—no matter how much money he could make. Tate's a lot like you, even if you won't admit it. If he wanted this coal, he would have dug it up a long time ago. Like you, he's probably known it was here all along and just rode right on past it."

"But times are hard now, Seth, since the blizzards took so many cattle and left most of us in financial straits. Who's to say he doesn't have his back up against the wall and has turned to the coal as a last resort to get himself out of trouble?"

"Maybe. But you didn't resort to digging up the coal. You rode out the hard times until you got back on your feet. My guess is that Ben Tate has done the same thing. There could be millions of dollars right under your feet, Maggie. Even if neither you nor Ben are interested in this, someone else might be. Someone who doesn't care about the land, only what it will reap for the short term."

Maggie lifted her eyes to the panorama of green rolling hills that lifted toward the Big Horn Mountains. This land meant so much to her. The news of a coal field under it was not what she wanted to hear. The preservation of the land was more important to her than the money. Cattle utilized the land; coal mining destroyed it.

"I've fought for twenty years to keep this land from those who would take it," she said. "Is this the beginning of a lifelong battle to hold onto the White Raven? Men are never happy to leave some things alone. As time goes by and more and more people discover it's here, how will I ever hold onto what I have? How will Lance do it after I'm gone?"

Seth scrubbed the coal off his fingers with a handful of loose, dry dirt. "Deal with one battle at a time, Maggie. You'll be overwhelmed if you don't."

"Is that how you've survived, Seth?" She searched his face for the answers she needed. "One battle at a time?"

He knew she was referring to the battle of his conscience, to all those things he had shared with her last night. "Yes," he said quietly. "And I just keep hoping the battles will end, or at least that they'll be small enough that I can win them."

"When should I confront Tate about this?"

"After we find Natalie. One battle at a time, remember?"

By the time they arrived back at the ranch, it was too late for Seth to take a meal at the cookshack. Maggie insisted he come to the house and she would fix something for the two of them. Before they went inside, though, they agreed not to say anything about the coal, just in case it turned out that it had nothing to do with the problems at hand.

Maggie had been clinging to the hope all day that Lance and the men might have found Natalie, but both parties were quickly let down when neither had news to report.

Catherine, Lance, and Alison joined Seth and Maggie in the kitchen and, although Dorothy offered to fix the meal, Catherine insisted taking charge. While she cooked up steaks and eggs and cut into a loaf of fresh bread, they all sat in the coziness of the small kitchen, saying little, but seeming to draw on the security of each other's company in this time of distress.

Maggie was the first to leave the group, dismissing herself for bed, but once there she didn't even attempt to sleep. How could she when everything that had been her life now hung in the balance, as fragile as a dandelion's puff waiting for the wind to blow it away? She didn't see Seth return to the tack building—although she sat on the chaise lounge at the window for what seemed hours. She wondered if her mother had once again put him up in the house.

A fleeting breeze of hopelessness brushed past her. What if she never saw Natalie alive again?

A cricket outside the conservatory's open windows was asking for the smashing toe of a cowboy boot, but Seth knew he'd never be able to find the pesky little insect in the tall grass among Maggie's flowers even if he went out there on his hands and knees with a lantern. His only hope was that another creature higher up in the food chain would eliminate it for him. But while he waited for such a miracle, thirty minutes passed, and then an hour.

Finally giving up on sleep, he left the house and slipped quietly out the back door, mindful that the screen didn't bang behind him. He went around to the front porch where he could study the ranch buildings awash in the moonlight. He made a mental note of the fact that since Natalie's disappearance the construction of the barn had come to a halt. They'd have to get back to it soon if they hoped to complete it before winter.

Positioning himself on the top step he removed a cigarette from his shirt pocket and lit it. His mind churned over the girl's disappearance and the reason behind it. Had she simply run away, possibly to Sheridan? Or had someone kidnapped her? And if they had, *why?* Was it tied to the coal? Was it one more ploy to get Maggie to give up and sell? Or could it possibly be not related?

A noise across the yard drew his attention. He

pinpointed it in the shadows, a man walking toward him. His hand slid to the gun on his hip, tensing for possible action, then relaxing when he saw who it was.

"You're out awfully late, Haig." He didn't have to lift his voice much. The night was so quiet that sound carried easily.

"So are you, Sackett."

Seth waited until Sonny stopped a few feet away. "What has you away from your bunk?"

Sonny propped a foot on the lower step. "Same thing as what has you away from yours, I reckon."

Seth offered Sonny a cigarette, but the younger man declined. "I prefer to roll my own. Those new readymades may be easy but they aren't to my liking. Thanks anyway."

Silence filled the gap between them while they found things to look at other than each other.

"That girl always was a spunky one," Sonny finally said, glancing at the dark bulk of the mountains rising against the western sky. "Hard-headed and stubborn she is and prone to demanding her own way. I always figured she could have used a paddle on her fancy behind a few times."

Seth wondered what Sonny really wanted to get out of this conversation. He wasn't here to be congenial. He'd made it clear, even when he'd tracked Seth down in Deadwood, that he wasn't in favor of Maggie hiring a gun. And he hadn't made a move since to be friendly. If anything, he'd been downright hostile.

Seth studied the foot on the bottom stair, Sonny's foot. It was small for a man's. "Looks like you could use a new pair of boots, Haig. Don't tell me Maggie doesn't pay you enough."

Sonny glanced at his boot and chuckled. "I've never liked breaking in new boots. I'll get these resoled before I buy another pair."

Another silence fell between them and once again Seth wondered why the man was forcing conversation, why he'd come to join him in the first place. Haig looked up at Maggie's window. "How she's handling it?"

"As good as can be expected." Seth took another drag on his cigarette.

"Well, I hope we find that girl soon. I hate to see Maggie distressed."

Seth didn't respond.

"Well, I guess I'll go warm my bunk." Sonny took a few steps in that direction and stopped, glancing back. "Where you throwing your bedroll now, Sackett?" he asked sardonically. "Is Maggie lettin' you stay in the house again?"

Seth curbed a smile. At last, the real reason for Haig's visit. "I wouldn't even if she offered, Haig. I'd hate to see this big house go up in smoke just because somebody wanted me dead. There's easier, less costly ways to kill a gunfighter."

"Such as?" Sonny hooked his thumbs in his gun belt. His eyes held Seth's longer than they ever had before.

"I'm sure you can figure something out," Seth replied. "But don't lose sleep over it. Maybe it'll come to you in your dreams."

Seth wondered if he might have misread the look that flashed in Sonny's eyes just before he'd turned and hurried, bow-legged, back to the bunkhouse. Had it been a look of startled fear, or just plain surprise at the insinuation that Seth knew Sonny was the one who had tried to kill him out at the line shack? He'd had his suspicions all along and had finally laid his trap the other day. He had written that note to Maggie, sending it via Sonny, fully expecting the foreman to read it. Apparently he had, and then he had come to the line shack, accurately guessing it to be the one where he knew Seth and Maggie had spent their first night together. The boot prints had proven it further. Seth's only question now was why Sonny had seemed to dislike him from the beginning even before Maggie had come between them?

He headed around the side of the house to the conservatory. Just because Haig had tried to kill him didn't mean he was behind anything else. And surely not the attempt on Maggie's life, unless that bullet had actually been meant for Seth. Haig wanted Maggie, and Seth was standing in his way. It could be that Haig figured if he killed Seth, it would be blamed on Tate's hired guns. One way or the other, Seth couldn't turn his back on Haig again.

He stepped inside the conservatory but immediately sensed he wasn't alone in the dark room. Knowing he was a perfect target silhouetted in the doorway, he faded into the shadows, reaching for his gun as he did. But no attack came. Only a melodic, feminine voice that sent pleasant tingles of anticipation surging throughout his body.

"It's just me, Seth," she whispered.

He heard the rustle of clothing and heard the chair in the corner squeak as she moved out of it and stood up. Even though it was dark, he could make out her form in a pale gown with her long hair flowing over her shoulders. The seductive way she stood sent a shiver of anticipation through his body. He closed the door quietly, just in case Haig was still lurking about in the shadows, watching him.

"Maggie, is something wrong?"

She moved a step closer to him, deciding even as she did so that she must be crazy for coming here tonight, to meet him like this in her own house with her family just upstairs. But images of him at the hotel, and again in the golden sunlight of the line shack, kept coming back to haunt her mind and to keep her awake. Her body ached with a need for him, a need that went beyond simple sexual fulfillment. She needed his companionship and the security of his arms to help her fight the fear and pain growing like an ugly monster inside her. There was the small hope that he might somehow make it go away, or at the very least keep it at bay.

"I can't stand to be alone tonight, Seth," she said urgently. "I just keep thinking of all the horrible things that might be happening to Natalie. I'm afraid. Afraid for her. Afraid for the White Raven. Afraid for myself." She moved closer to him and he could see the fear in her eyes. "Hold me, Seth. Help me forget it all for awhile."

He hesitated, but not because he didn't want her in his arms. No, he wanted her there from now until eternity. It was just that he never would have thought she would seek him out after hearing the confession of his dark and ugly past—and especially now since her daughter had left because of him. He tried to squelch his own foolish hope that she might truly care as deeply for him as he did her. He told himself she was only asking him to hold her because she was afraid, nothing more. He would be crazy to read anything else into it.

"It would cause you more trouble if another of your children sees us together," he reminded her.

He hadn't meant to plant the seed of doubt that would turn her away, but she walked back to the door separating the conservatory from the main part of the house. Expecting her to exit, he was surprised to hear the lock turn with a slow, quiet, and solid click. He knew in that moment she wanted more than to just be held.

"Lock the outside door," she whispered.

He reached behind him and did it. Then he closed the windows so that any sounds they might make would not drift outside to the curious ears of Sonny or anyone else who might be lurking around. The blinds were drawn last.

In the darkness they found each other. Maggie drew him to the center of the braided rug and lost herself in the hope his arms offered. He kissed her tenderly at first, truly soothing the pain in her heart and her mind that was caused from the disappearance of her daughter. But Maggie had come for more than just comfort, and slowly he filled her with the physical satisfaction that would, for a time, help her forget the fears.

Later they lay side by side, holding hands and silently enjoying the closeness of each other. Despite the darkness they had enveloped themselves in, Maggie's eyes had adjusted, and she was able to see something of his face. It was in repose, and she wondered if his confession might have cleansed his soul and brought him a degree of peace. This was one of the few times the stark harshness was gone from his features. The other time was while he slept, before the nightmares took over.

He was special, a unique and complex man. She had once thought him a necessary evil. And she still did, only in a different way. Now it was his love-making that had become necessary even though some might consider their affair evil. Hard as granite and looking as if he'd been chiseled from it, she had nonetheless felt the gentleness of him, the great passion he so expertly concealed to the world.

She found herself wanting to tell him just how much he had come to mean to her, and how much a part of her life he had become—even how much a part of her family's lives he had become. She hadn't wanted to question what that feeling was—it seemed safer not to. But her heart began an insistent little whisper, "You love him, Maggie Cayton. You love him. It may be foolish, but you can't deny it. Another man has slipped into the place you never thought anyone could occupy but Trent."

But she couldn't risk his reaction being anything less than love, too. He had stated boldly right from the beginning that they would be lovers. For him, she was sure that was all the relationship was.

So all she could do was lie next to him, shoulder touching shoulder, hands gripping hands. And all she could say was, "Thank you for understanding."

In the end she was glad she said no more, because his only response was silence.

Maggie had hoped to see Seth at the breakfast table, and apparently the rest of the family had, too, because Lance came in from the conservatory looking glum. "Seth's gone," he said. "I guess he went out to the cookshack."

They ate in silence, no one having much to say as long as Natalie's plight was predominant in everyone's minds. Even Alison was not her usual cheerful self. She said little, but had become extremely withdrawn since her sister had disappeared. Like the rest of the family, she only picked at her food.

From the first moment Maggie had awoke in the gray dawn, one thought had been on her mind—go back to the last place where she'd last seen Natalie. Maybe there would be a clue, a message that Cleve hadn't seen that would tell her where her daughter had gone. She had wanted to tell Seth, ask him what he thought.

Deciding she would follow her instincts, she excused herself. Alison's face lifted somewhat with a ray of hope. "Are you going to go looking for Natalie again?"

Maggie moved to Alison's chair and drew the girl into her embrace. "I'm going to keep looking until I find her," Maggie whispered against the girl's soft hair. "Will you stay here again today and help Grandma? I really need for you to do that."

Alison turned her face to Maggie. "We're making a new quilt for Natalie's trousseau."

Maggie understood that her mother needed to keep busy and keep the hope that soon, very soon, the girl would be found and that all would be all right with her. Catherine did it not only for her own mental peace, but to keep everyone else thinking positively as well.

"That's an excellent idea," Maggie said to Alison. "I'm sure Natalie will be very happy to know you and Grandma are doing that."

Maggie kissed her again, then went around the table and left a light peck on her mother's cheek, silent gratitude for everything she did. "I'll see you all at supper tonight."

Lance followed his mother outside and they walked to the corrals. "What do you want me to do today?"

"Talk to Seth. See if he's got plans."

"What about Sonny?"

Maggie had nearly forgotten Sonny was still in charge. It just seemed so natural to turn the authority over to the person more capable of handling it—Seth. "Well, check with him, too. Tell Seth I want to go back to town and talk to Cleve."

Maggie watched Lance stride to the cookshack then she went to the corral and caught and saddled her horse. But she hadn't led it from the corral when a rider came hell-bent-for-leather from the west. She recognized him as Benteen—one of the young cowboys who had went out yesterday to the line shacks on that part of the ranch. Hope leaped inside her that maybe he'd found Natalie. She ran out to meet him, as did the men.

"Mrs. Cayton!" He skidded his horse to a dusty

stop in front of everybody, seemingly as out of breath as his horse. "We've got more trouble!"

Maggie's heart sank with fear and then began to beat even more violently than before. "What is it, Benteen?"

He pulled a deep breath. "More dead cattle. Fifty head. And this time they've been shot!"

The men simultaneously released a roar of anger and then they were all talking at once.

"This is it!" Clements shouted, raising his fist, his face twisted with rage. "I say we get our guns and go have it out with Tate. He's gone too far this time!"

To Maggie's amazement all the men joined in—all the men except Sonny, who stood quietly watching the proceedings as he usually did. And Seth, doing the same. In a rush the men all headed for the corral, having just formed their own vigilante force and angry enough to carry it out to whatever ends they deemed necessary.

"Wait!" Maggie shouted. "Think about what you're doing!"

Clements, self-appointed leader, turned back to face her. "We know what we're doing, Mrs. Cayton. We're going to end this range war the only way possible. Tate wants to fight, well he's going to get exactly what he asked for."

"He's got hired guns—professional killers."

His expression never altered. "Just because we aren't being paid to kill doesn't mean we can't do it. Your hired gun hasn't done a thing so far." He turned accusing eyes to Seth, along with every other man on the place.

Seth sauntered over next to Maggie, contemplatively allowing his gaze to search each man's angry face. "Maggie's right. Tate's professional guns will more than likely see you coming and meet you with gunfire before you even know what hit you."

"Then what do you suggest? Sitting back and watching all the White Raven cattle be slaughtered, one by one, while we're waiting for you to find your *evidence!"*

Seth's lengthy time in replying made them all begin to shift nervously. "I've got my evidence," he finally said. "Not as much as I'd like, but enough. What I want you men to do is get on those horses and keep on searching for Natalie. Sonny and I will head over to Tate's."

The men exchanged questioning glances. Sonny's expression revealed a trace of surprise, then irritation, but he kept his thoughts to himself.

"Do you think you can just go riding in there by yourself?" Clements lips twisted into a sneer. "Unless you plan on wearing a suit of armor, they'll gun you down so fast you won't know what hit you."

"Maybe," Seth quietly acknowledged. "And maybe not. But with Haig with me, I don't think it'll be the latter. Now, unless Maggie disagrees with me, I think all of you would be better served today to keep looking for Natalie."

"You'll find that girl at Tate's. He's kidnapped her—or killed her!"

"That's enough," Seth snapped, his eyes flashing now. "Maggie doesn't need to hear talk like that."

"We want to go with you, Sackett," Benteen

spoke up. "We ain't afraid to fight. They want to start a war. I say we give it to them!"

Sonny finally stepped forward. "All of you calm down. Mrs. Cayton's the boss here, not Sackett. I say we let her give the orders." He turned cold eyes to Seth, effectively reminding him of his place. The men rallied around his attitude and turned to Maggie for her decision.

She lifted her eyes to Sonny's and saw the gleam of smug satisfaction. He was doing whatever he could to undercut Seth, to make him look bad in the eyes of the men. He wanted the men to turn against him—either that or he was afraid to go over to Tate's without an army around him. But what he was asking for was war. Did he want all these men to be killed, possibly himself? Surely it wasn't Sonny himself who wanted her off? Did he have his eyes on the White Raven? Did he know about the coal that was hidden beneath the long, swaying grasses?

She felt Seth's waiting gaze over and above that of all the other men. At least Seth was concerned about her future and about her. He knew that with the men dead in a range war she'd be left vulnerable to a succession of attacks which, if resumed over a period of a week or two, would break her once and for all.

Sonny seemed so sure of what her answer would be. He'd been a loyal hand and a good friend, but she had no choice now but to disappoint him. "I'm sorry, Sonny, but I have to agree with Seth." She thought about explaining her reasons, but remembered that Trent wouldn't have justified his decisions.

Sonny's back stiffened. "All right, whatever you say. Let's ride, Sackett." He stalked to the corral to get his horse, not waiting for Seth.

Maggie gave the rest of the men her attention. "I know you've searched everywhere you think you possibly can, but I would greatly appreciate it if you would continue looking for Natalie."

When the men had dispersed, Seth's gaze touched her in the gentle way his hands had touched her last night. "Thank you, Maggie."

"Likewise."

"They're not happy about not getting to fight."

"No." She glanced at the corral, watching them collect their horses. "What's this about having evidence, Seth? Why didn't you tell me?"

"Because I'm not sure it is evidence. I was mostly bluffing to make the men back down. It's best if I don't say anymore until I know for sure."

"Does it have something to do with Sonny?"

Seth's hesitation was an answer in itself, but he only said, "It could."

Maggie knew there was no point in trying to pry the information from him. Like Trent, he would tell her in his own good time. She could surmise with some confidence that he didn't want to unjustly accuse a man until he was guilty beyond a shadow of a doubt.

"I'd better go," he said.

She tried not to show her fear for him. What if, like Trent, Sonny brought him back slung over a saddle? She wanted to tell him she loved him, something she wished she would have told Trent that fateful morning and hadn't. But this was different.

This was Seth Sackett, a hired gun, a man who would soon be out of her life, one way or the other.

"Don't turn your back on Morrell," she said softly.

Those gray eyes flickered. What was that look she saw in their stormy depths? Was it love?

He brushed her cheek caressingly with the back of his hand. "Don't worry, Maggie. God's business is saving sinners."

Chapter Twenty-Three

Maggie waited until the men had all left the ranch before returning to the house. There she quickly strapped on her gun belt and checked the revolver's load. She was tugging her hat down on her forehead when her mother appeared in the foyer.

"And just where do you think you're going, Maggie? Don't you think you should leave this mess up to the men?"

"I certainly would, Mother, but since I'm the owner of the White Raven I hardly think it would be appropriate for me to take on the role of helpless female. I'm not going to sit idle while my men are out risking their lives for me and you and the children.

"I'm going to Cleve's," she continued. "It was the last place I saw Natalie and I'm just hoping she left something there that Cleve missed, a note or something telling where she went."

Catherine's tone changed from authoritative to one of pleading. "For the love of God, Maggie, you're as impetuous as Natalie! It's simply too dangerous. I forbid you to go. Wait for Seth, or one of the other men. For heaven's sake, if you insist on this insanity, then *I'll* go with you, but you shouldn't be going out by yourself. You were nearly killed once, if you'll remember."

"Yes, I remember. All too well. But as soon as Tate's lookouts announce that Seth and Sonny are on White Raven property, they won't give a tinker's damn what I'm doing. And you can't go. You need to stay here with Alison."

"I'm afraid this mess has her very upset," Catherine stated. "And you're going out alone isn't going to help."

"Then don't tell her."

"Maggie," Catherine reproached. "You have to think of your children."

"That's exactly what I'm doing." Suddenly she took her mother's hands and pleaded with her. "You've got to understand, Mother. I have to do this. The White Raven is all we've got, but finding Natalie is even more important. If I have to give up the ranch to get her back, then I will, gladly. Precious time for her is slipping by. It might already be too late. I cringe to even think beyond that."

Catherine pulled her daughter against her bosom and laid a comforting hand to her back. "I know, Maggie. I know. I would do the same for you. I would do it for Natalie, too, if you would just let me come with you. But I most likely would only slow you down. I can't ride the way I used to," she said with a sigh.

Maggie searched her mother's eyes. "I know you

would come with me, Mother, but if anything happens to me, you're all the children have."

"And that isn't much." She chuckled.

Maggie smiled. "Don't say that. Don't even believe it. You're the center of this family, even if you aren't aware of it. You hold us all together, Mother. You always have."

Catherine's eyes filled with tears, and so did Maggie's. She gave the older woman a quick kiss on the cheek then rushed from the house before she changed her mind.

Three miles from Tate's ranch headquarters, Seth directed Sonny off the road and into a clump of cottonwoods.

"What's wrong?" Sonny asked suspiciously, glancing behind them for the first time.

"Why so nervous, Haig?" Seth folded his hands over his saddle horn. "Are you afraid I came out here to execute you for trying to kill me?"

Sonny's eyes narrowed, but not before Seth saw wariness leap into them. "I don't know what you're talking about, Sackett."

Seth shrugged. "Well, maybe I'm wrong." He nodded his head toward the road. "We're being followed. Anybody you know?"

Sonny squinted down the road toward the approaching rider and started to pull his Winchester from the saddle scabbard. Seth caught his arm. "Not so fast. He's one of ours. Been following us since we left the White Raven."

Sonny tried to brush Seth's hand off his arm. "It

doesn't matter. He could be working for Tate with intentions of bushwhacking us."

"Or he could be your accomplice and you're afraid he'll implicate you."

Sonny glared at him. "You're talking nonsense, Sackett. I never tried to kill you."

Seth ignored his denial and focused on the approaching rider again. "It's Lance."

Sonny's eyesight apparently wasn't as good, something Seth made a mental note of. Whoever had fired on him and Maggie that day outside of town would have had to be able to see a farther distance to even come close to his target. It was beginning to look like there was more than one person trying to kill him and the Caytons. He was positive Sonny had been the one who had tried to kill him in the tack building and out at the line shack, but could it be that Sonny had a personal vendetta that had nothing whatsoever to do with the range war? Maybe Sonny just wanted him out of the way so he'd have a clear path to Maggie. If that was the case, though, the foreman would have to kill Cleve, too.

"What in the hell is that kid doing out here?" Sonny said. "He's going to get himself killed."

"He's a Cayton," Seth replied nonchalantly. "I think they pretty much do what they damn well please."

They rode their horses from the trees and Seth lifted a hand of greeting to Lance who was surprised to see them. Seth sidled his horse up next to Lance's and gave the boy a hard scrutiny that had him fairly squirming in the saddle.

"I guess you want to know why I'm out here," Lance finally said sheepishly.

Seth folded his arms over the saddle horn. "That would be my first question, yes."

"I was afraid someone would try to backshoot you guys, or else you might ride into a trap. I was only coming along to watch your back trail."

Seth straightened and gathered his reins. "Well, Lance, if I had to have anybody watching my back trail, you'd be the one I'd want. Since you're here, I think the best thing for you to do is just ride in there with us. They already know you're here anyway."

Lance looked around uneasily. "How do you know? I haven't seen anybody."

"Morrell's men don't let you see them if they don't want you to see them."

"Damn it, Sackett," Sonny said. "He's a kid. Send him home."

"He's got a better and quicker aim with that six-shooter than you do, Haig. I'd just as soon have him along, if you don't mind. Personally, I don't think Tate will open fire on us as long as we look like we're going in there to talk. If we go in with guns blazing and an army of men and . . . well, he won't have any choice but to shoot back, now will he?"

"You're a damned fool, Sackett, riding in there alone."

Seth's gave him a humorless smile. "Maybe I don't have as much at stake as you do, Sonny. Now, let's get this bronc broke, shall we?"

As before, Seth was aware of guns popping out of every available hole in every building as they passed through the main gates of the Broken Arrow. Tate was running scared, for sure, keeping the place so heavily armed. Seth couldn't help but wonder how many more men were out policing the range. They'd picked up two men just outside of the ranch who were following them closely, not even trying to remain concealed. Sonny was getting so visibly nervous that sweat had broken out on his face.

Seth didn't get as far as the house this time. Big Ben came out in the center of the yard with a Winchester across his chest, feet spread in a stance that suggested a body would have to kill him to move him.

"What brings you trespassing again, Sackett?" he hollered.

Seth kept riding until he was close enough to talk without shouting. He drew rein and looked down at the big man who still looked like a giant even though Seth had the advantage of his horse. "We came to talk, Ben, just as before. I'm not really a man who believes in firing first and asking questions later. That never does seem to accomplish anything."

Ben's face drew up hard. "All right, step down from that hoss and let's talk. I see you brought Maggie's boy. Think that'll save you from gettin' killed?"

"You're not going to kill anybody, Tate. You're as scared as a chicken in a henhouse with a weasel running loose."

Tate's eyes narrowed and the grip on his rifle tightened. "Watch your mouth, Sackett. I don't like your words."

"No, most people don't like the truth. I don't like it much myself when it pertains to me."

He swung to the ground and waited until Haig and Lance had done likewise. "The reason I'm here, Ben, is because I found one of the culprits that's behind this mess. And he came with me all nice and peaceful, ready to surrender." Seth turned to Sonny. "Didn't you, Haig?"

Sonny suddenly reminded Seth of a chicken-eating dog backed into a corner with a long-barreled shotgun staring him in the face. He took a step back toward his horse. "You conniving bastard, Sackett. I don't know what he's talking about, Tate. He's trying to frame me. I'm not involved in anything but trying to keep the White Raven from going under."

He turned to his horse, gathering the reins. He had a foot in the stirrup when Tate spoke up.

"I wouldn't ride out of here, Haig, if I was you. All I have to do is give the signal and those guns out there will start blazing. Now, how about you just coming back over here and start explaining?"

The sweat poured down Sonny's face with new profusion and Seth knew it had very little to do with the heat. "There ain't nothing to confess. If anybody's double-crossing Maggie Cayton, it's Sackett. He just wants a way out."

Tate took two steps closer, backing Sonny up against his horse. "I never liked you, Haig. Never liked a man who wouldn't look me in the eye when he addressed me. Sackett is what he is, but at least when he opens his mouth, I believe what utters from it. I can't say the same for you, and I've known you a lot of years."

"Tell him about the coal, Haig," Seth prodded. "Isn't that why you're trying to run both him and Maggie off their places so you'll get rich off that coal?"

Seth had only been playing a hunch where Sonny was concerned, but from the evasive look on the foreman's face, Seth decided he played it right.

"I don't know anything about any coal," Sonny denied.

"And neither do I," Ben said, glancing at Seth.

Seth explained to Tate what he'd found and his belief that someone knew about the coal and knew they'd never get it as long as the White Raven and the Broken Arrow were under present ownership.

Tate considered it thoughtfully and finally agreed that Seth might just be right. "It would surely explain what's been going on. I've told you all along I didn't kill Maggie's cattle. I cut a few fences just to get even with what she was doing, and I damned up a creek once. But I haven't poisoned nothing nor shot nothing. I didn't burn that woman's barn down either."

"And Maggie hasn't done anything to you, so it only leaves somebody from the outside."

They both turned to Haig again. "I know you tried to kill me, Haig," Seth said. "That night at the line shack you left plenty of clear tracks. Small feet with a hole in the bottom of the boots. They match yours. You were probably the one who tried to cook me alive in the tack building, too, weren't you? And what about that bullet that got Maggie?"

"I didn't try to kill Maggie! That wasn't me."

"Oh, so you admit you had an accomplice?"

By now, all of Tate's men had come out of their hiding places and were gathering around. One of them had brought a rope and was twisting the end into a too-familiar shape. "Maybe he'd talk with a noose around his neck," the man said.

Sonny's eyes darted over the men, moving closer, threateningly. Seth was afraid the foreman was going to bolt and run, which if he did, would more than likely be fatal.

"Tell us who's in on it with you, Haig," Seth said, "and it could be you'll go free. After all, if you only *tried* to kill someone, maybe the court will go easy on you. Otherwise, you might just hang here and now. These boys don't look like they would care if we waited for a trial—especially if all the evidence points to you."

Sonny licked his lips nervously while his eyes darted over the gathering congregation. "You've got to understand I didn't do it to hurt Maggie. I'd never hurt Maggie."

"You're not making a whole lot of sense," Seth added dryly. "Exactly what did you do, and what didn't you do?"

"Are you going to hang me?"

"I'll try my best to see that these boys don't, but I can't promise much. I can promise one thing, though. I'll let them hang you if you don't start giving us some information."

Sonny took a breath, but suddenly a shot was fired from the crowd, hitting him in the chest. Guns leaped from holsters, all pointing to Tate's foreman, a man by the name of Garnett.

"He's guilty!" Garnett quickly defended his

deadly action, not knowing if any second one of those guns pointing at him would put him down just as his bullet had put down Haig. "He's the one who's been killing our cattle, boss. I know it cause I saw him sneaking around over by the Long Valley water hole."

Tate walked over and grabbed the gun from his foreman's hand. "You damned fool. The man had something to say. You had no call in killing him."

"He isn't dead," Seth said as he lowered himself to a knee next to Sonny. Tearing open his shirt, Seth looked at the wound. He'd seen enough of them to know Haig wasn't going to make it.

Sonny grabbed the front of Seth's vest and pulled him closer. "I didn't know about the coal." His voice was so weak only Seth and those within a few feet of him could hear. "Williams hired me to turn them against each other. He was going to pay me big money. Enough that I could have bought my own place . . . and ask Maggie . . . to marry me. He hired Garnett, too . . . ."

"Did you shoot Maggie?"

"I couldn't see that far . . . . I was aiming at you. Sackett?"

"Yeah, Haig?"

Sonny's grip tightened and loosened on Seth's vest. Finally his hand fell to his side. "Tell Maggie I . . . love her . . . ."

A flash of surprise was the last light that flickered in his eyes. Seth stood up slowly. He hadn't intended for it to end this way when he'd brought Haig with him today, and silently he cursed himself for having made a poor decision. All he'd been after was a confession, not another death. But somehow he wasn't surprised to hear that Williams was behind it all. He was that sort of snake.

He turned to Tate. "Did you hear him?"

Tate nodded and grabbed Garnett by his shirt front. "I ought to kill you with my bare hands, you lowlife bastard. You've worked for me for years. You would have been the last man I would have ever thought would doublecross me. How much did Williams pay you to do it?"

Garnett looked at the hateful eyes of his fellow cowboys. Tate's big hand was pressed into his throat and his heels were off the ground. "Ten thousand."

Tate shook his bullish head with disgust and flung the man away from him with such force that he fell on his back in the dirt. "You'd sell me out for a measly ten thousand? I ought to let them hang you here and now." He glared at Garnett a moment or two longer, as if seriously considering making quick work of them. But finally he said, "Tie him up. He'll stand trial . . . and *then* he'll hang."

Tate turned to Seth. "Let's get Williams and get this over with. Do you want me to bring my men?"

Seth's glance slid over the motley crew of cowboys and professional killers. They could create more problems than they might solve and more bodies would be on the ground. And Morrell was missing.

"Where's Morrell, Tate?"

"He quit me. Came home from the dance with a broken nose and just packed his gear and left. He said something about there not being enough action around here to keep him interested. I don't suppose you'd want him along anyway, would you?"

"No. I'd prefer to handle Williams by myself. We can't risk tipping him off, and if we all ride into town he'll probably take off. I think our best bet would be to catch him unaware."

"You're not leaving me behind, Sackett." Tate tilted his head back stubbornly. "I'll leave these boys behind, but Williams has done some terrible damage to the Broken Arrow and I want to be the one to shove his skinny ass behind bars."

"All right, Tate," Seth finally conceded. "But only you and Lance. Nobody else."

Maggie nervously waited on the veranda of Cleve's mansion for one of his servants to answer the door. When it was finally answered she was met with a pleasant smile.

"Mrs. Cayton. What a pleasure to see you again."

"Is Mr. Williams in?"

The maid shook her pretty blonde head. "No, he went down to the office today to finish up a few things that needed to be done before Monday morning. But if you'd like to wait, he shouldn't be long now. I'll get you some tea while you wait."

"It must be an important deal," Maggie said, stepping into the house. "Cleve usually refuses to go to his office on Saturday and Sunday."

The maid smiled. "That he does, even to the point of making clients irritated with him."

Maggie stepped into the cool interior of the house

and the maid closed the door behind her. "I'm sorry to hear you haven't found your daughter yet, Mrs. Cayton. I wish there was something we could do to help."

"There might be," she said anxiously, relieved that the subject had been broached so easily and that the woman was so willing to help. "Since this was the last place where anyone saw Natalie, I was wondering if you would mind if I looked through the room to see if she might have left a note or something."

Apprehension clouded the woman's features. "Oh, I've cleaned the room thoroughly, Mrs. Cayton. There was nothing, not even a ribbon or a barrette left behind." Seeing Maggie's disappointment she hastened to add with a cheerful smile, "But why don't you come with me and we'll look again."

Maggie followed the woman to the guest room and together they searched it from top to bottom, but no trace remained of Natalie's occupation.

The maid led the way back to the first floor and offered to make some tea while Maggie waited for Cleve, but Maggie declined, preferring to go directly to his office. She had to see if there was something, anything, that Natalie might have said or done that would give an indication of where she'd gone. Something that Cleve hadn't thought important, or something that had meant nothing to him.

Maggie thanked the maid for all her help and left the residential district. Outside of Williams & Co. on Main Street, she tied her horse to the hitching rail. The office building was a two-story red brick, one of the most prestigious in town. Cleve didn't use all the rooms for his current enterprises, but he'd built the building with expansion in mind.

He wasn't in his main office and Maggie wondered if he was in one of the back rooms that he used for storage. Wandering back down the hall, she checked every room. At the end of the hall, however, the last door was locked. She thought that curious and the first thing that crossed her mind was what did he have in this room that needed to be kept under lock and key.

Deciding it was really none of her business, she started back to the main office when a loud clatter from the locked room caused her to whirl around in alarm. With heart hammering, she laid a hand on the doorknob and tried it again, calling, "Cleve, are you in there?"

Her question was answered by a loud thumping and distinctly muffled cries. The commotion continued in a fashion Maggie interpreted as sheer desperation. Had someone come into the office, robbed Cleve, and locked him in the room?

"I'll get you out!" she called. "Just wait until I can find the key."

Maggie raced back down the hall to Cleve's desk, but all she found were locked drawers. Abandoning the desk, she returned to the storage rooms, and in the second one found various tools, including a crowbar, an ax, and a hammer. She chose the ax.

At the locked door, she said, "I'll have you out in a minute. Just hold on."

The ax made quick work of the thin wood and soon she had it chopped away enough that she could get her hand inside to unlock the door. In another second, she was swinging it wide.

She was hit with darkness. The windows had all been boarded up and only slivers of light came through between the boards. With the light from the hall, her eyes soon adjusted enough that she could see the room was piled with old boxes and crates.

"Where are you, Cleve?"

The thumping began again, behind the crates. Maggie had to move several of them out of her way before she could get to the captive. What she didn't expect to see was her own daughter, huddled in a corner, gagged, and bound with ropes.

A cry of anguish rose up from her throat and she fell to her knees beside her daughter, grabbing her up in her arms. "Natalie! My God." She was so moved at seeing her that she could barely think clearly. She hastily removed the gag from her mouth and the girl began to cry.

"He kidnapped me, Momma! Cleve kidnapped me. Please get me out. I think he's going to kill me."

Maggie could barely believe her ears. Cleve? But why? Still, there was no time to ask questions. She had to get her daughter out of here. Cleve could return any moment. She started on the cotton ropes, wishing she had had a knife to slice through them quickly. They were tight, nearly cutting the girl's circulation off, but at last Natalie was free and she flung herself into her mother's arms. For as much as Maggie would have liked to hold her forever, she felt the push of urgency. She took Natalie by the arm and helped her up, but the girl had been so long in her cramped position that she could barely stand.

"Come on, Natalie," Maggie urged. "We've got to get out of here before he comes back."

With her arm under her daughter's shoulder, Maggie helped her around the crates. Suddenly a shadow filled the doorway. Natalie screamed and Maggie reached for the gun on her hip.

"Don't try it, Maggie," came Cleve's voice from the doorway. "Unless you want to see your daughter die right before your eyes."

Chapter Twenty-Four

Maggie stepped protectively in front of Natalie. "What's going on here, Cleve? Why have you done this?"

"Lose the gun, Maggie, and do it carefully."

Seeing that she had no choice, Maggie slowly lifted the gun the rest of the way from the holster and let it fall to the floor. "What could you have possibly gained by kidnapping my daughter? If you've touched her . . . so help me I'll kill you with my bare hands."

He was amused. "You're hardly in a position to do anything, Maggie. But don't worry, I didn't touch her. And she's been fed and watered properly, too. I must tell you, I hadn't planned this. However when she ran away, I couldn't deny that it was the final brick that would topple your wall. The only bad thing is that now I'm going to have to kill you, too, and I really didn't want to do that. I was actually hoping you would come to your senses and sell the White Raven—or at least marry me so I could become owner the legal way."

Maggie was appalled that Cleve was so underhanded, so murderous, but she was quickly beginning to make sense of it. "Does this have anything to do with the coal?"

Cleve was impressed by her ability to find the last piece of the puzzle. "So you knew the coal was there?"

"Seth believed it was the reason someone wanted me off the ranch. Were you going to kill Tate to get the Broken Arrow?" she ventured.

"I had hoped you'd give in before I had to do that."

She swallowed softly before she asked her next question. "And Trent?"

"He had to be killed. As I said, with him out of the way there was the possibility you'd turn to me, marry me. But I had to get rid of Tate first so I—"

"So you staged the range war," she interjected, "hoping he would get killed by my men. And if he didn't, then you planned to kill him yourself and make it look as if someone on the White Raven had."

"Quite correct, Maggie. And I think I nearly had everyone incited to riot, from what my informers tell me. Did you know Sonny Haig is one of them?"

"Sonny!"

"Yes, good old Sonny. Easily coerced, easily bought. He was so in love with you that all I had to do was tell him that if you lost the White Raven he would have a very good chance at making you his wife." He chuckled to himself. "Little did he know he'd soon be dead and I would step into the position as husband."

"That would never have happened."

"Don't be so sure, Maggie. You might have married me . . . if Sackett hadn't come along. I saw your interest in him right away and I knew he was going to have to die, too. My apologies for that bullet in your shoulder—it was meant for him. I hired Sonny to do the job and he didn't quite hit his target. He was quite sick about it, thinking he'd nearly killed you. He almost quit me then, so I sweetened the pot by upping his wages from ten thousand to twenty. A small price to pay for all the coal that I'll get out of that ground.

"Now, Maggie," he moved farther into the room. "You and Natalie just sit tight until tonight and then we'll go out on the range and . . . well, I hate to say it, but I'll have to do away with both of you. Then, maybe Lance. But once he's out of the way, your mother will be easy to convince that she'll have to sell."

Maggie glanced at the revolver on the floor, knowing it would be useless to reach for it. Helplessly, she moved back into the middle of the crates with Natalie.

A board in the hall suddenly squeeked, and almost instantaneously Natalie yelled, "Help! He's going to kill us!"

Cleve yanked the girl up against him, putting a choke hold around her neck and the gun to her head. "Say another word and I'll kill you right now," he hissed.

Maggie took a step toward Natalie, instinctively reaching out to help. The hammer came back on the revolver, clicking loudly.

"Don't try anything, Maggie," Cleve warned, "or believe me, I *will* kill her, the same way I killed Trent."

Natalie began to sob, looking desperately to her mother who was completely helpless. But the determination in Cleve's eyes told Maggie she would be wise not to doubt his threat. She wondered if someone was really out in the hall. She hadn't heard the main door open or close. Nor had they heard any footsteps in the hall, but Natalie had been here for days and she had probably heard that board creak more than once when someone stepped on it.

Maggie's question was suddenly answered when in the next instant Seth lunged into the doorway, his gun immediately leveled on Cleve. "You can't get away with it, Williams. This place is surrounded by Tate's men."

Maggie had never been so happy to see him, but how was he possibly going to get Cleve to lower his gun and give up without killing Natalie? Maggie was so frightened of the outcome of the confrontation she was nearly paralyzed. If it was herself Cleve was threatening to kill it would have been different, but she would go mad if she saw him kill her child.

He smiled in an evil way and ignored Seth's words. "Do you expect me to believe that, Sackett? You're here by yourself, and you'd better put your gun down right now if you don't want Natalie's death on your conscience."

Like a band of unbending steel, Seth's outstretched arm held steady on his target. "If you kill her, Williams, you won't get far. As soon as she falls, you're a dead man."

Maggie's head snapped up higher as a startled gasp of dismay came from her throat. A whimper came from Natalie's. How could Seth be so careless about her daughter's life? But from the way his eyes burned with concentrated intent she could only hope he knew what he was doing by bluffing Cleve. And surely he had to be bluffing.

Cleve pressed the gun harder against Natalie's temple and tightened his grip around her neck until she could barely breath. She was gasping for air, clutching his arm in an attempt to loosen it. Maggie feared he was going to choke her to death.

"I mean it, Sackett," he reiterated. "Drop your gun or I shoot on the count of five. I'm leaving here with Natalie as a hostage and you'll step aside and let us pass. It begins now. One . . . two . . ."

"Maybe you'd better do as he says," Maggie said frantically. "Please, Seth. He'll kill her."

Seth kept his eyes on Cleve and his gun arm still showed no signs of weakening its aim. "If he leaves this room, Maggie, you'll never see her alive again."

"Three . . . four . . ."

The gunshot boom exploded in Maggie's ears. She screamed, and Natalie screamed. In confused horror, Maggie watched as Cleve was thrown back against the boarded-up window, clutching his upper chest where Seth's bullet had neatly made its entrance. Another gunshot boomed and his forgotten revolver was snapped from his other hand and sent clattering across the floor. Natalie fell forward onto her knees, crying in fear. Maggie ran to her and pulled her safely into her arms. She looked up and saw Seth's gun smoking. It was still leveled on Cleve.

Running feet thundered down the hall and Ben Tate and Lance burst into the room. Tate hurried forward and gathered up the guns, both Maggie's and Williams'. Lance trained his Colt on Cleve, just in case he had notions to try anything else that was totally stupid.

Seth moved closer to Cleve then dropped his Peacemaker back in its holster. "I don't like ultimatums, Williams. It's too bad you didn't know that."

Natalie leaped to her feet then, her hysteria having turned to a stream of relieved tears. She flung her arms around Seth and buried her face in his chest. "Oh, Seth," she sobbed. "I'm sorry I said those mean things to you. Please forgive me."

Seth had never held a crying young girl in his arms before and he didn't know quite what to do. But instinct took over and he placed his hand on her tangled hair, smoothing it with gentle strokes that comforted her the best they could.

"I was never angry at you, Natalie."

She looked up at him, her soiled face streaked with tears. "Never?"

He gave her a quarter grin then held out an arm to Maggie. Like her daughter, she found a place against his solid chest. Never had it felt so good. "It's over now, ladies. We can go home."

Big Ben awkwardly turned to Maggie. "I guess we've got a lot of apologizing to do to each other, Maggie."

"Just promise me you won't sell out to some damn coal company, Ben."

His grim expression lifted into a smile that eased the perpetual hardness. "You've got my promise, Maggie. Course, everybody will soon know why Williams wanted our property. I don't know how long we'll be able to stave off the wolves."

"I don't either," Maggie replied, "but maybe we'll be able to at least have some say in what happens in the future."

Ben looked at the toe of his boot, looking terribly sheepish. When he spoke again, his deep voice was rougher than usual and laced with a quiver of emotion. "Maggie, if this sort of thing happens again, what do you say we just get together over dinner and hash it out."

It was Maggie's turn to smile. "I'm all for that, Ben."

Seth positioned one arm around Maggie and the other around Natalie. "You can get up now, Williams. I don't think you'll die before we get a chance to hang you. That is, if we can get you over to doc's before you bleed to death. Lance, escort him out."

Maggie wandered aimlessly from one piece of furniture to another. The house was dark and quiet; everyone was asleep, confident that nothing disastrous would befall them in the night. For the first time in over a year, the burden of fear had been lifted from everyone's minds.

She fingered the keys of the piano in the parlor, wondering if she could even remember how to play it, it had been so long. But tonight she was too restless to try again, and she was sure that even the softest, melodic piece would wake everyone on the ranch.

Impatient with her own restlessness, she went to the library bookshelves and pulled out several books, but almost immediately she thrust them back into their dusty places. They were too boring to settle her mind and ease her turbulent mood. Then one book, *Antigone,* caught her eye. She fingered the narrow spine and removed it from the shelf, wondering if Seth had enjoyed it.

Why hadn't he come to see her tonight?

She tossed the book on the sofa. Tears stung her eyes as she paced the floor. He was going to leave tomorrow. Just like that. No last tryst to say goodbye. Nothing.

Had she expected something more? Had she expected him to propose marriage to her? He had come to do a job, and now it was done. Tomorrow he could collect his pay and get on down the road to the next job, the next woman.

She could go to his quarters. Yes, she certainly could. But she wouldn't. Why bother? Why make the pain just that much worse, the goodbye that much harder? Their time, so short and sweet and tumultuous, was over. It was better to leave it at that.

"Mother?"

Natalie's appearance in the dimly lit room startled Maggie. She had heard nothing but the agony and indecision whirling in her own mind. It had thoroughly blocked out the sound of Natalie's slippered feet on the stairs and in the hall.

Hastily Maggie brushed her tears aside with the palm of her hand. "Yes, dear?"

"Is something wrong, Mother?"

The girl moved further into the room and took a seat on the settee, curling up next to *Antigone*. She picked the book up, turning it over and finally opening it.

Maggie, always conscientious of her children's needs, cast aside her own for the time being and settled at the other end of the settee, drawing her knees to the side and tucking her dressing gown down around them. "I'm fine. But what brings you out of bed at this hour?"

Natalie traced the name of the book with the tip of her finger. Ignoring her mother's question, she said instead, "You don't want him to go, do you?"

Maggie looked away from her daughter's knowing eyes. How could she deny the truth? It hurt so much, she didn't even want to deny it. She wanted to tell somebody. "No, I don't, Natalie. It's been nice having a man around who could handle a difficult situation and keep the men in line."

"That isn't the only reason, though. Is it?"

The tears puddled in Maggie's eyes again. Was she going to spend the rest of her life crying every time a thought of Seth came to mind, or every time someone in the family mentioned his name? She wiped the tears away, thinking it was such a different sort of pain to lose a man to death and to just lose one. To have him walk out of your life and to know he's still out there in the world somewhere, but you don't know where, and you don't know if he's with another woman. You don't know if he's dead, or if someday he might come back. It was harder to let go.

"No, it isn't the only reason," she admitted softly.

Natalie opened the book, riffling the pages with her thumb. "It's funny how we change our minds, isn't it? I mean, you didn't used to like Seth and now you do. I used to like Andy, but now I don't."

Maggie searched her daughter's face. "Then you found out about Andy taking Cecilia to the dance?"

Natalie nodded. "Yes, while I was at Cleve's before he—" she halted at the memory but then flippantly added, "before he decided to be a crook and lock me up."

Maggie laid a comforting hand to the girl's knee. "You were brave and handled it well. I'm very proud of you."

Natalie's eyes filled with a new wisdom and maturity. "He was going to kill me, Mother. I was never so scared in my life. And while I was in there, just hoping he'd put if off for a day longer, all I could think of was wishing I'd told you and Seth I was sorry for being such a selfish little snit. I was also sorry for not telling Daddy how much I loved him that morning he rode away for the last time. Being away from home made me realize that you can't wait to tell people you love them. You can't just think they'll know how you feel." Natalie left the sofa and curled up on the rug at Maggie's feet, resting her head on Maggie's knees. Maggie stroked the loose cascade of dark hair. "I came to appreciate everything a lot more while I was locked up," Natalie whispered. "I love you, Mother, and I just wanted to tell you."

Maggie drew her daughter into her arms. The tears started all over again for them both. "I love you, too, honey, more than you can ever know."

Natalie smiled through happy tears. "Oh, I think I'm beginning to know." With a grave expression, she searched her mother's face deeply and held her hand tightly. "Mother, maybe you need to tell Seth how you feel. Some things just won't wait, and you may never get another chance."

Maggie didn't know what to say to her daughter's wisdom, nor what to do. Natalie didn't seem to expect an answer. She gave her a kiss, another hug, and returned to her room. Maggie stared at the door long after Natalie was gone. Should she follow her heart?

She rose and got as far as the front door before stopping. The light in the tack building was still on. So he wasn't sleeping either. But she couldn't go to him. She couldn't lay her soul bare to a man who had from the very beginning planned to make love to her as a mere pastime. Their relationship had been nothing more than a diversion for him. To try and make more of it would be truly juvenile on her part. She was a grown woman and she had known from the beginning what the outcome of their relationship would be.

Besides, it was a man's place to approach a woman. Seth Sackett was a man of the gun, a wandering man who wouldn't want to settle down with a woman her age and take on three grown children, and possibly a couple of his own. He had come into their lives and he had touched them all in a very special way, but it was time now to say goodbye.

The lantern light cut a frail path up the stairs to her room. Inside, Maggie went directly to the night table, set the lamp there and blew it out. With the room in darkness she began to remove her gown. Then suddenly she felt something. Some*one*.

She whirled to the armchair that was backed into the corner on the other side of the door. It was a chair she seldom used, but she sensed someone was in it now.

Her heart began to dance with fear. Surely Cleve hadn't escaped jail? She backed closer to the small table. In the drawer was her derringer.

Then the chair squeaked from movement and she gasped, but a male voice immediately whispered, "Don't be afraid, Maggie. I just came to tell you goodbye."

Maggie could never mistake that voice. She found the edge of the bed and sat down, her quivering legs having suddenly given out. "Seth." she breathed a sigh of relief. "You nearly frightened me to death."

In the next instant she heard the rustle of clothing, the muffled sound of footsteps across the rug, and the distinct scent of tobacco touched her nostrils. Seth stopped just inches in front of her, his legs touching her knees. It was pitch black in the room with the blinds and curtains completely drawn, blocking out all possibility of starlight or moonlight. She hadn't closed the curtains, so he must have.

"How did you get in?" she queried softly.

He put his hands on her shoulders and drew her to her feet in front of him. "I came in the back way." His words were spoken so quietly Maggie didn't fear that they would be heard beyond the walls of her room. "You were gone so I decided to wait."

His voice flowed over her in the darkness, soothing and warm like clover honey over hot bread, melting into her stream of awareness. His hands moved up along her neck and into the heavy length of hair tumbling down around her shoulders.

She had wanted to see him one last time, to have this last rendezvous. It hadn't seemed to matter that there was no hope he would stay beyond the night. But now that her prayers had been answered and he was here, it hurt almost too much to face it, and she wondered if she should just tell him to go. What was the use in prolonging the pain of his departure? How many other women had he said goodbye to in this same fashion? It was only a crazy hope that she might be special to him in some way.

"I was in the library," she whispered. "I was—"

But even as the last word slipped out, he had pulled her into his arms in a bruising embrace. His kiss silenced her explanation. In the next instant he had slid the gown off her shoulders. It fell into a dark puddle of cloth at her feet, quickly followed by the remainder of her garments as well as his.

He lifted her into his arms and placed her in the center of the bed. Then he was next to her, shielding her nakedness with his. She thought about lighting the lamp so she might see him this one last time, but as quickly as the idea emerged she suppressed it. A light would make the parting even more difficult. If he looked into her eyes he would surely see the pain written there, and he would know he had succeeded in making her love him. She, who was probably only another in a long line. And it would make no difference in his ultimate decision to go.

So her hands became her eyes, and her lips the instrument of photography. And while she claimed him as hers before releasing him forever, she longed to hear just once the muttering of some sweet words of love. But he said nothing. He only made love to her with a quiet passion that seemed to her, at times, to be almost as hopelessly desperate as what she herself was feeling.

Once, she almost spoke those telling words, going so far as to discard her last raiment, the frail one that protected her heart. Instead she closed her eyes and simply held him. For she knew now, without a doubt, it would be the last time.

Alison's shrill laughter, drifting in through Maggie's open window, was the thing that finally penetrated her sleep. Maggie sat up with a start. Seth was gone. The part of the bed he'd warmed was cold, indicating he must have left some time ago.

Feeling as dismal as a rainy March morning, Maggie rolled to her back and pulled the covers up over her head. She didn't want to get up. Not ever again. How could she face the rest of her life without Trent *and* Seth? She closed her eyes and tried to force herself back to sleep so she wouldn't have to think about the aloneness.

It might have been Alison's laughter that had awakened Maggie, but it was the other voices, one in particular, that finally drew her from bed and to the open window. She pulled back the drapes and was stabbed with the sunshine of a new day and the wonderful image of the man she loved.

Below in the yard, Seth stood by his horse. The bay was saddled and ready to go. Seth was surrounded by not only the ranch hands, each shaking his hand and giving him a final farewell, but her children and mother who were there, too, talking and laughing. He looked as if he belonged there, not as if he should be leaving. Her mother said something to him and then handed him a book. The youthful grin that burst out on his face made Maggie's heart fall to her toes. The tears sprang anew.

Seth kissed her mother on the cheek, then gave a turn to Natalie and Alison before putting the book in his saddlebags. He shook hands with Lance, his words drifting up to the window.

"Keep practicing with that gun, Lance, but don't ever forget to give the other man's gun the respect it deserves."

"Yes, sir," Lance replied solemnly. "I'll remember."

Alison clutched Seth's hand. "Oh, please, Seth. Do you have to go?"

He lowered to his haunches to talk to her and his words were lost to Maggie. She couldn't bare watching him and yet she couldn't take her eyes off him. Wouldn't everybody be expecting her to come down and say her farewell, too? She hadn't even paid him what she still owed him. And he hadn't asked.

Miserable, she forced herself from the window and back to the bed. She sat on its edge, wondering whether to just let him ride away and let last night serve as their final goodbye, or whether to face up to her job as owner of the White Raven and go down there and see him off.

She began to crawl back into bed, deciding on the cowardly alternative, when she saw the piece of paper, folded in half and propped on the night stand. Her name was on it, written in the elongated hand she easily recognized as Seth's.

Tentatively she reached for it. What were his final words to her? Would they ease her heart? Or break it?

She could scarcely breath as she opened it. The missive leaped out at her, bold and startling:

I love you, Maggie. I always will.
Seth

A wrenching sob of pain mixed with ecstasy tumbled from her throat. Suddenly she was in flight, removing her dressing gown, fumbling into her nightgown, then pulling the dressing gown back on as she flew down the stairs. The screen door slammed behind her and she finally stopped short on the porch. He was still there.

All eyes turned to her and she became aware that it wasn't proper for the men to see her in her night clothes, but she gathered her composure and the hem of her dressing gown and started down the porch stairs on her bare feet with as much demeanor as if she had been attired in her Sunday best.

"Why didn't someone wake me?" she scolded them all in general. Then to Seth, "Surely you didn't intend to leave without your final payment?"

Abandoning his conversation with Alison, Seth came to his full height. His fathomless gray eyes locked with hers and the rest of the world and its onlookers suddenly faded from sight and mind. For Maggie, only the two of them existed, facing each other across three dozen feet and an abyss of unspoken words.

"I guess I figured I didn't do much to earn it," he said. "I only fired two shots."

"We want him to stay," Alison announced loudly, closing her small hand around his as if she had absolutely no intention of letting go, ever. "Please ask him to stay, Mama. *Please*. He can be our new foreman."

Natalie moved to her mother's side. "Please, Mother," she said in a whisper. "Ask him to stay. I think he wants to."

Maggie wasn't so sure. What if he had written his confession of love but still planned on leaving? She had heard there were certain types of men—loners, drifters—who couldn't settle down, not even for love.

The hot, dark glow in his eyes reminded her of how his hands had felt on her body. But like all the others, he waited, saying nothing. The next move was hers.

"That would have to be Seth's choice," she finally

said. "But he would be welcome to take the position of foreman if he is inclined to do so."

Clements spoke up. "What do you say, Sackett? We'd all like you to stay on."

With everyone agreeing, Maggie waited. Seconds ticked away but time stood still as Seth's gaze penetrated hers. Was he trying to gauge her reaction to his note? Was he wondering if she'd even seen it? Had he hoped he would be long gone by the time she did?

And then he stepped away from the crowd and came toward her on slow, purposeful steps. His eyes held hers and her heart began to thud crazily. She thought it would run away with itself when he took her hands in his.

"I'll stay, Maggie," he said softly, "but only on one condition."

Hope leaped inside her. "And what is your condition, Seth?" She lowered her voice so no one could hear but him, and Natalie who was standing just a few feet away. "Could it have something to do with the note you left?"

"It has everything to do with the note, Maggie," he whispered back. "I can't stay here as your lover. And I won't stay as your foreman. I could only stay if you would allow me to become a part of your life and your family. Maybe I have no right to be asking this, because I have nothing to offer you, only my heart. But will you marry me, Maggie? Will you be my wife?"

Natalie gasped and squealed with delight, but Maggie barely heard her daughter's outburst. Mesmerized by Seth's eyes, glowing with the love he spoke of, her heart took command. She put her arms around his neck and whispered, "I never thought you would ask."

Natalie squealed again. "Yes! She said yes! She's going to marry him, everybody!"

While the hired men and Maggie's family clapped and laughed with delight, Maggie sank into the wonderful world of Seth's embrace and the joy of his lips taking hers in a gentle but passionate kiss that promised everlasting love.

Amid the distant hum of voices Maggie picked up phrases and words such as: "Wedding." "Oh, we'll make it a big one!" "Grandma, you design the dress." "We'll have to have a dance."

Seth reluctantly drew his lips from hers and searched her eyes deeply. "My mother, who was my only salvation in life, always said that love covers all sins, but I never really knew what she meant until now," he whispered. "Maggie darling, you stripped my soul bare and then you turned around and covered it with unconditional love. You made me take another look at myself, at who I really am, and it's not who I thought I was at all."

"And who are you Seth? Really?"

"I'm a man who had a lot of dreams that he thought he had no right to pursue. And all because my father made me believe my soul was so hopelessly lost it couldn't possibly be destined for anything except Hell. But Ezra Sackett was wrong. And now I'm going to make all those dreams come true with you by my side. I'm free at last. Your love has set me free."

Arm in arm they turned to the house and went inside. They had more than wedding plans to make. They had those dreams that were going to start coming true, right now.

FROM THE AUTHOR

I hope you enjoyed Seth and Maggie's story. If you would like to know about my previous or upcoming books, please send your letters to me, with a self-addressed stamped envelope to:

P.O. Box 3555
Idaho Falls, ID 83403

—Linda Sandifer

Debi Dulak